KT-386-849

Lynne Graham was born in Northern Ireland and has been a keen romance reader since her teens. She is very happily married, to an understanding husband who has learned to cook since she started to write! Her five children keep her on her toes. She has a very large dog, who knocks everything over, a very small terrier, who barks a lot, and two cats. When time allows, Lynne is a keen gardener.

Michelle Smart's love affair with books started when she was a baby and would cuddle them in her cot. A voracious reader of all genres, she found her love of romance established when she stumbled across her first Mills & Boon book at the age of twelve. She's been reading them—and writing them—ever since. Michelle lives in Northamptonshire, England, with her husband and two young Smarties.

A BABY ON THE GREEK'S DOORSTEP

LYNNE GRAHAM

THE BILLIONAIRE'S CINDERELLA CONTRACT

MICHELLE SMART

MILLS & BOON

First Published in Great Britain 2020
by Mills & Boon, an imprint of HarperCollins*Publishers*
1 London Bridge Street, London, SE1 9GF

A Baby on the Greek's Doorstep © 2020 Lynne Graham

The Billionaire's Cinderella Contract © 2020 Michelle Smart

ISBN: 978-0-263-27833-0

MIX
Paper from
responsible sources
FSC C007454

This book is produced from independently certified FSC™ paper
to ensure responsible forest management.
For more information visit www.harpercollins.co.uk/green.

Printed and bound in Spain
by CPI, Barcelona

A BABY ON THE GREEK'S DOORSTEP

LYNNE GRAHAM

CHAPTER ONE

TOR SARANTOS IGNORED his security head's frown at the news that he would require neither his car nor his usual bodyguards that evening.

'You know what day this is,' Tor said simply. 'I go out… I go alone.'

'With all due respect,' the older man began heavily, 'in your position, it is not safe.'

'Duly noted,' Tor breathed very drily. 'But it is what I do, as you well know.'

Every year without fail for the past five years, Tor had gone out alone on this particular date. It was an anniversary but not one to celebrate. It was the anniversary of his wife's and daughter's deaths. He considered himself to be neither an emotional nor sentimental man. No, he chose to remember what had happened to Katerina and Sofia because their sad fate was *his* worst-ever failure. His ferocious anger, injured pride and bitterness had led to that ultimate tragedy, which could not, in conscience, ever be forgotten. Out of respect for the family he had lost, he chose to remember them one wretched day a year and wallow in his shamed self-loathing. It was little enough, and it chastened him, kept him grounded, he acknowledged grimly. After all, he had screwed up, he had screwed up *so* badly that it had cost two human lives that could have been saved had he only been a more forgiving and compassionate man.

Tragically, the traits of compassion and forgiveness had never run strong in Alastor, known as Tor, Sarantos. Although he came from a kind and loving family, he was tough, inflexible and fierce in nature as befitted a billionaire banker, celebrated for his ruthless reputation, financial acumen and foresight, his advice as much sought by governments as by rich private investors. In business, he was a very high flyer. In his private life, he was appallingly aware that he had proved to be a loser. However, that was a secret he was determined to take to his grave with him, as was the truth that he would never remarry.

That was why he rarely went home now to his family in Greece. Not only did he have an understandable wish to avoid meetings with his Italian half-brother, Sevastiano, but he also didn't want to listen to his relatives talking with increasingly evangelical fervour about him 'moving on'. On his visits, a parade of suitable young women was served up at parties and dinners even though he had done everything possible to make it brutally obvious that he had no desire to find another wife and settle down again.

After all, he had long since transformed from the young man happily wed to his first love into a womaniser known throughout Europe for his passionate but short-lived affairs. At twenty-eight, he was generations removed from the naïve and idealistic man he had once been, but his family stubbornly refused to accept the change in him. Of course, his parents were as much in love now as they had been on the day of their marriage and fully believed that that happiness was achievable by all. Tor didn't plan to be the party pooper who told them that lies, deceit and betrayal had flourished, unseen and unsuspected, within their own family circle. He preferred to let his relatives live in their sunny version of reality where rainbows and unicorns flourished. He had learned the hard way that, once lost, trust and innocence were irretrievable.

Dressing for his night out, Tor set aside his gold cufflinks, his platinum watch, all visible signs of his wealth, and chose the anonymity of faded designer jeans and a leather jacket. He would go to a bar alone and drink himself almost insensible while he pondered the past and then he would climb into a taxi and come home. That was all he did. Allowing himself to forget, allowing himself to truly move on, would be, he honestly believed, an unmerited release from the guilt he deserved to suffer.

Eighteen months later

Tor frowned as his housekeeper appeared in his home office doorway, looking unusually flustered. 'Something wrong?'

'Someone's abandoned a baby on the doorstep, sir,' Mrs James informed him uncomfortably. 'A little boy about nine months old.'

'A…*baby*?' Tor stressed in astonishment.

'Security are about to check the video surveillance

tapes,' the older woman told him before stiffly moving forward. 'There was a note. It's addressed to you, sir.'

'Me?' Tor said in disbelief as an envelope was slid onto his desk.

There was his name, block printed in black felt-tip pen.

'Do you want me to call the police?'

Tor was tearing open the envelope as the question was asked. The message within was brief.

This is your child.
Look after it.

Obviously, it couldn't possibly be *his* child. But what if it belonged to one of his family? He had three younger brothers, all of whom had enjoyed stays at his London town house within recent memory. What if the child should prove to be a nephew or niece? Clearly, the mother must have been desperate for help when she chose to abandon the baby and run.

'The police?' Mrs James prompted.

'No. We won't call them…yet,' Tor hedged, thinking that if one of his family was involved, he did not want a scandal or media coverage of any kind erupting from an indiscreet handling of the situation. 'I'll look into this first.'

'So, what do I do with it?'

'With what?'

'The baby, sir,' the housekeeper extended drily. 'I've no experience with young children.'

His fine ebony brows pleated. 'Contact a nanny

agency for emergency cover,' he advised. 'In the mean-time, I'll sort this out.'

A baby? Of course, it couldn't be his! Logic stirred, reminding him that no form of contraception was deemed entirely foolproof. Accidents happened. For that matter, *deliberate* accidents could also occur if a woman chose to be manipulative.

Like other men, he had heard stories of pins stuck in condoms to damage them and other such distaste-ful ruses, but he had never actually met anyone whom it had happened to.

Fake horror stories, he told himself bracingly. Yet, momentarily, unease still rippled through Tor, con-nected with the unfortunate memory of the strange hys-terical girl who had stormed his office the year before...

Eighteen months earlier

Pixie used the key to let herself into the plush house that was her temporary home. Several glamorous, high-earning individuals shared the dwelling, and as a poor and ordinary student nurse she was fully conscious that she was enjoying a luxury treat in staying there. She was happy with that, simply grateful to be enjoying a two-week escape from living under the same roof with her brother and his partner, who, sadly, seemed to be in the process of breaking up.

Listening to Jordan and Eloise constantly fighting, when there was absolutely no privacy, had become se-riously embarrassing in the small terraced home she shared with them.

For that reason, it had been a total joy to learn that

Steph, the sister of one of her friends, had a precious
Siamese kitten, which she didn't want to abandon to
a boarding facility while she was abroad on a model-
ling assignment. Initially, Pixie had been surprised that
Steph didn't expect her housemates to look after her
pet. Only after moving in to look after Coco had she
understood that it was a household where the tenants
all operated as independent entities, coming and going
without interest in their housemates in a totally casual
way that had confounded Pixie's rosy expectations of
communal life with her peers.

But in the short term, Pixie reminded herself, she
was enjoying the huge indulgence of a private bathroom
and a large bedroom with the sole responsibility of caring for a very cute kitten. As she was currently working twelve-hour shifts on her annual placement for her
final year of nursing training, living in the elegant town
house was a treat and she was grateful for the opportunity. A long bath, she promised herself soothingly as she
stepped into the room and Coco jumped onto her feet,
desperate for some attention after a day spent alone.

In auto mode, Pixie ran a bath, struggling greatly
not to dwell on the reality that during her shift in A &
E she had had to deal with her first death as a nurse.
It had been a young, healthy woman, not something
any amount of training could have prepared her for,
she acknowledged ruefully. Put it in a box at the back
of her brain, she instructed herself irritably. It was not
her role to get all *personally* emotional, it was her job
to be supportive and to deal with the practical and the
grieving relatives with all the tact and empathy she
could summon up.

Well, she was satisfied that she had done her job to the best of her ability, but the wounding reality of that tragic passing was still lingering with her. She was not supposed to bring her work or the inevitable fatalities she would see home with her, she reminded herself doggedly, striving to live up to the professional nursing standards she admired. But at twenty-one, still scarred as she was by her own family bereavement six years earlier, it was a tough struggle to take death in her stride as a daily occurrence.

Dressed in comfy shorty pyjamas and in bare feet because the house was silent and seemingly empty, it being too early in the evening for the partying tenants to be home while others were travelling for work or pleasure. At this time of day and in the very early morning, Pixie usually had the place to herself, her antisocial working hours often a plus. She lit only the trendy lamp hanging over the kitchen island, hopelessly thrilled with the magazine perfection of her surroundings. Moulded work surfaces, fancy units and a sunroom extension leading out into a front courtyard greeted her appreciative gaze. Pixie loved to daydream and sometimes she allowed herself to dream that this was *her* house and she was cooking for the special man in her life. Special man, that was a joke, she thought ruefully, wincing away even from the dim reflection she caught of herself in the patio doors, a short curvy figure with a shock of green hair.

Green! What had possessed her when she had dyed her hair a few weeks earlier? Her brother Jordan's lively and outspoken partner, Eloise, had persuaded her into the change at a moment when Pixie was feeling low because the man she was attracted to had yet to even notice that she was alive. Antony was a paramedic, warm and friendly, exactly the sort of man Pixie thought would be her perfect match.

But the hair had been a very bad idea, particularly when the cheap dye had refused to wash out as it was supposed to have done and she had then checked the instructions to belatedly discover that the lotion wasn't recommended for blond hair. She had hated her blond curls from the instant she was christened 'Poodle' at school, and not by her enemies but by her supposed friends. In recent weeks, she had learned that green curls were far worse than blond because everyone, from her nursing mentor to her superiors and work colleagues, had let her know that green hair in a professional capacity was a mistake. And she couldn't afford to go to a hairdresser for help. She might be working a placement, but it was unpaid, and because of her twelve-hour shifts it was virtually impossible for her to maintain a part-time job as well.

Still preoccupied with her worries, Pixie dragged out her toasted sandwich machine and put the ingredients together for a cheese toastie. It was literally all she could afford for a main meal. In fact, Coco the cat ate much better than she did. She put on the kettle, thought she heard a sound somewhere close by and blamed it on the cat she had left playing with a rubber ball in her room next door. Coco was lively but, like most kittens, she tired quickly and would fold up in a heap in her little princess fur-lined basket long before Pixie got to sleep.

While she waited for her toastie, Pixie contemplated the reality that she was returning to her brother's house that weekend. She hated living as a third wheel in Jordan's relationship with Eloise, but she didn't have much choice and, since he had lost his job over an unfortunate expenses claim that his employers had regrettably deemed a fraud rather than a mistake, Jordan was having a rough time. All his rows with Eloise were over money because he hadn't found work since he had been sacked and naturally, the bills were mounting up, which in turn made Pixie feel terrible because she was only an added burden in her brother's currently challenging existence.

Jordan had become her guardian when their parents died unexpectedly when she was fifteen and he was twenty-three. Pixie was painfully aware that Jordan could have washed his hands of her and let her go into foster care, particularly when they were, strictly speaking, only half-siblings, having been born from the same father but to different mothers, her father having been married and widowed before he met her mother. Even so, Jordan hadn't turned his back on her as he could have done. He'd had to jump through a lot of hoops to satisfy the authorities that he would be an acceptable guardian for an adolescent girl. She owed Jordan a lot for the care and support he had unstintingly given her over the years, seeing her through her school years and then her nursing course.

'Something smells good…'

At the sound of an unfamiliar male voice, Pixie almost leapt a foot in the air, her head swivelling with a jerk to focus on the strange man slowly spinning round the recliner in the unlit sunroom, where he had apparently been seated unnoticed by her.

'Heaven must be missing an angel' was the cheesiest pickup approach Pixie had ever received, but for the very first time she was looking at a man who might legitimately have inspired such a line with his sleek dark fallen-angel beauty. He *was* otherworldly in his sheer masculine perfection. Her heart was still beating very fast with fright and, striving to crush those inappropriate thoughts, she stepped forward. She collided involuntarily with the eyes of an apex predator—sharp, shrewd, powerful and dark as the night sky. 'I didn't see you in there…who are you?' she asked as civilly as she could, fearful of causing offence to any of Steph's housemates or their friends.

'I'm Tor,' he murmured. 'I think I must have fallen asleep before I called a taxi to take me home.'

'I didn't know anyone was here. I've just come in from work and I was making some supper,' Pixie confided. 'Who are you visiting here?'

His brow furrowed. Slowly, he sank back down on the recliner. 'My apologies… I don't recall her name. A leggy redhead with an annoying giggle.'

'Saffron,' Pixie told him with concealed amusement. 'But why did she just leave you in here?'

He shrugged. 'She stormed off. I rejected her and it made her angry.'

'You rejected… *Saffron*?' Pixie queried in disbelief because Saffron, a wannabe actress, resembled a supermodel and turned heads in the street.

'A misunderstanding,' he corrected smoothly. 'I thought I was coming to a party. She thought something else. I'm sorry. I'm rather drunk, not in proper control of my tongue.'

No way was he drunk!

Pixie was accustomed to dealing with surly drunks at A & E and usually they could barely vocalise or stand without swaying or cursing. He was speaking with perfect diction and courtesy and remained astute enough to smooth over the unfortunate impression he might have made in saying bluntly that he had rejected the other woman. All the same, she hadn't thought there was a man born who wouldn't jump at the chance of having sex with the gorgeous redhead. Presumably, Saffron had either sought the privacy of her own room upstairs to handle such a blow to her ego or she had gone out again, but Pixie could only be impressed by a man particular enough in his tastes to say no to a beauty like Saffron.

'What are you cooking?' he shot at her unexpectedly.

'A cheese toastie,' Pixie responded in an undertone as she lifted the lid, waved away the steam and reached for her plate.

'It smells incredible…'

'Would you like one?' she heard herself ask and she wanted to slap herself for being so impressionable.

He was a complete stranger and she owed him nothing but, as her brother's partner had warned her, she was a 'nurturer', the sort of woman whom men, according to Eloise, would take advantage of. And Pixie had seen the evidence for that condemnation in her own nature. She *did* like to feed people; she *did* like to take care of them. Pleasing people, tending to their needs, satisfied something in her, a something that Eloise believed she should suppress out of self-interest.

'I'd love that. I'm starving.' He smiled at her and that smile locked her knees where she stood because it was like a galaxy of golden warmth engulfing her, locking his lean bronzed features into shocking beauty, releasing a flock of butterflies low in her tummy. Stupid, stupid, *stupid*, she castigated herself with self-loathing as she reached for the bread and butter again before saying, 'Here…have this one… I'll have the next.'

As she pushed the plate with a knife and fork across the island, he tugged out one of the high stools and settled into it. She busied herself with the sandwich maker, her pale skin pink while he watched her, and she could feel the weight of his regard like a brand. Nothing she had felt in Antony's radius could compare to the thrumming level of awareness assailing her beneath the stranger's gaze.

The hair was weird, there was no other word for it, Tor was reflecting, his gaze locked to those tumbling pale green curls lying tousled on her narrow shoulders, but if a woman *could* rock green hair, she was rocking it. She had the brightest blue eyes he had ever seen, the softest, pinkest mouth, the most flawless skin, but she was so undersized he could barely see her behind the barrier of the island.

'What height are you?' he asked curiously.

Pixie cringed. 'About four ten…no tall genes in my family tree.'

'How old are you?'

'Why are you asking me that?'

'I'm in an unfamiliar house with unknown occupants. I don't want to find out that I'm keeping company with someone's child, and you don't look very old…'

'I'm twenty-one,' Pixie provided grudgingly. 'Almost a fully qualified nurse. Totally grown-up and in-dependent.'

'Twenty-one is still very young,' Tor countered mildly.

'So, how old are you, old man?' Pixie enquired teas-ingly, putting down the lid on the second toastie and relaxing back against the kitchen cabinets to watch him eat. 'Coffee?'

'Black, sweet. I'm twenty-eight,' he told her.

'And married,' she noted without thought as the ring on his wedding finger glinted under the light and she switched on the coffee machine again. 'What were you doing with Saffron? Sorry, none of my business… I shouldn't have asked,' she muttered, backtracking in haste from that unintentional challenge.

'No offence taken. I'm a widower,' Tor volunteered.

Pixie turned back to him, stirring the coffee and passing it to him. 'I'm sorry for your loss.'

'It's OK,' Tor said with a stiffness she recognised, the awkwardness of someone unaccustomed to deal-ing openly with the topic of grief. 'It's been five years since my wife and my daughter died.'

Pixie paled. 'You lost your child as well?'

Pixie felt even more awkward, painfully aware of how she had felt earlier that evening when she had dealt with her first death at the hospital. The finality of a pass-ing and the grieving family left behind scarred the staff as well. For a man to have lost both a wife and a child together was an enormous double blow and her heart squeezed on his behalf at the idea of such a huge loss.

Pale too beneath his bronzed skin, Tor jerked his chin down in silent confirmation.

'I'm so sorry,' she whispered.

'Nobody ever mentions it now. For them it's like it happened a hundred years ago,' he muttered with perceptible bitterness.

'Death makes people uncomfortable. They avoid discussing it often out of fear of saying the wrong thing.'

'Or as if it might be contagious,' Tor slotted in drily.

'I know… My parents passed within a week of each other and even my friends avoided me at school when I went back,' she told him with a grimace of recollection.

'A car accident?'

'No, they caught legionnaires' disease on a weekend away. They were both diabetic with compromised immune systems and they didn't go for treatment soon enough. They thought they'd caught some harmless virus and none of us knew any different.' Pixie shifted a wordless shoulder in pained acceptance. 'My father went first and Mum a day later. I was devastated. I had no idea how ill they were until it was too late.'

'Is that why you're doing nursing?'

'Partially. I wanted to know more so that I could help people when they needed it and I like doing useful, practical stuff.' Pixie sighed, a rueful smile tugging at her generous mouth. 'And to be frank, I was also the sort of child who bandaged teddy bears and tried to raise orphaned baby birds. My brother calls it a save-the-world mentality.'

'I have a brother too but we're estranged,' Tor heard himself volunteer, and wondered for the first time if that old saying about alcohol loosening the tongue could actually be true because he was gabbling like a chatterbox, which he was not and never had been. He was innately reserved, rather quiet outside working hours. Or was it *her* affecting him? Unthreatening and studiously un-sexy as she was in her pale grey pyjamas adorned with little pink flamingos? And no sooner had he thought that than he had to notice the stupendously sexy thrust and sway of a pair of firm full breasts beneath her top as she clambered up on the stool to eat her toastie.

'You're estranged?' Her big blue eyes clouded with sympathy. 'That's sad.'

'No, it's not. He *slept* with my wife!' Tor bit out, shocking himself with that revelation, which had never crossed his lips before, not to anyone, not for any rea-son, a sordid secret he had planned to keep buried until the day he died.

Pixie's eyes widened in shock. 'Oh, my goodness...' she gasped. 'Your brother did *that*?'

'He and I didn't grow up together. We are not close,' Tor acknowledged grudgingly. 'But I could never for-give him for that betrayal.'

'Of course, you couldn't.'

That first confession having leapt from his tongue, Tor was discovering that for some inexplicable reason he could not hold back the rest. 'On the night my wife died she admitted that she had fallen in love with Sev *before* we married but that she fought her feelings out of loyalty to me and assumed she would get over him.'

'She still shouldn't have married you,' Pixie opined feelingly. 'She should've told you she was having doubts before the wedding.'

'That would certainly have been less devastating than the end result.' His lean, bronzed face could have been sculpted out of granite, his dark-as-night eyes flinty and hard. 'Finding out several years down the road that our whole life together was a fake, a *lie*, was much worse and…and I didn't handle it well,' he completed in a raw undertone.

'I should think you were in shock.' Pixie sighed, retrieving his coffee mug and moving to refill it.

'Still doesn't excuse me.' The eyes she had believed were so dark focused on her absently and she saw the gleams of gold lightening them to bronze. Such beautiful eyes, fringed and enhanced by ridiculously long black lashes. He was shockingly attractive, she thought, struggling to concentrate and avert her attention from the perfect slash of his dark brows, the exotic slant of his high cheekbones and the fullness of his mouth.

'Why? What did you do?' she prompted.

'When I arrived home, she was putting cases into her car. That was when she told me about the affair…at the very last minute. I had no suspicion that there was another man in her life but, after three years of what I had believed was a happy marriage, she was just going to leave me a note.' His nostrils flared with disgust. 'We had a massive argument. It was…chaotic,' he selected roughly. 'I barely knew what I was saying.'

'Shock,' she told him again. 'It intensifies everything you feel but at the same time you're not yourself. You're not in control.'

'I said a great deal I regret… I was cruel,' Tor admitted unevenly, biting back the final shameful admission that Katerina had made, which had torn him apart: her insistence that the daughter he loved was *not* his child but had been fathered by her lover.

'You weren't prepared. You had no time to think.'

Warmed by her compassionate need to console him, he reached for her hand where it rested on the counter and squeezed it gently before withdrawing his touch again. 'You may be able to save the world, but you can't save me from a world of regret. Katerina raced upstairs to lift our daughter out of her cot. My wife was very worked up by that stage and in no condition to drive. I tried to reason with her, but she wouldn't listen to me. Sofia was screaming and upset...'

His voice had become gruff and he lifted his hands to scrub at his face, wiping away the dampness on his cheeks, and her heart went out to him in that moment because she knew that he was recalling the guilt and powerlessness that grief inflicted. 'It was all madness that night, madness and chaos,' he continued. 'Katerina drove off far too fast and the car skidded on the icy drive and careened into a wall.'

'So, you saw it happen.' Pixie was lost for words, full of sympathy for him, able to see that he was still torturing himself for what he had said and done that night in his own shock and distress.

'And it was too late to change anything,' he completed in a curt undertone.

Her eyes connected with his, awash with fellow feeling and understanding. 'You recall every wrong thing you ever did or said to the person. Every emotion is exaggerated. When my mother was passing, I was beating myself up for being cheeky to her when she had told me to clean my room. That's being human.'

Tor sat back tautly. 'I don't know why I've told you all this. I've never talked to anyone about it before.'

'No one?' Pixie pressed in surprise.

'I didn't want to tell anyone the truth about what happened that night. I didn't want anyone judging Katerina or thinking less of her. The truth wouldn't have eased the shock of her death and my daughter's for anyone, least of all her own family. It would only have caused greater distress.'

'But staying silent, forcing yourself to go on living a lie made it harder for *you*,' Pixie slotted in with a frown.

'I've got broad shoulders…and I really don't know what I'm doing here,' Tor confessed, the smouldering, breathtaking appeal of his bemused eyes and drowsy smile washing over her, imbuing her with a sense of connection she had never felt with any man before. 'It must be true that it's easier to talk to a stranger. But I think it's time for me to order that taxi.'

'Possibly,' Pixie muttered self-consciously, scrambling off the stool in haste and beginning to tidy up to keep her hands busy. She stacked the dishwasher, darting round the island at speed to gather up the dishes before opening the tall larder cupboard to stow away the clutter of condiments that had been left sitting out.

'What's the address?' he asked her as he paced several feet away with his phone in his hand, a deprecatory smile of great charm curving his mobile mouth at his having to ask that basic question that divulged the reality that he truly didn't know where he was.

For a split second she couldn't drag her eyes from him, that half-smile somehow enhanced by the black shadow of stubble framing it and defining his strong jawline, his eyes gleaming a glorious tigerish gold. There was a condensed power to him, a leashed energy that sprang out at her.

Pixie had to think for a second before trotting out the address in a rush, stumbling and correcting herself with the number, and she was already scolding herself for her reaction to him. He was a very, *very* good-looking guy and naturally she had noticed, but she had also immediately recognised that he was way, way out of her league. She was ordinary, he was something far superior, not only in the looks department, but also with his instinctive assurance and ingrained courtesy.

'The taxi will be here in five minutes.' Tor dug the phone back into his jeans and walked towards her.

'I'll wait outside. Thanks for feeding me…and for listening,' he murmured ruefully. 'I didn't even ask you for your name.'

She laughed. 'Pixie…'

His brows pleated as he stared at her. *'Pixie?'*

'I was a very small, premature baby. Mum thought it was cute.' Pixie wrinkled her tip-tilted nose, eyes blue as cornflowers gazing up at him.

Marvelling at the truth that she was barely tall enough to reach his chest, for he stood over six feet in height, he extended a lean brown hand. 'I'm Alastor Sarantos but I've always been called Tor.'

'Pleased to meet you.'

As he swung away to leave, he walked head first into the larder cupboard door and reeled back from it, sufficiently stunned by the blow to his temple to grab the edge of the island to steady himself and stay upright. Pixie gasped and rushed over to him.

'No…no, stay still, don't move,' she warned him. 'You hit your head hard.'

His hand lifted to his temple in a clumsy motion and he blinked in bemusement. 'That hurt,' he admitted.

Guilt assailed Pixie as she glimpsed the still-swinging door, which she had neglected to close. It was her fault that he had been injured. 'Can I check your head?' she asked.

'I'm fine,' he told her, even as he swayed, and he frowned at her because, she reckoned, he was having difficulty focusing on her.

'No, you're not. Nobody could be fine after smacking their head that hard,' she declared, running light fingers across his temple, feeling the bump in dismay while being relieved that he hadn't cut himself and there was no blood. 'You're not bleeding but you are going to have a huge bruise. I think you should have it checked out at A & E because you probably have a concussion.'

'I will be absolutely fine.' Tor swore impatiently as he attempted to walk away and staggered slightly.

'You're still very dizzy. Take a moment to get steady. You can lie down in my room until the taxi arrives,' Pixie murmured as she planted a bracing arm to his spine and directed him down the hall to the room next door. He towered over her, his big powerful frame rigid as he attempted to put mind over matter.

'Are you feeling sick?'

'No,' he told her very drily.

No, big masculine men didn't like to be knocked off balance by any form of weakness, she thought, feeling guiltier than ever about his plight and his doubtless aching head as she pushed open the door of her room and guided him over to the bed.

He lowered himself down and kicked off his shoes.

Pixie set them side by side neatly on the rug. 'You can nap. You seem to be thinking coherently.'

From his prone position, Tor rested dazed, long-suffering dark golden eyes on her anxious face. 'I don't want to be saved right now. Go save someone else,' he urged.

It was a polite way of telling her that she was being irritating and she gritted her teeth on a sharp comeback.

CHAPTER TWO

'WHY GREEN?' Tor mumbled.

'The hair?' Embarrassed, Pixie touched a hand to her hair and grimaced. 'I wanted to be different.'

'It's different,' Tor confirmed, wondering when he had last seen a woman blush, and it looked like an all-over blush too, a slow tide of colour sweeping up from her throat to her hairline.

Pixie winced. 'There was a guy I was hoping would notice me at work. *And* he did notice,' she admitted with a slight grimace. 'Antony said I reminded him of a leprechaun.'

A spontaneous laugh broke from Tor. 'Not quite the effect you were looking for? I shouldn't tease you. *Diavole...* I am drunk,' he groaned, watching the ceiling revolve for his benefit. 'Where's my taxi got to?'

'It should be here soon,' she said soothingly. 'Just chill.'

'Don't have a lot of practice at just chilling. I'm naturally impatient.'

Pixie sat on her knees by the bed because there was nowhere else to sit in the room. She breathed in deep and slow. She was very tired but she had to stay awake until the taxi arrived and she saw him off. At least he had taken her mind off what had happened during her shift: the pointless death of a young life in a car accident, a young woman on the brink of marriage, deeply mourned by her heartbroken fiancé and her devastated family.

'What's he like? The guy you want to notice you?' Tor prompted without warning, startling her out of her reverie.

'What's it matter? Leprechauns aren't sexy,' she pointed out in a defeatist tone. 'Antony's a paramedic so I don't know much about him, only that he's a lovely guy. For all I know, he could have a girlfriend.'

'I think you look more like a forest fairy than a leprechaun,' Tor remarked, wondering when a woman had last told him that she was attracted to someone else rather than him. He didn't think it had *ever* happened to him. It was a startling, disconcerting novelty. He was used to walking into a bar and every beautiful woman there making a beeline for him. He was young, he was rich, he was single. That was how his world worked and casual sex was always easily available, not something he had to plan.

Before his marriage, though, he hadn't had much experience. He had grown up with Katerina. Their families had been and still were friends. He had known even as a teenager that he would marry Katerina and he had insisted on going ahead and marrying her when he was only twenty. Maybe his parents had been right when they had tried to talk him out of that, tried to tell him that they were too young. He had been ready for that commitment but evidently Katerina hadn't been.

Yet he had honestly believed that she loved him the way he loved her.

Forest fairy? That sounded rather more complimentary than a leprechaun, Pixie was reflecting ruefully. OK, she was fishing for hope! What he had already taught her without even trying was that what she had regarded as attraction with Antony was a laughable shadow in comparison to the way in which Tor drew her. Perhaps she had only focused on Antony because there was nobody else around and she had yet to find a boyfriend.

'Maybe that depends on your point of view. If I still look like I belong in a kid's storybook, it's not exactly seductive,' Pixie muttered. 'But you've definitely got the gift of the gab.'

'Gift of the gab? What's that?' he questioned.

'A ready tongue. You know the right thing to say. If you were interested in a woman, you would know better than to compare her to a leprechaun,' she guessed.

'That's true,' Tor acknowledged without hesitation.

Pixie studied him, liking his honesty in admitting that, where women were involved, he was as smooth and cutting edge as glass, instinctively knowing the right words to impress and please. That fitted. No guy as downright gorgeous as he was could be an innocent or clumsy with his words. He had already been married, which made her respect and trust him more because he had committed to *one* woman young when he must have had so many other options.

In his marriage, however, he had been badly burned, she reflected with fierce compassion, because the woman he had married had betrayed his trust and *hurt* him. And that was what he was *truly* struggling with, she decided thoughtfully. He wasn't only striving to handle the pain of loss, but he was also dealing with the pain of being betrayed by someone whom he had loved and trusted.

She went out to the front door to check for any sign of the taxi, but the street was quiet. She padded back into her room, colliding with watchful dark eyes shot through with accents of gold. He really did have the most beautiful eyes and the thickest, longest, blackest lashes and any woman would have noticed those attractions, she reasoned uncomfortably. The guy had dynamite sex appeal. 'Why were you on your own tonight?' she asked him curiously as she leant over him.

'I go out every year on this date and remember Katerina's and Sofia's deaths,' he confided, dismaying her.

'If you have to drink to handle those memories, it's a destructive habit,' Pixie told him gently. 'It would be wiser to talk about them and leave the booze out of it.'

Tor pushed himself up on his elbows. 'And what would you know about it?'

'I lost my parents six years ago,' she reminded him. 'I used my nursing course to work through those feelings of loss by helping other people. I have to deal with bereaved people at work on a regular basis. Sometimes their unhappiness makes me feel anxious and sad. Let me look at your head.'

She had the brightest blue eyes and a full soft pink mouth. Arousal slithered through Tor and he struggled to master it and concentrate on the conversation as he lowered his head. 'And how do you handle it?'

'I have a box with a lid at the back of my mind. At

work I cram anything that makes me uncomfortable in there and then close the lid down tight. I don't allow myself to think about any of it until the end of my shift.'

He shivered as gentle fingertips brushed his brow and delicately traced the bump. He was already imagining those soft fingers smoothing over a far more sensitive part of his body and he castigated himself for his arousal because she had been kind to him and she was too young for him, possibly not that experienced either. She didn't deserve for him to take advantage of her sympathetic nature.

'All that restraint sounds rather too taxing for me.' Tor tilted his head back again to look up at her.

And her heartbeat pounded like a crazed drum as their eyes met again, a wild fluttering breaking free in her tummy even as an almost painful ache thrummed between her thighs. It was lust, instant and raw and nothing at all like the simple sexual curiosity Antony had stirred in her. A man had never made her feel anything that powerful before and that shocking intensity stopped her dead in her tracks. Long brown fingers reached up to lace with care into her curls, tugging her head down to his.

'I want to kiss you,' Tor murmured almost fiercely.

'Do it,' she heard herself urge without hesitation, so greedy was she for more of the new sensations he had awakened.

And his mouth tasted hers, gently parting and seeking, startling her with that sensual testing appeal and warm invitation. His mouth sent a curling flame of liquid heat to the heart of her, which made her lean down, instinctively seeking more of the same. Long, lazy arms extending, he brought her down on top of him and effortlessly turned them both over, flipping her down onto the bed beside him without her registering any sense of alarm.

In fact, as he slid partially over her, the weight of one masculine leg parting hers, a naked thrill of excitement raced through Pixie and her entire body tingled as the tip of his tongue skidded over the roof of her mouth. Nothing had ever felt so good or so necessary as the hot urgency of his mouth on hers. She was no innocent when it came to kissing but never before had she enjoyed kisses that set her on fire. Beneath her top she was ridiculously conscious of the heavy swell of her breasts and the prickling tightening of her nipples while in her pelvis a combustible mix of heat and craving seethed.

He eased a hand below her top and cupped her breast, his thumb rubbing an urgently tender nipple, and her back arched and her hips bucked, and a breathless moan was torn from her lips without her volition. He thrust the top out of his path and locked his mouth to the straining, tightly beaded tip of her nipple and her whole body rose against his on the surge of tormenting sensation that darted straight to the hollow between her legs.

'I love your body,' he husked. 'It's so sexy.'

And her lashes almost fluttered open on surprised eyes because she had never been told she was sexy before. No, she was always the girl the stray men locked on to and shared their life stories with. They told her about their past break-ups and what sort of girl they were hoping to meet. It was never ever a short curvy blonde who liked to listen and didn't like exercise much. No, it was always someone tall, slim and into the gym. She had more gay friends than heterosexual ones, friends who told her she needed to be more confident, outgoing and chatty if she wanted men to notice her. That instant of clear thought and surprise faded as Tor divided his attentions between her breasts with a single-minded intensity that destroyed any control she had over her sensation-starved body.

Tor was making her feel sexy. He was making her feel good about herself and her body and the burning, yearning ache at her feminine core, making her hips writhe, cutting through every other consideration she might have had. He touched her *there*, where she needed that touch most, tracing her slick folds with skilled fingertips, toying with her to make her gasp and then circling her unbearably sensitive core until she didn't know what she was doing any more, only knew that her body felt like one giant yawning scream in desperate need of release. She was shifting, moving, out of control, feverish with a need she had never felt so strongly before.

'Want me?' he groaned as he skimmed off her pyjama bottoms.

'*Yes!*' she exclaimed, longing for that gnawing hunger to be satisfied.

'*Thee mou...* I've never wanted anything the way I want you right now!' Tor growled, shifting over her, rearranging her willing body to push her legs up and back and higher.

And then he was surging into her, partially sating that desire for more with a compelling rush of new sensations. There was the burn as he stretched her tight channel and then a sudden sharp sting of pain as he plunged deeper. It made her grit her teeth but before she

could linger on that development a whole host of new
reactions was washing her memory of it away.

'So tight, so *good*, you feel amazing, *moraki mou*,' he
framed raggedly, dark eyes sheer smouldering golden
enticement as he looked down at her, shifting his lithe
hips to send another cascade of sensual response travelling through her pliant body that made her breath catch
on a gasp of wonder.

What had momentarily felt new and disconcertingly
intense now felt absolutely right. Deep down inside,
her body was tightening and tightening while his every
passionate stroke inside her sent a sweet tide of rap-
turous sensation rippling through her. His urgency increased her breathless excitement. She thought her heart
was about to burst from her chest. Only quick, shallow
breaths came to her lungs and her body was rising up
to his until finally the unbearable tension gripping her
broke and she convulsed, her body clenching tight on
his as an exquisite surge of release sent her over the
edge and engulfed her in ecstasy.

In the wake of that shattering conclusion, Pixie
stirred, shifting out awkwardly from beneath Tor's
weight. 'Tor?' she whispered. *'Tor?'*

She scrambled out of bed, worriedly scanning him.
Breathing normally, he was fast asleep. Her fingers
grazed his brow, but his temperature was already cool-
ing from his exertions on her behalf. Her face flamed
hotter than hellfire.

Pixie was in shock as she eased back into her pyjama
shorts with a wince because a part of her that she didn't
want to think about just then was sore. Tor had kept on
warning her that he was very drunk, but she hadn't re-

ally believed him. Some people retained better control under the influence of alcohol, and he was clearly one of those individuals, capable of having a normal conversation and putting up a front. His conduct, however, was more revealing, she conceded uneasily. Intoxicated people were less inhibited, more liable to succumb to impulsive, uncharacteristic behaviour.

And having sex with her could only have been a random impulse and something he wouldn't have done under any other circumstances. She could feel the blood draining from her shaken face as she made that deduction.

Saffron had brought him home for sex and he had said no. While respectfully engaged in remembering the death of his loved ones, Tor had not wanted a one-night stand with anyone. Pixie completely understood that, so she could not explain how she had lost control of the situation to the extent of actually having sex with Tor. How had that happened? How had she contrived to take advantage of a guy who was drunk and probably concussed and confused into the bargain?

She hurried into the compact en suite bathroom and went for a quick shower, registering in consternation as she undressed that neither one of them had thought to use contraception. She lifted chilled hands to her distraught face because she wasn't on the birth-control pill or the shot or anything, having deemed such advance precautions unnecessary when she had yet to have even a relationship with a man and had never felt any urge to try more casual encounters.

Of course, she could ask for the morning-after pill, she reminded herself, and tensed at the prospect of having to make that decision. Why was that the exact moment when she had to recall her late mother tugging her curls and saying, 'You were my little surprise baby!' Although she hadn't been planned by her parents, both of whom had been in their forties when she was unexpectedly conceived, she had been welcomed into the world and loved all the same. How could she do any less for any child she conceived?

Well, she *was* being a little theatrical in imagining such a challenging scenario in the immediate aftermath of her *first* sexual encounter, she told herself in exasperation.

But in truth, she was in shock at what she had done. She wasn't an impulsive person and yet from that first scorching kiss she had succumbed to Tor and had encouraged his every move. She hadn't made the smallest attempt to call a halt, she reminded herself crushingly. Her body and the fiery seduction of her own eager responses had enthralled her. All these years, it seemed, she had totally underestimated the fact that sexual arousal genuinely could lead to seriously bad choices.

Tor was gorgeous and he had got her all excited and everything that had happened from that point had been *her* fault. He had told her that he was drunk, and she had seen for herself that he was probably concussed. She had chosen to have sex with a drunk, grieving man and could only thank herself for the powerful sense of humiliation and shame that she was now enduring. *She* had taken advantage of *him*.

Pixie moved back into the bedroom, where Tor still slept. In only a couple of hours she had to get up again and go to work. She got back on the bed and clung to her side of it, eyes so heavy they ached. She felt sad, ashamed that she had been so foolish as to get carried away like a wayward teenager with the excitement of sex. She knew better, she knew the risks to her health and happiness and knew she would be visiting a clinic as soon as possible to be checked and go on some form of birth control. Although the guilt currently assailing her warned that she was highly unlikely to make such a mistake twice.

His phone was buzzing in his pocket and she drew it out with careful fingers and gently switched it off before replacing it. She was in no mood to be confronted by an angry, confused man because she couldn't explain what had happened between them either.

Dawn was lightening the skies when she rose again and quietly dressed for her shift. Tor was still heavily asleep, and she decided to leave him to let himself out. That approach would neatly sidestep any embarrassing conversations or partings. She never ever wanted to lay eyes on the guy again!

CHAPTER THREE

TEARS WERE BURNING the backs of Pixie's eyes as she sat stiffly in the waiting area of the opulent office building. The receptionist was exasperated with her for refusing to take a polite hint and leave: Tor Sarantos was not available for an appointment or even a phone conversation with anyone whose name wasn't on the 'approved' list.

So, how was she supposed to tell the man that he had got her pregnant? Putting such a confidential disclosure in a letter struck her as foolish and careless. It would be read by office staff and likely discarded as the ravings of some desperate wannabe striving to importune the boss. And if it *was* given to him, he would be embarrassed that employees had been made aware of information that he would probably prefer stayed private.

Yes, Tor Sarantos, banker extraordinaire, had certainly been hiding his light under a bushel, a virtual forest of bushels, according to everything that Pixie had learned about him on the internet and in the media in the months since their meeting. He was an incredibly rich and important banker and as far removed from her ordinary world as a gold nugget would be in a waste-paper bin. Only the craziest accident of fate could have ever let them meet in the first place, never mind conceive a child together.

It had taken Pixie quite a few months to decide that she *had* to tell Tor that she was pregnant. It was his right to know that he was going to be a father again. She would never forget the devastation she had seen in his haunted eyes when he told her about his wife and daughter dying. He had loved and cared for his daughter and it was that fact more than any other that had forced Pixie to listen to her conscience and seek him out.

He might not want any sort of relationship with her, but he might well want a relationship with their child, and she could not bring herself to deny either him or their unborn child that opportunity.

She was almost six months pregnant now. And, so far, pregnancy was proving to be a long, exhausting haul. She had finished her nursing training before she even allowed herself to acknowledge her symptoms and do a pregnancy test. She had wasted weeks running away from a looming truth that frightened her, she acknowledged shamefacedly, afraid to face the trial of being pregnant, alone and unsupported.

Her brother had been incredulous. 'You're a nurse!' he had exclaimed when she had told him. 'How could someone with your training fall pregnant? Why weren't you on birth control? And why haven't you gone for a termination yet?'

Yes, there had been loads of awkward, painful conversations between her sibling and her, conversations mostly bereft of Eloise's more sympathetic input because her brother and his partner had split up and Eloise had moved out. Sadly too, although Pixie still saw Eloise as a friend away from the house, Eloise's departure had worsened their financial situation and made meeting the mortgage payments an even bigger challenge.

Thankfully, however, Pixie was now able to work and contribute to the household bills, but the larger she got, the harder she was finding it to work a twelve-hour shift. Her exhaustion had been another factor that had persuaded her that she needed help and that she had to approach Tor for it even if it was the very last thing she wanted to do.

After all, it wasn't as though she had even been a one-night stand who had fallen inconveniently pregnant. Tor hadn't sought her out, hadn't personally selected her from any crowd of available women, he had simply kissed her and ended up having sex with her because he had fallen asleep in the wrong kitchen. Proximity had been their downfall and every step of the way she had encouraged him with her willingness. She should have said no, she should have called a halt but, controlled by that crazy excitement, she had been greedy, immature and selfish.

Pixie was still convinced that Tor would not have chosen to have sex with her had he been in full control of himself. But alcohol, grief and a nasty blow to the head had made him vulnerable and she, who should have known better, had urged him on.

Even worse, she didn't want to be another problem in his life. She didn't want to upset him. But once she'd realised that false pride was keeping her from reaching out for the assistance she needed, she had finally seen common sense. Unhappily, getting a personal meeting with Tor was probably as easy as getting to have tea with the Queen.

'Miss Miller, I've called Security to show you the way out,' the receptionist informed her with a fixed, unnatural smile. 'There's no point in you sitting here waiting when Mr Sarantos is unavailable.'

And that was when Pixie appreciated that by following the rules she had got as close to Tor as she was ever likely to get. As soon as the receptionist returned to her desk, Pixie rose and began walking down the wide corridor that led to the imposing double doors, behind which she had estimated lay Tor's office.

A shout hastened her steps. 'Hey! You can't go in there! Security... *Security!*' The receptionist was screeching at the top of her voice.

Pixie thrust down the door handle and stalked right in. Tor swung round with a phone gripped in one hand. Impossibly elegant and tall, he wore a dark pinstriped suit teamed with a white shirt and a snazzy red tie. He looked indescribably sophisticated and intimidating, not remotely like the man who had sat at the kitchen island and eaten a cheese toasted sandwich with every evidence of normal enjoyment.

'What is the meaning of this interruption?' Tor demanded imperiously, studying her with frowning intensity.

And Pixie held her breath and waited...and waited... for recognition to colour that cool, distant stare. It didn't happen, and that absence of recognition flustered her even more.

'Don't you remember me, Tor?' she murmured almost pleadingly, cringing inwardly from that note in her own voice.

'I don't know who you are. How could I remember you?' he enquired cuttingly, his attention lowering to the prominent swell of her abdomen, his wide sensual mouth tightening when he registered that she was pregnant.

'That night you were with me last year,' she whispered uncertainly, tears involuntarily stinging her eyes at having to voice that lowering reminder. 'I came to tell you that I'm pregnant.'

Derision hardened his lean, darkly handsome features. 'I've never seen you before and if you want to make fanciful allegations of that nature, I suggest you approach my lawyers in the usual fashion.'

'Sorry about this, sir. She wouldn't listen to reason!' the receptionist snapped, a hand closing over Pixie's forearm to prevent her from moving deeper into the office. 'Security are on their way.'

Pixie had never felt so humiliated in her life.

I don't know who you are… I've never seen you before.

Perhaps it had been naïve of her not to expect that sort of rejection. Perhaps it had been ridiculously optimistic, even vain, for her to expect Tor Sarantos to remember her after a casual sexual encounter. To be strictly fair though, she supposed her appearance had changed since her green hair had faded and eventually washed out entirely.

Even so, she just hadn't been prepared for him to look through her as if she didn't exist, and then perceptibly wince when the tears her pregnancy hormones couldn't hold back flooded down her cheeks and a noisy sob was wrenched from her.

An older man began easing her back out of the office again and by then she was crying so hard, she could hardly see to walk. And what a terrible irony it was for her to hear Tor intervene loudly with the words, 'Be careful with her…she's pregnant!' As if he were the only person who might have noticed the vast swell of her once-flat stomach.

'Well?' Jordan had demanded expectantly, when he'd come home from his barista job that evening. 'What did he say?'

And for the first time she had told her brother a little more of the truth of how very fleeting her intimacy with Tor had been. Jordan had simply shrugged and said that such facts were irrelevant and that the father of her child still had obligations to meet.

'Not until the baby is born,' Pixie had protested, cutting through Jordan's insistence that she needed a solicitor to fight for her rights.

Jordan generally got aggressive and argumentative in difficult situations but that wasn't Pixie's way. It took her weeks to get over that distressing encounter in Tor's office, when he had denied all knowledge of her. She had wondered if Tor was telling the truth, or if indeed he remembered her perfectly well but just didn't want to be bothered or embarrassed or reminded of what had happened between them that night. And that wounding suspicion had cut her to the quick.

Admittedly, she wasn't a beauty like the women she had seen him with in the media. She wasn't a socialite, a model or an actress who swanned around in designer clothing and posed for photos. She was a very ordinary young woman. A handful of small, unexpected events and coincidences had put her on intimate terms with Tor and resulted in her ending up in bed with him.

He had been special to her, but she hadn't been special to him. They had both walked away afterwards, both of them probably feeling the same: that it shouldn't have happened. So, it didn't really matter whether Tor genuinely didn't remember her, she told herself, or whether he was simply *pretending* not to remember her. At the end of it, his distaste and derision that day in his office stayed with her and understandably coloured her attitude to him. After that experience, she was pretty convinced that even though she was pregnant by him, Tor would prefer *not* to know, and her conscience quietened. She decided that she didn't need his help and that she didn't want his financial assistance either, no matter what arguments her aggrieved brother put up!

Present day

Pixie wakened and revelled in the quietness of the house, smothering a yawn as she sat up and wondered if Jordan had taken Alfie out to the park.

She smiled as she thought of her son. He was nine months old, big and strong for his age, hitting every developmental target ahead of time and already trying to walk.

Coco slunk up the stairs to greet her with delighted purrs and she petted the cat with a warm smile. Steph had begun leaving Coco with Pixie whenever she went abroad, and weeks would pass before she finally reappeared to collect the little animal again. In the end, she had asked if Pixie would like to keep the Siamese because she was finding pet ownership too much of a tie.

Pixie crossed the landing to the bathroom and went for a quick shower before dressing. Everything she did was done by rote because she had been working night shifts since Alfie was born. In the morning she came home, fed and dressed her son and then went immediately to bed while Jordan took charge of Alfie for a few hours.

Working nights as a nurse, combined with Jordan's freedom to choose his shifts as a barista, meant that she didn't have to pay for childcare. Considering the amount of debt that her brother seemed to have acquired since he had lost his insurance job, that was fortunate. Clad in cropped jeans and a long-sleeved cotton top in raspberry pink and white stripes, she descended the creaking narrow staircase.

The terraced house was small, but she had managed to squeeze a cot into her bedroom and there was a little backyard she was currently cleaning up to serve as a play area for Alfie once he became more mobile. She was taken aback to find her brother sitting at the tiny breakfast bar with a beer.

'Where's Alfie?' she asked. 'And why are you drinking at this time of day?'

Jordan shot her a defiant look. 'I've sorted things out for you,' he said, compressing his lips.

As she took after her mother in looks, Jordan took after their father. He was tall with dark hair and a beard and spectacles, which gave him a slightly nerdy look.

'What things?' she questioned with a frown as she

glanced into the cramped lounge, expecting to see her son playing on the floor with his toys. The room, however, was empty and the toy box sat untouched by the wall.

'Your situation, the mess you made having that child…against *all* my advice!' her brother complained loudly.

'Jordan…where's Alfie?' Pixie exclaimed, cutting across his words.

And then he told her, and she couldn't believe her ears, was already snatching up her coat and her bag in sheer panic at the danger he had put her son in. 'Were you out of your mind?' she demanded in disbelief.

'Alfie's his kid. *He* should be looking after him and taking care of all his needs!' Jordan countered heatedly.

'You abandoned my son in the street, where anything could have happened to him?' Pixie yelled at him full blast.

'No, I stood out of sight and watched to see that he was taken into the house before I walked away. I'm not an idiot and he *is* my nephew. He may be a nuisance, but I do care about the little tyke!'

'What house?' she demanded in sudden sincere bewilderment.

There was another wildly frustrating hiatus while Jordan explained how he had paid some man he met in a pub to find out Tor's London address. By the time she'd dug that information out of her sibling she'd already ordered a taxi—because no way, no how, when her baby boy was in danger, was she heading out on a bus or a train to reclaim him!

Jordan pursued her right out onto the street, heatedly

arguing his point of view, which was that her attitude towards caring for Alfie had been wrong from the start.

'You could've made a killing out of having that child and now you *will*,' Jordan declared, striking horror into her bones. 'And it'll be all thanks to me for looking out for your interests.'

'Not everything is about money, Jordan,' Pixie breathed in disgust. 'And I did *not* have Alfie to feather anyone's nest!'

She slumped in the taxi, sick to her stomach. When had money come to mean more to Jordan than his own flesh and blood? Had she always been blind to that side of her brother? How had she contrived to ignore the fact that Jordan had only begun supporting her desire to have her baby *after* he had grasped that Alfie's father was a very rich man? Even back then, had Jordan been viewing her little boy as a potential source of profit? As the ticket towards an easier life? Her stomach shifted queasily. And what on earth was her brother expecting to happen now that he had confronted Tor Sarantos with the child he didn't want to know about?

Was Jordan hoping that Tor would pay handsomely for her and Alfie to go away and not bother him again? What other scenario could he be picturing? And how could she continue living with and entrusting Alfie's care to a man who could behave as he had done and put an innocent child at risk?

Still in a panic, Pixie leapt out of the taxi and rushed up the steps of the imposing town house. It was a three-storey Georgian building in a grand city square with a private park in the centre. She rang the bell and thumped the door knocker as well, so desperate was she to reach her son.

An older woman with an expressionless face answered the door.

'My son was left here…accidentally,' Pixie said with a shaky smile. 'I'm here to collect him.'

In silence the door widened, allowing her to step into a cool, elegant hall. A fleeting glance was all it took for Pixie to feel shabby, poor and out of her comfort zone as she stood there clad in her cheap raincoat and scuffed trainers. The aromatic scent of beeswax polish lingered in the air, perfectly matching the gracious interior of polished antiques and a truly splendid classical marble sculpture that looked as though it should be in a museum.

'I will ask if Mr Sarantos is free to see you,' the woman said loftily.

As Pixie hovered, she saw two men in suits standing almost out of sight down a short side corridor, both men avidly studying her, and she flushed and turned her head away, relieved when the older woman reappeared and asked her to follow her.

A clammy feeling of disquiet engulfed Pixie's body, quickening both her heartbeat and her breathing as she contemplated the unpleasant prospect of meeting Tor Sarantos again. A man who had utterly rejected her during her pregnancy, who insisted he didn't recall ever even meeting her before? Of course, she didn't want to see him again.

But, sadly for her, Jordan had made it impossible for her to continue sitting on the fence and avoiding the issue of Alfie's existence and his father's responsibility towards him. Now she had to come clean about events eighteen months earlier, regardless of how embarrassing or humiliating that might be. Pixie lifted her chin and reminded herself that all she should still feel guilty about was surrendering to a meaningless sexual encounter while neglecting to protect herself from the risk of a pregnancy.

That horrid little scene in Tor's office had clawed away the finer feelings of guilt that he had once induced in her. Going through a pregnancy and the delivery of her child with only Eloise's occasional support as a friend had made Pixie less self-critical. She had done all right alone; she might not have done brilliantly but there were many who would have coped worse and complained a great deal more. She had nothing to apologise for, she told herself bracingly.

Tor was in a very grim mood. He didn't like mysteries or unexpected developments and the instant the same woman who had forced her way into his office the previous year appeared in his office doorway, a chill of foreboding slid down his rigid spine. Who the hell was she? Stymied by the lack of information about her that day, he had failed to establish her identity after the event and had waited impatiently to see if any claim for child support arrived with his lawyers. When no such claim had arrived, he had written off her visit to a possible mental-health issue. But if she was the child's mother, who was the man surveillance had on tape who had left the child on the doorstep?

'I'm here to pick up my son,' Pixie announced stiffly, her slim shoulders rigid because being even the depth of a room away from Tor Sarantos was too close for

comfort. 'I'm sorry you've been dragged into this…
er…situation.'

There he stood, tall, poised, predatory dark eyes
locked to her like grappling hooks seeking purchase
in her tender skin. He was angry, suspicious, everything she didn't want to be forced to deal with but, even
with him in that mood, she wasn't impervious to how
gorgeous he was, clad in an impossibly elegant dark
grey designer suit, sharply tailored to his lean, powerful
frame. And while still being that aware of his movie-
star-hot looks annoyed her, it also reminded her of how
very strange it was that she could ever have conceived
a child with a man so far out of her league.

That night they had been together so briefly loomed
like a distant and surreal fantasy in the back of her
mind and her face heated with mortification because
that night was the very last thing she wanted to think
about in his presence.

'You need to come in, take a seat and explain what
you describe as a "situation" to me,' Tor said coolly,
watching her like a hawk.

She was incredibly tiny and curvy with a torrent of
golden curls that framed her heart-shaped face and enhanced her crystal-blue eyes. Something about her eyes
struck him as weirdly familiar; there was something
too about that soft, full, pink mouth and the stirring of
that vague chord of familiarity spooked Tor as much as
a gun held to his head. Because Pixie Miller, whoever
she was, was *not* his type. He had always gone for tall
brunettes and certainly not a tiny blonde, who from a
distance could probably still be mistaken for a child.

'I don't want to talk to you… I just want to collect my son,' Pixie told him truthfully.

'I'm afraid it's not that simple. I need to know what's going on here and then I need to contact social services.'

'Why would you need to contact them?' Pixie gasped in dismay, the colour draining from her face.

'Come in, sit down,' Tor repeated steadily, wondering why she was so skittish and reluctant to speak up when presumably the baby had been dropped as a most effective way of grabbing his attention and forcing such a meeting. 'And then we can talk.'

Pixie clenched her teeth together hard and steeled herself to walk into the book-lined room. He planted a seat down in front of his desk and tapped it.

Pixie slung him a mutinous glance. 'I'm not sitting down while you stand over me,' she warned him. 'Where's my son?'

'In a safe environment being cared for by a nanny. If it makes you feel more secure, I will sit down as well,' Tor breathed impatiently, stepping back behind his desk and dropping down into the leather office chair there.

'You mentioned social services,' Pixie reminded him tautly. *'Why?'*

Tor ignored the question. First, he wanted some facts. 'Who was the man who left the baby outside this house?'

Pixie stiffened. 'My half-brother, Jordan. We had an argument…er…a misunderstanding,' she corrected uncomfortably.

'Why here? Why this house?' Tor pressed.

'Jordan knows you're Alfie's father,' Pixie murmured flatly, focusing on a gold pen lying on the desktop.

'And how could he possibly know that when *I* don't know it?' Tor enquired very drily. 'Am I the victim of some silly story you have told your brother about how you got pregnant?'

Pixie compressed her lips and paled. 'No. I tried to tell you last year at your office, but I bottled out when you didn't even remember me,' she admitted plainly, feeling the shame and sting of that moment warming her cheeks afresh. 'That was a bit too much of a challenge for me.'

His sleek ebony brows had drawn together as he studied her, dark eyes flaming like melted caramel below his outrageous lashes, those beautiful eyes that she had been seduced by that unforgettable night. 'Let's get this straight.' In shock at her simple explanation, Tor regressed a step. 'You are saying that that baby is *mine*?'

'Yes,' Pixie said simply.

'I am finding that hard to credit when I don't remember you. Yes, there is a certain familiarity about your eyes, possibly your face, but that's *all*.'

'So sorry I wasn't a more memorable event,' Pixie countered thinly. 'But facts are facts. You were with me and you got me pregnant.'

'I never have sex without contraception.'

Pixie flung her head back, anger in her gaze. 'Well, you did with me and Alfie is the result. Maybe it was wrong of me not to see a solicitor while I was still pregnant and make some sort of formal approach to you but it's bad enough having to tell you about it, never mind some total stranger! But there it is, that night happened even though we both regret it.'

Tor sprang upright, outraged by the words spilling

from her lips. He didn't sleep around indiscriminately, and he was always careful and responsible when sex was involved. 'I still find this story almost impossible to credit and think it may be wiser for us to proceed through legal channels...'

'Oh, for goodness' sake,' Pixie groaned, tipping her head forward and then pushing her hands through her tumbled curls to push the strands off her face again. 'I'm not being fair to you, am I? If you honestly don't remember, it's *because* you were drunk and grieving... although, in my defence, I have to say that I didn't realise how drunk you were until afterwards.'

Tor had frozen in place, a darkening expression of consternation tightening his lean, dark features. 'Drunk? *Grieving?* I rarely drink to excess.'

'It was the anniversary of your wife and child's accident,' Pixie filled in heavily. 'You told me that you went out every year on that date and drank while you remembered them.'

With difficulty, Tor forced himself back down stiffly into his chair. Inside he was reeling with shock, but that she knew that much about him literally confirmed his worst fears and struck him like a hammer blow. How much had he told her? *All* of it or only some of it? He was affronted by his own failure to keep his secrets where they belonged.

'And it's probably very rude to say it...but when you're drunk, you're a much nicer, more approachable guy,' Pixie whispered apologetically. 'If you'd been like you are now, I probably wouldn't have made love with you, which of course would have been wiser for all of us…although I couldn't ever give up Alfie, even to make you feel better.'

'Make *me* feel better?' Tor echoed in disbelief. 'Nothing you have so far told me could make me feel better!'

'Yes, you're one of those glass half-empty rather than half-full types, aren't you?' Pixie sighed. 'Look, now we've got the embarrassing stuff out of the way, can I please see my son?'

'I'm afraid it isn't that straightforward.'

'Why not?' Pixie demanded. 'What's the problem?'

'Where were *you* when your brother took your son and left him in the street?'

'I was in bed.' Pixie flushed beneath his censorious gaze. 'I'm a nurse and I'd just come off night shift. I come home, feed and dress Alfie and then I leave him in Jordan's care while I sleep. I'm usually up by lunchtime. I can get by on very little sleep. And Jordan didn't leave Alfie in the street.'

'He *did*,' Tor interposed flatly.

'Yes, but he hung around somewhere nearby to ensure that Alfie was taken into the house before he left. Look, I *know* that what Jordan did was totally wrong and dangerous and that he shouldn't have done it. I'm still very angry about it too,' Pixie declared tautly. 'But the point is, Jordan has been helping me to look after Alfie and letting us live with him ever since Alfie was born. I owe my brother a lot.'

'I can understand that.'

'No, not really, how could you? You can't understand when you live like *this*…' Pixie shifted an expressive, almost scornful hand that encompassed all the opulent designer touches that distinguished the decor even in a home office setting. 'You and me? We live in very different worlds. In my world it's a struggle to keep a roof over our heads and pay the bills.'

'We will deal with all those problems at a more appropriate time,' Tor cut in. 'Right now I am more concerned about the child's present welfare and security.'

'Alfie's none of your business,' Pixie told him curtly, compressing her lips so hard they went white. 'Do you think I don't appreciate how you feel about this situation? Do you really think I want anything from a man who would prefer that neither I nor my child even exists? '

'This is all getting very emotional and again it is not the right time for this discussion,' Tor countered grimly. 'If your child is also *my* child, I obviously don't want to involve the social services in this issue. But neither am I prepared to hand over custody of a baby to someone who may not keep him safe from harm.'

'How dare you?' Pixie gasped, leaping up out of her seat in angry disbelief at that condemnation.

'Whether you like it or not, you have given me the right to interfere. Either I'm acting as a concerned citizen or as a possible father to ensure that the baby is protected. You can see your son but I will *not* allow you to remove him from this household or take him anywhere near your brother until I am convinced that that is in *his* best interests,' Tor completed with harsh conviction.

'You can't do that…' Pixie whispered shakily.

'Either you accept my conditions, or I contact the authorities, explain what has happened and allow them to make the decisions. If you choose the second option, be aware that neither of us can control events in that scenario,' Tor warned her.

'You don't even believe that Alfie is yours yet,' she protested tightly. 'Why are you trying to screw up our lives? Alfie's a happy child.'

'I want your permission to carry out DNA testing,' Tor admitted. 'I want irrefutable proof of whether or not he is my child.'

'Of course, you're not going to take my word for it,' Pixie remarked stiffly.

Tor was tempted to say that once, without even asking the question, he had blithely assumed that a child was his and had then learnt, very much to his shock, that it was not an assumption any man could afford to make. Now he took nothing for granted and he checked and double-checked everything and trusting anyone had become a serious challenge.

'Will you agree to the testing?' he prompted.

Pixie nodded jerkily for she could think of no good reason to avoid the process. He had the right to know to his own satisfaction that Alfie was his son and it would be wrong of her to deny him that validation, wouldn't it be? Unhappily, however, events were moving far too fast in a direction she had not foreseen.

She had been foolishly naïve when she'd raced to Tor's home to collect her son, too distraught to appreciate that there would be long-term consequences to such exposure. Tor would not let either of them walk away again until his questions were answered. And evidently, she had misjudged him that day at his office. He *had* forgotten her as entirely as though she had never existed and that was an unwelcome truth that could only hurt.

As she watched, he pulled out a phone, selected a number and began speaking to someone in a foreign language. She wondered if it was Greek while she scanned the eloquent movement of a lean brown hand, fingers spreading and then curling as he talked. For such a tall, well-built guy he was very graceful, but all his movements were tense and controlled, hinting at the darkness of his mood.

The night they had met Tor had been so natural, so relaxed and open with her. Sober, however, he was a very different person with his freezing politeness and disciplined reserve. But she could still read him well enough to recognise that her appearance and that of a potential child in his life were a huge surprise and a disaster on his terms. He didn't *want* Alfie. He might be talking impressively about needing to ensure that Alfie was safe, but he wasn't personally interested in her son, excited at the possibility of being his father, or indeed anything positive that she could see.

'I've organised the DNA testing,' he informed her grimly. 'Now I want you to sit back down and tell me about the night we met.'

'No…' Pixie's refusal leapt straight to her lips.

'But obviously I want to know what happened between us!' Tor slung back at her between gritted teeth.

'Why should you need to know anything when Alfie's the evidence?' Pixie dared, lifting her chin.

'So, you expect me to just live with this blank space in my memory?' Tor breathed with incredulous bite.

'Yes, I'm quite happy to exist in that blank and I don't see any advantage to raking over an encounter that upsets you so much.'

'I'm *not* upset,' Tor responded icily.

'Angry, ashamed, whatever you want to call it. It doesn't matter to me now,' Pixie told him truthfully, wishing he could bring himself to be a little more honest with her. 'All I want now is to see my son.'

Tor released his breath in a soundless hiss of frustration. He wasn't accustomed to dealing with opposition from a woman. Women invariably went out of their way to please and flatter him, keen to attract and retain his interest. But Pixie Miller?

She was more likely to raise her stubborn chin and challenge him with defiant crystal-blue eyes. And he wondered, *of course*, he wondered if it had been that difference in her that had attracted him to her in the first place. Was he attracted to stronger, more independent women? Certainly, he never had been in the past, had always played safe by choosing quiet, discreet lovers who understood that sex with him didn't ever lead to anything deeper.

But that he should have slept with another woman that night of all nights? That shook him, but it also filled him with intense curiosity. He might not know her, but he knew himself. Either Pixie had been extraordinarily seductive, or she was something a great deal more special than she was willing to admit or he was able to remember…

CHAPTER FOUR

'I THINK YOU could at least take your coat off before I take you upstairs to your son,' Tor told Pixie drily. 'You won't be returning home until we sort this out.'

With a stiff little twist of her shoulders, Pixie removed her coat. 'There's nothing to sort and I have to be back at work by seven.'

'Leaving the baby in your brother's tender care? Not on my watch,' Tor spelt out curtly, watching her bend to drape the coat over the chair and reveal an awesomely curvy bottom covered in tight denim. Grabbable, squeezable, touchable, every word that occurred to him startled him because he was no longer a sexually libidinous teenager and he didn't leer at women's bodies like one either, did he? Well, so much for Pixie Miller not being his type, a little devil piped up in the back of his brain, infuriating him even more as a throbbing pulse at his groin stirred.

She was sexy, *very* sexy, that was all it was, and her appeal was all the stronger because she didn't work at it. No, there was nothing remotely inviting or sensual about her presentation of herself, he conceded grudgingly, nothing in her appearance that sought attention.

She looked like what she was: a young mother on a restricted income. But that description did not encompass the whole of her or reveal the charm of those tousled golden curls, the clarity of her bright anxious eyes, the soft pink pout of her mouth.

Angrily aware of his burgeoning erection, Tor led the way out of the room and up the sweeping staircase. He hadn't even looked at the child, hadn't gone near it. If he was honest with himself for once, that was because he tended to avoid young children and the memories they roused of Sofia.

Now in many ways, though, he was being confronted by his worst nightmare: another child and a relationship with a woman that could not be denied, the sort of bonds he had been resolutely determined to avoid since the death of his wife and daughter.

Of course, her son could not be his! At the very least it was highly unlikely. Had he even *had* sex with her that night? There was still room for doubt on that score. He had few memories of that anniversary, had already acknowledged that he had behaved irresponsibly by getting dangerously drunk. He had wakened with an aching head in an unfamiliar bedroom, but he had *still* been fully clothed. That he could have had sex with anyone had not once occurred to him, only that he shouldn't have been reckless enough to get that intoxicated. As he had left that strange house in haste, someone had been coming downstairs behind him and he hadn't even turned his head because all he had wanted to do was get home. He had known even at that point that he would not be drowning himself in alcohol for that anniversary ever again. It had been a foolish, juvenile habit he had naturally decided not to repeat.

'They're in here...' Tor thrust open the door.

Pixie surged over the threshold. Standing up, Alfie was holding on to the side of a travel cot and bouncing with his usual irrepressible energy. He was the strangest mix of his parental genes, she thought fondly, because he had inherited her golden curls with his father's dark eyes and olive skin tone.

'Mm...mm...mm!' Alfie burbled excitedly, his sturdy little arms lifting as soon as he saw his mother.

'I think he's trying to say Mum,' the smiling young woman hovering said. 'Hello, I'm Emma and I've been looking after your...son?'

Alfie clawed up the front of Pixie's body in his desperation to reach her and held on as tight as a clam with his whole body wrapped round her, burying his little face fearfully in her shoulder, still muttering, 'Mm...mm.'

It was the moment when Pixie would have happily killed her brother for having subjected her child to such a frightening experience. Alfie wasn't normally clingy, and she had never seen him frightened before because he was one of those unnerving kids who jumped unafraid into unfamiliar situations and left her with her heart in her mouth.

'Alfie,' Pixie sighed, hugging him close. 'Hello, Emma. I'm Pixie and, yes, I'm his mum and this little boy got lost this morning and I was frantic!' She punctuated those remarks by tickling Alfie under the ribs in an effort to break him free of his anxiety and it worked. Alfie went off into paroxysms of giggles and leant back, the weight of him forcing Pixie to kneel down and brace him on the floor before he toppled both of them.

'He's a real little charmer,' Emma commented. 'How old is he?'

'Nine months.'

'And already getting ready to walk. My goodness, that'll be a challenge for you,' Emma chattered. 'The younger they are, the less sense they have.'

Tor had frozen where he stood as Alfie flung his head back, laughing, and his dancing dark eyes and slanting mischievous grin reminded Tor powerfully of his youngest brother, Kristo, who was only seventeen. Unnerved by that instantaneous sense of familial recognition, he looked hastily away, reminding himself that the child was very unlikely to be related to him. But if he *was*?

A faint shudder raked through Tor's tall, powerful frame because *that* would be a game-changer, the ultimate game-changer, forcing him to embrace everything he had turned his back on. Choice would have nothing to do with it.

'This is Alfie,' Pixie said simply as she looked up at Tor, so impossibly tall from that angle as she knelt. He looked pale, or as pale as someone as sun bronzed as he was could look, she adjusted uncomfortably.

Alfie settled back on the floor to explore a plastic truck with his fingers and his mouth, his attention unnervingly locked to Tor as if he was sizing him up. Tor wanted to back away. Countless memories of Sofia at the same age were engulfing him but he fought them off and got down on his knees, careless of his suit and his dignity.

'Shall I leave now, Mr Sarantos?' the nanny enquired.

'No, we still need you, but you can take a break while Alfie has his mother here,' Tor murmured, quite proud of the steadiness of his voice as Emma nodded and left the room.

Alfie settled the truck down on Tor's thigh and sat back expectantly, big chocolate-coloured eyes unerringly pinned to Tor, almost as though he could sense his discomfiture.

'Let me,' Pixie began to intervene awkwardly.

'No, I've got this.' Alfie chuckled as Tor ran the truck along the floor with the appropriate *vroom-vroom* noises even though his eyes stung like mad as he did it and he cursed himself for being a sentimental fool.

Alfie grinned and patted Tor's thigh to indicate that he wanted his truck back now that its magic had been demonstrated to his satisfaction. Tor handed it back and hastily backed away, vaulting back upright again.

'I'm sorry... I'm out of practice. I've avoided young children since, well, since Sofia's death,' he admitted grittily, determined to be frank because he had evidently been more than frank with this young woman when they first met and for once there was no reason for him to put up a front.

Pixie almost winced because that likelihood hadn't occurred to her, and she scolded herself for not appreciating that Alfie would resurrect memories that Tor probably preferred to bury. Even so, on another level and one she didn't want to examine, his sensitivity saddened her because Alfie was his child too. Of course, he wouldn't accept that until he had the official proof of it.

With a knock on the door the woman who appeared to be the housekeeper appeared and announced that Tor had a visitor downstairs.

'I'll send him up when he's done with me. It'll be the DNA testing I requested.'

'My goodness, how did you get it organised this quickly?' Pixie exclaimed in surprise.

'To put it simply…money talks,' Tor replied drily. 'But I'm afraid we'll still have to wait twenty-four hours for the results.'

'Well, I'm not going to be in suspense,' Pixie pointed out.

'You haven't the slightest doubt?'

Pixie reddened and then lifted her head high, her crystal-blue eyes awash with censure.

'No. You were my first and only, so there isn't the smallest chance that anyone else could have fathered Alfie.'

His lean, darkly handsome features tightened as though she had struck him, and she might as well have done, Tor acknowledged. He paused at the door and glanced back at her. 'How old are you?'

'Twenty-two,' Pixie answered. 'You asked me the same question the night we met. It's infuriating. It's because I'm small and people always assume I'm younger than I am.'

Tor went downstairs to have the swab done for the DNA testing with an inescapable sense of guilt. If that little boy was his child, he had hit on a twenty-one-year-old virgin, left her to struggle through her pregnancy alone, denied all knowledge of her when she'd approached him for support and generally treated her in the most unforgivable manner. The idea that he could have behaved like that shattered him and left him reeling with shock because the whole nightmare situation was making him appreciate that he hadn't been living in the *real* world for over six years.

He had been living in the past, seeing the world and the people around him through toxic lenses, believing that he was standing tall and strong in the face of adversity when in fact he was continually backing away from the wounding truth that his wife and his half-brother had betrayed him. He hadn't come to terms with it, hadn't dealt with it, hadn't put it behind him the way he should have done.

And in reacting in that inflexible way, it seemed he might have caused one hell of a lot of damage to an innocent bystander. He breathed in deep and slow as he made those deductions and hoped that the child turned out not to be his, because at that moment the alternative was just too much for him to contemplate.

The DNA test was carried out in minutes and Pixie was left alone with her son. After some energetic play, Alfie went down in the travel cot for a nap. She had put her phone on mute because Jordan had called her repeatedly and she wasn't in the mood to talk to him and didn't know what she would say when she did. He had destroyed her trust in him but to a certain extent she understood his frustration with her.

She had leant on her brother when she should've been seeking the support of Alfie's father because her pride had got in the way and that stubborn pride of hers hadn't done her any favours.

For months, Jordan had been forced to stay home

most evenings while she was at work, a considerable sacrifice for a young, single man. Worse still, he was unable to look for other employment because only casual barista work allowed him to choose his hours and mind Alfie for his sister. Her decision to go ahead and have her child had adversely affected Jordan's life. It was pointless to say that she had never meant to do that when she had still gone ahead and done what *she* wanted to do, which was to give birth to a child without a partner and depend on her brother's help.

If she could have gone back and changed things she knew she would have done it all differently, she conceded heavily. She had taxed her brother's patience for too long, forcing him to act in an effort to make her confront Tor. Yes, dumping Alfie on Tor's doorstep had been absolutely the wrong way to go about achieving that, but had she gone to a solicitor to claim child support from Tor, Jordan might have been released from the responsibility of having to help her look after her child months ago.

'Mr Sarantos would like you to come downstairs for a meal,' Emma told her, sliding into the room on quiet feet. 'I'll keep an eye on Alfie.'

Pixie checked the time and suppressed a sigh. Soon she would need to get home to get ready for work. As she came down into the hall the housekeeper was waiting to show her into a formal dining room, where a polished table set with silver cutlery and crystal wine glasses awaited her. Tor strolled forward, all lithe contained power, vibrant energy radiating from his dark golden eyes.

'I assumed you'd be hungry.'

'I've haven't got much time before we have to leave,' Pixie responded uncomfortably.

'I still want to know what happened that night between us,' Tor admitted, disconcerting her.

'But it's not important now,' Pixie reasoned stiffly.

'If you're telling me the truth and that night led to the conception of my son, it's *very* important,' Tor contradicted as a man in a short white jacket entered and proceeded to pour the wine, mercifully silencing him on that subject.

'Not for me, thank you,' Pixie said, refusing the wine while watching the man leave again with wide eyes. 'You are surrounded by staff here.'

'I have to concentrate on work. Domestic staff take the irritating small stuff out of my day. How do you feel about leaving Alfie here in Emma's care tonight?'

Pixie paled. 'I'd prefer to take him home.'

'Which would mean your brother taking charge of him again. Give your brother a night off,' Tor urged.

Her slight shoulders stiffened. She had to talk to Jordan before she could feel that she could trust him again with her child. 'If I didn't have to go to work, I wouldn't agree,' she muttered ruefully. 'But just one night, and I'll have to go home and get Alfie's things before.'

'Anything the baby needs can be bought.'

'Bunny, his toy rabbit, can't be, and he won't go down for the night without it. Babies like familiar things around them. It makes them feel secure.' Pixie sighed. 'I also need to feed my cat and if Alfie stays, when am I supposed to get him back tomorrow?'

'I'm expecting you to return here in the morning and stay. A room beside his will be prepared for your use.

It would also mean that you'll be here when the DNA results become available.'

He already had her movements and Alfie's all worked out on his schedule, but letting him interfere in their lives to that extent disturbed Pixie. On the other hand, Tor contacting the authorities to share his concern about Alfie's safety in her brother's custody would cause a firestorm, which would be a great deal worse, she conceded wryly. In truth, with that 'concerned citizen' threat of his, Tor Sarantos had trapped her between a rock and a hard place and deprived her of choice.

'That night…' Tor said again, shimmering dark golden eyes locking to her and making it hard for her to find her voice.

And Pixie gave way but stuck to the bare bones, telling him about their meeting in the kitchen, the cheese toasted sandwich she had given him and the accidental collision he had had with the cupboard door. While she talked, a deliciously cooked meal was served, and she began to eat.

'Yes… I had a bruise above my eye,' Tor commented with a frown. 'I wondered if I'd fallen or got into some sort of altercation.'

'The taxi didn't arrive and that was my fault too,' Pixie explained in a rush. 'I was only staying there for two weeks and when you asked me for the house number I got it wrong. I only realised that a couple of days afterwards.'

'These are dry facts,' Tor remarked, cradling his wine glass elegantly in one lean brown hand as he lounged back in his chair like a king surveying a recalcitrant subject. 'You've stripped everything personal out of this account. Nothing you have yet shared explains how we ended up in bed together.'

'I should think your imagination could fill in that particular blank,' Pixie dared.

'Surprisingly not. That particular night I wouldn't have been looking for sex with anyone,' Tor asserted coolly. 'It was out of character.'

'Blame the alcohol.'

'And as you were a virgin, presumably it was out of character for you as well.'

Pixie went red as fire and hated him for throwing that in her teeth. 'Obviously, I was overwhelmingly attracted to you.'

An entirely spontaneous grin slashed Tor's wide sensual mouth, chasing the gravity from his startlingly handsome features. 'OK.'

'Was that *personal* enough for you?' Pixie slammed back at him sharply as she rose from the table, furious that he had embarrassed her and that she had been that honest with him in her response.

As Tor also sprang up, smouldering dark golden eyes collided with hers and she stopped breathing and froze in her retreat to the door. She couldn't drag her attention from him as he stalked towards her, all lean predatory grace and masculine power.

'No, in the interests of research I'd like to get a lot more personal,' Tor confided. 'I want to kiss you.'

Pixie was knocked off balance entirely by that familiar phrase. 'You said that that night.'

'And what did you say?'

Do it,' she recalled weakly as he reached for her. The tip of his tongue licked along the closed seam of her mouth and she shivered violently, wanting more, craving more, outraged by the flood of instant awareness cascading through her treacherous body. She didn't know what he did to her self-discipline, but it was lethal because with one touch her whole body switched on as though he had pressed a magic button. Her skin felt too tight round her bones, her breath shortened in her throat and her heart began to pound. The light play of his splayed fingers across her spine somehow made her breasts swell and stir inside her bra, letting her feel the straining tautness of her nipples. Her lips parted and he took advantage, delving between to explore the moist interior of her mouth.

The immediate rush of heat and dampness between her thighs took her by storm, prickling, tingling awareness shooting through every nerve ending she possessed. She jerked in helpless response. It was one kiss and her body leapt on it as though it were her first meal after a famine.

He pressed her back against the table and her hands lifted up, her fingers spearing into his springy black hair to hold him fast while his firm lips moved with compelling hunger on hers. The bottom could've fallen out of the world at that moment and she wouldn't have noticed. Her surroundings had fallen away. All she was aware of was him, the hard, demanding bar of his erection against her stomach, the passion of his mouth on hers, the glorious heat and strength of him that close.

Breathing raggedly, Tor dragged his mouth from her and pulled back from her, dark eyes flaring with bright golden intensity and full of new knowledge. 'Well, I don't need to ask *how* it happened, do I? We have explosive chemistry…and I'm remembering things now. The taste of you…and green hair? *Diavole*…where does *green* hair come into it? And I said that you reminded me of a forest fairy? *Thee mou*…spouting nonsense of that calibre, I must've been incredibly drunk!'

Pixie reeled back from him, deeply shaken by the passion that had betrayed her in his arms, exposing a vulnerability that mortified her. She didn't even feel relieved that he was starting to remember stuff, only more mortified and exposed than ever.

'I had dyed my hair before we met…it stayed sort of pale green until it finally washed out,' she muttered tightly. 'And you *did* compare me to a forest fairy, but only because someone else said I reminded them of a leprechaun with my green hair and I told you that.'

Tor shot her a glance of concealed wonderment because she was on another plane entirely, too naïve to even register how unusual it was to find a sexual connection that strong. He had gone up in flames with her. She was a dynamite charge in a tiny package and all he had wanted to do was spread her out on the table and thrust inside her hard and fast.

The ache of having to deny and control his libido was new to him. Sex had become something Tor snapped his fingers and received with minimal effort. Persuading or coaxing had never been required from him. But no woman had ever aroused him to the extent that Pixie did. Her effect on him, however, certainly explained what must have happened that night and his own unusual recklessness…

But he had recalled enough of his own reactions to be thoroughly disconcerted by what he was both learning and remembering. *Best sex I ever had...* That was what he had fallen asleep thinking that night, satiated by the glory of her silken, tight depths. He breathed in deep and slow, tamping down those thoughts and forcing himself back to the present.

'A limo will take you home and bring you back here again. Do you want me to accompany you? At some stage, I will need to speak to your brother,' Tor imparted, while thinking that within a couple of days he would know everything he needed to know about the siblings because he had told his head of security to have them checked out.

'Why would you need to speak to Jordan?'

Tor compressed his lips. 'Because you don't appear to have sufficient control over him.'

Her face flamed with annoyance because she was in no position to argue after what Jordan had done with Alfie.

'Look, with Emma here I'll let Alfie stay here tonight and I'll come back in the morning as you asked but, to be frank, once the emergency is over, I hope we can all settle back down and get on with our lives,' Pixie admitted, hoping that if she gave a little, he would too. 'But I don't want you to speak to Jordan. I'll take care of that.'

'How?' Tor challenged.

'I can't defend what Jordan did this morning when he left Alfie here,' Pixie conceded. 'But he's my half-brother, my only surviving family and he's been good to both of us when there was nobody else willing to help, so please cut him some slack...'

'If that baby *is* my son, it's going to change your lives,' Tor retorted in a growling undertone, ignoring her plea on her brother's behalf. 'I'd be a liar if I said anything else.'

Pixie set her teeth firmly together on a hasty and ill-judged response to that statement. She saw no reason why he should interfere with *her* life. She was willing to accept him as a masculine role model in Alfie's world and hopefully a better one than Jordan had so far proved to be. Presumably, Tor would expect to spend time with Alfie. He would also expect to contribute towards his support, she assumed, but she hoped that that would be as far as his interference went because there was nothing more personal between them than that single night and Alfie's unintentional conception.

Really? a little voice sniped, unimpressed, deep inside her. What about that kiss? What about that response you gave him? That had gone way beyond masculine role models and child support, that had been personal and intimate to a level that filled Pixie with guilt and discomfiture. That kiss had smashed through the defensive barriers she had forged and blown her away.

'Why did you call him Alfie?'

'I named him after my grandfather. He was a wonderful character. He died when I was six, but I never forgot him.'

Tor accompanied her to the front door, waiting there in silence until a sleek black shiny limousine pulled up outside. 'I have an appointment now, so I won't see you before you leave for work. Hopefully, I'll see you in the morning for breakfast,' he murmured silkily.

Pixie nodded and went down the steps, wide-eyed as the driver climbed out to open the passenger door of the limousine for her. She got in, sinking into the

pearl-grey leather upholstery and scanning the embel-
lishments in front of her, wondering what the various
buttons and switches she could see did, but restraining
herself from experimenting lest she embarrass herself.

The house was empty when she got back. Jordan had
gone out, probably to avoid dealing with her recrimina-
tions, she reflected with a wry shake of her head. She
rushed around, gathering up her son's belongings, and
changed for work, conscious that she didn't have much
time to waste.

If that baby is my son, it's going to change your lives.

That declaration had aggravated her. Tor Sarantos
could only change what she *allowed* him to change,
she reminded herself bracingly. He didn't own her; he
didn't own either of them. He couldn't force her to do
anything she didn't want to do…

CHAPTER FIVE

ELOISE SAT ACROSS the table in the hospital canteen from Pixie during their break and said, 'About the only thing your brother got right was when he advised you to take what you can get to make raising Alfie easier. His father *should* be sharing the responsibility.'

Pixie stiffened and blinked, taken aback by the pretty brunette's frankly offered opinion. Since the other nurse and her brother had broken up, by mutual agreement both women had avoided discussing Jordan. 'I never thought you'd say that.'

'It's gloves-off time. The best thing for both you and Alfie would be to get as far away from Jordan as you can because if you don't, he'll rob you blind like he did me.' Eloise sighed. 'I'm sorry to be that blunt, Pixie, but Jordan left me broke. Although I could never get the truth out of him, money was always disappearing, and I didn't believe the stories he told me. I suspected he was gambling but he laughed in my face when I accused him, and I couldn't prove anything. If Alfie's father gives you financial help, grab it with both hands and step away from your brother.'

'*Gambling?*' Pixie whispered, aghast.

'What else could he be at? Where do you think the debts he's always complaining about are coming from?' Eloise prompted in an undertone, mindful of the diners at tables nearby. 'He doesn't live the high life or smoke or use drugs. The money has to be going somewhere and, if you're not careful, you and Alfie will end up on the street because when I moved out that mortgage was already in serious arrears.'

Pixie frowned. 'But I give him most of the money to cover it every month.'

'Check it out for yourself. Your name's on the mortgage too,' Eloise reminded her drily. 'Stop trusting Jordan to take care of the budget because I suspect he's been pulling the wool over your eyes as well.'

'You think he's dishonest. That's why you dumped him,' Pixie finally grasped and that new knowledge made her feel grossly uncomfortable. 'But if he *was* that kind of cheating, lying person, why would he have looked after me for so long?'

The brunette rolled her eyes ruefully. 'Everyone's a mix of good and bad. But you had better believe that your brother dumped your son on his rich father's doorstep because he decided that there was something in it for *him*!'

'I wish you'd told me what you suspected sooner,' Pixie admitted heavily, having been given a lot to think about. It was an empty wish, but she found herself wishing that her parents were still alive because she would have turned to them for advice. She felt gutted by the suspicion that Jordan might have been up to no good behind her back and that he could not be trusted with money.

'Jordan and I split up and bad-mouthing him to his sister afterwards struck me as bitchy and unnecessary because I've moved on now.'

After that conversation, it was a struggle for Pixie to concentrate on work and when she was leaving the hospital, with her brain buzzing with conjecture, she was dismayed to see Jordan waiting for her outside the door because she still wasn't ready to deal with him. At the same time, though, she knew it was necessary.

Her brother gave her a sad-eyed sideways glance. 'I'm sorry,' he said awkwardly as he walked by her side. 'But I didn't have a choice—'

'There's *always* a choice, Jordan!' Pixie cut in thinly.

'No, on this occasion there truly wasn't,' Jordan told her, dropping down onto a stone bench that overlooked the busy car park. 'You ignored all my advice. You refused to go to a solicitor and apply for child support.'

'I know *but*—' Pixie deemed it too early in the conversation to admit that she now accepted she had leant too heavily on him for support.

'The house is about to be repossessed,' Jordan told her heavily.

Pixie turned bone white. 'That's not possible. There would have been letters.'

'I've been hiding the letters. I hoped that I could stop it happening, but I can't, and I *had* to force you to deal with Sarantos some way, so that he could be there to look after you and Alfie. I didn't want you ending up in some homeless shelter because I've been stupid!'

Pixie's knees finally gave way and she sat down beside him, plunged deep into shock by that blunt confession. 'But I've been giving you money towards the payment every month.'

'It's all gone. I'm sorry but we're going to lose the house,' Jordan muttered heavily.

As he confirmed Eloise's misgivings, Pixie was reeling in horror and disbelief at such a betrayal of her trust. 'But how could that happen?'

Her brother sprang up again, refusing to meet her stricken gaze. 'I'm very sorry,' he said again and he walked away at speed.

Pixie splurged on another taxi to return to Tor's town house. She was in a state and her exhaustion wasn't helping. Worry about her brother's state of mind and the fear of impending homelessness had overloaded her brain. Only a couple of days ago she had been secure and now all of a sudden, and without warning, her life was falling apart. Once again she craved parental support. Jordan had lied to her and could no longer be trusted. In the aftermath of that acknowledgement, walking into the gracious luxury of Tor's home gave her a surreal feeling and, more than ever, the sense that she did not belong in such a setting.

She went straight upstairs and found Emma bathing Alfie. That reunion got her very damp, but she insisted on taking over because early mornings had always been her fun time with Alfie, and she treasured those moments when he was fresh for the new day and full of energy and nonsense.

She took him downstairs for breakfast, wincing at the formality of the dining room and the prospect of Alfie's mealtime messiness, but Mrs James, the housekeeper, did at least have a smile for her as a high chair was brought in—complete, she was amused to see, with a protective mat for it to sit on.

Tor, it seemed, was already long gone from the house, which was a relief for Pixie in the mood she was in.

After she and Alfie had both eaten their fill from an array of breakfast dishes that would not have shamed a top-flight hotel, she handed her son back to Emma and retired to the beautiful room next door to them, smothering a yawn.

Nothing would seem so bad after she had had a decent sleep, she soothed herself as she climbed into the wonderfully comfortable bed and set the alarm on her phone. Perhaps some solution would come to her while she slept, she thought hopefully, striving not to stress about the future but knowing in her gut that she did not want to be dependent on Tor.

She could share Alfie with him, but she wanted any other connection between them to be remote and unemotional and most definitely *not* physical. The last thing she needed was to get attached to a man still in love with his dead wife, even though she had cheated on him. She hoped she had more sense than that, but a hot, sexy Greek like Tor Sarantos played merry hell with a woman's common sense. She had made a huge mistake once with Tor, but she had no intention of repeating that mistake, she assured herself firmly.

The results of the DNA testing had been delivered to Tor at his office, but he resisted the urge to rip open the envelope. On another level, he knew he didn't really need to open the envelope to know that Alfie was *his* child. That truth had shone out of Pixie when he'd realised that she had no doubts about who had fathered her child, but, even more potently, Tor had felt the family connection the instant he saw Alfie's smile and was reminded of his little brother. The preliminary file he received on Pixie and her brother, however, posed more of a problem. The contents bothered Tor and while he also appreciated that those same facts would make Pixie more reliant on him for assistance, Tor didn't really want to be the bearer of such bad news when his relationship with Alfie's mother was already strained and difficult. On the other hand, he couldn't see that he had much of a choice on that score.

He went home at lunchtime, needing to be within reach of the child he believed to be his, before the results confirmed it. Telling a flustered Mrs James, taken aback by his sudden appearance, that he didn't need lunch, only coffee, he strode into his home office. He tore into the envelope then, and breathed in deep before he looked down at the page in his hand.

Ninety-nine point nine per cent likelihood that he was Alfie's father. Ironically, the shock wave of confirmation left him light-headed and then galvanised him into heading straight upstairs. He glanced down at his immaculate city suit and silk tie and frowned, striding into his bedroom to change.

He was a father, genuinely a father, for the first time. It shook him how much that meant to him. Of course, the first time around he had taken fatherhood for granted. He hadn't realised that until the night Katerina and Sofia died.

Katerina had put the little girl into the car against his wishes while informing him that he had no right to object because Sofia wasn't *his* daughter, but her lover's. Rage had burned in Tor's gut like a bushfire. Never again would he allow a woman to put him in so powerless a position, he'd sworn to himself.

He was a father, and fathers had rights…didn't they? He was an unmarried father, though. That was a different situation. He needed to talk to his legal team to find out exactly where he stood.

But that wasn't an immediate priority, he told himself impatiently, heading straight off to see his son.

Frustratingly, however, Alfie was sound asleep, his little flushed face tucked up against a battered rabbit soft toy, his bottom in the air. Tor studied the slumbering child intently, wanting to pick him up, wanting to hold him, knowing he could not. Phone the lawyers, his ESP was urging as the recollection of his own family history returned to haunt him.

His elder brother, Sevastiano, had grown up outside Tor's family circle because his Italian mother, Francesca, had changed her mind about marrying Tor's father to marry another man instead. Tor's father, Hallas, had moved heaven and earth to try to gain access to the child he had known Francesca was already carrying, but he had failed because a child born within marriage was deemed to be the husband's child and DNA testing had been in its infancy back then. Without evidence that there was a blood tie, the law and an antagonistic stepfather had excluded Hallas from his son's life. That sobering story in mind, Tor phoned his lawyers and, from them, he learned facts that startled him. In the

UK, an unmarried father had virtually no rights. He had no right to either custody or even visitation with his child without the mother's consent.

Pixie was emerging from the en suite bathroom wrapped in a capacious towel when a knock sounded on the bedroom door. She had slept like a log but the instant she wakened her mind began seething with anxiety again. If the house was to be repossessed, where was she going to live? How was she going to manage to work without Jordan to rely on for childcare? Checking the towel was secure, she opened the door a crack.

'It's Tor…can we talk?'

'Right now?' Pixie muttered doubtfully, stepping back a few feet without actually meaning him to take that retreat as an invitation.

Tor strode in without skipping a beat. 'Give me five minutes,' he urged.

His gorgeous black-lashed dark eyes locked to her, golden as heated honey, and she froze, scanning his appearance in faded jeans and a black top with almost hungry eagerness. He looked so good in denim he stole her breath from her lungs, the jeans showcasing lean hips and long powerful thighs. She dredged her attention from him again with pink spattering her cheeks and said uneasily, 'I need to get dressed.'

'You're pretty much covered from head to toe,' he pointed out gently.

It was true. The large towel stretched from above her breasts to her feet and she sank down on the side of the bed and endeavoured to relax and behave less awkwardly around him.

'I got the DNA results,' he volunteered. 'And as you said, Alfie's my son.'

'So?' Pixie prompted.

'We have a lot to talk about.'

'I suppose we have…that is *if* you're planning to play an active part in his life,' Pixie responded.

'So far I may not have made much of a showing in the father stakes, but I plan to change that,' Tor swore with impressive resolve.

'I believe that would benefit Alfie,' Pixie commented quietly.

'I hope that it will benefit *both* of you,' Tor countered with assurance, his attention welded to her because she was so tiny and dainty in the towel, her curls damp from the shower, bare pink toes peeping out from beneath it. Impossibly pretty, incredibly cute and sexy. All of a sudden, this tiny blonde was becoming the most fascinating woman he had come across in years. It was *because* she was Alfie's mother, he reasoned with himself, nothing at all to do with the fact that he wanted to rip the towel off her and spread her across the bed. That was just lust, normal, natural lust. It didn't relate to anything more complex.

Colouring at the tenor of his appraisal, Pixie shifted uneasily. 'I'm not sure I understand what you mean… obviously we can learn to be civil to each other,' she murmured. 'It's probably a blessing that we were never in an actual relationship. We've got none of the baggage that can go with that scenario. That's a healthy start.'

Tor didn't agree at all. He didn't want to be reminded that they had never been in a relationship. Nor did he want to be held at arm's length like a stranger.

'I'd like to have my name put on Alfie's birth certificate, but I understand you have to fill in forms and go to court to achieve that.'

'Then you already know more than I do,' Pixie admitted, stiffening a little at that reference to going to court, nervous of that legal step without even knowing why. 'I only know that when I registered his birth I couldn't put your name on the certificate without you being there and agreeing to it.'

'We'll look into it.'

'Look, can I get dressed now?' Pixie pressed. 'I'll come downstairs straight away.'

Tor departed, thinking about the contents of that file and the brother she semi-idolised for his supposed sacrifice in becoming her guardian. What he had to tell her would hurt, but he could not conceal the truth from her when her safety and his son's could be at risk.

Pixie got dressed, pulling on ankle boots, a flouncy skirt and a long loose sweater. She was off work for a few days and she liked to make the most of her downtime, usually commencing her break with a trip to the park with Alfie and a fancy coffee somewhere. But she didn't have the money to cover fancy coffees any longer, she reminded herself, feeling guilty about the taxis she had employed in recent days. Now she had to carefully conserve what money she had because she had to be prepared to find somewhere else to live. And there and then, the whole towering pack of cards on which her life and security were built began to topple, she acknowledged with a sinking in the pit of her stomach. Her salary was good, but it wouldn't stretch to cover both rent *and* childcare.

Tor awaited her in the opulent drawing room, which had oil paintings on the walls and sumptuous contemporary seating. A tray sat on the tiered coffee table. 'We'll serve ourselves,' he told the housekeeper smoothly.

Tor scanned the outfit Pixie wore, which was eclectic to say the very least, his gaze lingering on her slender, shapely legs and then whipping up to her flushed face beneath the curls she had haphazardly caught up in a knot on top of her head, the hairstyle accentuating her brilliant blue eyes. Natural, artless, everything he had never looked for in a woman, everything he had never guessed he would find appealing.

Pixie dished out the coffee, remembering that he took his black and sweet and handing it to him. She sank down into the depths of a capacious sofa, one knee neatly hooked over the other, her legs slanted to one side while tension thrummed through her, making her small body rigid while she wondered what he wanted to say and what demands he might try to make of her. His name on the birth certificate? She saw no reason to object to that.

'As soon as I realised that you were saying that I was the father of your child yesterday I asked my head of security to have your background investigated—'

'*Investigated?*' Pixie repeated, cutting in, her dismay unhidden.

'I'm sorry if that annoys you, but I needed to know more about you. It's standard in my life to take that sort of precaution,' Tor proffered unapologetically.

Pixie forced an uneasy little smile. 'I've got nothing to hide.'

'No, but unfortunately your brother did,' Tor revealed ruefully.

'If you're about to tell me that the house is about to be repossessed because of Jordan's debts, I already know. He came to see me after I finished work at the hospital today. It was a major shock because I wasn't aware that there was even a problem. He had hidden that from me.'

'His web of deception goes much deeper than that, I'm afraid,' Tor told her reluctantly.

Fully focused on his tall, powerful figure by the fireplace, Pixie sat forward with a frown. 'What do you mean?'

'When your parents passed away, your mother's house was left entirely to you.'

'No, the house was left to both Jordan and me,' Pixie corrected.

'Obviously, it was in your brother's interests to make you believe that, but that house, which originally belonged to your mother's parents, was left solely to *you*. In fact, so keen was your mother to ensure that the house went to you only that she wrote her will soon after she married Jordan's father, in the event that they should have any children. Social services were aware that the house belonged to you but at the time that Jordan applied to become your guardian he was decently employed and would have seemed to be a fine upstanding citizen, capable of taking care of his little half-sister…'

Her brow furrowed in growing surprise. 'Jordan didn't get a share of the house *too*?'

'No. But by taking on caring for you he gained access to a free roof over his head and as soon as you were old enough he got you to sign documents which enabled him to take out a large loan against the house.'

Pixie frowned. 'The bathroom and kitchen were badly in need of an update. We both had to sign for the loan.'

'I suspect he gave you forged documents. You were young, inexperienced. I doubt that it took much effort for him to fool you, and at the same time he got you to put him on the mortgage, which enabled him to do a great deal behind your back.'

Pixie blinked rapidly. What he was telling her was much worse than anything she could have dreamt up because he was suggesting that her brother had defrauded her, had taken advantage of her ignorance and *used* her to try to steal *her* inheritance. 'The loan was honest. There was nothing questionable about it,' she argued tightly, seeking a strand of comforting truth to cling to in her turmoil. 'The work needed to be done and there was no other way of paying for it.'

'But Jordan pocketed most of the loan and, I imagine, spent only a small part of it on home improvements. From what I understand that's when the gambling started. He bet, he lost, he borrowed more and more money from various sleazy sources, and he sank deeper and deeper into debt. He's a gambling addict.'

'Then he needs professional help,' she whispered painfully, appalled that Jordan could have sunk so low without her even noticing and wondering what could possibly be done to cure him of such an addiction. She was gutted and she felt horribly alone, for he was her only relative. Yet in her heart her fondness for Jordan still lingered deep down, even though the man he was now wasn't the man he had been a few years earlier.

'He should be punished for what he's done to you,' Tor contradicted, his firm mouth compressing into a taut line.

'Mum *should* have left the house to both of us,' she protested on her brother's behalf. 'It must've been very hurtful for Jordan to realise that he'd been left out.'

'He wasn't her son, he was her stepson,' Tor pointed out drily. 'Generally parents do choose to leave their worldly goods to blood relatives.'

'And you think Jordan targeted me because I was left the house?' Pixie demanded angrily, jumping to her feet. 'Well, I think that's nonsense! Maybe he did cheat to get his hands on the money, but he cared about me.'

'I'm not saying that he didn't, but using you to get his hands on more money quickly became his main motivation. Before he got involved you had a secure future with the ownership of that house. Instead he ensured you were loaded down with mortgage payments and student loans,' Tor sliced in in a harsh undertone. 'And now some very dangerous men are chasing him for repayment, which puts both you and Alfie at risk. You *can't* go back to that house. You can't risk meeting up with Jordan in public again either.'

'You can't tell me that!' Pixie gasped. 'You can't tell me where I can live and what I can and can't do!'

'When it comes to your security I will tell you, particularly if it affects my son.'

'You didn't want to know about your son when I was pregnant last year!' Pixie slung at him vengefully. 'Don't expect me to have faith in you now!'

'You know now that I didn't remember you and that I'm only telling you what you don't want to hear because you need to know those facts,' Tor countered in his measured level drawl. 'But you *can* have faith in my determination to ensure that neither you nor my son are further affected by Jordan's bad choices.'

'But I *have* to go back to the house… I've got a cat to look after…and then there's all my stuff.' Pixie gasped, the ramifications of what he was telling her finally beginning to sink in.

'I'll make arrangements for you to remove your cat and your possessions immediately. There's a good chance that your brother's creditors will ransack the property and take anything that they can sell.'

Pixie went pale and broke out in nervous perspiration. 'Oh…my…word,' she whispered in horror. 'This is a nightmare.'

'With my support it doesn't have to be.' Tor pulled his phone out and began to make calls while she stared at him wordlessly.

He was on the phone for about ten minutes and it sounded as though he was rattling off instructions to someone. 'When you go to the house you will take my security team with you to protect you and you will leave Alfie here.'

Slowly, painfully, it was dawning on Pixie that, faced with impending homelessness, she was in no position to call any shots. 'But I can't move in here!' she exclaimed.

'I am more than happy to have you and Alfie here.'

'Well, possibly for a few days until I can move on. I'll have to find somewhere I can rent. Maybe there's someone at work I can share with. Thank goodness

I'm not due back at work until next week,' she gabbled, covering her clammy face with her spread hands in an expression of near desperation as the true meaning of her position hit her hard.

'I'd prefer for you to stay on here,' Tor admitted. 'It will make it easier for me to get to know Alfie.'

'That's important to you, is it?'

'The most crucial thing in my life right now,' Tor disconcerted her by declaring. 'I can't begin to tell you how much his existence matters to me.'

And Pixie almost scoffed at that turnaround in attitude on his part until she recalled the man with the haunted eyes telling her about his daughter's death, and she compressed her lips and said nothing, shame silencing her because she recognised sincerity when she saw it. Tor had only needed confirmation that Alfie was his to develop a serious interest in his son.

'You and I have had a very troubled start…but we don't have to continue in the same vein,' Tor framed almost roughly.

'We don't,' she agreed, welded to his beautiful eyes, bronzed by golden highlights and strong emotion.

'In time I genuinely believe that we could make something of this…attraction between us, potentially even marriage,' Tor spelt out almost curtly, so tough did he find it to broach the concept of a new relationship, particularly when he had promised himself that never again would he make such an attempt with a woman.

Pixie flushed and froze, not quite sure she had heard those words but keen to nip any such toxic notion in the bud. 'Oh, no…you and me? We're *not* going there,' she told him without hesitation.

His fine ebony brows drew together. He was not vain, but he was confident and arrogant, and he knew his own worth. He was richer than sin, reasonably good-looking and most women loved him. He wasn't remotely prepared for Pixie's blunt and woundingly *instant* rejection. 'Why not?' he asked equally bluntly.

A strangled laugh that was not one of amusement was wrenched from Pixie. She stared back at him wide-eyed, as if his proposition had been shocking.

'*Why not?* How can you ask me that?' she exclaimed. 'Five years after you lost your unfaithful wife you're *still* not over her and you're *still* wearing your wedding ring. No woman in her right mind would risk getting involved with you!'

For once in his life, Tor was silenced because it was a direct strike he hadn't been expecting. His ultimate goal was to marry Pixie and legitimise his son's birth and he had expected to proceed to that desirable conclusion by easy stages; the possibility of rejection had not once crossed his mind. Now it dawned on him that he could well be facing a long and stony road, toiling uphill every step of the way, because this was a woman who knew stuff no other woman had ever known about him and there would be no fooling her, no fobbing her off with something less than she felt she deserved.

'So, to sum up, you and me…well, you bury that idea,' Pixie advised him briskly. 'You and Alfie? Speed ahead…and I'll stay here until I get sorted out.'

It was a tragedy that he was so emotionally unavailable, so wrapped up in the past, she acknowledged unhappily. Marriage to Tor would have changed her life and Alfie's out of recognition but marrying a man still unhealthily attached to a past love would be a daily punishment for her. She could still remember the love between her parents and their relationship had struck her as a shining example of what marriage should be. She cringed at the prospect of being Tor's second-best and the likelihood that she would always be compared to her predecessor, whom he had loved. No, she had made the right decision, putting her own need for security and happiness above her son's needs...*hadn't she?*

CHAPTER SIX

IT WAS THE middle of the night or at least the early hours of the morning, Pixie guessed, when Tor shook her awake.

'Your brother's in hospital,' he told her grittily.

Pixie forced herself up on her elbows, shaken out of a sound sleep, and stared up at Tor, fully dressed and formidable. 'He's...*what*?'

'He's been beaten up by his creditors,' Tor divulged thinly. 'I wasn't sure whether or not to tell you.'

Pixie searched his lean dark features in wonderment. 'Of course, you tell me,' she protested. 'He's my brother and he screwed up, but I still love him!'

That bold statement of affection seemed to unnerve Tor slightly. His shimmering golden eyes hooded and cloaked as if she was showing him a softness that he didn't want to see in her. 'Does that mean that you want to see him?'

'Of course, I do,' she confirmed, clambering out of bed, suddenly uneasily conscious of the reality that she was only clad in pyjamas and of how incredibly uncomfortable Tor could make her feel when she was anything less than fully dressed.

In recent nights, she had encountered Tor in the nursery when teething was making Alfie fractious and unwilling to settle and he would cry and cry. She usually told Emma to go back to bed and that she would take care of her son, but Tor had proved to be surprisingly invested in Alfie being upset, persisting with his presence when she had expected him to lose patience and leave them alone. And gradually, it had dawned on her that Tor was a father prepared to take the rough with the smooth and willing to help out when Alfie was less than his cheerful smiling self. Was that the result of his previous experience with young children or simply his drive to make up for that poor start in fatherhood that he had acknowledged? Whichever, Pixie was unwillingly impressed by Tor's ability to cope with his son even when he was whiny and miserable. Add in the reality that Tor was half-naked during those encounters, clad, as he was, in only a pair of faded jeans, and she was a woman, heaven forgive her for that truth, but suddenly she was fully on board with him pushing in where before she had had nobody but herself to depend on.

There was Tor, a six-pack of impressive musculature on parade, all bronzed and lethally built and sensual. With that temptation before her, being got out of bed in the middle of the night had, without warning, become a thrilling kind of adventure. She had to struggle to keep her attention on Alfie when Tor was there, bare-chested and sleepy, those gorgeous eyes drowsy and somehow even more compelling, the black spiky lashes strikingly noticeable and his eyes on her. Hot, hungry, interested. But she wasn't stupid and she wasn't going there—wasn't going to make that mistake *again*.

She was a pushover for Tor, she reckoned unhappily. One hint that he wanted something more and she was ready to jump on the chance. But that would only complicate things between them, she warned herself sagely. Tor was open to having sex with her, nothing more lasting, nothing deeper, she reckoned ruefully. She believed the idea of marrying her had been his knee-jerk conventional overreaction to the discovery that he was a father again, not a proposition that he was properly serious about. In the short term, however, Tor was a typical male, programmed to seek sexual satisfaction, and for the present he didn't seem to be seeking that outlet with any other woman, so she was convenient and available, but his apparent interest didn't mean anything more than that. It was wiser to keep her distance, retain her barriers and stay uninvolved while letting him build his relationship with Alfie separate from hers.

'A car will be waiting for you when you're ready.'

'You're not coming with me?' she heard herself say and reddened fiercely.

'I want to punch your brother too. He put you and Alfie in danger. You could've been in that house with him. You could've been hurt, and it would've been his fault,' Tor breathed rawly.

Pixie compressed her lips. It was several days since she had returned to the empty house and packed up their belongings and Coco. The move had been executed at frightening speed because Tor's aid had included a professional removal team and a van as well as a squad of Tor's security men to protect her. Within little more than an hour and a bit, everything she possessed had been transferred, much of it now stowed in an attic room on the top floor of the town house. Some day she would have to go through it all and she would probably dump a lot of what she had grabbed in haste, stuff that Jordan wouldn't value but she did. There had been the family photo albums, and her mother's treasured bits and pieces as well, items she would never part with, the objects that reminded her of her happy childhood and favourite moments, which she would, one day, share with Alfie.

'But Alfie and I have been with you, *safe*, and Jordan's my brother,' she muttered ruefully.

'Your *half*-brother,' Tor stressed.

'He was eight when I was born. He's been with me all my life. He might as well be my full brother,' Pixie countered steadily.

'A family connection isn't a forgive-all escape clause,' Tor objected, marvelling at her ongoing loyalty to a male who had let her down so badly. His half-brother, Sev, had betrayed him and Tor knew that he would never pardon him for his behaviour. Of course, his outlook had always been very black and white on such matters, he conceded, and clearly Pixie's was not.

And Pixie instantly knew that he was thinking of *his* brother, who had slept with his wife and whom he could not forgive.

'Jordan loves us. He's got nobody else,' Pixie stated almost apologetically in the face of Tor's disapproval. 'I need to be the bigger person here and try to help him.'

'Even if he's already burned all his boats?'

'He tried to tell me, warn me away to keep Alfie and me safe, but I think he was too ashamed to tell me the whole story.' Pixie sighed.

In spite of his attitude, Tor joined her in the waiting limo. It was barely dawn and the drive to the hospital was accomplished in silence. 'You don't need to do this,' she said awkwardly on the way in.

'If you're here, I'm here.'

Jordan was in a cubicle in A & E. He had been badly beaten, his face swollen, his eyes black. He had a broken arm and cracked ribs too and he couldn't meet her eyes. 'I knew they'd be coming for me,' he said thickly. 'That's why I wanted you and the baby out.'

'You can come back from this,' she told him.

He twisted his head away, a tear leaking from one eye before he closed it and shuddered. 'It's too late. I've lost everything—the house, you and Alfie…there's nothing left. It's all my own doing.'

'You can come back from this,' she repeated.

'Jordan needs help, he needs therapy,' Pixie muttered to Tor, who had remained in the waiting room, an island in a distant corner, surrounded by security men and normal humanity. 'He's at his lowest ebb.'

'He's got what he deserves,' Tor opined unsympathetically, walking her back outside and tucking her into the waiting limo.

Her gaze was full of reproach. 'Do you have to be so hard?'

'That's who I am. And after what Jordan did to you, you shouldn't be feeling sorry for him,' Tor told her grimly as he swung in beside her.

'You don't have an ounce of compassion in you,' Pixie complained.

'You could persuade me otherwise,' Tor informed her,

dark eyes bright as gold ingots below the velvet sweep of his black lashes. 'But I wouldn't advise you to try.'

The power of those eyes holding hers unleashed a flock of nervous butterflies low in her tummy. 'Why not?'

'The world turns on negotiations and agreements. If you want me to help your undeserving brother, there would be a price...and you wouldn't *want* to pay it.'

Bewilderment gripped her. 'Try me...' she invited.

'You're appealing to my dark side and that's not a good idea,' Tor warned her.

'You mentioned negotiation,' she reminded him.

'Essentially, you give me what I want and in return I give you what you want.'

'I'm not stupid. I understood that without the explanation!' Pixie slung back impatiently. 'Jordan needs help.'

'He needs therapy, his debts paid off, a fresh start,' Tor enumerated without skipping a beat. 'You're asking me for money and that's easy because I've got a lot of it, even though I don't believe that Jordan *should* be dug out of the hole he dug for himself.'

'Shut up!' Pixie cried, out of all patience with that unemotional assessment. 'What do you want from me? And *no*, you can't have *that*.'

Rare amusement lightened Tor's gaze, making his eyes sparkle and dance and his firm mouth slant upward. *'That?'* he queried sardonically. 'Are you referring to sex?'

'Yes,' Pixie retorted tightly. 'And you can't have that in return because I'm not for sale and I'm not the sort of person who would trade sex for anything.'

Tor's self-discipline cracked and he grinned. 'I'm glad to hear that and I can work with what you've just told me.'

Pixie shot him an unconvinced glance. 'You…*can*?'

'I wouldn't want a woman who would use sex as a bargaining chip,' Tor traded smoothly. 'For the right price, I want *more* than sex.'

Pixie studied him in complete shock.

'You're so innocent. Why do you look so surprised?' Tor quipped. 'Virtually everything has a price.'

'Jordan's my family.'

'Who stole from you and put you and our son at risk of harm.'

'What did you mean about "the right price"?'

'My terms would be simple. That you agree to visit Greece with me to introduce Alfie to my family and consider marrying me.'

'Marrying you?' She gasped incredulously.

'You only have to consider the idea. When I first broached the idea, after all, you dismissed it without even considering it. I'm not going to try and force you into anything,' Tor proclaimed defensively. 'But I do want my family to meet Alfie.'

'I have to go back to work tomorrow.'

'Give me that trip to Greece and you'll never have to work again,' Tor murmured sibilantly. 'Seriously, the world will become your oyster.'

Breathless, Pixie whispered, 'And Jordan?'

'He gets therapy and a new start, but he has to be in the mindset to change, otherwise, I warn you, you're wasting your time,' he warned her flatly.

'I want him to have that chance…'

'Marry me and we'll be a family,' Tor told her.

And it was the perfect promise because Pixie longed to be part of a family again more than she wanted anything else. Jordan's deception had hit her hard and, while she still regarded her brother as family, he was now somewhere on the outside of that charmed circle until he could prove himself decent again.

'OK… I'll go to Greece with you for a visit and I'll apply for unpaid leave from my job. I don't want to just give it up. I *like* working,' she admitted, while scarcely able to credit that she was willing to take that leap of faith into the unknown with him.

But her world and its boundaries had changed irrevocably, she acknowledged ruefully. She could no longer trust Jordan because, clearly, he was addicted to gambling. He had stolen her inheritance from her, frittered away her hard-earned cash, destroyed her trust. Even if Jordan recovered, it could be years before she could have faith in him again because addiction was a slippery slope and he would always be fighting temptation. And Jordan had put both her and Alfie at risk. Tor, at the very least, was keen to put Alfie's best interests first, and that Tor was keen to introduce their son to his family impressed her. He could've kept Alfie as a dark little secret and visited him discreetly and nobody would ever have known that the little boy existed.

Instead, Tor had chosen to be open and honest with his relatives and he was making room for his son everywhere in his life. Only, what did that mean for her? Not marriage, she couldn't marry a man simply because he had got her pregnant, could she? But everything in her once stable world was shifting, she conceded apprehensively, and it was happening so fast that it left her breathless.

'You and Alfie will need new clothes. It's much warmer out there,' Tor completed. 'A shopping trip is on the cards.'

But Pixie was still thinking over his insistence that she consider marrying him. She had noticed that he had finally removed his wedding ring but naturally she hadn't said anything about it. 'Why do you want me to consider marrying you?' she asked bluntly.

'Two parents would be better than one for Alfie. I want him to have my name and my family, to become part of that support system. I want to be fully involved in his upbringing, not standing on the sidelines. Without taking him away from you, I want to share him,' he delineated tautly. 'But that's all for him and me. For us—well, we'd be a work in progress but we'd be a family and the attraction between us is strong.'

'I would need love.'

'I have to be honest. I don't think I could do love again.'

'Because you're scared,' Pixie breathed in a softer tone of understanding.

'It's nothing to do with fear,' Tor asserted between gritted teeth of repudiation, insulted by that interpretation of his natural reservations. 'I grew up with Katerina. She was my first love. I was young, naïve and idealistic. I'm not that boy any more. I'm a man and my expectations of a woman are much more practical and prosaic. You have abilities that I respect and value. Loyalty to your brother, in spite of the fact that he's let you down badly. You have compassion for the weak because, make no mistake, Jordan *is* weaker than you and in trying to help him you could be setting yourself up for a world of hurt and disappointment.'

'I'm willing to take that chance and, even though some of what you've said makes sense, I'd want more than practicality in marriage. I'd want passion.'

'I can give you passion,' Tor told her boldly, shimmering eyes welded to hers, and all the oxygen in the car suddenly seemed to be sucked up. 'I can give you as much passion as you can handle.'

'Passion *and* love from a guy who's willing to take a risk on me.'

'Successful bankers estimate the risks they take in advance and without emotion getting involved.'

Pixie nodded in acceptance and sighed. 'I'm not a cold person.'

'No, you're not…and my family are not cold either. For Alfie's sake, I'm glad you are the way you are, but that doesn't change the fact that you and I are very different. We would only work as a couple if you could accept those differences.'

'I'd always be wanting more,' Pixie told him, wondering why her eyes were prickling and stinging, why she suddenly felt all worked up about a perfectly innocent and unthreatening conversation. Aside of that sexual sizzle between them, they didn't suit and that was that—better by far to see and accept that now than try to fight it. So, Katerina had been his first love, his *only* love, which was probably why her treachery had been so massively damaging. After all, if he couldn't trust the girl he had grown up with, who could he trust?

'I have every hope that you'll change your mind,'

Tor murmured. 'Should I have lied and said that I could give you what you want?'

'You can't fake emotion. I'd have seen through you.'

'Most people can't read me.'

'I saw you at your lowest. You have certain tells,' she told him gently, thinking of his body language that night when Alfie had been conceived: the haunted dark eyes, his lean, restless hands shifting with the grace and eloquence that were so much a part of him, the emotion that seethed inside him, the emotion that he denied and suppressed.

Tor elevated a fine ebony brow. 'We're definitely going to have to discuss the tells.'

Emerging from that disturbing recollection of their first meeting, Pixie went pink, trembling a little as that unavoidable flood of physical awareness shifted like melted honey down deep inside her, warming her from the inside out as she pressed her thighs together and stiffened defensively. She wanted to slap herself for even those few moments of remembrance, for an indulgence she no longer allowed herself. To maintain boundaries, she too needed to put that intimate past knowledge of Tor behind her.

'No, we're not arguing about this any longer…you are *not* buying me clothes!' Pixie told Tor heatedly. 'You can pay for Alfie's clothes, but *not mine*.'

'Have you any idea how much money I must owe you in terms of child support?' Tor enquired calmly.

And it was precisely that calm and lack of embarrassment that riled Pixie. She didn't want to discuss money with Tor. She didn't want to admit that she was pretty much broke because she'd never had sufficient cash to manage to save. Paying what she had believed to be her share of the mortgage and buying food every month had cleaned her out and reduced her wardrobe to 'must-have' slender proportions.

She had forgotten what it felt like to buy something just because she liked it or fancied something new because, nine times out of ten, Alfie had needed something more. And now Tor was trying to hand her credit cards, open accounts for her, put her in the hands of some fancy stylist so that she could do him proud in Greece, and it was all too much for her to handle. Registering that she was on the brink of silly tears because he wasn't listening to her, Pixie pushed her trembling hands down on the arms of her chair and stood up.

'I can't listen to any more of this… I'm out,' she said thinly, and walked out of the dining room.

Tor released his breath in a groan and drained his wine glass, pushing away the plate in front of him because his appetite had died. For long minutes he sat and pondered his dilemma. How was she planning to buy clothes without money? Why was she so resistant to his financial help when it came to her personal needs? Had he ever even heard of a woman refusing a new wardrobe before?

When the table was being cleared, and after he had politely refused his housekeeper's suggestion that she make something else for him to eat, Tor vaulted upright and followed Pixie upstairs. There was nothing more frustrating than someone who walked away from a dispute, he registered in frustration, although he could not recall *ever* having an argument with a woman before the night on which Katerina had died. He and Katerina had never argued prior to that, had had no differences of opinion, minor or major. In essence they had not talked that much. Maybe those had been revealing signs of an unhealthy or, at the very least, boring relationship, he conceded grimly. How did he know? He hadn't had a single relationship since then and if he had ever had any skills in that field, they had to be distinctly rusty.

He knocked on her bedroom door and scowled. That was another problem: the whole 'separate bedrooms' thing was tying him up in knots. Why did she make such a big deal of sex? Sex was physical, not a pursuit anyone needed to imbue with magical properties or meaning. Was it because the only time she had indulged in sex she had ended up pregnant? Or could she simply be resistant to his advances because that one-off experience with him had been lousy? That drunk, how considerate could he have been? Tor clenched his teeth together and wondered if he could bring himself to ask. He knocked again. He *needed* to know, he *needed* details. He recalled sufficiently to be aware that he had enjoyed himself thoroughly, but that did not mean that his partner had also enjoyed the experience.

'*What?*' Pixie demanded aggressively as she flung the door wide on him. Dragged out of the shower by the knocking on the door, she was in a thoroughly bad mood.

There she was, not even five feet tall and barefoot and wrapped in a stupid towel, which covered her delectable curves from neck to toe. Why did his housekeeper buy such *huge* towels in his household? Tor wondered absently. And why did the angry fire of challenge in Pixie's bright blue eyes turn him on?

'We need to talk.'

'No, we don't,' Pixie argued, trying to close the door on him.

'Yes, we *do*,' Tor decreed, stalking over the threshold, automatically gathering her up into his arms, a warm, struggling, fragrant bundle of damp femininity that fiercely aroused him. He was shocked by that reaction as he carefully laid her back down on the bed. 'You explain to me now why you won't allow me to buy you clothes when you need them…'

'Where's your furry loincloth? You're behaving like a guy who just walked out of a Stone Age cave!' Pixie snapped back at him.

'I need to understand the problem before I can fix it,' Tor breathed in a raw undertone.

'I don't need you to fix *everything* in my life,' Pixie muttered. 'I mean, you've already spent a fortune trying to sort out Jordan. Isn't that enough?'

'That was our agreement and I haven't spent a fortune. You wouldn't let me buy the house for him.'

'No, because that would have cost too much and Jordan needs to rebuild his life somewhere new,' Pixie reasoned. 'He has to become self-sufficient again and he shouldn't be rewarded for what he's done. You don't need *all* of us hanging on your sleeve like scroungers.'

Tor gave up the ghost and groaned out loud in frustration, sinking down on the edge of the bed and raking impatient fingers through his cropped black hair. 'Why would you think for one moment that I would look on the mother of my child as a scrounger? Have I done or said anything to give you that impression?'

'Well, no,' she conceded grudgingly. 'But it's how I feel… Why is the clothes thing so important to you?'

'I want you to feel comfortable with my family and friends. I don't want you to feel inappropriately dressed or out of place.'

'Are you afraid my appearance is going to embarrass you?' she whispered, thinking that if she flew out with her well-worn winter wardrobe there was a good chance that it would, and that there was an even stronger chance that she might be mistaken for one of the cleaners that came into the town house to clean several times a week. And that would definitely embarrass everybody, not just her. He was winning the argument, she thought ruefully—he was winning without even trying.

Tor closed a large hand over hers. 'Nothing you could do would embarrass me. I'm thinking of your comfort, your ability to relax.'

'Maybe it would help if you told me about where you're taking me.'

'An island called Milnos. I bought it a few years ago. The property I built is large enough to house my family when they come to visit. They live on Corfu. One of my brothers, Kristo, is still at school. Dimitri is at university and the eldest, Nikolaos, works for my father in his shipping company.'

'No sisters?'

'None. And so far I'm the only son who has married. Sofia was my parents' first grandchild and her death hit my family as hard as it hit me,' Tor confided tautly, trying to ignore the small fingers gently smoothing over his thigh in a gesture that he knew was intended to offer comfort but which was, instead, travelling straight to his groin and winding him up. 'That's why I want them to meet Alfie. My family are overdue for a glimpse of a brighter future.'

'Yes, I'm pretty sure you haven't been a bundle of laughs to be around,' Pixie mumbled, and then flushed at having made that tactless comment. 'Sorry—'

Tor grinned down at her, relishing the flushed triangle of her animated face beneath the tousled curls. 'You could be right… I've been all about work and nothing else for a long time, but I'm lighter-hearted around you…when we're not arguing, of course.'

'OK. I'll see the stylist and pick clothes,' Pixie muttered with a slight grimace. 'But I'd much prefer not to have to let you pay.'

Tor stared down at her, dark golden eyes unashamedly hungry. 'Do you think you could include some sexy underthings in the selection?' he murmured thickly.

Her cheeks burned. 'What would be the point?'

'My imagination thrives on fuel,' Tor husked, bending down slowly.

Her fingers skimmed up from his wide shoulders into his luxuriant black hair. He smelt amazing to her, fresh and earthy and male, a faint hint of citrus fruit in his designer cologne, that scent achingly familiar to her, achingly evocative. It was the same cologne he had worn *that* night. Her brain was telling her with increasing urgency to push him away, to sit up, to *stop* touching him, but her body was rebelling against common sense with Tor that close. She could feel the heat of his big body through the towel she was wrapped in, the stinging sensation of her nipples snapping taut, the warm damp ache making her feel hollow between her thighs. Every nerve ending was sitting up and taking screaming notice. It was like a wave of physical insanity taking her over.

'I like your fingers on me,' Tor muttered raggedly as he lowered his mouth to hers, let those sensual lips play across hers in a wildly arousing fashion that brought her out in a fever of awareness and damp heat. 'I'd like them all over me, your mouth as well—'

'We said we weren't doing this.'

'*You* said. I didn't make any promises,' Tor said urgently against her parted lips before his tongue delved between, and suddenly speech of any kind was beyond her. And she was bargaining shamelessly with herself: a few kisses. Where was the harm in that? And he was such an amazing kisser, it would be foolish to deny herself the experience.

Her hand slid off his thigh over his crotch, tracing the hard thrust of his erection, and he shuddered against her, his mouth hotter and harder than ever on hers, and she wanted nothing so much as for him to whip off the towel, lay her back and sate the unbearable longing as he had once before. She wanted him and he wanted her, no denying that. But when it went wrong, she thought frantically, Alfie would be caught up in the fallout and her relationship with Tor would become fatally toxic. Having sex with Tor again would come with a price tag attached and a series of risks. One or both of them would ultimately be disappointed and that would lead to discord.

'We can't do this,' she groaned against the urgency of his mouth.

'I can do this fine,' Tor contradicted.

And discomfiture washed over her because she had encouraged him, given him expectations, and she didn't like to be provocative. 'You shouldn't touch me,' she told him.

'You shouldn't touch me either.'

Her face burned so hot she was afraid that she would spontaneously combust. 'I'm acting like a tease and that's not me.'

'No, you need time to decide what you want and I'm not giving you space the way I promised because you're too damn tempting,' Tor growled, setting her back from him, scorching golden eyes smouldering over her discomfited face. 'I'm just naturally impatient and assertive when I want something. You need to push back hard to handle me when I get too enthusiastic.'

'But how does that work when I'm enthusiastic too?'

'You marry me,' Tor said simply.

CHAPTER SEVEN

'Not without love,' Pixie protested.

'I've got lust covered,' Tor said almost insouciantly as he reclined back on her bed, completely unashamed of the arousal tenting his tailored trousers. 'I've got lust in spades.'

And Pixie thought about it in that moment—seriously thought about marrying a man because she couldn't keep her hands off him—until all her common sense stood up and screamed at her to get her brain back in gear.

'We need more,' she told him heavily.

'We've got Alfie, and Alfie will benefit from having an equal share of both of us. Two parents together, *united*.'

'You're still hung up on Katerina.'

'No. I've taken the ring off. That's behind me. I can't promise love because that's an emotional state and I don't know if I'm capable of feeling like that again,' Tor told her frankly. 'But I can tell you that I'll be faithful and trustworthy and secure.'

And she wanted him, dear heaven, Pixie had never wanted anything as she wanted Tor at that moment because she saw that he was willing to try, she saw that he had moved himself on, indeed that the eruption of her and Alfie into his life had fundamentally changed his outlook. But was it enough?

'I'd be taking a chance on you…and I don't do that,' she whispered honestly. 'I always play safe.'

'I'll *make* it work. You marry me and I'll make it work,' Tor intoned fiercely. 'We can be married within a couple of days and you can meet my family as my wife.'

And that offer had undeniable power because she had naturally been nervous of meeting his family. Being a wife would give her more status than merely being his illegitimate son's mother, a position that would only leave his family questioning exactly what their relationship encompassed. If she went to Greece with him, the two of them would be very much under scrutiny, which made her uneasy. She had watched Tor with Alfie, watched him being patient and caring. She could look for no more than that in the father of her son.

Even though it had gone against the grain, Tor had extended a helping hand to Jordan because that was what *she* wanted him to do. Even if she only married him for Alfie's sake and security, she would be making the right choice, she reasoned. But that wouldn't be the only reason she married him, her conscience piped up, and her face heated. She could have him in bed, if she married him, no worries about what he might think of her for succumbing, no worries about where that intimacy could be heading because marriage would give them the solid framework that they lacked.

Pixie breathed in deep and fast. 'OK… I'll marry you, so that we can be a real family.'

Tor lowered lush black lashes over stunned eyes at

that seemingly snap decision, wondering what he had said right, *done* right to ultimately convince her round to his point of view. 'I'll get it organised.'

Pixie nodded slowly. 'I want a proper wedding though,' she warned him. 'I know you've already done it before, but this is my first time.'

'*Last* time,' he qualified. 'And I understand. If you have no objection, my mother will be ecstatic to be asked to organise a wedding reception and we'll get married in Greece.'

'You're looking for trouble,' Eloise pronounced after Pixie had finished breathlessly sharing her insecurities on the topic of marrying Tor. 'Why are you doing that?'

Pixie's smooth brow furrowed as yet another model strolled out wearing a dream wedding dress, only unfortunately, not one she had seen so far matched *her* dream. She lacked the height and shape to do puffy or elaborate or dramatic. But concentrating even on something as superficial as choosing her wedding gown was a challenge when her brain was eaten up by so many other worries.

'Am I?'

'Yes,' Eloise confirmed without hesitation. 'Tor is hotter than sin and richer than an oil well. So, he comes with some baggage like a first wife he may not be over... Well, who *doesn't* have baggage? Start appreciating what you've got, Pixie. Even if he gets bored and dumps you a few years down the road, you'll be left financially secure and Alfie will still have his father. You can't expect to get a man like Tor, a wedding ring and undying love too. Life isn't a fairy tale.'

'I know it's not, but do you think he can be faithful?' Pixie whispered. 'I mean, from everything I've read online about him, he's been quite a womaniser.'

'I think if Tor plays away, he's clever enough to be discreet and you'll never know about it,' Eloise countered cynically. 'And I know that's not what you want to hear but if you can content yourself with what you've got you'll be far happier.'

Pixie swallowed hard, well aware that the brunette was not the person to turn to for reassurance because Eloise had been hurt and disappointed by men too many times. She was a good friend, but she always spoke her mind and she was correct—she had yet to say anything that Pixie had wanted to hear. Eloise had already pointed out that she was boxing above her weight with Tor, that she had landed the equivalent of a super tanker when by rights on the strength of her attractions she had only been due a tugboat. Pixie hadn't needed those reminders of her own essential insignificance, her ordinariness and her lack of any surpassing beauty or talent.

Perhaps unwisely, she had researched Tor's first wife online and had read about the tragic accident that had occurred at their London home, which had later been sold. And she had seen what Katerina looked like: a truly beautiful slender brunette with almond-shaped dark eyes and a mane of dark, glossy hair. She had been on board a yacht, her wonderful hair blowing, looking all athletic and perfect and popular with a bunch of friends around her. After that first glimpse, something inside Pixie had died along with curiosity and she had looked for no further photos.

Tor was in Brussels attending a banking conference

and Pixie had been kitting herself out with a new wardrobe and her wedding gown. In the end she had only invited three people to the Greek wedding, Eloise and a couple of gay friends, male nurses she had trained with, who had accompanied her to the stylist and laughed her out of her attempts to go light on Tor's wallet. Jordan had refused to come to Greece, which had hurt, but at the same time she had understood that, in his current mood as he underwent counselling for his addiction and was forced to face all his mistakes, the idea of having to put on a front for strangers at her wedding was more than he could bear. Tor's comments on the same score had, predictably, been a good deal more critical.

Pixie had also had to find and engage a new nanny because Emma was only temporary and preferred moving between different jobs. Actually, having to interview potential employees had been nerve-racking for her, but Tor had pointed out quite rightly on the phone that she wouldn't be happy leaving the task to him. She had found Isla, a cheerful young Scot, who had struck up an instant connection with Alfie that impressed her and who couldn't wait to make a trip to Greece.

'Oh, that's *it*,' Pixie said warmly, focusing appreciatively on the slender sheath dress with the pretty scalloped neckline that the current model was displaying. 'That's definitely the dress.'

'But it's very plain. A bride needs more pizzazz,' Eloise opined in surprise at the choice.

'It's got enough pizzazz for me.' Pixie laughed, knowing that the dress probably cost a small fortune even though it was unadorned, because they were in a designer bridal salon.

'Don't you think you should go for something fancier for a big society wedding?' Eloise made one last attempt to sway her.

'No, it's not going to be a large event. Tor said it would be small and it's my day and I'm not going to worry about trying to impress people.' *As if she could*, she was thinking ruefully, having decided that the only sensible way to behave was to be herself without any false airs or graces.

Three days later, Pixie flew out of London with her friends and Alfie and Isla on board Tor's private jet. It was her wedding day and all she had to do was show up with her dress and a magic wand would take care of all the other necessities—at least according to Tor, that was. In reality, she was pretty apprehensive about what was coming next. They landed in Athens to VIP treatment and they were ushered straight onto a helicopter to complete the journey to Milnos. She had her friends to comment out loud on the luxury and ease of their journey and what life was like on the five-star side of the fence. And all she could think, thoroughly intimidated as she was by the champagne offered on boarding by attractive stewardesses and the constant service, was how on earth was she ever going to fit into this new world where wealth provided so many of the extras she had never enjoyed before?

For that reason, arriving in the lush landscaped grounds of the Sarantos property on the island, a massive white villa with wings radiating out from it, and meeting up with her future in-laws came as a huge relief. Pandora Sarantos was reassuringly motherly and friendly, and she lit up like a firework display the instant she laid eyes on Alfie. Alfie suddenly became the eighth wonder of the world and Pixie could not be uncomfortable with an older woman that keen to admire and appreciate her son. By her side, Hallas, a shorter, greying version of his sons, was less vocal but truly welcoming. He apologised for the absence of his younger sons, who were with Tor, he explained, and he asked if he could have the honour of walking her down the aisle. Pixie agreed, pleased not to have to undergo the stress of having to walk that aisle alone in front of strangers and touched by the offer, a pang of pain arrowing through her as she thought how much her father would have enjoyed fulfilling that role for her. It would have been wonderful to have her parents with her to share the day, she conceded, but Tor's parents were a comfort and their enthusiasm for Alfie was very welcome.

'Alfie is so beautiful, with your hair and Tor's eyes,' Pandora enthused in fluent English as Alfie tottered upright, gripping the edge of a metallic coffee table in the foyer. 'Tor will have to tackle childproofing everything here. Let me show you up to the nursery…'

As Pixie left her friends being shown to their rooms with wide eyes fixed to their palatial surroundings, she followed Pandora Sarantos upstairs with Alfie and the nanny, Isla.

'Wow, this is some place,' the nanny remarked in a shaken undertone.

Pixie was relieved to have someone else comment on the sheer splendour of the marble stairs and hallways and the airy grandeur of the sunlit walkways left open to balconies and fabulous island and sea views.

'This is *your* home now,' Tor's mother announced,

disconcerting Pixie. 'I may be here to host your wedding but I'm not the interfering type. I won't be visiting without invitation or anything of that nature. Tor's father, Hallas, and I are really happy that Tor is settling down again.'

Because that's the agreement, Pixie reflected, thinking that she and Tor really were going to have a marriage based on the most practical rules. He would settle down in order to gain regular access to his son and have Alfie become a Sarantos by name. Alfie's mother, Tor's bride, was more or less an afterthought, a necessary step towards reaching those all-important goals. Clearly, Tor's chatty mother had assumed that their marriage was of a more personal, normal nature and she could hardly be blamed for that when most couples married because they were in love with each other, Pixie reasoned ruefully.

Pandora spread open the door of a room furnished as a nursery but not the usual nursery, Pixie adjusted, scanning in wonderment shelves of new toys and every luxury addition known to early childhood. It was a nursery arranged for a little prince, not a normal toddler. 'I can't tell you what a thrill I had furnishing this room for Alfie,' the older woman explained volubly. 'I was so excited to find out about him and you and Tor. You and Alfie are exactly what I was hoping would arrive in his life…a new family.'

And you couldn't get much more of a welcome mat than that, Pixie conceded, warmed to the heart by that little speech and finally appreciating, as her soon-to-be mother-in-law looked yearningly at Alfie and smiled, that her son was so welcome and that she was equally welcome because obviously Tor's parents had assumed that he had fallen in love again. Any parents that loved their son and had seen him heartbroken by the tragic end to his first marriage would want to see him embark on a fresh relationship. Yet even they didn't know the truth of how very tragic and soul-destroying that prior marriage had been for Tor, she acknowledged ruefully, because they didn't know about the infidelity and heartbreak involved.

'I mustn't keep you back from your bridal beautifying,' the older woman remarked with a sudden smile. 'It's a wonderfully exciting day for all of us.'

'She's lovely,' Pixie told Eloise when she arrived in the suite of rooms designated as the bridal suite.

'"Mothers-in-law" and "lovely" don't go together in the same sentence,' Eloise told her in dismay at the statement. 'There's probably a hidden agenda there and it'll take time for you to work it out.'

'I don't think that's true this time,' Pixie said with assurance, because she had recognised the genuine warmth in Tor's mother. 'Wait until you meet her properly. I think she's just happy that her son has found someone and that there's a grandchild. Alfie's going to be spoilt rotten.'

A pair of strangers entered, accompanied by a young, very pretty brunette, who seemed to be there to act as an interpreter and who introduced herself as Angelina Raptis, a friend of the family. One of her companions was a hairstylist, Pixie learned, and the other a make-up artist.

'I don't wear a lot of make-up,' Pixie began uncertainly.

'But today you *do*,' Eloise whispered in her ear.

'Today is special. You want to look your very best and feel good.'

Pixie acquiesced, wanting to at least fit nominally with Tor's expectations. The stylist wanted to cut and straighten her hair and she mustered the courage to say that she preferred her curls and simply wanted to wear her hair up in some fashion.

'I love curls. They're *so* natural,' Angelina commented. 'How brave of you to leave them like that for a formal occasion.'

Encountering the steely glint in the brunette's eyes and noting the scornful curve of her lips, Pixie reddened and turned her head away again, recognising that Angelina was a bit of a shrew while conceding that she couldn't expect everyone she met at her wedding to be a genuine friendly well-wisher.

'I can't wait to meet your son,' Angelina told her brightly. 'Does he look like Tor?'

'Yes, although he's fair-haired like me. He has Tor's eyes though.'

'A very handsome little boy, then. I admire you for being so calm.'

In the background, Eloise was grimacing but, mercifully, her other friends Denny and Steve had come in to join the bridal preparation team and lighten the mood.

'Pixie's looking forward to enjoying a wonderful day,' Denny said cheerfully, earning a relieved smile from Pixie, who loved his positive attitude.

'Even with that awful story in the press?' Angelina burbled, startling Pixie. 'I really admire your strength, Pixie.'

'What press? What awful story?' Pixie repeated in consternation. 'What are you referring to?'

Denny groaned out loud while Eloise stared at Angelina as though she wanted to strangle her where she stood. 'Until you spoke up, we were keeping that story to ourselves, flower,' Denny told Angelina.

'What story?' Pixie whispered afresh, her heart sinking although she had done nothing that she knew that she should be ashamed of.

'Some viper called Saffron sold a story to a tabloid newspaper about the night you met Tor,' Steve explained. 'And the newspaper did a little digging and made a fluffy story out of it.'

Saffron—the wannabe actress who had brought Tor back to that house Pixie had temporarily stayed in; Saffron, the redhead he had rejected and a woman who would probably relish publicity exposure. What on earth could she have to say about anything? Had she seen Tor leaving the bedroom the next morning? That was the only explanation, Pixie decided unhappily.

'Let me see it,' she said to Denny, who was already tapping his phone.

'I'm so sorry. I didn't mean to upset anyone,' Angelina said plaintively.

'You don't dump that sort of stuff on a bride,' Steve said stiffly.

'I'm sure you didn't mean anything by it,' Pixie said politely, forgivingly, her heart racing until Denny had handed her his phone and she glimpsed a very glamorous photo of Saffron next to a brief article about the billionaire banker about to marry the nurse he had got pregnant on a one-night stand. News of her pregnancy had probably got back to Saffron by way of her house-mate, Steph, who had given Pixie her cat, Coco. Steph was also the sister of one of Pixie's former colleagues. A stray piece of gossip had probably exposed Pixie's secret pregnancy, she thought heavily, and Saffron had put two and two together to register that they made a very neat four.

'Then I suppose that I shouldn't say that Tor is absolutely furious,' Angelina revealed. 'Look, I feel awkward now... I'll leave you to get dressed with your friends.'

'And you'll not be making a friend of that toxic piece,' Eloise breathed wrathfully.

'If there's nothing untrue in the article I'll just have to live with it,' Pixie pronounced with a stiff smile as she struggled to conceal how mortified she was that Tor's family and friends should have access to the bare shameless facts of their first meeting. 'Let's just forget about it for now.'

'Why on earth would Tor be furious?' Eloise scoffed.

'Because I expect he likes his private life to stay private, like me.' Pixie sighed as the make-up artist fluttered around her, one soft brush after another tickling her brow bone and her cheeks and every other part of her face.

'You're going to look totally amazing,' Eloise told her bracingly.

Denny gave her a fond appraisal. 'A complete princess...'

'A trophy bride,' Steve completed, not to be outdone on the soothing-compliment front.

After presenting her with a beautiful bouquet of

roses, Hallas Sarantos accompanied her down to the church in the village down by the harbour. They travelled in a flower-bedecked vintage car that he confided belonged to him as he admitted to a passion for classic cars. Pixie thanked him for all that he and his wife had done to make the wedding possible, and then she was stepping out with a smile into the warmth and brightness of the day outside the small village church. Her smile lurched a little when she saw how packed the church was and the sea of faces that turned to look at her because being so much the centre of attention unnerved her.

Instead, she chose to gaze down the aisle at Tor and, reassuringly, he didn't look angry, only his usual cool self-possessed self. And so incredibly handsome that he stole her breath away at that moment just as he had the very first time she saw him, her attention lingering on the slashing black sweep of his brows, the sculpted high cheekbones that lent his features that perfect definition, the straight nose and the masculine fullness of his sensual mouth. It was as if looking at him lit a whole row of little fires inside her, flushing her face with warmth, filling the more sensitive areas of her body with heat and sexual awareness.

There was a smile in the stunning bronzed eyes that met hers at the altar, no, not absolutely furious about anything, Pixie decided, liberated from that apprehension. If he even knew about the newspaper piece, and she doubted that he did, it evidently hadn't annoyed him in the slightest. He eased the wedding ring over her knuckle and the ceremony was complete. Tor had

become her husband and she was now his wife, a conclusion that still shook her.

'You look ravishing,' he murmured on the way out
of the church, dark eyes sliding over the shapely silhou-
ette that the elegant gown somehow accentuated, noting the way the fine silk defined the lush plumpness
of her breasts and the full curve of her derrière, and
more than a little surprised to realise that he was cat-
egorically aroused by the prospect of taking his bride
to bed, even though he *was* furious with her for the
choices she had made. Bad choices, wrong decisions,
the sort of mistake he had to expect from someone as
youthful and inexperienced in the world as she was, he
reminded himself grimly.

'Your parents are brilliant,' she told him chirpily.
'You lucked out there. Neither one of them asked me a
single awkward question.'

'Wait until you meet my three brothers, none of
whom are known for their tact,' Tor parried smoothly.

And the car swept them back to the enormous villa,
where a throng far larger than Pixie had anticipated
awaited them in a vast room with ornamental pillars that
could only have been described as a modern ballroom.
'You married someone who's got a freaking ballroom!'
Denny gasped in her ear. 'And his mother is *still* calling this affair "a very small do"!'

Possibly by Sarantos standards it was small, Pixie
conceded as she was tugged inexorably into a receiving line to meet their guests and the long procession
of names and faces quickly became a blur. Personal
friends, business acquaintances, family friends and relatives. Tor's three brothers were remarkably like him

in looks. There truly was a very large number of people present and the only light moment of the experience for Pixie was when Isla appeared with her son and Alfie made a mad scramble out of her arms to reach his mother, smiling and chattering nonsense. Dressed in the cutest little miniature suit she had ever seen, Alfie was overjoyed at the reunion and it was a shock to her when, after giving her a hug, he twisted and held out his arms to greet Tor as if it was the most natural thing in the world.

Her baby boy was growing up and there was room in his little heart for a father now, and the immediacy of Tor's charismatic smile and pleasure at that enthusiastic greeting from his son warmed Pixie as well. It was just at that moment that a tall dark man appeared in front of them and Tor froze, his grasp on Alfie tightening enough that the baby complained and squirmed in his hold.

'Pixie, this is my half-brother, Sevastiano Cantarelli... I didn't realise you were attending,' he said flatly.

'I was determined to drop in and offer my congratulations. I can't stay for long,' Sevastiano responded in his low-pitched drawl. 'It means a lot to Papa.'

'Yes, yes, it would,' Tor acknowledged with a razor-edged smile as the other man moved on past, as keen to be gone, it seemed, as Tor was to see him go.

'If you would simply tell your family the truth, you wouldn't have been put in the position of having to entertain him,' she whispered helplessly.

'Don't interfere in what you don't understand!' Tor countered with icy bite and she paled with hurt and surprise and looked away again, suddenly appreciating that she had spoken too freely on what was a controversial topic in Tor's life. He might have spilled his guts the night they first met, but alcohol had powered those revelations, she reminded herself doggedly. His reaction now was a disquietingly harsh reminder that she was *still* an outsider, a virtual newcomer in Tor's world, not someone who should have assumed that she had the right to wade in and offer an opinion on a matter that private and personal.

CHAPTER EIGHT

A PERFECTLY CATERED MEAL was served by uniformed staff. Speeches were made by some of Tor's relatives and he translated them for her.

'You're very quiet,' Tor murmured then. 'I was rude earlier. I'm sorry.'

'No, sometimes I have no filter and it was a sensitive subject.'

'Let me explain,' Tor urged, skating a fingertip across the back of her clenched fingers, letting her know that *he* knew that she was still as wound up as a clock by his rebuke. 'For various reasons, Sev didn't get to know our father until he had grown up and their relationship now means a lot to Hallas. My mother has become very fond of him as well. If I spoke up, it would tear them all apart. My father is a very moral man and he would feel he had to choose between his sons and exclude Sev. What good would that anguish and disappointment do any of us now?'

'Your attitude is generous.' Pixie was impressed by his unselfish, mature outlook while recognising the sense of family responsibility that he had allowed to trap him into silence. 'But if your family had understood what you were *really* going through back then, they might have been able to offer you better support.'

'All of that is behind me now,' Tor insisted with impressive conviction. 'Meeting you gave me something of a second chance.'

'No, Alfie did that,' Pixie contradicted without hesitation.

Tor gritted his teeth at that response but said nothing. Knowing that he was to blame for every low point in their relationship was a new experience for him and not one anyone could have said he enjoyed. His bride wasn't in love with him, didn't think he was the best thing ever to happen to her and didn't even particularly crave what he could buy her either. His rational mind argued with that appraisal, reminding him that Katerina's supposed love, which, ironically, he had never once doubted, had been an empty vessel. Love didn't need to have anything to do with his marriage. And Pixie was naïve, honest though, loyal, everything Katerina had not been. For the very first time, he mulled over the truth that Katerina had lied to him and conducted an affair with another man that had begun even before their marriage. Three years of lies including Sofia's birth, he reflected angrily, and even the anger was new because he was making comparisons and he saw now so clearly that his first marriage had been all wrong from the very outset.

So, this time around, Tor reflected grimly, he wasn't compromising, he wasn't making any allowances for misunderstandings or mistakes. He was going to be who he was, tough, and when it came to telling his wife that she had gone wrong he was going to grasp that hot iron and go for the burn.

* * *

'Where are we going?' Pixie questioned breathlessly some hours later as she climbed out of the car down at the small harbour. 'And what about Alfie?'

'Alfie and his nanny will join us tomorrow. We can manage one night without him…*right?*' Tor arrowed up a questioning black brow as he bent down, curving an arm to her spine, and even in moonlight she felt the heat of embarrassment at being exposed as an overprotective mother.

As her gaze clashed in the moonlight with those stunning dark glittering eyes of his, her heart jumped inside her chest and her lower limbs turned liquid. His fierce attraction rocked her where she stood and almost instinctively she leant into him for support, literally mortified by the effect he could have on her because the feelings he inspired in her were so powerful and so far removed, she believed, from his reaction to her.

'It would be cruel to lift Alfie out of his cot at this hour,' she agreed, deliberately stepping back a few inches from him, striving to act cooler.

'Especially after he was exhausted by his social whirl.' Tor's expressive mouth quirked as he recalled his son being passed around like a parcel between groups of cooing women during the reception. Alfie certainly wasn't shy, and his unusual combination of golden curls and dark eyes attracted attention as much as his smiles and chuckles. 'At least he wasn't scared and shaken up like he was the day Jordan abandoned him,' Tor completed, knowing he would never forget the sight of his son clawing his way up his mother's body and clinging in the aftermath of an ordeal that had visibly traumatised him.

Pixie gasped a little in surprise as he bent and simply lifted her off her feet to lower her down into the launch tied up by the jetty. She winced at his words though, wishing he wouldn't remind her of her brother's lowest moment and worst mistake. 'You still haven't said where we're going… You said I didn't need to get changed and now I'm wearing a wedding dress in a boat.'

'To board a much larger vessel,' Tor sliced in, indicating the huge yacht anchored out in the bay and silhouetted against the starry night sky.

'You own a yacht?'

'No. It belongs to a family friend and his wedding present is the use of it. If you like cruising we can always buy one,' he told her as the launch bounced over the sea at speed, driven by the crew member in charge of the wheel.

Pixie studied the yacht with wide eyes, struggling to accept that she was now living in a world where her bridegroom could talk carelessly about purchasing such an enormous luxury. 'Why haven't you bought one already?'

'To date, I haven't taken much time away from work and a yacht would have been a superfluous purchase for a workaholic. But that has to change with you and Alfie in my life now,' Tor traded calmly.

She wanted to ask him if he had been an absentee husband and father during his first marriage, but on their own wedding day it felt as if that would be tacky and untimely. He had made her wary of impulsive speech as well when he had reacted badly to a tactless question earlier that day. For that reason, she made no comment and bore up beautifully to being hoisted on board the enormous yacht in her fancy gown and greeted by the captain and a glass of champagne before being guided up to the top deck and a bedroom that took her breath away.

'I'm afraid that we now need to have a serious discussion about your brother,' Tor murmured levelly then, utterly taking her aback with that announcement.

Bright blue eyes widening in bewilderment, Pixie slowly swivelled, silk momentarily tightening across her slender, shapely figure to draw his magnetic gaze. 'What on earth are you talking about?'

'Today of all days, I don't want you to be upset,' Tor informed her smoothly. 'But I believe that Jordan was the source of a rather sleazy story about our first night together and Alfie that appeared in a British newspaper this morning—'

A fury unlike anything Pixie had ever felt, or indeed had even guessed she *could* feel, burned up her backbone like a licking flame and she went rigid with the force of it. 'Is that so?' she almost whispered.

'Who else could it be but Jordan?' Tor derided. 'He'll do anything for money. He has no decency, no backbone.'

'Shut up!' Pixie practically spat at him in her outrage at that denunciation.

His brows knotted, a look of incredulity in his smouldering golden eyes, such incivility not having featured very often in his experience. '*Diavolos*, Pixie. There is no reason for you to treat this as though it is some kind of personal attack on *you*. It is not intended as such.'

And Tor stood there, smokingly handsome, thrillingly sexy and towering over her. He was utterly sure of his ground in a fashion that she supposed came entirely naturally to him and yet she wanted to kill him in that instant, smite him down with heavenly lightning for blaming her poor brother for the tabloid article as well. As though Jordan had not already sinned enough and *paid* the price for his mistakes! He had lost her respect and the only home he had ever known, and his self-esteem was at basement level. And yes, he had deserved that punishment, but right now he was trying very hard to fix himself and pick himself up again, only he hadn't yet mustered sufficient strength to make more than a couple of tottering steps back towards normality. At present, in her view, Jordan was more to be pitied than condemned.

'Yes, shut up and stop talking down to me in that patronising way!' Pixie let fly at Tor angrily again. 'I gather you haven't actually *seen* that article. Well, before you hang, draw and quarter my brother for the story, acquaint yourself with the article and the facts first.'

'Have you seen it? I assumed you didn't know about it,' Tor confided in disconcertion. 'I didn't mention it because I didn't want to destroy the day.'

'So, you just destroyed it now instead by assuming that Jordan is to blame when in fact it is *your own choices* that brought the humiliation of that article down on the two of us!' Pixie flung back at him in a furious counter-attack.

'How could it be anything to do with *my* choices?' Tor shot back at her icily, his own temper rising because he had not been prepared for either her attitude or the argument that had erupted. Unsurprisingly, he would never have chosen to mention the article on their wedding night had he foreseen her response.

'Look it up online and find out, as I had to,' Pixie urged him curtly.

Tor did nothing so basic. He shot an order to one of his personal assistants to send him an exact copy of the item, still outraged that *his* assumptions, *his* conclusions, were being questioned.

First, a photo of a woman he had never seen in his life before arrived on his screen, and he turned it towards Pixie and breathed, 'Who is she?'

'Saffron Wells—an actress. The beauty who brought you back to the house that night. You allowed her to pick you up and bring you back there and I suspect that she saw you leaving the room I was using the next morning.'

'I don't know what you're talking about and you know it!' Tor thundered at her, while grudgingly recalling that vague memory of someone coming down the stairs in that house that morning. Disorientated and in a bad mood, he hadn't even turned round to see who it was. 'Because you flatly *refused* to tell me everything about that night!'

Pixie was in no mood to compromise when she was still so angry with him. On a level she didn't want to examine, some of her anger related to the weirdest current of possessiveness inside her. It still annoyed her that he had allowed Saffron to pick him up, even if he hadn't done anything with the other woman, and even though she knew she would never have met him otherwise, that annoyance went surprisingly deep.

'Saffron brought you back to the house in the first place. You apparently believed you were accompanying her to a party, but she thought she was bringing you home for the night. You rejected her because supposedly you weren't in the mood and she stormed off... At least that's what *you* told me happened. But for all I know,' Pixie breathed with withering bite, 'you slept with her too before I came into the kitchen, where you were waiting for a taxi!'

Tor swore in vicious Greek at being slapped in the face with that character assassination. 'I may have been drunk, I may have slept with you that night, but I'm no playboy and you know it.'

'According to your online images, you've been around...*a lot*,' Pixie emphasised, unimpressed. 'However, I'd say it's unlikely anything happened between you because I think you offended her and that's one good reason why she sold that story. Her being passed over for someone as ordinary as me would have been the last straw. The other reason is that, being a media person, she lapped up the opportunity to get her picture into a newspaper.'

Tor was frowning now. 'But if she was some random woman in that house, how could she possibly have known about you getting pregnant and all the rest of it when you left the property only a couple of days later?'

'There were other connections involved. I was using Steph's room that night. Steph was one of the other tenants and I worked with her sister. I had ongoing contact with Steph because of my cat, Coco. Steph only finally gave Coco to me when I was pregnant,' Pixie recited wearily, the fury draining from her without warning.

'Someone somewhere talked and connected the dots and that's how the story about us got out. It had nothing at all to do with my brother, who knew less than you did about what happened that night until very recently.'

His lean dark features hard and forbidding, Tor jerked his chin in acknowledgement of that likelihood. He was angry because he had got it badly wrong again with his bride. He was angry because he had been so *sure* of his facts when a thieving, dishonest, greedy character, such as he regarded Jordan to be, had been in the mix and available to blame. But he was still stunned by the level of her loyalty to her brother, her childhood memories of the other man evidently sufficient to restore some measure of her faith and affection for him.

Her attitude made him think of his own response to Sevastiano, the older brother he had only met when they were both adults. Tor had found it an unnerving experience to go from being the eldest son in the family to the discovery that his father's eldest child had actually been born to another woman before his marriage to Tor's mother. If he was honest, he had never really given Sevastiano a fair crack of the whip and learning that Katerina had been unfaithful to him *with* Sev had been the last nail in the coffin. No semblance of sibling affection had ever developed.

Shaking off that momentary attack of self-examination, Tor straightened his broad shoulders. 'I owe you an apology,' he breathed between gritted teeth. 'But make some allowances for the difference between our natures. When it comes to your brother, I'm less forgiving of his wrongs towards you and my son and much more about punishment, while you're overflowing with compassion and a desperate desire to rehabilitate him. But please accept that *my* strongest motivation is to protect you from Jordan and ensure that he cannot take advantage of you or hurt you again.'

Pixie nodded jerkily, tears stinging the backs of her eyes because this was not how she had imagined her wedding night would turn out, with them at logger-heads, angry words having been exchanged and now all the subsequent discomfiture of the aftermath. 'Apology accepted,' she said stiffly, crossing the room to explore through a door and discover to her relief that it led into a bathroom where she could excusably escape for long enough to regroup. 'I'm going to treat myself to a bath…if you don't mind?'

'Of course not,' Tor murmured tautly, wondering how to dig himself back out of the hole he had dug for himself and coming up blank from lack of practice in that field.

'I need your help to undo the hooks on this dress,' Pixie admitted even more stiffly. 'I don't want to damage it. Being a sentimental sort, I want to keep it.'

Tor breathed in deep and slow, questioning how the hell he had once again screwed up with her when such errors and misunderstandings had never occurred with any other woman. He was all over the place inside his head: he could *feel* it and it unnerved him more than a little to appreciate that, with her, he lost his focus, his self-discipline and his logical cool. She had shouted at him and he had not even known she was *capable* of shouting because in so many ways she was his exact opposite, being gentle and caring and softer in every way. Softer but *not* weak, he grasped, grateful for that distinction, because her weasel-like brother's weakness had turned his stomach.

'I like that,' he admitted honestly. 'You're not thinking of me having a successor.'

Pixie twisted her head round to survey him in shock. 'You thought that might have been likely?'

'It's not uncommon in my world for a woman to use her first marriage as a stepping stone to better.'

'You're Alfie's father. I couldn't get better,' she insisted awkwardly.

'Even though I messed up?'

'Everyone does that occasionally,' Pixie pointed out, shooting him a sideways smile as he embarked on the hooks on her silk gown. 'Sooner or later I'm going to do it too…nothing surer.'

'You always say the right forgiving thing, don't you?'

'Well, it's better than being all bitter and cynical and always expecting the worst from people, which seems to be your MO…*not* trying to start another argument!' she added in haste.

'I see the world through a different lens. I'm not bitter,' Tor asserted.

Pixie would have begged to differ on that score, but she compressed her lips and said nothing at all. Of course, Tor was bitter that his first love had let him down so badly, but if he was determined not to recognise the fact, that was *his* business, not hers. It wasn't his fault that he didn't know enough about his own emotions to label them, was it? Because she had decided that *that* was what she was dealing with: a guy utterly unable to recognise his own feelings for what they were, blind as a bat to his own emotional promptings. He had concentrated on the guilt he'd experienced at his wife and daughter's deaths, beat himself up for his mistakes rather than on the huge betrayal that had preceded and powered that tragic loss.

Tor's usually nimble fingers began to get inexplicably clumsy as he unhooked the back of Pixie's dress. Pale pearly shoulder blades, narrow and delicate, were revealed, and as the hooks worked down, something frilly and lacy and absolutely Tor's favourite sort of lingerie began to appear and he snatched in a startled breath, wondering why it felt vaguely indecent to find his bride quite so sexually potent. It was a tiny corset, as tiny as she was as long as she didn't turn round and show off the front view, which he imagined would be spectacular. He reminded himself that she was heading for a bath and that the last thing she needed now was to be mauled by a sexually voracious bridegroom, who had already infuriated her. He spread the corners of the gown back and succumbed involuntarily to temptation, pressing his lips softly against an inch of pale porcelain skin.

'Tor…?' Pixie prompted, but only after a helpless little quiver as that unsought kiss on her skin travelled through her.

'Working on the hooks,' Tor ground out thickly, watching the corset hooks appear, the pulse at his groin speeding from interested to crazed because he was realising just what he had wrecked. The fancy lingerie had been for *his* benefit because he had made that remark about how much he liked such adornments.

'I find you incredibly tempting,' he breathed with a ragged undertone as he traced the line of her shoulder to her nape with the tip of his tongue and lingered there, drinking in the fruit scent of her skin, some kind of peachy scent that absolutely did it for him. 'I'm sorry.'

Pixie wasn't really speaking to Tor, not in a child-ish way but in a grown-up-quiet way. She had been en route to a bath and a serious rethink about where she stood with him, but nobody had ever told her that she was incredibly tempting before. No man's hand had ever trembled before against her shoulder and that she could have the power to affect Tor to that extent was a dream come true for her. Slowly, Pixie turned round and let the silk dress drop down her arms to her wrists and fall, so that the whole thing dropped round her ankles and he was gratifyingly entranced. It was written all over him, brilliant dark golden eyes locked to her like magnets, and she liked that, really, *really* liked that.

'Kiss me,' she said abruptly, not thinking about it, *refusing* to think about it, just acting on natural instinct.

'That's where we started out before.'

'Nothing wrong with a repeat,' Pixie told him squarely. 'But you're far too tall to kiss standing upright, so I think we should move…er…lie down, whatever.'

'You were going for a bath.' Tor husked the reminder reluctantly.

'A lady can change her mind,' Pixie told him, drowning in the dark golden smouldering depths of his black-fringed eyes, revelling in the truth that the gorgeous guy was actually *her* gorgeous guy and not someone else's.

'Did I say sorry *that* well?' Tor asked, sucking in a quick shallow breath, quite unbelievably enthralled by her change of heart and shocked by himself.

'I'm softer than you but selfish too,' Pixie whispered

shakily. 'I want you. I probably want you more than I ever wanted anything in my life.'

And that was the green light that Tor needed to snatch her up out of her fallen gown and carry her over to the bed, where he laid her out to admire her in all the glory of the white corset, panties and white stockings she had worn for his benefit. He couldn't take his eyes off her tiny figure lying on display, the full mounds of her breasts cupped in lace for his delectation, the tight white vee of silk between her thighs, the slender grace-ful line of her thighs. He was enchanted by that view. Dimly, he registered that sex had, evidently, been rather boring before he met Pixie, something only his strong libido had driven him to do on a regular basis, and that was a fine distinction he had not recognised before. *She* made him burn with lust, *she* added another entire di-mension to his concept of sexual desire.

Without warning, Pixie scrambled up and off the bed and began to help him out of his jacket. 'You've got too much on,' she mumbled, half under her breath, belat-edly embarrassed by her own boldness.

Tor smiled, shed the tie, the jacket, peeled off his shirt and toed off his shoes. He was getting rid of the socks and unzipping his trousers when he saw her seated at the foot of the wide divan watching him as though he were a film. 'What?' he queried with a raised brow.

'You didn't undress the first time,' Pixie admitted starkly.

And in that single admission, Tor knew how badly he had got it wrong the night his son had been conceived and he almost grimaced. 'Precautions?'

Pixie winced and reddened. 'No, neither of us

thought of that, so that wasn't entirely your fault. I was foolish too.'

His black brows drew together. 'I was fully clothed when I woke up the next day, which is why I had no idea I had been intimate with anyone,' he breathed in a driven undertone, because nothing that he was discovering was raising his opinion of himself when he was under the influence of alcohol and he knew it would be a cold day in hell before he got in that condition again.

Pixie dropped her curly head with a wincing motion of her slight shoulders. 'I…er…tidied you up. I was… I was embarrassed… If I'm honest, I didn't want you to know or remember me. I felt I had let myself down and taken advantage of you.'

'Of…*me*?' Tor cited in disbelief.

'Well, you'd been quite clear about not wanting to be with anyone after you had rejected Saffron,' she reminded him ruefully. 'I should've heeded that and drawn back.'

Tor set his teeth together. 'We both got carried away and I know why. You turn me on fast and hard and neither of us was able to call a halt.'

Pixie nodded in a rush, seeing that he had grasped what had happened, the sheer explosion of hunger that had seized her. But while they had been talking, Tor had also been getting naked and her mind was wandering because she was very much enjoying the view. Stripped down to black boxers, he had the build of a Greek god garbed in living flesh instead of marble and the lean, powerful lines of muscle etching his chest and abdomen made her mouth run dry. He was amazingly perfect and beautiful. In Eloise's parlance, it was a case of the super tanker and the tugboat comparison again. What on earth had he *ever* seen in her ordinary self? Or was that kind of physical attraction simply unquantifiable and impossible to explain? she wondered. The pull between them that night had been so strong, so irresistible and already she could feel the same thing happening to her again, her body warming and quickening down deep inside and her heartbeat speeding up.

'Tonight will be different from that first night,' Tor swore with an edge of raw anticipation and masculine resolve that sent butterflies cascading through her stomach while a hot, tight feeling clenched her pelvis.

CHAPTER NINE

'It wasn't a bad experience…er…you and me,' Pixie reassured him with hot cheeks. 'Physically it worked for me.'

'I can do better than that,' Tor husked, staring down at her, at the high plump mounds peaking from the lace edge of the corset. 'I love this lingerie, *hara mou*.'

'You're acting like it's something special to you… me wearing this stuff,' Pixie muttered tensely. 'When we both know it's *not* special because you've had many women in your life and a great deal of experience.'

'After Katerina I never stayed with anyone for more than a few days, so I was never around long enough for anyone to make the effort to dress up for me,' he countered bluntly as he gazed down at her with heavily lashed, half-hooded, dark brooding eyes. 'We're married now. This is a whole different relationship.'

Yes, very different from the one he must once have had with the woman he loved, Pixie's brain sniped, and she stifled that thought, knowing that such thoughts, such pointless, tasteless comparisons, would drive her mad if she let them in. Katerina was his past and *she* was his present and she had to be sensible and view their marriage in that positive light, not give way to envy. *Envy?* That was what she was discovering inside herself, a sense of envy relating to his late wife, who had had it all with him and simply thrown it away. Why *was* she envious? Why was she feeling more than she should about an old relationship that was none of her business?

But that knotty question fled her mind as Tor brought her down on the bed and crushed her mouth under his. If there was one thing she had learned the first time Tor kissed her, it was that Tor knew how to kiss, indeed, Tor knew so well how to kiss that he made her head spin and sent a ripple of craving shooting through her with every dancing plunge of his tongue. Her fingers laced into the thick silk of his hair and held him to her, smoothing down over his wide, strong shoulders, exploring over the satin skin of his back because that first night she hadn't been able to touch him while he was still clothed.

Tor came up on an elbow, a long forefinger skimming back an edge of lace to bare a rounded breast crowned by a straining pink nipple. 'You excite the hell out of me,' he admitted gruffly, hungrily closing a mouth to that tempting peak, using the tip of his tongue, the tug of his teeth and his warm sensual mouth to pleasure her.

The motion of his mouth on her breasts tightened her, as if there were a chain leading to the hot, liquid centre of her body, and her hips shifted upwards, all of her awash with more craving. He sat her up with easy confidence and began to unhook the corset. Her cheeks flushed and she looked away from him, wanting so much to own that confidence of his. It had been dim that first night, never mind his lack of awareness: he had not been looking for flaws.

'What's wrong?' he asked her, disconcerting her by noticing her anxiety.

'It was sort of darkish that night and now I feel like I'm under floodlights.' With one hand she made an awkward motion towards the fancy lights above, the mirrors on the units adding their myriad reflections to the brightness.

Tor shifted up and hit a switch above the bed and the illumination dimmed. 'Better?'

'It's really stupid being shy when we've already got a kid,' Pixie muttered guiltily, wishing she could get a grip on her self-consciousness before it wrecked the atmosphere.

'No, it's not.' Tor tugged her back down to him, moulding his big hands to her full breasts. 'But you do stress a lot, don't you?'

'Yes,' she admitted ruefully.

'So, it's up to me to ensure you have more to think about, *latria mou*…' Tor skated a fingertip across the taut triangle of her panties and she gasped, the pulse of arousal between her slender thighs kicking on to an intense high.

In that moment everything else melted away along with her insecurities. Suddenly, she was twisting round to find that wicked mouth of his, so sensually full and yet hard and soft at the same time, that so enthralled her. He was peeling off her panties and she quivered at the prospect of him touching her again, for the merest instant mortified by her own eagerness, but then she was already maddeningly conscious of the swollen, slick readiness of her own body.

Even the lightest brush of his fingertips aroused her, and she was knocked off balance when he slid down the bed and began to use his mouth on that most tender area. Of course, she knew about that, knew the specifics of everything sexual, but she hadn't ever imagined that anything could feel as good as what he made her feel then. Every nerve ending in her body seemed to be centred there and before very long she was quivering with little reflexive tremors running through her and breathless little sounds she couldn't silence falling from her parted lips as her head thrashed back and forth on the pillow.

As the pressure in her pelvis rose and tightened, her hips began to writhe to a spontaneous rhythm and the great gathering whoosh of sensation surged and she cried out and then lay there, discovering her fingers were knotted in his hair and slowly withdrawing them, a great lassitude sweeping her.

'No, you don't get to sleep now, *moraki mou,*' Tor told her with a slashing grin that banished every shred of dark, forbidding tension from his lean, darkly handsome features. He kissed her with devouring hunger as he stretched up over her with the lean, powerful, predatory grace of a stalking panther. She tasted herself on his lips and still moaned beneath that sensual assault as he hooked up her knees and settled her back, pushing his hot, sleek shaft against the still-tingling entrance to her body and plunging in hard enough to make her gasp in delight.

He angled down his hips and sank so deep into her

that she didn't know where he began and she ended and that was only the beginning, the wildly arousing beginning while she was still in control. But the excitement of his fluid, driving thrusts into her sensitised body smashed her control, smashed it and broke it into tiny pieces until she was rising against him with her heart pounding and her body arching, craving his every move. She could barely breathe, she could certainly not speak, but had she had her voice she would only have urged him *not to stop*. The burning rise to orgasm began all over again, forcing her higher and higher, stimulated almost beyond bearing and seething with a physical sensual energy she had not known she possessed. And then at the zenith of sensation she shattered, electrified by the blazing excitement that convulsed her every limb, and she was utterly captivated by the drenching slow, sweet pleasure that flooded her in the aftermath.

Tor froze as Pixie cuddled into him, her little hand spreading across the centre of his damp heaving chest, and for an instant he almost lost control and pushed her away from him in a knee-jerk reaction. For five years, he had been pushing women away the instant they tried to be affectionate because, rather than pleasing him, it chilled him. It had always reminded him of Katerina's superficial affection, which had, in the end, proved to be so false, not only towards him, but towards her daughter as well, he acknowledged grimly. But he would not make vile comparisons that Pixie did not deserve, and he would make a really big effort to pretend that this was his first marriage *before* he learned to question almost everything a woman said and did.

That sounded bitter, he conceded in surprise as he extended an arm round Pixie's slight, pliant body and pulled her close. But he wasn't bitter—*was he? Thee mou*, his bride was as good as a witch when it came to slotting odd ideas into his mind! Only, she didn't need a book to cast a spell, only her body, her response, her warmth, all of which she offered so freely. If he wasn't very careful he would hurt her again, because she was much more fragile than the women he was accustomed to dealing with and he wasn't of a sensitive persuasion.

'Is it always that amazing?' Pixie whispered.

'No, it's not,' Tor answered truthfully, and he was almost but not quite tempted to tell her that it had never been that good for him before, but she didn't need to know that, did she? Theirs was a marriage of convenience and practicality and that was *all* he wanted it to be. He didn't want the legendary highs or the fabled lows, he would be content with his son and a marriage on an even keel.

Pixie felt blissfully relaxed, relieved that the silly newspaper story had been dealt with and set aside without causing more trouble. Being in a relationship, being one half of a whole, was very new to her and she was beginning to see that there were no hard and fast rules and that she had to learn to compromise and smooth over the rough spots where she could. Even now, though, she was aware that even if Tor didn't see it, he was still damaged by what Katerina had done to him.

Pixie had felt him freeze when she'd snuggled up to him and she had held her breath, waiting to see what he would do, and she had only relaxed when he'd pulled her the rest of the way into his arms. But that didn't mean that she wasn't aware that she had married a wary, bitter, suspicious man with a tendency to expect everything to blow up in his face when he least expected it. Hopefully, time and experience would teach him differently when it came to having her and Alfie as a family. Should how he felt matter to her as much as it did? Well, she knew what her problem was: she was halfway to falling madly in love with Tor, possibly even further than halfway, she conceded ruefully.

Almost a month later, Pixie watched Tor climb, still dripping, from the pool, after the acrobatics he had performed there to entertain Alfie, and cross the main deck to speak to the yacht captain, a bearded man currently sporting an apologetic smile.

While they were chatting she lifted Alfie, who was already half-asleep, and moved down to the cabin where her son was sleeping to change him and put him in his crib for a nap. Their nanny, Isla, was probably sunbathing on the top deck because Pixie and Tor usually kept Alfie with them in the mornings. She went for a shower and was towelling herself dry when Tor reappeared in the doorway.

'We have an unscheduled stop to make this evening to take on supplies. While the crew are dealing with stocking up, we'll be enjoying a sheltered cove and dining in a restaurant which the captain assures me is a hidden gem,' he related lazily as he peeled off his shorts.

Heat mushroomed in her pelvis as she watched and dimly wondered if she would ever become accustomed to Tor's utterly stunning masculine beauty. His gleam-

ing bronzed gaze struck hers and she stilled, her heartbeat quickening, her breath catching in her throat. '*Se
thelo,*' he breathed, thick and low.

I want you—one little Greek phrase she had become
hugely familiar with over the past four weeks.

Hunger lightening his eyes to gold, he reached for
her, disposing of the towel with an aggressive jerk to
release her small body from its folds and hauling her
up against his hard, hot length.

'I *always* want you,' he breathed with a slight frown,
as if he couldn't quite work out why that should be so.
'You're turning me into a sex addict.'

Pixie flushed, knowing that she matched him there.
She couldn't keep her hands off him, couldn't back off
from the allure of that raw masculine magnetism he em-
anated if her life depended on it. It flared in her every
time she looked at him, every time he reached for her,
like a flame that had only been fed into a blaze by constant proximity. A month was a long time for a couple
to be alone together, she acknowledged, just a little sad
that they would be returning to London the following
day. It had been a wonderful holiday though, *her* hon-
eymoon, something she had not been quite sure it was
when they'd first set sail on their wedding night. But
they had both needed that time and space to get to know
each other on a deeper level and it had worked. Tor had
probably planned it that way, she conceded, having finally come to understand that Tor planned most things.
It was just the way he operated. Only with sex was Tor
spontaneous or impulsive.

'What's wrong?' Tor husked as he backed her into

the cabin again, all hungry predatory resolve and indescribably sexy in the role.

'Absolutely nothing,' she told him truthfully, because
she reckoned that she would have to be a very demanding person to want more from him than she already had,
and she refused to allow herself to feel discontented.

He spread her out on the bed and she tingled all over,
her skin prickling with high-voltage awareness and anticipation as he feathered his sensual mouth over her
protuberant nipples, making her moan. He stroked a
provocative fingertip between her legs, where she was
already swollen and damp, and a fierce smile of satisfaction slanted his lean, darkly handsome features.
Without any further preamble, he thrust into her hard
and fast and a shot of dynamite pleasure ravaged her
pliant body. His compelling rhythm sent her to a stormy
height of need faster than she would have believed. It
was good, it was *so* good she climaxed crying out his
name...and something else. 'I love you!' she gasped,
just seconds before her brain could kick in again and
make her swallow those words.

And Tor said...*nothing*. Pixie told herself that possibly he hadn't heard or that he was just politely ignoring that accidental word spillage of hers and that that
was better than forcing her to discuss the issue. For Tor
would see that declaration as an issue, not a benefit,
not a compliment, not something he should treasure
and be grateful for. In turmoil, she turned away from
him, her face literally burning with mortification and
a sense of humiliation. Why? *Why* had she had to let
those words escape?

Maybe it was pathetic to be so happy with a guy

who didn't love her when deep down inside her there was still this dangerous nagging need to have *more* from him and, of course, it bothered her. After all, love couldn't be turned on like a magic tap by anyone but perhaps, over time, Tor would come to care for her more, she had recently soothed herself. Life wasn't a fairy tale, Eloise had warned her, but, in truth, Pixie couldn't help still yearning for the fairy tale.

Yet at the same time, honesty lay at the very heart of her nature and she had wanted to share her feelings with Tor, give him that warmth and validation. After all, she knew for a fact that life could change in a moment with an accident, an illness, some other terrible event, and she needed to live in the moment. Secrets weren't her style.

It was true though that there were still little black holes in their relationship where she didn't dare travel. He never ever talked about Katerina or Sofia, not even accidentally. It was as if he had locked that all up in some underground box on the night of the crash when he'd lost his wife and child and, sadly, only an excess of alcohol had unleashed his devastating emotional confessions the evening he and Pixie had first met. The rest of the time? Tor might as well have been a single man rather than a widower when she'd married him.

Yet Tor had asked her so much about her parents and her childhood memories, had freely satisfied his own curiosity and it had brought them closer, of course it had. Why couldn't he do the same for her when it came to his first marriage? His silence was a barrier that disturbed her. Why was he still holding back? It was because of her honesty that Tor now understood a great deal better why she was so attached to her half-brother, the boy who had stood up for her in the playground when other children had teased her about her diminutive size, the adult male who had comforted her after the death of their father and her mother by promising that he would always be there for her.

'Need a shower,' she muttered, pulling free of the arms anchored round her and heading for the bathroom as though her life depended on it because his silence hurt her. Was it possible that he was still in love with his dead wife? Or was she being fanciful?

Tor rolled over and punched a pillow, perfect white teeth clenching now that Pixie was out of view. For a split second he was furious with her for putting him in that position. Just because he wasn't prepared to lie, wasn't prepared to pretend! Those three words were so easy to say, had routinely featured between him and Katerina and they had been absolutely meaningless and empty on her side.

But was it fair to punish Pixie for Katerina's lies and pretences?

He froze as that possibility penetrated his brain for the very first time. He wasn't punishing anybody, he roared defensively inside himself. He was simply insisting on a higher standard of honesty in their marriage, which meant that there would be a smaller chance of misunderstandings occurring between them. They needed a lot of things in a successful marriage, but love wasn't a necessity, not as respect and loyalty and caring were, he reasoned in exasperation. Pixie was just young and rather naïve and had yet to grasp such fine distinctions. And it wasn't as though believing that she loved him was likely to do her any harm, he rationalised, denying the warmth spreading through his chest and the smile tugging at the corners of his mouth.

That evening Pixie dressed to go ashore for dinner in a glorious white sundress that flattered her new tan, her blond curls tumbling round her shoulders in abundance. Her wardrobe had expanded over the month because Tor had taken her to more than one exclusive shopping outlet where he had insisted on buying her stuff. Jewellery such as she had never expected to own sparkled in the diamonds at her ears and throat, the slender gold watch on her wrist, the glittering rings on her fingers. On the outside she looked like a rich woman; on the inside, though, she still felt like an imposter, she acknowledged unhappily. She had won Katerina's place only by the other woman's death and an accidental conception. She was basically just Katerina's imperfect replacement and even Alfie was only a replacement for the little girl who had died.

The launch delivered her and Tor to a beach, where he insisted on carrying her across to the steps that wound up the cliff to where the restaurant sat. Pixie examined her feelings for him as he set her carefully down on the steps, so attentive, so honourable, so everything but *not* loving. How could she condemn him for that lack? she scolded herself sharply, annoyed that she was letting her own humiliation linger and twist her up to the detriment of their marriage. That was foolish, short-sighted, and in the light of that reflection she linked her arms round his neck before he could straighten and stretched up to kiss him. He didn't have to love her because she loved him; they could get by fine as they were.

Relief coursed through Tor, who had remained insanely conscious of how quiet and muted Pixie had become throughout the day. He didn't know when he had become so attuned to her moods, but he noticed the instant the sparkle died in her eyes and she withdrew from him. It had disconcerted him to appreciate how much she could put him on edge. He smiled at her as he urged her up the steps, careful to stay behind her in case she stumbled in her high heels. They took seats out on the terrace with its panoramic view of the sea and had only received their menus when Tor swore softly in surprise under his breath.

An older couple had walked out onto the terrace.

'My godparents,' he breathed. 'Basil and Dimitra... *not* a happy coincidence.'

'I think I dimly remember them from the wedding... but we didn't actually speak,' Pixie whispered. 'Don't you like them?'

'It's not that,' Tor parried with a frown before he stood up to greet the other couple.

Pixie rose as well, walking into a hail of Greek being exchanged and smiling valiantly. Dimitra introduced herself in easy English, explaining that she had grown up in London before moving to Greece in her teens, where she had gone to school with Tor's mother, Pandora. Their meeting was not quite the coincidence Tor had stated, Pixie thought once she learned that the other couple owned a holiday home nearby. Tor insisted that the couple join them for their meal, and it passed pleasantly with talk of their cruise round the Greek islands until Tor became increasingly involved in talking business with his godfather. By the coffee stage, the men had shifted to the outside bar across the terrace and the two women were alone.

'I feel guilty that we've intruded on your last night away.' Dimitra sighed.

'I'm really surprised that I didn't get talking to you at the wedding when you're so close to Hallas and Pandora,' Pixie confided, wondering how that oversight had come about.

'I suppose because we felt it would've been inappropriate to put ourselves forward too much. I wasn't even sure about us accepting the invitation to your wedding,' Dimitra admitted and, seeing Pixie's frowning, puzzled look, added, 'You don't know, do you? Tor's first wife was *our* daughter…'

'*Oh…*' Pixie whispered, bereft of breath by that revelation but equally quickly grasping the difficulties of that situation. 'But you're all still good friends, aren't you?'

'Of course, although it's a shame that Tor chose to conceal the truth about their marriage,' Dimitra shared in a troubled undertone. 'After what he'd endured, we've never wanted to tackle that subject with him directly, but we're straight-talking people and it would've been easier for us had he just admitted that our daughter was having an affair and that Sofia was not his. At first I was grateful for that silence but with such close friends I would've preferred the truth rather than feeling forced to live a lie.'

Pixie settled startled eyes on the other woman, swiftly suppressing the shock of learning that Sofia had *not*, after all, been Tor's child. 'I don't think Tor realises that *you* know.'

'We knew. We tried hard to stop it, but we got nowhere. Katerina was obsessed with Devon.'

Pixie's brow furrowed. 'Devon?' she queried.

'Sevastiano's half-brother, Devon. Katerina called him Dev. Ironically, they met at a prewedding party Hallas and Pandora threw for Tor and my daughter. Devon was already married with two young children,' Dimitra revealed heavily. 'But once Tor and Katerina moved to London, where Devon lived, the fact that they were both married didn't influence either of them and we didn't know it was happening until two years after the marriage when we caught them together. It was on that horrible day that my daughter admitted that she was pregnant with Devon's child. I won't go into our feelings, but you can imagine how treacherous I felt when Pandora wept over the passing of a child who was not of their blood. But it was not *our* secret to tell.'

And Tor hadn't revealed that final secret even when he *could* have told it that first night they met, Pixie reflected painfully. Even more revealing was his silence on that score, a silence so complete, so unyielding over the entire sordid business that he had been erroneously blaming his brother, Sevastiano, for being his late wife's lover when in fact it had not been him. How on earth had he contrived to get *that* wrong? Yet it served Tor right, a part of Pixie declared *without* sympathy. He had far too busy hugging his damaged ego and his secrets, and Tor and his family had remained in dangerous ignorance long after the event. And that was very unhealthy, wasn't it?

A welter of differing thoughts and deductions assailed Pixie on the launch that wafted them back to the yacht. What she had learned from Dimitra had put her in an awkward position. She had to tell Tor not only that his former in-laws were already fully acquainted with their late daughter's peccadilloes, but also that he had misjudged his brother, Sevastiano, who had not been Katerina's lover. How could she keep quiet about such matters? They were too important to ignore yet too personal for her to want to tackle them...aside of that revelation about Sofia, who had not been Tor's daughter, as he had led her to believe.

But did Tor even know that Sofia had not been his child? It was perfectly possible that he didn't know, Pixie reasoned uneasily. On the other hand, if he *did* know, Pixie believed that Tor should have told *her*— because such an issue *did* matter to the mother of the baby she had assumed to be his second child.

However, if Dimitra was to be believed, Alfie was Tor's firstborn, and if he had known that all along and kept quiet about it, deliberately misleading Pixie in relation to her son's status, she *did* have a bone to pick with him. Just at that moment Pixie felt very tired of following in Katerina's footsteps and suspecting that her beloved Alfie was a mere replacement for Tor's lost daughter. All of a sudden that felt like a burning issue for her. But at the same time she was consumed by the awareness of what Tor must have suffered when he'd realised that the child he loved was not his child, and she felt quite sick at the prospect of having to broach that topic with him.

'You're very quiet. Did Dimitra say something that

upset you? I didn't intend to leave you alone. Basil had a tricky financial problem he wanted my advice on and I lost track of time.'

'No, nothing she said upset me,' Pixie lied, because she didn't want him misinterpreting her meaning. 'Although I could've done with you just biting the bullet and telling me that your godparents are your former in-laws. It's not such a big deal.'

'It feels awkward now that I've remarried,' Tor countered a little stiffly. 'Especially with all that happened five years ago. I've known them all my life but I'm aware that they feel uncomfortable as well. It's unfortunate. They're a lovely couple.'

'Yes. I liked them,' Pixie confided, on surer ground.

'It's a mystery to me why their daughters turned out as they did. Maybe they spoilt them, never told them no… I don't know. I feel like I should know, though, when I grew up with them running around my home, but you have a different viewpoint as a child.'

'I didn't know there was another daughter.'

'Angelina. Didn't you meet her at the wedding?' Tor asked casually.

'Oh, yes, I met her, but I didn't realise the connection.' Pixie understood Angelina's bad attitude then, or thought she did: a sister being confronted by her dead sibling's replacement bride and child. The brunette had been unpleasant but her identity granted her some excuse for her behaviour, in Pixie's opinion.

Her mind moved on as she mulled over Tor's remark about it being a mystery how the Raptis daughters had turned out as they had. That was the closest he had ever come to criticising Katerina and it surprised her, for she had assumed that he still viewed his first wife as some kind of misunderstood martyr.

'We have to talk when we get back,' she breathed softly as Tor settled her down in a seat on the launch, having carried her across the beach to save her from the task of removing her shoes.

'About what?'

'Stuff,' she framed flatly.

His ebony brows pleated, bronzed eyes narrowing with a dark glitter in the moonlight, and she thought how gorgeous his sculpted bone structure was and of the marvel that she was actually married to such a man. All that electrifying sexiness and caring and she was still finding fault? Was she crazy?

CHAPTER TEN

TOR HAD SPENT much of the evening lazily watching his wife across the depth of the terrace, drinking in her natural animation, the shine of her naturally blond curls below the lights, the deep ocean blueness of her eyes and the amazing curves hinted at even below that perfectly modest sundress. Where she was concerned, he was like a junkie in constant need of a fix, he reflected grimly, because that lack of control, that burning hunger that continually seethed in him, bothered him. Something about Pixie revved his libido to absurd heights and, always a fan of everything in moderation, he had already tried and failed abysmally to switch off that reaction or at the very least turn it down to a more acceptable level.

And what did she want to talk about? He could think of nothing amiss and that put him on edge as well because he didn't like surprises. In his past experience a surprise had rarely led to anything good and yet Pixie regularly surprised him in the most positive of ways. She was a terrific mother to his son, protective without overdoing it, loving and caring and willing to share Alfie. She was unsophisticated, naïve, utterly ignorant of the exclusive world he inhabited and yet she moved through that same world with disconcerting grace and assurance, relying on ordinary courtesy to smooth her path. When he least expected it, she impressed him, and she had done it over and over again.

On board the yacht again, Pixie walked ahead of him up to their master cabin, where most of their luggage had already been packed ready for their departure back to London. First thing in the morning they were being picked up by a helicopter, which would deliver them straight to the airport.

'We can talk when we get back to London,' she suggested rather abruptly, apprehensive about the confrontation that she knew awaited her. It cut her to the heart that Tor had *not* chosen to confide in her about the truth that he had not been Sofia's father. That revelation on top of Katerina's infidelity must have devastated him. Yet Pixie had believed that she and Tor were getting really close, but how could she go on believing that comforting conviction when he continued to hide such a dreadful secret from her? His silence on that score hurt her a great deal, showing a dangerous fault line in their relationship, making her feel more insecure than ever about how he still viewed Katerina.

Tor was frowning now, his lean, strong features taut and a little forbidding. 'No, say whatever you have to say now.'

'I'll just spit it out, then,' Pixie murmured reluctantly. 'I found out some pretty shocking things listening to Dimitra this evening.'

'But you said—'

'I couldn't explain unless we had privacy,' Pixie interposed wryly. 'For a start, Katerina's parents are fully aware that their daughter was having an affair and was in the process of leaving you when she died. They tried to stop the affair, but she wouldn't listen to them.'

Tor was stunned.

'I can't credit that…are you sure?'

'Unequivocally. Dimitra actually said that pretending everything was fine in your marriage put more of a strain on them because they felt as though they were being forced to lie. But at the same time, she acknowledged that it was your right to maintain that pretence if that's what you preferred. She didn't have any axe to grind. I appreciate that you believed you were protecting them from distress by not telling them the truth but, really, I think it would have been easier all round if you'd just spoken up at the time,' she confided gently.

'You know nothing about it. I told you about the situation with Sev though,' Tor bit out angrily, taking her aback because that anger seemed to come out of nowhere at her.

'According to your ex-mother-in-law, Sev *wasn't* Katerina's lover,' Pixie stated even more uneasily. 'It wasn't him, it was his brother, Devon.'

Tor stared back at her, his eyes dark with seething incredulity. 'That's not possible. Dimitra must have misunderstood.'

'I don't think so. They knew about the affair before you did and presumably, if they tried to stop it, they did discuss the man involved with their daughter,' Pixie pointed out quietly. 'Look, I know you hate all this being raked up again and I appreciate how difficult all of this is for you, Tor—'

'How the hell could you?' Tor demanded with ferocious bite. 'You're standing there giving forth about issues that are nothing to do with you and naturally I resent that.'

'I resent being plunged into the middle of your secret, sordid past when I didn't want to be involved in any way!' Pixie fired back at him, embarrassment and pain at his attitude combining to send her temper over the edge as well. 'As far as I'm concerned, I feel like Katerina might as well still be alive because you still think of her as your wife and protect her good name so carefully. Well, what about me? Where do *I* come in? I've only been married to you for a month and already I feel like I'm living in her shadow!'

'*Thee mou*…that's rubbish!' Tor blistered back at her, bronzed eyes shot through with smouldering lights of gold disbelief at that charge.

Pixie raised a doubting brow. 'Is it? Why are you still so guilty about her death that you took all the blame for it on your own shoulders? Were you a rotten husband? Were you unfaithful as well? And why didn't you tell me that Alfie was your *first* child? I feel that that's something that I should have known. Maybe because it's the only thing out of all of this mess that relates to me personally. But you should've told me that Sofia wasn't your daughter by blood. I understand and fully accept that you loved her and that you probably didn't discover that truth until Katerina was leaving you, but I do believe that you *could* have shared that with me.'

Tor had frozen where he stood, shaken at that hail of spontaneously emotional censure emerging from mild-tempered Pixie. 'I wasn't a rotten husband and I wasn't unfaithful. As to why I didn't tell you about Sofia's paternity…?' He spread lean brown hands. 'I can't really answer that. Maybe because it was the last straw, the ultimate humiliation for a man to learn that the child he has been raising and loving is not his. Maybe I was still in denial because, yes, I did love that little girl a great deal. But I still don't see how Sofia's paternity has anything at all to do with you or Alfie.'

'Well, that news doesn't surprise me,' Pixie retorted tight-lipped in her distress, furiously swallowing back the thickness in her throat and the warning sting at the backs of her eyes. 'All along you haven't once understood how I feel about anything because you don't really care about me. So, let's leave it there for tonight, Tor. I'm exhausted and I'm going to bed.'

'That's not true,' Tor declared as she snatched up her toiletries bag and cosmetics from the en suite and walked to the door. 'Where are you going?'

'I don't want to share a bed with you tonight. I don't want to be anywhere near you,' Pixie countered stiffly, determined not to reveal her distress in front of him. 'I'll sleep in one of the other cabins.'

'That's ridiculous… I don't want that. You're blowing this nonsense up out of all proportion,' Tor proclaimed rawly.

But Pixie didn't believe that. She was horribly upset, all her feelings flailing with pain inside her and he was the blind focus of them. And she didn't even know exactly what she wanted from him, only that she wasn't receiving it. Was she blaming him for not loving her as he had loved Katerina? She stopped dead in the empty cabin next door, stricken by that suspicion because that would be absolutely unfair to Tor. And she thought of what she had thrown at him without warning and almost cringed where she stood. When had she ever acted with so little compassion before? Where had her sympathy, her understanding gone?

Dear heaven, she had thrown in his teeth the reality that his poor little daughter had not been fathered by him. Had he even known that fact before she'd hurled it at him? Or had he only suspected that he might not be Sofia's father and had she confirmed his misgivings with her attack? Her stomach tightened and swirled with nausea at that possibility. She was horrified. Kicking off the high heels now pinching her toes, she trekked back barefoot to the master cabin.

A dim light glowed on the deck terrace beyond the French windows.

Through them she could see Tor leaning up against the rail, luxuriant black cropped hair ruffling in the breeze, his jacket discarded, the fine fabric of his shirt rippling against his lean, powerful torso, and her mouth ran dry the way it always did when the sheer beauty of him punched her afresh. Lifting her chin and suppressing that reaction, Pixie went outside to join him.

'Were you already aware that Sofia wasn't yours?' she pressed bluntly, her troubled face pale and tight in the low light.

Tor gritted his teeth. 'Yes… Yes, I knew. When I tried to prevent her mother from removing her from the house that night she told me then that Sofia wasn't my daughter. At first I didn't believe her because she was hysterical. But afterwards…' He breathed with difficulty. 'I had the tests done because I had to know the truth and it was confirmed.'

'I'm still really sorry I hurled it at you like that though,' Pixie muttered shakily. 'I also think that that little girl was very fortunate to have your love and care while she was alive. Like you, she didn't know the truth, but you loved each other anyway. You were still her father, Tor, in every way that mattered.'

Tor drained the tumbler in his clenched hand, whiskey burning down into the chill inside him because he was still in shock from their exchange. 'That's a really kind thing for you to say in these circumstances. But I'm sorry that you were inadvertently dragged into my secret, sordid past tonight. Just go to bed now, Pixie. I've got nothing else to say to you right now...'

And that was true. The tormenting belief that he could have wrongly believed his half-brother, Sevastiano, had betrayed him for so many years sickened Tor. In retrospect it struck him as unbelievable that he had chosen not to confront Sev. Did he blame his pride for that silence? His desire to let sleeping dogs lie for the sake of family unity?

Yet the instant Pixie had named Devon, pieces that had never made sense to Tor had locked together neatly to provide a much clearer picture of that secret affair. And suddenly, for the first time, it had all made sense.

Devon was Sev's English half-brother and he would already have been a married man when Katerina had first met him. No doubt that was why she had gone ahead and married Tor, because she had been unable to foresee and trust in a future with a lover who already had a wife and children. Easier access to Devon would explain why she had been so keen to live in London as well.

And Sevastiano?

Tor swore under his breath, recognising that his older brother would have been placed in an impossible situation, stuck in the middle between two half-brothers: one who had never really made an effort with him—Stand up, Tor, and own your mistakes, he urged himself—the other whom presumably he'd had a warmer relationship with because he had grown up with Devon.

How could Sevastiano possibly have chosen loyalties between them?

Dismissed, and feeling like a sleepwalker, Pixie went back next door, undressing where she stood, deciding that, yes, she could go to bed with make-up on because she didn't care, she really didn't care just at that moment. Her eyes were prickling and throbbing, the tears she had been holding back burning through her defences and finally overflowing, a painful sob tearing at her throat. He had thrown her own unjust words back at her…his 'secret sordid past'. And she should never have said such words to him when the sordid aspect had related to his wife's behaviour and had had nothing at all to do with his.

Why had she done it? Why had she dragged up all that messy stuff from the past and thrown it at him as though he were the worst husband in the world? And the easy answer twisted inside her like a knife and made her groan out loud because there was nothing very adult or admirable about her envy of Katerina, her possessive vibes about her son's status or her embittered attitude to Tor's grief over the death of his first wife.

In reality, she was a nasty jealous cow and now he knew it too. She had unveiled herself in all her immature, selfish glory for his benefit, all because she had admitted she loved him and he had ignored that confession. That disappointment had wounded her and put her in the wrong state of mind, releasing turbulent emotions that had quickly got out of her control. She had said things she didn't believe, demanded truths she wasn't entitled to receive and roused memories of a tragedy she truly hadn't wanted to bring alive for him again. And she had told him that she loved him and then acted in a very unloving way. Her eyes burned and ached as she recalled his tense chilliness towards her out on the terrace. Well, what had she expected from him? Bouquets and praise?

Tor stayed up thinking for most of the night and when dawn lightened the skies, he felt amazingly light as well. It had been so many years since he had felt like that that it was almost like being reborn. Reborn? Tor winced at that fanciful concept, but he was still smiling, still wondering how he had got everything so wrong for so very long and if it was even possible that he could have set a new record for sheer stupidity.

Pixie rose heavy-eyed in spite of the exhaustion that had finally sent her to sleep and grimaced at the tackiness of waking up without having removed her make-up. It sucked to have mascara ringing her eyes and smears of make-up on her pillow and she fully understood too late why she shouldn't have done it in the first place. She was in a funereal mood, eyes swollen and red behind strategically worn sunglasses, mouth tight, a wintry outfit chosen to suit her mood.

Tor surveyed her approach for an early breakfast, noting the jeans and the black sweater and how much they enhanced her petite yet curvy figure that drove him crazy with desire. Then there was the glorious glitter of her silky curls in sunlight and the sweet delicate lines of her troubled face. An uphill climb then, he recognised grimly, exactly what he deserved because he had done everything wrong, got everything wrong, merited nothing better.

In comparison to both parents, Alfie was brimming with energy and love. He bounced in his high chair with a huge smile at them both, held out his arms pleadingly to his mother, who for the very first time failed to notice his need, and succumbed to his father instead, who not only noticed but also swept him up and made him giggle and smile and gave him kisses.

'He needs to eat, Tor,' Pixie breathed curtly.

'He wanted a cuddle,' Tor breathed with perfect assurance. 'He's a very affectionate child. Sofia was much more reserved in nature.'

Disconcerted by that reference, Pixie lifted her head. 'She was?'

'Yes. Katerina kept us apart. I thought she was a possessive mother. Even when she kept me out of the delivery room when she was born I assumed the wrong things,' he told her, taking her utterly aback with those revelations. 'I didn't smell a rat.'

'A rat?' she echoed, nonplussed.

'I wasn't a suspicious husband,' he clarified wryly.

'But right from the beginning, she tried to keep me apart from Sofia. She knew she wasn't mine and she felt guilty.'

'Oh...' Pixie replied, her confusion only deepening at what could be driving his desire to be disclosing such facts when he had never been that confiding in relation to Katerina before.

'I didn't see it at the time. I didn't even see it afterwards,' Tor admitted starkly. 'I wasn't very good at seeing that sort of thing...in advance, as it were...or even in retrospect.'

'No, you're not very switched on that way...empathy-wise,' Pixie extended awkwardly. 'You're obviously very efficient in the business line, but in personal relationships you kind of lose the plot a little.'

'Or maybe don't even see the plot to begin with,' Tor added.

Pixie steeled herself to say what she still felt she had to say. 'I wasn't fair to you last night.'

'No, you got it right,' Tor broke in grimly. 'I got it wrong.'

That silenced Pixie, who had been trying to make amends without embarrassing herself. She didn't understand. She didn't want to get it wrong again either, though, and it was the fear of doing that that kept her quiet throughout their trip to the airport and their subsequent flight back to London.

'I want you to think about whether this house is right for us,' Tor remarked as the limo drew up outside the town house. 'I didn't buy it as a family house.'

'It's a blasted amazing house,' Pixie told him sniffily, because it was enormous and fancy and everything she believed suited him to perfection. 'It's even got a garden out back. What are you talking about?'

Tor mustered his poise and a decided amount of valour and breathed in deep and slow to say, 'Some day we may think of extending the family.'

Pixie sent him a wide blue-eyed glance of naked disbelief. 'Oh, you can forget that,' she said helplessly. 'Seriously, just forget that idea!'

Another baby? Was he kidding? Whatever, his expectations were seriously out of line with her own. She would be perfectly happy just to settle for Alfie…and… er…what? she asked herself. And she couldn't come up with a single goal because, in truth, without the love she craved, Tor had nothing to offer her. She was an unreasonable woman, she told herself squarely. He was gorgeous, amazing in bed and he did all the right things as if they had been programmed into him at birth. Seriously, he was the sort of guy who would never ever forget your birthday. It wasn't love but it was the best he could offer.

So, who was she to say it wasn't enough? Who was she in her belief that she ought to have more than the basics? This was a guy who had told her from the start that he didn't think he could fall in love again…that he could give her everything else but that.

Tor had been honest.

She had been dishonest, accepting him on those terms while secretly yearning for exactly what he had told her that he couldn't deliver. Appreciating that, she swallowed hard and struggled to suppress all the powerful hurt reactions that were making it virtually impossible for her to behave normally again with Tor. She had to stop acting that way, concentrate on the future he was holding out to her, not dwell on the downside, because everything had a downside to some extent. And that future Tor was suggesting included a larger family, which was something she would eventually want too, so why had she snapped at him when he admitted it?

Isla already had Alfie tucked in his crib when she entered the nursery.

The nanny was going home to stay with her own family for a few days and while Pixie loved and relied on having help with her son, she was, conversely, looking guiltily forward to having him all to herself again for a few days. Wishing the other woman a happy break, she went into the master bedroom, stiffening into immobility a few steps in when she glimpsed Tor poised by the tall windows.

'I have something I need to tell you,' he breathed as he swung round.

And Pixie wanted to run, didn't want any more stress, any more bad news. She was full to the brim and overflowing with insecurity, regret and worry as it was.

'This is important. Perhaps you should sit down,' Tor told her tautly. 'I may not be great in the empathy stakes, but I do know that we need to clear the air.'

And he was right, of course, he was, Pixie conceded, sinking down on the foot of the bed and folding hers arms defensively on her lap while watching him like a hawk to try and read his mood. But all she could read was his tension because his beautiful eyes were screened and narrowed in concentration. His uneasiness screamed at her because not since their very first meeting had she seen Tor look less than confident.

'What's wrong?'

'I finally worked some things out and it's changed the way I see everything,' he volunteered almost harshly. 'Try not to interrupt me. I'm not good at talking about this sort of stuff and I don't want to lose the thread of what I need to explain…'

'You're scaring me,' she whispered and then she clamped a guilty hand to her lips because she realised she had said that out loud even though she didn't intend to do so. 'Sorry.'

And for a split second his wide charismatic smile flashed across his serious features and her heart jumped inside her before steadying again, because nothing could be that serious if he could still smile like that. 'There's nothing to be scared of.'

Pixie nodded rather than speak again.

But the silence stretched way beyond her expectations as Tor paced with the controlled but restive aspect of a man who would rather be anywhere than where he was at that moment. His lean, impossibly handsome face went tight. 'I feel ashamed even saying it, but I can see now that Katerina and I didn't love each other the way we thought we did when we married, but that she had the misfortune of finding that out long before I did…'

Pixie was transfixed because whatever she had been expecting, it had not been that admission. She had always believed that Katerina had been his childhood sweetheart, his first deep love, his everything.

'There was no great passion between us. I didn't think that mattered. I assumed that being friends, getting on well, the similarity between our backgrounds and even our parents being so close was more than enough to make a really good marriage.' Tor shifted a pained lean brown hand. 'I was only twenty but considered mature beyond my years because I wanted to settle down and marry young. I thought I knew it all on the basis of very little experience. My parents tried to stop me, but I wouldn't listen to them either. I believed that what I felt for Katerina was love, but I can see now that it was more of a friendship, familiarity, admiration, loyalty, many decent things but not necessarily what a husband and wife need to stay together. I can only assume that it was the same for her and that when she met Devon, she quickly realised the difference.'

'Presumably, Devon wasn't initially prepared to leave his wife for her, or their affair wouldn't have lasted so long,' Pixie murmured uncertainly.

Tor shrugged. 'Who knows? But being able to finally see that different picture has made those events easier for me to accept. I think I felt so guilty about Katerina for so many years because in my brain somewhere, I knew I didn't love her the way she deserved to be loved.'

'But it was mutual, so you can't take on all the blame for that,' Pixie interposed soothingly, worried by his continuing tension. 'It's a very positive thing for you to be able to take a less judgemental view.'

'The guilt made it impossible for me to let go of the past. I felt responsible. I did care for her, but I shouldn't have argued with her that night.'

'No, stop it,' Pixie urged anxiously. 'No more blaming, no wishing you could change it all when you can't. Katerina made her choices as well and she chose to lie about everything. She chose not to tell you beforehand that she had fallen for another man or about Sofia. She drove off late at night in an emotional state of mind and that was the fatal decision which caused the accident.'

'I agree with you,' Tor admitted, startling her. 'It would never have happened as it did if she had not lied. I would have let her go, with great misgivings, but I would never have tried to keep her with me when she was unhappy and Sofia's paternity would have settled that. Be warned though...' Dark golden eyes locked to her hard and fast and her mouth ran dry. 'I would lock you up in a tower and lock myself in with you. I wouldn't be reasonable or compassionate or responsible. I would be possessive and enraged and jealous as hell!'

Pixie flushed and tilted her head back to look at him, blond curls tumbling back from her cheeks. 'And why would I get the tough treatment? Not that I'm thinking of straying,' she hastened to add.

Tor laughed half under his breath. 'The reason I finally understood that I didn't love Katerina was because I know what love feels like now. I've never been in love before, but it knocked me for six. For weeks since you came back into my life, I've been acting oddly because I didn't understand how I felt about you. So, while I was telling you that I couldn't fall in love again, I was actually falling in love for the first time, with you.' He grimaced. 'No prizes for my failure to recognise that happening. I'm not the introspective type. I don't analyse feelings, I just react, which is why I've been all over the place...emotionally speaking,' he completed with a harsh edge of discomfiture in his voice.

Pixie blinked, so shocked she wasn't quite sure what

to say. He was telling her he loved her, a little voice screamed inside her head.

'I thought telling you would fix things!' Tor bit out in frustration. 'You love me… I love you. Isn't that enough?'

Pixie glided up out of paralysis like a woman in a dream because she was still telling herself off inside her head. He might not have known what he was feeling but she felt that she should have recognised in his desire to constantly be with her, to constantly touch her and connect, that he was feeling far more for her than a man merely striving to be an attentive partner. 'I've been blind,' she whispered. 'I was so envious of what I believed you must've felt for Katerina. It made me irrational. And yet I loved you anyway. I was always just wanting more.'

'Nothing wrong with wanting more.' Tor closed strong arms round her, dragging her close with the fierceness of his hold. 'But at the end of the day I just want you any damned way I can have you and it's much more powerful than anything I ever felt in my life before. I can't stand seeing you hurt or upset or unhappy,' he confided, crushing her soft parted lips under his with a revealing hunger that shot through her like a re-energising drug.

Clothes were discarded in a heap. His mouth still hungrily ravishing hers, he tugged her down onto the bed and drove into her hard and fast. The wild excitement engulfed her but there was a softer, more satisfying edge to it now because she knew he loved her. She felt safe, secure, happy, no longer sentenced to crave what she had believed she couldn't have because that had decimated her pride. Completion came in a climax of physical pleasure that shot through her in an electrifying high-voltage charge.

Afterwards, Tor cradled her close. 'I'll never forgive myself for not remembering you that day in my office.'

'No negative thoughts,' Pixie urged, fingers tracing his wide sensual mouth in reproach. 'We can't change the way we started out.'

'I think the absence of the green hair didn't help,' Tor teased. 'And I was more fixated by the fact that you were very pregnant, so I didn't look at you as closely as I should have done. But what I do understand is that we were incredibly lucky to find each other that first night because, for me, you are that one-in-a-million woman, who sets me on fire with a look. I love you so much...'

One in a million? That made Pixie feel good and she smiled up into the dark golden eyes welded to her with such fierce appreciation. 'Why didn't you respond when I told you I loved you?'

Tor laughed. 'Because I was a very late arrival to the party. I only realised last night. You talked of being in Katerina's shadow when you had never been and I sat up thinking about all of it, the past and the present. That's when what was really happening became clear to me. I understood how I truly felt after Katerina's death and why I hadn't got over that guilt. I also understood what I was feeling for you.'

'I probably would like another baby in a year or two,' Pixie told him, gently shooing away Coco, who was trying to climb into bed with them. 'Sorry I snapped over that idea. It's been a very emotional twenty-four hours.'

'But worth it,' Tor countered with a scorching smile,

and he was bending his tousled dark head to toy with her lips again when a faint sound alerted Pixie and made her pull away from him.

'Alfie's awake.' Pixie slid off the bed and began to dress in haste. 'Isla's on holiday…remember?' she prompted.

'So, we get to be real parents,' Tor teased, rolling off the bed, naked and bronzed.

'Yes, Tor,' Pixie said with eyes filled with amusement. 'And the first lesson in being real parents is, you have to put on clothes.'

'Did I tell you how much I love you?' Tor asked, hitching an ebony brow.

'It was practically love at first sight for me.' Pixie held up a finger in unashamed one-upmanship. 'I win hands down.'

'I'm not so sure. I was a pushover for you and I'm not a pushover,' Tor declared. 'But maybe it was the green hair…'

'Well, we're never going to know for sure because I'm not going green again,' Pixie assured him with a chuckle, bending forward to kiss him as he pulled up his jeans and dallying there, Alfie having quieted again, her keen hearing assured her.

'And I'm never ever going to be without you again, *agapi mou*,' Tor husked, gathering her to him with all the possessiveness of a male determined never to let her go.

EPILOGUE

OVER TWO YEARS LATER, Pixie was presiding over a busy Christmas gathering at the mansion she and Tor had moved to overlooking the Thames. Surrounded by acres of gardens and possessed of numerous bedrooms, it was the perfect home for a family who enjoyed entertaining. Tor's relatives were frequent visitors.

Although that had not been her original intention, Pixie had never returned to work. At first, she had revelled in the luxury of being able to be with her son whenever she liked. But as she had begun to adapt to her new life, she had also become much busier. Having taken an interest in the charities that Tor supported, she had become actively involved with one in a medical field. She had soon realised that she could do a lot of good helping to raise funds and that fired up greater interest in such roles.

Moving from the town house into a much larger property had consumed a lot of her time as well, although she had thoroughly enjoyed the opportunity to decorate and furnish her first new home. That her first new home should be a virtual mansion still staggered her.

And now she was pregnant again, six months along and glowing with an energy she had not benefited from the first time around. Of course, she acknowledged, everything was different now for her. She was incredibly happy and secure and supported every step of the way. Tor's love had changed her, lending her new confidence and boosting her self-esteem. Discovering that she was carrying non-identical twins had been a bit of a shock at first, but a shock she and Tor had greeted with pleasure because they got so much joy out of Alfie, who was now a lively little boy of three.

Now she watched as Alfie dragged his grandfather, Hallas, outside to show the older man his ride-on car where it was parked on the terrace. Tor's father grinned as he visibly tried to explain in dumbshow to the little boy that he was far too big to get into the vehicle and take the wheel. Looking long-suffering with an expression that was pure Tor, Alfie climbed in instead to demonstrate his toy. Pixie smiled, feeling very fortunate that Tor's parents were so loving.

Tor had finally stopped being secretive about his first marriage and, although his revelations had roused shock and consternation, Pixie was inclined to believe that everyone was much more relaxed now that the truth was out and they were able to understand how Tor had felt for the five years that he had endured being treated like a heartbroken widower. Of course, he *had* been heartbroken in many ways, just not in the way that people had naturally assumed. She was particularly fond of her husband's half-brother, Sev, whom she had only got to know after Tor had cleared the air with him.

Just then she was wondering if Sev would manage to

spend Christmas with them. Or if he was off somewhere else with some gorgeous beauty on a beach, drinking champagne and carousing, for Tor's Italian half-brother Sev was an unashamed womaniser, chary of any form of commitment and deeply cynical. Even so, he and Tor had eventually grown closer, in spite of the fact that at the start that development had looked unlikely.

A huge Christmas tree embellished the front entrance hall while a log fire crackled in the grate. Richly coloured baubles twirled at the end of branches decorated with glittering beaded strings, multicoloured reflections dancing off the marble hearth. It looked beautiful and so it should, Pixie conceded, because she had spent so much time seeking out special ornaments since her very first precious Christmas with Tor and Alfie. And every year she would bring them out and hang them, enjoying the memories that particular decorations evoked. Here and there on the branches hung the less opulent ornaments she had inherited from her late parents, enabling the tree to remind her of her happy childhood as well.

Her attention roamed to her brother, Jordan, where he was kneeling on the floor beside a little girl of about five. Tula was his girlfriend Suzy's daughter. It was a fairly new relationship, but Pixie was crossing her fingers and praying that it would work out for Jordan—because although he had rebuilt his life, she knew he needed someone to do it for and to ground him, and hopefully Suzy was that woman.

Jordan had suffered a long hard road in rehabilitation. There had been relapses and episodes of depression and various other obstacles for him to overcome, but in the end he had succeeded. He had found somewhere to live at his own expense and, a year ago, he had found work in a charitable organisation where he had no access to money. He had met Suzy through his job soon afterwards. Tor was very slowly warming up towards her sibling and generally becoming, under Pixie's influence, a little more compassionate with regard to other people's failings.

Tor came through the door with Alfie clinging to him like a limpet while his father chatted to him, but Tor's stunning bronzed eyes sought out and instantly settled on his wife. There was a welter of talk and greetings as his entire family converged on him, for they had only arrived earlier that day and he had been at the office.

'My son adores you,' her mother-in-law, Pandora, pronounced with satisfaction at Pixie's elbow. 'You are the woman I always wanted for him and every woman deserves to be adored.'

'I adore him back,' Pixie whispered chokily.

'And another two grandchildren on the way together,' Pandora teased, fanning her face to lighten the atmosphere. 'What more can I say?'

'Three's enough!' Pixie laughed.

'We will see…'

Tor finally made it to Pixie's side. 'I need a shower and to change,' he groaned, raking his fingers up over his unshaven jaw with the attitude of a man suggesting that he resembled a down-and-out.

'Off you go,' his mother urged, her smile emerging as her son ensnared his wife's hand and tugged her upstairs with him.

'A shower?' Pixie lifted a dubious brow.

'Afterwards,' Tor suggested meaningfully, guiding her straight into their bedroom and peeling off his jacket in almost the same motion.

A pulse stirred between her thighs and turned into an ache as she saw his arousal through the fine expensive cloth of his trousers. It was a hunger that never quite dimmed, never ever got fully satisfied, she acknowledged, studying him from the crown of his cropped black hair to his shimmering dark golden eyes to the electrifyingly sexy dark shadow of stubble on his jawline. And something gave within her and she just stepped forward and flung herself at him with all the exuberant passion that he revelled in.

'*Thee mou*... You are beautiful, *agapi mou*,' Tor husked raggedly, struggling for breath as he emerged from that kiss.

Not half as beautiful as he was, she thought, but she had long since learned not to embarrass him with such words of appreciation. 'This is going to be a wonderful Christmas,' she told him happily. 'I feel so lucky. We've got everybody who matters to us here to celebrate with us.'

'I really only need you,' Tor told her truthfully. 'And Alfie...and our twins,' he extended as he turned her round and splayed large possessive hands over the swell of her stomach. 'I never realised I could love anyone the way I love you.'

'It was the green hair,' she teased.

'No, it was the first dynamite kiss. I'm a very physical guy,' Tor breathed hungrily, divesting her of her dress. 'Do you think we're having boys or girls this time? I think boys because they seem to run in my family.'

'I think girls.'

They were both right. Three months later, Pixie gave birth to a boy and a girl, whom they christened Romanos and Zoe.

* * * * *

THE
BILLIONAIRE'S
CINDERELLA
CONTRACT

MICHELLE SMART

This book is dedicated to Simon the Window Cleaner.
Thanks for the inspiration!

CHAPTER ONE

Mᴵᴬ Cᴬʟᴰᴡᴱʟʟ ɢᴬᴢᴱᴰ at the nondescript central London building before her then double-checked the address she'd been given. She'd never heard of Club Giroud, but this ordinary, black, slightly shabby front door did not look like the entrance of any club she'd been to before. The address matched, and the app on her phone indicated she was in the right place.

She put her finger to the doorbell, tightened her hold on her handbag and waited, trying hard not to bounce on her toes.

At the end of last night's performance she'd been in her tiny shared dressing room barely minutes when her normally useless agent had called. She hadn't spoken to Phil in over a month, so the call had been as unexpected as his news that she'd been invited to audition for the director of a new theatre company intending to tour a show in the south of the country.

The only catch was that the audition was being held first thing the next morning in a private club rather than in a theatre. Oh, and Phil had forgotten to get the name of the theatre company. And the name of the show. Or to ask how much the pay would be.

She really needed to think about getting a new agent.

As she was on the last leg of her current tour and had

nothing else lined up there was no way she was turning the audition down. Whatever the pay was, it couldn't be less than she was currently earning. If she was lucky, and they intended to play bigger theatres, she might earn a little more, hopefully enough to save a little cash. The boiler in her flat kept making ominous noises whenever she turned the hot water on, there was damp coming through the walls, plus there was no way her car would pass its next MOT. Right now, she didn't have the money to pay for any of these things.

The door opened. A huge man mountain with shoulder-length greasy hair dressed in a too-short and too-tight black suit stood in the threshold and stared at her with no expression whatsoever.

'Is this Club Giroud?' Mia asked when the man mountain made no effort to speak.

'And you are?'

'Mia Caldwell.'

'ID?'

That was something else, apart from the venue, that she'd found curious about this audition. The request for her to bring identification.

The man mountain examined her driving licence closely, gave a grunt, passed it back and then stepped aside to admit her with a curt, 'Follow me.'

She hesitated before stepping into a lobby as dingy and nondescript as the building's exterior, and followed Mr Man Mountain to a door at the far end. When that door opened…

Her eyes widened and for a moment she stood still, taking it all in. If there was a polar opposite of the dingy, nondescript lobby this was it, but she barely had time to soak in the richly decorated Gothic reception room when Mr Man Mountain grunted at her to continue and she was led through another door into a wide Gothic-inspired corridor. Up a flight of hardwood stairs, they came to another corridor. Some of the doors they passed were open. Mia caught a glimpse of a casino then a little further on a tantalising peep of a bar with a grand piano. Mr Man Mountain finally came to a stop, pushed a door open and indicated for her to enter.

She fixed the sunny smile to her face that now came as naturally to her as breathing and crossed the threshold.

This room was a fraction of the size of the others she'd passed and contained only two dark leather sofas separated by a small table. A man sat reading through a paper file. Their eyes met as the door closed behind her.

Prickles laced her spine at the unabashed scrutiny she found in his stare but, before the prickles could be defined, he rose from his seat and strode to her.

'Miss Caldwell?' he clarified, extending his hand. 'Damián Delgado. It's a pleasure to meet you.'

She held her hand out and found it gripped by the firmest handshake she'd ever been on the receiving end of.

'Likewise,' she murmured. Mia rarely found herself flustered but there was something about this man that set all her nerve endings pinging.

He was gorgeous. As tall as Mr Man Mountain but half the width, he had a muscular physique wrapped in a crisp white shirt, navy trousers and a silver striped tie but it was his eyes that really captured her attention. It was like staring into melted obsidian. Thick black hair styled in a classic crew cut framed a chiselled face with a broad yet defined nose and a generous mouth, all of which was enhanced by a trim black goatee beard.

And he smelled amazing.

'Can I get you refreshment?'

As her throat had suddenly gone dry, she asked for a glass of water.

'Still or sparkling?'

'Still.'

He walked to a cabinet. 'Please take a seat.'

Fearing she was in danger of swooning over his voice as well as his looks, she sat on the sofa opposite the one he'd been using. But honestly, his voice…it matched his eyes, all dark and rich, and his *accent*! This was a voice she would gladly have read her a bedtime story.

'Let us get straight to business,' he said as he popped the lid of a glass bottle of water. 'What have you been told about why you're here?'

For the beat of a moment Mia wondered what he was talking about. And then she realised she'd been on the verge of drooling over this man and pulled herself together sharply. 'That I'm here to audition for a role…' She looked more closely at him. At the immaculate way he was turned out, right down to shoes so buffed he could use them as mirrors…

Damián Delgado did not look like any theatre director she'd met before. And nor did his name mean anything to her. There was not a performing arts magazine or blog that Mia didn't subscribe to. His name should mean something.

Suspicions suddenly zinging through her, she narrowed her eyes. 'I'm sorry, I don't know the name of the production.'

'That's because there is no production.'

'Sorry?'

He placed her glass of water on the table and folded himself back on the sofa. 'The audition was a cover story.' He inclined towards her, his scrutinising stare unblinking. Unsettling. 'I need an actress to accompany me for a weekend to my family home in Monte Cleure.'

She drank half her water, unable to tear her gaze from his face even while she tried to take in his words. Mia had never been to Monte Cleure, a tiny principality sandwiched between France and Spain. Widely regarded as one of the wealthiest and most glamorous countries on the planet, only the stinking rich could afford to live there.

'If you agree to my proposition, I am prepared to pay you two hundred thousand pounds and cover all your expenses.'

Her mouth dropped open. So stunned was she at the astronomical figure quoted, which was ten times the amount she'd earned over the past year, that it took a few seconds for her brain to process it. 'You want to pay me *two hundred thousand pounds*?'

He gave a sharp nod of his head.

'Wow.' She blew a whistle. 'That's a lot of money...' Fresh suspicions zinged to life. 'What would I be expected to do for it?'

'There are aspects to be discussed after we reach agreement but the main thing I will require is for you to act as if you're in love with me.'

Mia's twenty-four years on this earth had left her no stranger to shocks but this was in a different league and so unexpected that it was difficult to compute what this man, this stranger, was asking of her. She drained the rest of her water while trying to clear the clutter in her brain. If not for the seriousness of his expression she would be searching the room for hidden cameras. This had to be a wind-up. 'Sorry if I seem dim, but run that by me again. You want to pay me to pretend to be your girlfriend for a weekend with your family?'

'*Si*. But in my world we say partner or lover. Never girlfriend.'

That jolted her further. 'Lover...?' The minor stupor that had numbed her brain cells vanished. 'Would I be expected to share a room with you while we're there?'

His gaze was unflinching. 'And a bed. My family must believe we are serious about each other.'

Disgust curdled swiftly in her stomach and she rose to her feet. 'I think you've mistaken me for someone else. I'm an actress, not an escort.'

'I know exactly who you are, Miss Caldwell.' The way his mouth curved at this sent a frisson of ice racing up her spine. 'It is an actress I need. I will require affection and devotion only when in the presence of others. Behind closed doors things will be strictly platonic.'

She hugged her bag tightly to her stomach and inched her way backwards. 'I'm not sharing a bed with a stranger who's twice my size and taking his word that things will be platonic. No way. I'm not for sale. Find someone else.'

He shrugged sardonically and steepled long, tapered fingers. 'I don't want someone else, Miss Caldwell. I want you. Do you know who I am?'

Having backed herself to the door, she wrapped her fingers around the handle and gave a brittle smile. 'Nope. And I don't care. Goodbye, Mr Delgado.'

'Before you throw away the opportunity of a lifetime, search it. Search my name. You will find that accepting my proposition will be more than a financial advantage to you. It will give your career the turbo boost it needs too.'

A sudden vision of this man being a wealthy backer of theatre productions made Mia loosen her hold on the door handle. Who *was* this man?

Damián saw the curiosity and indecision cloud her beautiful features. 'Search my name,' he repeated. He'd not gone to all this trouble finding the perfect candidate only for her to dismiss it out of hand. Time was running out. In less than three weeks, the family business he'd spent his adult life working for and which should already be under his control would be taken from him and his reputation destroyed. The business itself would likely be destroyed too. If he had any chance of stopping this happening, he needed Mia's agreement and he needed it today. He'd been certain the mention of two hundred thousand pounds would be enough to entice her into further discussion.

Mia Caldwell, formerly known as Mia Clarke, had struggled for work since graduating from drama school three years ago. Her main source of income was with a provincial theatre company touring the UK's smaller towns, her dry spells supplemented by working in a coffee shop. To say she was hungry for her big break would be an understatement.

Slowly, she reached into the cheapest and shabbiest handbag he'd ever seen. She pulled out a phone then settled bright blue eyes on him. 'How do you spell your name?'

He recited it then settled back to watch her scroll through the overload of information his name would bring. Her back pressed against the door, she read quickly, eyes flickering from the screen to him, disbelief and amazement blazing from them.

For the role he required, Damián had done his homework. He'd set his lawyer the task of compiling a shortlist of beautiful, hungry London-based actresses—he didn't want to have to worry about language problems—looking for their big break, with one extra requirement added. He'd been presented with the portfolio of four actresses who met the criteria. With her honey-blonde hair and sparkling, intelligent bright blue eyes, Mia Caldwell had captured his attention immediately. There was something about the look of her that would fit in the world he inhabited. To satisfy himself of her acting abilities and to have a believable first encounter, he'd attended a performance of *My Fair Lady* at the tiniest theatre he'd ever been in, fully expecting an evening of boredom. Instead, he'd found himself captivated. Mia had lit up the stage and utterly convinced as a cockney flower girl. She'd been funny, vulnerable, charming and could sing like an angel. Damián had known before the interval that he'd found his own real-life Eliza Doolittle.

He hadn't expected to find her more attractive and captivating in real life. The photographs in her portfolio didn't do her justice. A classical oval face framed beautiful almond-shaped eyes, a straight nose and a wide, generous mouth. Add to that a lithe figure, currently hidden beneath a loose knee-length shirt dress, and she would look at home on a catwalk. If she had a couple of extra inches of height that was. On stage, she'd appeared magnified. Up close, she was far more waif-like.

The intelligence he'd detected in her photographs shone through in person too. There were people in Damián's world blessed with wealth and looks at the expense of brain cells. Mia was blessed with looks and brain cells without the wealth. Exactly as he required. The job he required of her was far more than being an adornment on his arm.

'I have your attention?' he asked after she'd spent a couple of minutes scrolling through the information on him.

When her bright blue eyes met his again there was a dazed sheen in them. She blinked the sheen away and nodded.

Of course he had her attention now that she was aware of his wealth and power. No doubt that clever, if suspicious, brain was already imagining the boost being photographed on his arm would give her career.

'Good. Now sit down and let us finish this discussion.'

Phone clutched in her hand, she obeyed.

Assured he had her full attention, he rested his elbows on his thighs. 'Listen carefully. The weekend after next, Celeste—my mother—is hosting her annual summer party. Hundreds of the world's richest and most important people attend but immediate family visit for the whole weekend.

You and I will arrive there on the Friday and then leave and go our separate ways on the Sunday. We will need to go on a few public dates, and I will require you to be available for the whole of next week. That will give us the time we need to be seen together and get to know each other well enough to make our story believable and for me to fill you in on everything I require.'

'What else *do* you require of me other than to act as if I'm madly in love with you?'

'That is something I will divulge when we have made an agreement.'

Her eyes narrowed with fresh suspicion. 'Would the role involve doing anything illegal?'

And now they came to the extra 'something' he required of the actress he'd selected for the role.

'Nothing illegal but your criminal record proves you have the lack of scruples I require.'

Her face drained of colour so quickly it was like someone had pulled a plug on her blood.

'How do you know about that?' she croaked.

'Your criminal record?'

Her head barely moved in a nod.

'I have the means to discover anything.'

Her eyes widened. Her mouth opened then closed but no sound came out.

'Your secret is safe with me, Miss Caldwell,' he assured her. Damián cared nothing for her past, other than what it made her as a person. For this role, he needed someone with a distinct lack of morals.

She gave no response, sat staring at him as if a ghost had suddenly appeared before her.

With a sharp tut, he reiterated all she stood to gain by taking the role. 'Celeste's party is a high society event. The press swarm all over it. Being photographed on my arm is guaranteed to raise your profile. The money I'm prepared to pay you is far more than you would get for selling any story about me but, as I'm sure you'll understand, I've had a non-disclosure agreement prepared along with the contract of terms for your services. My family business depends on secrecy. Our discretion is what sets us apart from other financial institutions. You will be privy to information the press would pay a fortune to hear.'

Still she gave no response. He didn't think she'd blinked once since he'd mentioned her criminal record. Irritated, aware of time pressing, he tapped the table. 'All the cards are on the table, so are you with me or not? I'm afraid I require an immediate answer. If the answer is no then leave and that will be the end of the matter. I haven't revealed any sensitive information to you and I have no wish to ruin you through petty spite.'

It was Damián's last ten words that pulled Mia out of the heated fog she'd fallen into. Everything else he'd said from the moment he'd revealed he knew of her criminal conviction had been white noise in her head. His mouth had moved but the whooshing in her ears had deafened her to the words.

Her belly churned, her brain awhirl, consequences flashing before her eyes.

'I have no wish to ruin you with petty spite...' Dear God, he was *threatening* her.

She wanted to cover her ears and squeeze her eyes shut and then wake up far from this nightmare she'd unwittingly walked into.

Don't panic. Stay calm. Don't panic.

Don't panic? This man couldn't ruin her. The acting world wouldn't care about her past; she would escape professionally unscathed, but emotionally… Any attempt to ruin her could easily destroy the two people she loved most in the world. Ghosts from the past would be resurrected. Everything she'd tried to protect her family from could blow up all over again.

She should have listened to her instincts and walked away when she had the chance but she'd foolishly searched Damián's name and what she'd found had blown her away. The man made Croesus look poor. Curiosity at why a man like Damián Delgado would want to pay her a ton of money to pretend to be his girlfriend had been the reason she'd sat back down to listen. Stupid, foolish curiosity.

She'd listened to him explain how the weekend with his family would unfold, all the while intending to make her excuses and leave when he'd finished.

Mia wasn't an actress for the fame or the money and never had been. This was not the kind of career boost she needed and definitely not the boost she wanted. She didn't want the spotlight. The consequences were just too big for her to risk: the main reason she plied her trade in provincial theatres rather than seeking bigger stages. But the theatre was her love. She'd found it when her world had caved in and it had saved her from her grief. On the stage she'd found a new home. Acting was all she knew how to do. All she hoped was to one day make a regular income from it.

The chance to walk away from Damián Delgado had gone and she hadn't even known it. This gorgeous man she'd been in danger of swooning over...

'When do you need an answer?' she asked, desperately trying to buy herself time: time to think, to plan, to escape...

'I need an answer *now*, Miss Caldwell. Our contract and non-disclosure agreement are ready for signing. Sign or leave. Embrace a better future for yourself or continue to sink into nothing.'

His obsidian eyes held hers, his handsome face a tightly controlled mask.

How could anyone be so emotionless while making such threats?

Thirty minutes ago, Damián Delgado's name had meant nothing to her. She'd walked into this building unaware she was about to be propositioned by one of the world's richest and most powerful men. He must have gone to enormous lengths to discover her conviction. She'd still been a minor during the court case, her name forbidden by law from being published.

His eyes dipped to his watch and then back to her again. 'Time is ticking, Miss Caldwell. Give me your answer or...'

'Okay, okay, I'll sign it,' she said in a panicked flurry. If the only way to guarantee his silence was to agree to his proposition then she had to take it. And then pray the spotlight didn't find her and that all the ghosts from her past stayed where they belonged. She didn't want to think of the repercussions if they didn't.

CHAPTER TWO

MIA WAS APPLYING her lipstick when the loud rap on the door informed her Damián had arrived. She squeezed her eyes shut and took a deep breath. The hot panic that had engulfed her earlier had slowly seeped away, leaving only anger, fear and a million questions.

Everything had passed in a whirl. No sooner had she agreed to his terms than the contract and non-disclosure agreement had been shoved in front of her. Then no sooner had she signed them than an envelope stuffed with cash had been thrust at her with the instructions to buy herself an outfit and get ready for their first 'date'. Damián had then bowed his head, excused himself and left Mr Man Mountain to show her out of the building.

If not for the thick wodge of cash in her hand, she could've easily believed she'd dreamt the whole thing. She wished it had been a dream. Instead, she'd sleep-walked into a nightmare.

Swallowing back her bitterness, Mia had done as he'd instructed, stopping at a boutique she'd passed many times but never entered, bought herself the required outfit then hurried home. The rest of her day had been spent researching everything she could about him. If she hadn't needed to get ready for their 'date' she would still be reading. The internet had thousands of articles about the Delgado family. That was if most of the articles could be believed because none of the Delgados had ever done a press interview. Pretty much everything she'd read of a personal nature was gossip, innuendo and speculation.

What was irrefutable was that the Delgados were one of the richest families on earth. The Delgado Group, founded in 1960 by Damián's grandfather, was reputed to be one of the wealthiest private institutions in the world. It was indisputably the most secretive.

As for Damián himself... The only concrete facts she'd found were that he was thirty-six, two years younger than his brother Emiliano, and that he ran Banco Delgado, a division of the Delgado Group and believed to be the second largest private bank in Argentina. She'd found a handful of photos of him through the years with a handful of different women but there was nothing to suggest he'd been in any long-term relationship or had any children. It was rumoured he'd been in overall charge of the Delgado Group too since his father's death nearly six months ago. Eduardo Delgado's funeral had been attended by world leaders. Presidents. Monarchs.

Every word she'd read only added to her fear. Not even the down-payment of half the two hundred thousand pounds hitting her bank account shifted it. If anything, it heightened her fears. There was no backing out now. She had to approach the next few weeks as just another job with her performance being watched by only a select few. She was the actress. Damián was the director. The choreographer. The puppeteer.

But what the heck was she being dragged into? And why? And why her when there were literally thousands of actresses to choose from? Those were only a few of the million questions racing through her head as she walked to the front door. The Delgado family had more power than most of the world leaders who'd paid homage at their patriarch's funeral. Damián had the power to squash her like a bug and crush her family too.

Her belly full of weighted dread, she opened the front door.

Damián stood dressed in a black velvet suit and black shirt, holding the most enormous bunch of roses she'd ever seen in her life.

Their eyes clashed. A tempest of emotions shot through her. Her heart thumped violently, blood pumping hot and rabid. She held onto the door to stop herself from launching at him like a cat with its claws out, a reaction that frightened her as much as everything else that had happened that surreal, nightmarish day. She'd never had such a primitive, ferocious reaction before, had never wanted to hurl herself at someone and scream and pound and scratch at them.

Dark, dark eyes held hers. 'For you, *mi vida*,' he murmured before brushing his lips against her cheek. 'You look stunning.'

Her senses were immediately assailed by his exotic spicy cologne. Smelling it again hit her as vividly as it had the first time.

'Thank you.' She snatched the roses from him and took a sharp step back. The skin on her cheek tingled manically where his lips had caressed it. 'Let me find a home for these.' A home that didn't involve slapping them around his face first.

She was three paces up the hallway when she realised he'd stayed on the doorstep. 'Aren't you coming in?'

He flashed a smile that could have powered her flat on its own. From their earlier meeting she'd assumed he didn't know how to smile. 'You haven't invited me.'

'I didn't think it was necessary,' she retorted. 'But please, come in. Make yourself at home.'

'Sarcasm?'

'Bravo.'

He raised a black brow. 'Not an auspicious start when we're about to embark on the date in which we fall in love.'

That explained the full-wattage smile. Damián had clearly decided to go the method acting route.

'You told me I have to play devoted lover in public,' she said coldly, desperate to hide the heat flowing through her veins his presence had ignited. 'We're not in public.'

Did he think she was going to be polite and nice to him when he was blackmailing her with the one thing she couldn't bear people to know? He might be the sexiest man she'd ever encountered but he was also the cruellest and the most arrogant. If she had only herself to think of she would tell him to get stuffed but she had her sister and mother to think of. The thought of going through the dark days that had come so close to destroying them again was too terrifying to contemplate. She would gladly throw in the acting towel and work in a coffee shop for ever if it meant protecting her family.

Be careful what you wish for, she thought grimly as she filled pint glasses with water for the roses and tried not to think of Damián turning his haughty nose up at her meagre possessions.

Damián took his surroundings in. He'd never been in a home of such tiny proportions. The entire flat, he estimated, would fit in the reception room of his Buenos Aires home. But it was clean and smelled nice, a scent that made him think of fresh laundry. He took a seat at the tiny table in the living room and admired the furnishings, most of which were threadbare and none of which matched yet somehow fused together to create a tasteful and homely vibe. It was a home put together on a minuscule budget by someone with a keen eye and flair. He admired it.

Mia walked into the living room carrying two glasses filled with roses. 'You don't own a vase?' he asked.

She shook her head and placed one of the glasses above the fake fireplace. The other she placed on the table then disappeared again, only to reappear moments later carrying another pint glass and a huge mug full of roses too.

'Are you done? Our table's booked for eight and traffic's heavy.'

'Give me one minute.' She disappeared again before he could say another word.

When she returned, she'd slipped her feet into a pair of gold heels and sprayed perfume on, for his lungs filled with the most delicious fruity scent that immediately made his mouth water.

He cast a critical eye over her. She wore a white dress with strappy sleeves; it plunged in a V to her midriff without actually displaying any breast, a thin gold belt separating the top half from the skirt, which flared slightly and fell to her calves. With her hair knotted in a loose chignon and lots of tendrils framing her face, artfully applied make-up and simple hooped gold earrings, she looked classy and understated.

'Well?' she snapped, colour high on her cheeks. 'Satisfied with what your money paid for?'

He stared at her meditatively, biting back the burn of anger her belligerence provoked. No one spoke to him in that tone and it was time Mia Caldwell learned that. He'd made it very clear she didn't have to accept his offer: that she could walk away and her criminal record would stay secret. She'd chosen to take the money and career boost of her own free will. To behave as if she'd been put into this position under duress was inexcusable.

'I'm very satisfied, thank you. Looking at you makes me wonder if I'm not underpaying you. Still, I'm sure there will be men at Celeste's party who will happily pay a great deal more for a more *intimate* arrangement. Name your price with them—you can earn yourself a fortune.' Before the dark stain of angry colour on her face could translate on her tongue, he got to his feet. 'Provoke me, Miss Caldwell, and you will learn I *always* bite back. Now wipe that ugly look from your face and let us see if you're as good an actress as I think you are.'

Humiliation flushing through her blood, Mia stormed to the front door, teeth clamped together to stop her mouth firing expletives at him. While she checked she'd put her keys in her new clutch bag, she took some very deep breaths and worked on transforming her features into something soft and loving. The first role she'd ever played had been Juliet in a school production. The boy who'd played Romeo had been a vile braggart with halitosis who'd believed himself to be God's gift to women. She still considered convincing the audience that she'd been madly in love with him to be her finest acting achievement. If she could pull that off she could pull this off. She had to.

When Damián joined her in the hallway, she slowly tilted her head and fluttered her eyelashes at him. 'There you are. For a horrible moment I thought you'd flown back to Argentina.'

His eyes narrowed.

Making sure her voice was soft and verging on simpering, she put her hands to her chest and said, 'I can't tell you how excited I am for our date. It feels like I've spent my life waiting for you and now you're finally here…' She let her voice trail off and gave another flutter of her eyelashes for good measure.

His firm mouth twitched before he inclined his head. 'Much better.'

She smiled dreamily and opened the door. 'Shall we?'

They stepped out into the cool evening air. When Damián put his arm around her waist she made sure not to flinch, kept the same dreamy smile on her face all the way to the waiting car. The driver jumped out to open the back door for them.

Only when they were secure in the car's confines, the driver hurrying to climb back in, did she look at Damián and, with the dreamy smile still firmly in place, say, 'Don't even think of touching me in private.'

His dark eyes held hers before he slowly dipped his face to her ear and whispered, 'I'd rather touch acid. It would have less of a burn.'

When Mia got out of the car and saw the name of the restaurant Damián had brought her to for their 'date' she choked back a gasp. Never in a million years had she dreamed she would dine here, in a restaurant widely regarded to be one of the finest in the world.

'Am I allowed to be star-struck?' she murmured when he reached her side.

'No.' Then, slipping his arm around her waist, he swept her inside, where the maître d' greeted him like a long-lost Messiah.

Affecting nonchalance at the glorious interior, she clamped her vocal cords shut so as not to squeal when the first person she spotted was an A-list Hollywood actress and her director husband. Even though Mia kept her gaze fixed on the maître d's back as they were led to their table, she couldn't fail to notice all the heads turning as they walked past and the sudden flurry of impeccably dressed women smoothing their hair and dabbing under their eyes to catch wayward mascara.

Strangely, although the place was full, there was none of the noise she associated with busy restaurants. The background music was pitched at just the right level and the owner must have done some tricks with the acoustics because she couldn't hear a word of any surrounding conversations, only a low-level buzz.

To play it safe, she waited until they were alone before leaning forward to say in a low voice, 'Can we speak freely here?'

Damián, who was reading his menu, raised his gaze to hers. 'Yes.'

'In that case, tell me what it is, exactly, that you're forcing me into.'

To her immense frustration, the waitress came to their table to take their order. Having not eaten anything since the slice of toast she'd had for breakfast—after her awful meeting with Damián, food had been the last thing on her mind—Mia realised she was starving. And, for the first time since she'd left home for drama school almost six years ago, she didn't have to worry about the cost. She could choose anything she liked.

If Damián could blackmail her she might as well take advantage of the perks. This might be her only chance to eat in a three Michelin star restaurant, and she quickly selected the lobster and langoustine ravioli starter and the roasted monkfish for her main course. Considering the only seafood she'd eaten these past six years had been tins of tuna, these felt like decadent choices and she was happy to take the waitress's advice on the best wine to pair with them.

'Well?' she said when their wine had been poured for them and they'd been left alone.

He leaned forward and covered her hand. Unprepared for the gesture, unprepared for the sudden clatter of her heart at his touch, she only just stopped herself from tugging it away.

As if sensing her internal war, he murmured, 'Remember to keep your features soft and loving. People can't hear what we're saying but have no doubt we're being watched.'

She forced the dreamy smile back on her face. 'Better?'

He flashed another mesmerising high-voltage smile and nodded.

'Then please get on with it before the suspense kills me.'

Speaking as casually as if they were discussing the weather, he said, 'There are documents hidden in Celeste's villa—important documents—that I need to find as a matter of urgency. Your job is to help me find them.'

'Celeste? As in your mother?'

He nodded.

She studied him closely. There was no way it was as simple as he'd just made out, not with all the subterfuge and money he was spending. 'What kind of documents?'

'You don't need to know that.'

'Why not?'

'It isn't relevant. All you need to know is that the documents are hidden somewhere in Celeste's villa.'

'She's hidden them?'

'No. And I am not going to tell you anything more about them. It is not relevant to your job. What *is* relevant is that the villa is like a fortress and designed for concealing secrets. It was designed to Celeste's specifications when she married my father, and I have all the necessary blueprints and video tours of the interior for you to study. I will need you to become as familiar with the villa's layout as you are with your own home before we go there.'

'Why?'

'The weekend we're there, the villa will be packed with staff. It takes a team of hundreds to organise the party and this will work in my favour as it means I can search for the documents. With bodies everywhere, it will be hard to keep track of us but I don't like leaving things to chance. I need you to be my eyes and ears while I'm searching.'

Their conversation stopped as their starters were brought to the table, giving Mia the excuse she needed to remove her hand from under his. She resisted the strong urge to shake it and rid herself of the warm impression his fingers left on her skin.

After a few bites and a sip of wine, she said, 'If the documents are in your mother's home and she's not the person who's hidden them, why don't you just go over to the villa and look for them instead of all this deception?'

'That is not possible.'

'Why not? Just pop over one afternoon on your private jet. It's not hard.'

Something that sounded remarkably similar to laughter escaped his mouth. Similar to laughter but too cutting to be real.

'What's so funny?'

'You'll understand when you meet Celeste. Trust me, she's not someone you drop in on.'

'I drop in on my mum all the time.'

'Celeste is not like a normal mother. Our appointments are made by her staff.'

It took a beat for her to understand what he meant. 'You have to make an appointment to see your own mother?'

He inclined his head as if this were perfectly normal.

Trying very hard not to let her mouth drop open, she murmured, 'This sounds like something out of a soap opera.'

Damián's fingers tightened around his fork but he tilted his head in the manner of a man whispering sweet nothings to his lover. 'I assure you, this is no soap opera. This is my life and unless I find those documents my life as it stands is over and everything I've spent my life working for will be taken from me.'

'How?'

'That isn't relevant.'

'Of course it is. You're dragging me into it. How do I know the documents you're searching for aren't actually proof of something illegal you want to cover up?'

'Criminal acts are your speciality, not mine.'

Her indignation at this was immediate, and it must have shown on her face for he covered her hand again and pressed his fingers into her skin. 'Soft and loving, Mia. Do not forget we are being watched.'

Swallowing her feelings back, she rested her chin on the hand not being held by his and gazed adoringly at him. 'You say criminal acts are not your speciality and yet the only reason I'm here is because you've blackmailed me.'

Damián stilled and narrowed his eyes at this heinous slur. 'I haven't blackmailed you.'

Anger flared from the bright blue eyes gazing into his but her voice kept its sweet modulation. 'Yes, you have.'

'No, *mi vida*, I have not.'

'You said that if I walked away you didn't want to ruin me through petty spite. That sounded like a threat.'

'If you interpreted that as a threat then that's on you.'

'"I don't *want* to ruin you." That's what you said. That implies you *would* ruin me but the fault would be mine for walking away.'

Damián found himself fighting his own swell of anger. As someone used to his word being taken as gospel, Mia's cynicism was infuriating, her assertion that he was blackmailing her doubly so.

'Again, your interpretation of my words is on you,' he said tightly. 'If I'd wanted to blackmail you I wouldn't have bothered with the financial inducement.'

Her gaze continued to hold his speculatively while she chewed her food. There was something about the fire that smouldered behind the speculation that made his blood thicken and stirred his nerve-endings, and he took a large drink of his wine to quell it.

She swallowed, dabbed her lips with her napkin and then bestowed him with a smile that could melt an iceberg as quickly as the fire in her eyes. 'Then why choose an actress with a sealed criminal record? You must have gone to a heck of a lot of trouble and expense to unearth mine.'

Dios, the evening was not playing out at all as he'd imagined. Mia was playing ball with the role he'd given her but, instead of listening dutifully to the information he relayed, she was arguing the toss on everything.

Trying hard to speak through a jaw intent on clenching at her stubborn disbelief, he forced his mouth to curve into a smile to match hers. 'Because, *mi vida*, as I explained earlier, I need an actress without scruples. There is a good chance our search for the documents will involve looking through personal, private spaces. A convicted self-confessed drug dealer does not have scruples...' He enjoyed the flash of anger this reminder of her criminality clearly provoked. 'But that was only one of my requirements. I need someone who can fit into my world without anyone looking twice. Look at you now—one new outfit and already you look the part. But you have intelligence too, although I think you need to keep a lid on the overactive part of your imagination. The job requires someone with a sharp brain. There are times, I'm sure, when you will need to think on your feet. On top of that, I needed an actress who was unknown but talented. You were one of only a handful who fit all the criteria.'

She laughed. Anyone listening would believe it genuine. Only Damián heard the bite behind it. 'The unknown part is obviously accurate but what makes you think I'm talented?'

'I watched your performance last night.'

Her mouth dropped open. After all their verbal jousting, it was hugely entertaining to see her suddenly lost for words.

It took a few attempts for her to croak, 'You were there?'

'I needed to see with my own eyes whether you were good enough to pull this off.' He covered her hand again. Adopting a caressing tone, he said, 'Seeing you on that stage was the moment I fell in love with you, *mi vida*.'

Mia shook her head in disbelief. '*You* should be on the stage.'

Damián smiled. 'Believe me, the weekend at my mother's is too important for either of us to give anything less than a convincing performance.'

CHAPTER THREE

As soon as they were in the back of Damián's car Mia pressed herself against the door to keep maximum physical distance from him. After three hours of locked eyes and hand-holding it was disconcerting to find her eyes wanted to stare some more and her fingers felt all tingly...*everything* felt tingly.

Resting her cheek against the window to cool her overheated skin, she rubbed her lips with her thumb and tried hard to tune him out. Her brain was too overloaded to cope with anything else that day.

Strangely enough, the thing playing on her mind the most out of everything was Damián's indifference towards his family. It was an indifference she guessed was reciprocated. Who called their mother by their first name? How utterly alien was *that*? And what kind of mother only saw her children if they made an appointment through her staff? That wasn't just alien. That was… She couldn't think of the word to describe how mind-blowing she found it, but figured it explained a lot about his icy persona.

Mia spoke to her mum every day. They met up at least once a week. She didn't see her sister as much but that was only because Amy worked shifts and Mia tended to work evenings, their days off rarely coinciding. They still spoke lots and messaged all the time and got together whenever they could.

It hadn't always been like that. Their father's sudden death almost a decade ago had had the effect of a grenade being thrown at them. That grenade had detonated and caused what Mia had once feared was irreparable damage. Slowly though, the damage had repaired. There would always be scars but Mia, Amy and their mum were now as whole and as tight a family unit as they could be. She had to pray there would be no fallout from this job she'd been given...

She straightened. In a flash, it came to her how she could get out of this.

'Damián...' Speaking his name aloud for the first time was as strange an experience as everything else she'd been through that day. It seemed to just roll off her tongue, which immediately longed to have it roll off again. She shook the strange notion away and focused. 'You said you'd short-listed other actresses for this job.'

'And?'

'Let one of them do it. I only agreed because I thought you were blackmailing me, but as you're not then—'

'It's too late,' he interrupted tonelessly.

'I won't say anything,' she pleaded. She would beg if she had to. 'Please? I'll give you the money back and sign anything you want.'

'I said it's too late.' His face turned to hers. The darkness in his eyes glittered. 'We've been seen together.'

'But we've only had one date.'

'Believe me, *mi vida*, I would gladly swap you for another actress but it's too late. The wheels of our love affair have been set in motion.'

'After one date?' she asked in disbelief.

'I'm being watched and my communications monitored.'

'By who?'

'My brother.'

She stared at him in utter shock. Her head was ready to explode with all that had happened that day and this little nugget of information could have ignited it.

His jaw clenched, anger etched deep into his features. She had the feeling the anger was directed at himself. He hadn't meant to reveal that. It had been a slip of the tongue, and for the first time she felt a pang of sympathy for him.

'*Emiliano* is the one behind all this?'

His answer was silence, broken only when the car came to a stop outside her door.

'Tomorrow we will eat in my apartment,' Damián said curtly. 'My driver will collect you at seven.'

Her sympathy vanished at his arrogant assumption. 'I'm performing tomorrow night.'

'I fly back to Buenos Aires on Wednesday. It has to be tomorrow.'

'I'm working.'

'Get your understudy to fill in for you.'

'Why don't you get *your* understudy to fill in for you in Buenos Aires?' she retorted pointedly.

'I do not have an understudy,' he informed her through what sounded like gritted teeth.

'Guess what? I don't have an understudy either. I've got eight shows left and then on Sunday the tour's over.' And she still didn't have another job lined up. 'I'm not pulling out of any of them, so don't even think of asking me to— or, in your case, ordering me to. I've agreed to be available for you next week so don't push me any further.'

His eyes narrowed to tiny points. She could almost feel the lasers of affronted dislike shooting from them.

'I will collect you after your performance,' he said, his voice now clipped. 'Pack an overnight bag.'

'I'm not staying the night.'

'Then cancel your performance and spend the evening with me.'

'No.'

A sudden breeze kissed her cheeks as the driver opened the door for her. Before she could get out, long warm fingers closed around her wrist and Damián's face was inches from hers, close enough that she could see the individual hairs of his trim black goatee and the beginnings of stubble breaking out across his jawline. Close enough too for the exotic cologne he wore to dive into her airwaves and send her pulses surging.

A smile played on his lips as his eyes swirled menacingly. 'You *will* spend tomorrow night in my apartment, *mi vida*,' he said in a low voice. 'And you will spend next week in it too, as per the contract you signed. I'm paying you a fat fee to do a job and I expect you to fulfil it, and fulfil it to the best of your abilities. Is that understood?'

Swallowing back the moisture in her mouth, dimly aware of his driver waiting for her to get out and likely paying attention, Mia smiled back and brought her mouth to Damián's ear to whisper, 'Let go of me right now or I will scream.'

She didn't mean to touch him but the tip of her nose brushed against his earlobe and, frightened of the jolt that crashed through her, she quickly reared back.

Eyes clashing, his nostrils flared. Barely a second passed in that look before he loosened his hold and dipped his head to place his mouth against *her* ear, and it was enough for her stomach to flip over and for a fuzziness to envelop her brain.

'The only screams a man wants from a woman's mouth are the screams of pleasure,' he whispered cuttingly. 'The only thing a man will want to do with *your* mouth, though, is zip it up.'

With the warmth of his breath lingering against her skin, it took another beat before she realised Damián had let go of her wrist and settled back on the seat. While she tried to open her contracted throat and get her lungs to function properly, he was staring at her with the look of a man who knew he'd dealt a zinger of a finale.

A thick black brow rose as he bestowed her with a sardonic smile. 'Goodnight, *mi vida*. I will dream of you.'

Their eyes clashed again, fire and ice raging between them. And something else. A pulse. A charge she'd never felt before but which she instinctively knew spelled danger.

'Don't have nightmares,' she said in the sweetest voice she could muster before jumping out of the car, thanking the driver and doing her best not to run to the sanctuary of her flat.

Damián's smile vanished as he watched Mia disappear into the rundown building she called home. He rapped on the partition to let his driver know they could go, then rested back on the seat and closed his eyes. The beats of his heart thudded with such strength he felt the echoes through his heated skin.

He could count on one hand the number of serious mistakes he'd made in his life. Convincing his father to give the untested Emiliano a senior role in the business had always been the top one, a mistake that had cost Damián and his father half a billion dollars of their private wealth. The weight in his stomach told him Mia Caldwell could easily topple that.

He'd not even known her a day but he'd never met anyone outside his immediate family who pushed his buttons as easily as she did. For the sum he was paying her he'd assumed she would be deferential to him. In Damián's world, people moulded themselves to fit his expectations.

While Mia had played her part in the restaurant beautifully, she clearly had no intention of moulding herself to fit his expectations when they were alone. She *wanted* him to know the contempt she held him in. She'd gazed at him throughout their meal with the soft, dewy expression he'd demanded but her eyes had told their own story. She'd made no effort to hide her loathing. Like the character he'd watched her play the evening before, she had a wilfulness about her.

This alone would not be an issue, not so long as she played the role he was paying her for when he needed her to.

The biggest problem, he was forced to admit grimly, was his undeniable attraction to her. This was not something he had factored in when desperation had forced him to go down the route of paying an actress to help him. And what the hell had compelled his tongue to reveal that it was his brother he was up against? His answer to her question had come from nowhere.

It had been indoctrinated in Damián from birth that emotions were for the bedroom not the boardroom. Never mix business with pleasure on a sensual level. And all for very good reasons, namely that the man who allowed his head to be turned took his eyes off the ball. That, he'd always been certain, had been the reason behind Emiliano's disastrous time working for the business. Rumours had flown throughout the Delgado Group that he'd been having an affair with one of the staff. Damián had never found proof of this but, considering Emiliano's lust for life and lust for beautiful women, had believed it. True or not, something had turned Emiliano's head far enough away from the job in hand that his eyes had lost sight of the ball altogether.

In all his thirty-six years Damián had never had a problem separating the boardroom from the bedroom. Like his father, he'd never taken his eyes off the ball. Yet now, at the time he most needed to keep his famed focus, when his entire fortune and place in the world were at stake, he kept finding himself staring at the woman he was relying on and forcing himself not to strip her naked with his eyes. Every word exchanged between them came with a charge that raced through his veins and an uncomfortable heat that stirred his loins.

Even now, when the space she'd sat in in the back of the car had been empty for twenty minutes, he could still feel the charge rippling through him.

How he wished he could have agreed Mia's request to terminate their agreement. He didn't know if her request had been some kind of game to force more money out of him; he'd put her straight before she could ask. Terminating the agreement was out of the question. It really was too late to turn back. The wheels really had been set in motion. They'd been seen together. The world was vast but rumour could shrink it to the size of a snowball. If they weren't already aware, whispers would soon reach his family that he'd taken a new lover. Having always been fussy about the women he chose to bed, suspicions would be raised if he dumped Mia and immediately hooked up with another actress.

For all the dangers he could see himself having to navigate in the coming weeks, he was stuck with her.

The theatre audience the next night was a particularly enthusiastic one who laughed uproariously and applauded with gusto. This was the kind of audience Mia, like all stage performers, adored. It made the curtain call at the end of a performance a joy and made her cheeks hurt from smiling so widely and for so long. That night, though, she needed all her acting skills to fake her smiles during the curtain call. Right at the end of the song 'I Could Have Danced

All Night' she suddenly spotted the hulking figure sitting on the far right of the third row. Her heart clattered and the nightgown she'd been twirling around the stage dropped out of her hands. How she recovered without any of the audience noticing anything amiss she had no idea.

As she bowed, she made sure to keep her gaze far from the right, just as she'd done for the rest of the performance. But, just as had happened throughout the evening, Damián's stare burned straight through her. She couldn't get off the stage fast enough.

The chatter amongst the female cast members she shared the dressing room with was a distant buzz in her head and she could only smile and nod at any conversation directed at her, trying hard to control the tremors in her hand as she removed her stage make-up.

A loud rap on the door made her heart clatter all over again. There was not a single doubt in her mind as to who was knocking, and she frantically smoothed the loose stripy top she'd changed into over her skinny black trousers while Nicole, who played Mrs Higgins, opened the door, still continuing her conversation with the others. Her words came to an abrupt halt.

'Well…' Nicole said after letting out a very low yet very obvious whistle. 'What can we do for *you*?'

Mia squeezed her eyes shut as Damián's deep, distinctive voice rang through the sudden silence. 'I am here for Mia.'

Behind her, she heard someone, probably Jo, mutter, 'Lucky Mia.'

Clutching her overnight bag to her chest, Mia fixed a smile to her face and spun around. Damián stood at the threshold, dressed down in a navy polo shirt and black jeans, hair impeccably groomed, dark eyes fixed on her. She knew perfectly well what he expected of her.

'Damián!' she cried, hurrying over to stand before him. 'You made it!'

The smile he gave could have powered the Eiffel Tower but, before she could appreciate its full effect, a wave of his cologne hit her as he hooked a giant arm around her waist, pulled her against him and, before she could blink let alone think, covered her mouth with a kiss that managed to be both fleeting yet hungry.

'I wouldn't have missed it for the world,' he murmured. '*Mi vida*, I couldn't keep my eyes off you on that stage.'

Dumbstruck at the unexpected intimacy and the tingling rush of heat it sent careering through her lips and straight into her bloodstream, Mia could only stare into the dark, dark eyes and pray her legs didn't give way beneath her.

Noting the bright stain of colour flush over Mia's cheeks, Damián conceded that she really was a superlative actress. Aware too of the open-mouthed shock on the other actresses' faces, he released his hold around her waist and took her hand. 'I hope you ladies will not be offended if I take Mia from you now? This is my last night in the UK so we want to make the most of the time we have left together.'

Minutes later, hands still clasped together, they left the building through the stage exit and into his waiting car. The moment his driver shut the door, Mia snatched her hand away and edged as far from him as she could before glaring at him with enough venom to poison the whole suburban town they were in.

'What the hell are you playing at?' she demanded.

'I told you I would collect you after the performance.'

'You said your driver would collect me. You said *nothing* about attending it.'

'Did you find my presence a distraction?'

'Of course not.' She sniffed airily. 'I didn't even notice you in the audience.'

'Of course you didn't, Pinocchio.' He'd seen the night-gown drop from her hands in the moment her eyes had fallen onto him. Everyone had seen it, the only mishap in an otherwise spellbinding performance, but she'd covered it so well that no one would have realised. Only he'd known it for what it was and it had made all his sinews tighten to witness the effect he had on her.

Her glare deepened. 'And what the hell were you playing at, kissing me like that? How dare you? You do not kiss me, not ever.'

He contemplated her coolly. 'We were in public. I made it very clear that I expect you to show me affection in public. It's what I am paying you for.'

'And I made it very clear that I'm not an escort.'

'Do you refuse to kiss on stage if the role calls for it?'

Her pretty full lips clamped together, fury firing from the bright blue eyes.

He held the gaze and shook his head disparagingly. 'I thought not. Get used to the idea of us kissing in public, *mi vida*. When we are with my family you will be glued to my side, if not to my mouth.'

'Lay one finger on me in private and I swear to God…' Her voice trailed away as whatever threat she'd been about to utter vanished into the ether.

'Get over yourself,' he drawled. 'The kiss meant nothing.' If she could only see the tingling on his lips, still there from that one fleeting brush of their mouths, she would know it for the lie it was. Mercifully, his iron control hadn't let him down and he'd stopped the tingles spreading anywhere more intimate. 'As it is, we are stuck together for next few weeks so grow up and get over it.'

Damn it but this was the last thing he needed. He'd watched her perform on stage for the second night in a row and been as captivated as the first time. More so. He'd been unable to tear his eyes from her, unable to stop his mind running riot as he mentally undressed her, unable to stop his heart throbbing in response to her melodious singing.

He could not afford to have his mind distracted. When they were at the villa he needed to keep his wits about him and focus on finding the documents. The last thing he needed was to have his mind occupied with fantasies of Mia Caldwell naked and the cells in his body stirring and straining in anticipation of being alone with her.

The attraction would go nowhere even if he wasn't trying his damnedest to stop his brother stealing everything from him and destroying the Delgado legacy. Forget her criminal record and lack of money, both huge crosses against her for a man of his means and interests; Damián made it a point to only sleep with women he believed he could one day trust and whose interests aligned with his. That had been the basis of his parents' marriage and it had served them well for thirty-seven years.

Only a fool would trust a chameleon who played make-believe for a living.

CHAPTER FOUR

MIA HAD NEVER been to Canary Wharf before. Far removed
from the arty, if rundown, area of London she called home,
Canary Wharf was crammed with skyscrapers that mingled
with converted ironwork buildings, and yachts and boats
moored where the River Thames meandered. There was
zero surprise to learn Damián owned a penthouse apartment in the tallest of the skyscrapers or that the apartment
itself was as far removed from her own home as its location. It was so much like she'd imagined that she couldn't
help her bark of laughter when she stepped in it.

'What's funny?' he asked.

She shrugged and rummaged in her overnight bag for
her phone. 'I was just wondering where all your stuff was.'

Obviously, the apartment was ginormous and had the
requisite exquisite views accessed by floor-to-ceiling windows across every wall overlooking the Thames. All the
furniture was clearly bespoke. Everything was sparkling
clean and white, apart from polished oak flooring. Everything screamed money in flashing neon lights. There just
wasn't very much of it. The living area, which could fit her
entire flat in it, contained the biggest television she'd ever
seen, two white leather sofas and a glass coffee table. Ap-
proximately a mile away on the other side of the vast space
was a glass dining table and eight chairs. And that was it.

'This is a base to sleep when I'm in London,' he answered stiffly as he flipped a laptop open. 'My home is in Buenos Aires.'

She pulled a face and turned her phone on. 'I assumed you owned it.'

'I do own it. Now, excuse me a moment; I need to run a security check.'

'What for?'

'To make sure no one has tried to enter my apartment… What are you doing?'

She held her phone up. 'Say cheese.'

He blinked as the flash went off. 'Did you just take a picture of me?'

'I took a picture of my *lover*…' she stressed the word for effect '…for my sister.' Ignoring Damián's glower, she attached the picture to Amy's email and pressed send. Then she looked back at him and smiled brightly. 'The location on my phone's switched on but, just in case, I've sent her your address, so if my body's dumped in the Thames the police will know where to find you.'

His jaw clenched so tightly she wouldn't have been surprised to see the bones poking out. 'What have you told her?'

'Amy? Only that I've met someone.' She'd told her mother too, and it wasn't just for self-preservation. Mia didn't know if the press would ever publish pictures of her with Damián, but if they did she wanted her family prepared for it. With any luck, the press Damián had told her would be camped outside the villa for the party would be too intent on getting snaps of the glamorous playboy, polo-playing Emiliano to bother with them.

The last thing Mia wanted was for the paparazzi to focus on her. Being seen on Damián's arm might bring the kind of attention usually reserved for celebrated film actresses.

If Damián could dig out her old criminal record, what was to stop the press?

It was too late now. Damián had made that very clear. She was committed: stuck between the devil and the deep blue sea. Her priority was to protect her family and herself, and in that order. Protecting her family came in many guises and not adding undue worry to their shoulders was the biggest part of it. There was no way she could disappear for a weekend to Monte Cleure and not have them worry. She felt awful about lying to them and building their hopes up that she'd finally met someone, but this was a lie of necessity.

'I thought you wanted the world to think we're in love?' Batting her eyelashes, she smiled again and theatrically added, 'Our love will burn like a flame and then it will, sadly, extinguish itself.'

There was zero amusement in his expression. 'The terms of the non-disclosure agreement includes your sister.'

'I know.' Eyeballing him back, she gave him her most withering stare. 'You've made a liar of me.'

Now he was the one to conjure a fake smile before he switched his attention back to his laptop. 'We can add it to your list of attributes.'

Suddenly afraid she might slap the laptop's lid onto his fingers, she spun around and poked her head around a partition wall. Behind it she found the whitest, cleanest kitchen she'd ever seen. Unsurprisingly, it was functional over beautiful. The only gadget on display was a coffee machine that probably cost more than her monthly mortgage. She looked back at Damián. 'If you own this place, why does it look like a decluttered show home?'

'I use it as a convenient base, nothing more. Banco Delgado has offices on the thirty-first and thirty-second floor of the building opposite us.'

She sighed in mock disappointment.

His eyes narrowed. 'Now what?'

'I'd guessed you lived in the same building as your offices. Just as well I never made a bet on it. Where's your staff?' Surely a man of Damián's wealth had live-in staff?

'The building's concierge service includes staff when I need them.'

Great. That meant they were truly alone. 'Do you get them to spy on your front door for you too?'

His jaw clenched. 'I'm paying you to do a job, not make endless speculation.'

'Then maybe you should have chosen an actress with a blunter brain,' she stated sweetly. 'Can I be nosy and look through your kitchen cupboards?'

'If it shuts you up for five minutes, be my guest.'

'Cheers.'

Suspicion now in his eyes, he followed her into the kitchen and put the laptop on a work surface. 'Why do you want to look?'

She opened the nearest cupboard. It was empty. 'I'm curious what a billionaire's cutlery is like.' She opened another cupboard and found that empty too. 'Where's your food?'

'Are you always this nosy?'

'Only on special occasions. I'll be able to tell anyone who asks how a billionaire lives that the answer's soullessly... Unless discussing your decluttered show home apartment is a breach of the NDA?'

His look became meditative. 'Are you always so antagonistic?'

'Not at all.' The next cupboard was also empty. 'Consider yourself special.'

'Why?'

'You have to ask?'

'I'm paying you handsomely to perform a role that is no

different to what you perform on a stage. You are certain to get a career boost from it. I do all this and still you act like I'm El Cuco.'

Aha! A cupboard with a set of plates and bowls. And what a surprise. They were all white. 'El who?'

'El Cuco. He's like your bogeyman.'

'Right… Well, considering you won't let me quit this role even though you know I only took it because I thought you were blackmailing me, can you blame me for thinking of you as an El Cuco figure?'

He raised a brow. 'You expect me to believe you would have turned all that money down?'

'I offered to pay the money back, remember? Whether you believed that was genuine or not is on you. I don't care what you believe. Have you got anything alcoholic to drink?'

'When did you last eat?'

'An hour before the performance.'

'I will order food.'

'Drink first.'

'Not a good idea on an empty stomach.'

'Who made you my mother?'

'Mia…' Damián sucked a large breath in and closed his laptop. From the moment they'd stepped into his apartment there had been a manic energy about her. 'Have you been taking drugs?'

She looked affronted at the question. 'Of course not.'

'You're sure?' There had been no suggestion from the reports he'd had compiled on her that she still used drugs and he'd been prepared to give her the benefit of the doubt on that score because she had the talent and the look he needed and he'd been desperate. For possibly the hundredth time he wondered how great a mistake he'd made in choosing her.

'I don't take drugs.'

'You used to. You cannot deny that.'

A spark similar to the flashes he'd seen whenever he mentioned her criminal record flew from her eyes but her lips clamped together.

Holding onto his temper by a whisker, he scrutinised her more closely. Damián knew what drug addiction looked like. He knew too many people who relieved the pressures that came with a high-octane career in the banking and finance industries with cocaine not to recognise the signs of a user. Mia's eyes were bright and her cheeks flushed with colour but there was no sign of dilated pupils or a runny nose, and nor did she do the obsessive sniffing he associated with drug use.

'You are displaying edgy behaviour.'

She pressed her back against a worktop. 'I'm not edgy, I'm nervous. And can you blame me?'

'Are you afraid of me?'

She stilled as her eyes found his, the animation in her features dulling. Then her head dropped and she said in a low voice, 'I'd be a fool not to be afraid.'

And in that instant her antagonism made perfect sense. Pinching the bridge of his nose, Damián swallowed back rising guilt.

It hadn't occurred to him how threatening being here in his territory must be for her. He was a physically imposing man and still a stranger to her. The short time he'd spent in her flat he'd been aware of external noises, of bodies walking up and down the stairs that led to the other flats in the building, of bodies moving around in the adjoining flats, of people walking past outside. Help had been on hand if she needed it. In comparison here, in his apartment, the silence within the thick walls was stark. Here, there was no sense of the community he'd felt in Mia's building.

Damián would never take advantage of a vulnerable

woman, but how was Mia supposed to know that? He was deeply attracted to her and sensed she had an attraction for him too but, attraction or not, reciprocated or not, he would never force himself on a woman. He'd rather cut his heart out.

'Mia, look at me.'

She raised her stare to his slowly. Reluctantly.

'I gave you my word that when we were alone things between us would be platonic and I meant it. Sex is a complication I don't need. You are safe with me. Okay?'

Something glistened in her eyes but she blinked it away before he could read anything further in it.

'If I haven't already made it clear, you will sleep in the guest room. The only nights we will sleep together will be in Monte Cleure and if you choose to bring a chastity belt with you for it I will have no objection.'

Her lips quirked.

'But if it makes you feel better for tonight, take a knife and put it under your pillow. Hell, you can take it now if you want. If I get within a foot of you, jab me with it.'

Her shoulders rose and she covered her mouth as if stifling a laugh.

'I'm serious.'

She nodded but kept her mouth covered.

'Are you hungry?'

Her eyes met his. She gave another nod.

'Shall I order us something?'

'That's probably a good idea.' A giggle escaped her mouth but there was none of the bitterness he'd heard in her other bursts of laughter. She swept an arm around the kitchen. 'I'm pretty sure there's nothing to eat in this showroom.'

'There's an Italian restaurant on the third floor that delivers good, freshly cooked food. How does that suit you?'

'That's fine by me.'

He opened the drawer he kept all the local takeaway and restaurant menus in. Mia was right, he was forced to concede. His apartment was kept like a showroom. But then, he hardly spent any time in it. On average he visited the UK every two months, rarely spending more than a working week there. He had neither the time nor the inclination to make this apartment into a home.

He passed the menu to her, making sure not to allow their fingers to touch, then stepped aside. 'Name your poison.'

Her eyes lit up. 'Gin and tonic.'

'Large?'

She smiled. Like her laughter, it was the first genuine smile she'd given him. 'Yes please.'

It was only while he fixed their drinks, leaving her to read through the menu, that he realised what an arrogant thing it was for him to assume her smile had been genuine. Or that her laughter had been. For all he knew, her display of edgy fear might have been an act too.

And yet something inside him told him none of that had been Mia acting.

All the same, there was no earthly reason her smile had made him feel that he could climb Mount Everest in a single bound.

Mia, her third gin and tonic of the night in hand, curled up on one of the white sofas. It was long past midnight, usually the time when the adrenaline from a performance had worked its way out of her system and she went to bed. Tonight, even with the lights in the apartment's living room dimmed, energy still zapped through her veins and it had nothing to do with the performance. It was all to do with Damián.

Since their talk in the kitchen, things had been far more cordial between them. In truth, she felt like a naughty schoolgirl who'd been chastised by the headmistress. She had been deliberately antagonistic towards him. A very large part of her still wanted to be, and it disturbed her to remember the last time she'd behaved this way to a member of the opposite sex.

She'd had her first crush when she'd been nine. His name had been James. She'd daydreamed about him constantly. In her overactive imagination, she'd dreamed up adventurous scenarios where she put herself in danger in the pursuit of something marvellously worthy like rescuing a cat from a tree, and then needing James to come bounding in to rescue her. Sometimes it would be the other way round and she would rescue him. The ending of those daydreams was always the same: James would declare his love for her and kiss her cheek.

Alas, her daydreaming powers hadn't extended to influencing James to reciprocate her feelings. Looking back, she thought the fact she'd been consistently horrible to him in the playground might have had something to do with his failure to fall in love with her. She remembered a day at school when it had snowed. She'd made the biggest, tightest snowball she could fit in her hands and lobbed it full power into his face. From only two feet away. Fully expecting him to throw snowballs back and for their snowball fight to end in declarations of love, she'd been baffled when he'd called her a witch and gone off crying.

The way she was acting towards Damián strongly reminded her of her long-ago playground behaviour towards James but she had no idea why she reacted like this around him. She certainly wasn't trying to entice Damián into falling in love with her. The only thing she knew with any certainty was that when she'd told him she would be a fool not to be afraid she hadn't actually meant that she was afraid of *him* as he'd assumed.

It was the non-physical power he had over her that frightened her. When she was with him all her nerves were set on edge, every emotion heightened. Even now, when she was making a concerted effort to drop the antagonism, her heartbeats couldn't settle into a rhythm and all her senses were attuned to his every move. She hadn't been this scared since she'd appeared in court for sentencing and that had been a very different kind of fear.

'Tell me about your life,' she said when he settled onto the sofa opposite her. They'd exchanged only basic pleasantries during their shared meal, which hadn't helped her nerves in the slightest. She needed conversation to stop herself thinking. 'What's it like growing up a rich boy?'

What she really wanted to ask was why he thought his brother was watching him and accessing his electronic communications, and what those documents that were so important to him contained. She'd spent hours searching again on the internet and had her suspicions but, as Damián liked to remind her, he was paying her to do a job and not ask questions.

He had a large drink of the beer he'd poured for himself and wiped the froth on his lips away with his thumb. 'Next time. Tonight I want you to tell me about yourself.'

'You already know everything about me.'

He gave a faint smile. '*Mi vida*, I know very little about you. I know you're twenty-four, that you're an actress looking for her big break and that you have a sealed criminal record for possession of drugs with intent to supply. Nothing more.'

'I thought you'd dug into my history?'

'Only your recent history and only to satisfy myself that you are free of drugs.'

'What criminal records did the other actresses on your shortlist have?'

'I don't remember.'

Mia might only have known Damián a short time but of one thing she was certain: he was a man who noticed everything and, more importantly, remembered everything.

Damián noted the narrowed, suspicious stare his answer provoked. 'As soon as I saw your photo I knew you were the one I needed,' he explained evenly. His attention had been captured so completely by Mia's picture that he couldn't remember what the other actresses looked like. 'As I explained last night, you had the look I was after. Once I was satisfied you were clean—there were no rumours of you taking drugs any more—I had only to satisfy myself that you were an actress of talent. But, if we are to convince everyone that we are in love, I need to know personal things about you.'

'That works both ways.'

'Agreed, but today I want to talk about you.'

'Aren't you afraid the press will dig into my background and learn about my criminal record? Your name would be associated with a drug dealer.'

'They won't. And, even if they did, they wouldn't be able to do anything with it. Your record is permanently sealed. I was assured of that before I approached you.'

She had a sip of her drink, eyes wary.

Damián pinched the bridge of his nose and sighed. 'Please, *mi vida*, that document…put it out of your mind.'

'How can I?' Knowing her criminal record was in someone else's hands and could be used against her at any time was like having a permanent weight lodged in her chest.

What if she mucked the job up? Would he use her record as a weapon against her as punishment? While she knew zero about the documents he needed to find, she knew they were incredibly important to him. He was a man at war with his brother whereas Mia was a woman desperate to protect her sister. The way they lived and their outlooks on life were just too divergent; how could she trust someone whose mind worked in such a different way to her own?

He inhaled deeply and got to his feet. 'One minute,' he muttered.

He disappeared, returning shortly with a large envelope. He handed it to her. 'Here. This is my copy of your conviction. Take it.'

CHAPTER FIVE

DAMIÁN SAW THE hesitation before Mia took the envelope from him.

'This is proof I have no intention of using it against you.' He sat back down and stared into her wide, disbelieving eyes. 'I only wanted it for the information it contained. You will have to take my word that I made no copies.'

Expecting her to automatically demand proof regardless of his assurance, he was pleasantly surprised when she continued staring at him, time stretching between them, before the shadow of a smile curved her cheeks.

'Thank you,' she said simply, and laid the envelope on the table. Biting into her bottom lip, she said, 'If your communications are being monitored, how can you be sure Emiliano hasn't seen it and copied it?'

His chest filled, although whether it was because she seemed to have actually taken his word for something or her mention of his brother he couldn't say. He still couldn't believe he'd given her that information. 'My security team have provided me with a state-of-the-art phone which they monitor for me. Everything concerning you has been done through it. I have used Felipe and his team for my security needs for over a decade and I trust them implicitly. It was them who discovered my communications had been hacked.'

Her eyes held his for a little longer before she nodded, seemingly accepting his assurance and, masterfully keeping her glass straight, curled back into the sofa. 'Okay, so what do you want to know about me?'

Everything...

The wayward thought caught him off-guard, and he had another drink of his beer while he composed his thoughts. 'Your family. Tell me about them.'

'There's not much to tell. We're just normal.'

'Define normal?'

'Well, Amy and I never call our mum by her first name. And we don't need to make an appointment to see her. And I don't think she's following me or hacking into my communications. That kind of normal.'

Damián had no idea why this obvious slight against his family and dig at his situation, something he would normally take as a heinous crime, made him laugh.

As a man who rarely found humour in life, hearing his own laughter sounded strange to his ears.

'Is Amy older or younger than you?'

'Two years younger.'

'Any other siblings?'

'No.'

'Is Amy an actress too?'

'She's just qualified as a nurse.' Mia said this with unmistakable pride. 'Our mum works as a school teaching assistant. See? Normal. I grew up in a three-bedroom semi-detached house in an old market town where nothing much happened, all very ordinary and...'

'Normal?' he supplied with a quirk of his brow. Unbelievably, he found himself relaxing, something that was as alien to him as the sound of his laughter. Maybe it was the soft lighting or the way Mia had relaxed into the sofa, the two of them conversing as…well, not friends, but not foes either.

She sniggered. 'Exactly.'

'What about your father? What does he do?'

She had a quick drink before answering. 'He died nine years ago.'

The lightness of their conversation darkened in an instant.

'Oh.' He blinked. 'I'm sorry.'

Her smile became brittle. 'Don't be. It was a long time ago.'

But the pain was still there. He could see it in the way her knees pulled closer to her chest and in the sudden tautness of her features.

'How did he…?' He found the question flailing on his tongue.

'Die?' She swallowed but the brittle smile remained. 'His car broke down on the motorway. He was trying to pull over to the hard shoulder when he was hit by a lorry.' She had another drink. 'He didn't stand a chance.'

'I'm sorry,' he repeated. With his own father having recently died suddenly—although not unexpectedly as he'd suffered ill health—his chest twisted to imagine the devastation it had wrought.

'The coroner said he died instantly so that's a comfort. He didn't suffer.'

No, he thought. The dead didn't suffer. It was the ones left behind who bore the suffering.

'What was he like?' he asked.

Her tight frame loosened and her features softened. 'He was wonderful. He was a physics teacher and mad as a box of frogs. Very loving and very funny and hugely intelligent. He doted on us.'

'You saw a lot of him?'

'Err…' He caught the wry bafflement his question caused. 'Of course I did. We all lived under the same roof. We were a family.'

He grimaced. 'I'm sorry. My family…we were a family too but not, I think, as you experienced family. It wasn't unusual for us all to be on separate continents when I was growing up.'

Damián and his brother had been raised by their own personal nannies and a fleet of dedicated staff, and educated in an English boarding school. An annual skiing trip in Switzerland had been the only sacrosanct family time, and even that had been full of his parents disappearing to take calls. He remembered numerous occasions when he'd flown to one of their family homes on a school holiday only to find one or both of his parents had already moved on to another country. To Damián, that had been normal. He'd grown up longing for the day he could take his place as his father's side within the business. When that day had finally come, the day his father had appointed him head of Banco Delgado, his father had patted his back and said, 'You've made an old man proud.' After a lifetime of antipathy from his brother and being made to feel second best by his mother, those words had validated his entire existence. When, within a year, he'd increased Banco Delgado's profits by forty per cent, his father had looked through the accounts confirming this, risen from his desk and shaken Damián's hand. That was the moment he'd known he'd made his mark and that the respect he'd always craved from a father who was neither emotional or demonstrative had been his.

What would it have been like to be together as a family for more than a few weeks a year? To share meals every day? To go to bed every night knowing your parents and sibling were safe under the same roof as you?

'His death must have been hard for you,' he said heavily. He missed his father but their relationship had been too distant during his childhood for them to be close. As adults, they'd worked tightly together but there had always been a formality between them. The grief he felt for his father, he knew, was nothing to what Mia must have gone through with the loss of her father.

She nodded then downed the remainder of her drink and swirled it in her mouth before swallowing.

'Another?'

She put her glass on the table. 'One more then I'm going to have to call it a night.'

He fixed them both another drink. By the time he laid her glass on the table between them, she'd stretched her legs out and placed a cushion under her head. For a moment, he found his attention caught by her bare feet, which were resting slightly off the edge of the sofa. They were pretty feet, the toes painted a pretty coral colour. Did they ache, he wondered with a pang, after an evening spent on stage? Did they ache now? Did the rest of her ache…?

He took a deep breath and removed his gaze from her feet. These were not thoughts he should be having. Keeping his attention fixed on the conversation between them while ignoring the swell of desire that was constantly pulsing through him was proving incredibly hard.

Mia was just too damn desirable, that was the problem, and the stillness of his apartment and lack of external distraction was amplifying everything he felt. Every movement she made stirred his senses. He'd never before been in the position where his desire had to be stifled, and his weakness at overcoming it infuriated him. He'd always been able to compartmentalise. With Mia, though, he was failing to compartmentalise in a spectacular fashion.

He sat back on the sofa and hooked an ankle on his thigh,

feigning nonchalance. He must not let his wayward feelings show on his face or in his body language. Mia was finally relaxed in his company and he had no wish to put her back on edge.

'How did the daughter of a physics teacher become an actress?' he asked. 'Was it something you always wanted to do?'

'Not really.'

He waited for her to elaborate.

She sighed. 'After Dad died…things at home…they changed.'

'Understandable.'

Her eyes met his. 'It was awful,' she said softly. 'We all pulled together to begin with but then I guess we all got lost in our own pain for a while. I signed up for the school production of *Romeo & Juliet* on a whim. I couldn't believe it when I was given the role of Juliet, and I still don't know if I got it because they felt sorry for me or if they saw some kind of talent in me. Whatever…it doesn't matter. I got the part and…' Her throat moved before she continued. 'It's hard to explain but being on that stage… By inhabiting Juliet, I lost myself. I stepped into her shoes and for that short time all my worries and pain were gone. It was an escape. I knew that, even then. But it helped me.'

He digested this. 'Then why did you turn to drugs?'

Her eyes widened fractionally and suddenly he realised what it was he saw whenever he mentioned her criminal past. Fear. A rabbit momentarily frozen in the headlights.

She stretched an arm out for her drink. 'I don't want to talk about that.'

'Why not?'

'It's too personal.'

More personal than discussing her father's death?

Somehow she managed to drink from her gin and tonic

while laying flat out without choking or spilling a drop. When she laid her cheek back on the cushion she rested her hand beneath it and drew her knees in before her eyes locked back onto his.

'You don't have to tell me about the drugs if you don't want to,' he said. 'But I'm glad you're clean now. That must have taken a lot of strength.'

Her face contorted and she pressed her face into the cushion. 'Please, Damián,' she said. 'I can't talk about it.'

A lump formed in his throat at the distress he detected in her muffled voice.

'We need never speak of it again,' he promised quietly while his mind raced as to *why* she wouldn't talk about it and why she found it so distressing. 'Not unless you want to.'

Her shoulder blades rose before she turned her cheek to face him again. 'Thank you,' she whispered.

He stared closely at her. 'Are you okay?'

Her lips drew in tightly but she nodded.

'Okay.' He drank a third of his pint, then, in a lighter tone, said, 'Tell me your long-term plans. What do you want from life?'

He read the gratitude in her eyes at his change of subject. Her voice back to its usual melodious strength, she said, 'Another role would be a good start.'

'Haven't you got anything lined up after this tour?'

She pulled a face. 'Nada. I've got an audition Monday morning—and, before you get cross about it, it'll be over before you get back to London—but I know who I'm up against so I don't rate my chances.'

'Why so negative?'

'Realistic,' she corrected.

'If you were being realistic you would know you have an excellent chance. Remember, I have seen you on stage, *mi vida*. Twice. You are a natural.'

'That's nice of you to say but I like to prepare myself for the worst and hope for the best. That way I'm not disappointed when things don't go my way.'

'It will. One day I will walk past a billboard of the hottest movie and your face will be on it.' The image flashed vivid in his mind. Mia had the talent and the looks, plus she had that rare star quality.

She gave a theatrical shudder. 'Never going to happen.'

He threw her a stern look that he was gratified to find her lips twitching at. 'Don't be so negative.'

'In this case, I'm not being negative. I don't want that life. I have no wish to become public property.'

'An actress who doesn't want to be a star?' he said cynically.

'It's being on stage that I love. I love the sense of family you get being part of troupe… I love everything about it.'

'Maybe one day I will see you on Broadway.'

She pulled a rueful face that turned into a wide yawn that she hastily covered with the back of her hand. 'Not going to happen. I don't want to leave England and, even if I did, I wouldn't have much chance getting a visa to the US, not with my record. And that really is me being realistic.'

Making a mental note to make some discreet enquiries about this, he stared into her eyes. He could see the lethargy taking over her. The cynical part of him, which he fully admitted constituted the major part, wondered if it was shame over her drug-dealing past holding her back from pursuing a career in TV or the movies rather than her love of the stage as she professed. But then he thought of his reaction to seeing her on the stage and thought of the comments whispered from the other audience members, all of whom had raved about how fantastic she was, and he knew she was right. Mia belonged on the stage.

She yawned again, pulled herself upright and stretched, inadvertently pushing her breasts forward. 'I need to get some sleep.'

With his blood thickening all over again at her innocent movement, Damián got straight to his feet. 'I'll show you to your room.'

Overnight bag and envelope in hand, she followed him up the hallway to the apartment's sleeping quarters.

He opened her door briskly and stepped in. 'This is your room,' he said, doing his damnedest to keep his tone no-nonsense. 'You have a private bathroom. Help yourself to anything you need or want. If you need me, I'm in the room opposite.'

She kept her eyes on the floor and gave a murmured, 'Thank you.'

'Right... I'll leave you to sleep.'

She nodded before raising her gaze to his. 'Damián?'

His heart slammed. His chest tightened. 'Yes?'

'I'm sorry. For how I behaved earlier.'

He swallowed hard. 'It was understandable.'

Their eyes stayed locked for a moment that seemed to last an age before he took a deep breath and broke it. And then he made the fatal mistake of stepping out of the room at the exact same moment she chose to step into it.

'Excuse me.'

'No, excuse me.'

And then they were past each other on the opposite sides of the threshold to where they'd started but not without Mia's breasts brushing against his arm in the process.

For one final time their eyes locked.

The colour flaming her face was unmistakable.

He cleared his throat. 'Goodnight, *mi vida*.'

Her whispered goodnight in response was lost as he closed the door sharply behind him.

* * *

Arms covering her tingling breasts, the beats of her heart a painful staccato, Mia closed her eyes and dragged air into her lungs. A door closed and then there was silence.

Once she felt reasonably in control of herself, she sat on the edge of the huge bed and covered her burning face.

Intensely private about her personal life, she'd just unloaded things to Damián that she never spoke about. She talked about her dad with her mum and sister all the time but not with strangers. The pain of his death had eased through the years but it never really went away, was always carried in her heart.

The most unsettling part was the yearning to tell Damián the truth. The past had seen her develop a thick skin but every mention of her conviction made her want to scream the facts at him. She hated him thinking such things about her, which was a frightening notion in itself. Why should she care what he thought?

It was the unflinching intensity of his stare, she thought, cheeks burning afresh remembering how it made her feel: as if he were stripping her naked with his eyes and reaching deep inside to touch her in a place no one had ever been before. Nothing had ever made her feel like that, and she'd had to bury her face in the cushion to break the spell.

After a quick shower she crawled into bed. But it wasn't fear of Damián slipping into the room that had her wrapping the duvet around her like a cocoon. It was the fear that she might be the one to slip out of bed and seek him out.

CHAPTER SIX

MIA SHOOK THE director's hand, thanked him for the opportunity then pulled the strap of her handbag around her neck and headed for the theatre exit. There'd been nothing in the director's demeanour to suggest she'd overly impressed with her audition. The tour was over and she had nothing lined up...apart from the role she was currently playing for Damián.

She'd already spent most of the hundred thousand he'd transferred to her but had a little left over for emergencies. She'd bought herself a second-hand car—no point blowing it on a brand-new car when a decent second-hand one did the job—paid a large chunk of her mortgage off, ordered a new boiler for the flat and spent a small fortune on damp resistant paint. Sometimes she thought she should have rented rather than use the small inheritance she'd received from her father's insurance pay-out as a mortgage deposit, but she'd wanted security. Finally, she had it. She was going to save the next hundred thousand after the weekend in Monte Cleure. She'd worked it out and, so long as she was careful with the remainder, she could live off it for at least five years even if she failed to get another role.

Bright sunlight greeted her when she stepped outside with two of the other actresses who'd auditioned, the three of them discussing where they should get some lunch. Mia lifted her face to the sky, greedy to feel the sun's warmth on her face after the darkness of the theatre's interior.

About to reach into her bag for her sunglasses, she suddenly noticed a large figure propped against a nearby wall.

She blinked to clear the vision. He remained against the wall, arms folded across his considerable chest, dressed in dark grey trousers and a black shirt, top button undone, the sleeves rolled up. A sardonic smile played on the wide, firm lips.

'Mia?' Tanya, one of the other actresses, nudged her. 'Where do you think we should go?'

Swallowing, she finally managed to get her mouth working. 'I'm sorry. I'm going to have to give it a miss. My boyfriend's here.'

She would not call him her lover. That was not the language she or her friends used.

Two sets of eyes followed her gaze. From the periphery of her vision, Mia saw Tanya's mouth drop open. '*That's* your boyfriend?' she asked faintly.

She nodded, her heart too full for words to form.

Even with the considerable distance between them she caught the glint in Damián's eyes before he strode towards her.

Knowing exactly what was expected of her, Mia forced her legs to walk towards him.

Except that was a lie. She didn't have to force her legs to walk. She had to force them not to run. Or skip.

She hadn't seen him since they'd shared a quick coffee for breakfast in his apartment before he'd left for Argentina five days ago. But those five days had not been without his presence in her life. He'd messaged her before every performance, including the weekend matinees, with wishes that she break a leg. And he'd called her after every performance too, asking how it had gone.

She knew the messages and calls were for show because he suspected his brother of hacking his communications. That hadn't stopped her heart skipping to see his name flash on the screen of her phone.

Their conversation last night had gone on for thirty minutes. To Mia, it had passed in the blink of an eye. She'd snuggled into her sofa and allowed his wonderful voice to infuse her senses, safe that he was thousands of miles away and unable to see the pleasure she took from speaking to him.

And now, even though they had an audience to perform for, she found she didn't have to fake pleasure at seeing him.

How had that happened? She hated him…didn't she?

Their eyes stayed locked. The smile on her face widened by the second as they closed the distance until he was right in front of her.

Mia found she needed to dredge none of her acting skills to loop her arms around his neck and tilt her face to his.

His dark eyes glinted as he wrapped his arms around her waist. 'Now this is what I call a welcome greeting, *mi vida*,' he murmured. The warmth of his breath whispered against her lips and then his mouth fused onto hers.

At the first touch it felt as if a thunderbolt had gone off in her heart.

The sigh she expelled came from nowhere but, before she could melt into him, the kiss was over. She had the delicious sensation of his lips brushing over her cheek before he stepped back and she found herself gazing at him and finally having to use her acting skills to mask the disappointment ricocheting through her.

What was *happening* to her?

She cleared her throat quietly then injected brightness into her voice. Her colleagues were watching and, no doubt, listening intently. 'This is a nice surprise. I wasn't expecting you back until the evening.'

A smile played on his lips but a shutter had come down in his eyes. 'I wanted to surprise you.'

'You succeeded.'

'Can I buy you lunch?'

'That would be great.'

Waving a quick goodbye to Tanya and Eloise, Mia let her hand be enveloped in Damián's much larger one and fell into step with him.

'Where would you like to eat?' Damián asked, striving to keep his voice casual. But *Dios*, never in his wildest dreams had he imagined a greeting like the one Mia had just given him.

She'd sighed into him. He hadn't imagined it. It had been a cold reminder of what a great actress she was. If he'd been an outside observer he would have believed she was thrilled to see him. He'd have believed her affection to be genuine.

'Surprise me,' she said. Now their audience was gone he thought she'd drop his hand. But she didn't.

Mia Caldwell was an actress. She played make-believe for a living. He'd given her a role to play and she had stepped up and thrown herself into her performance.

If only he could explain his own thrill at seeing her again as easily.

His five days home in Argentina had dragged by, which was unusual as his life was so busy. He tended to stick to the same daily routine when in Buenos Aires: an early workout in his gym and then business for anything between ten and fifteen hours before calling it a day. His hunt for an actress these past few weeks had eaten into his precious time so he'd had catching-up to do on top of his daily routine. Despite the snail-like pace his life had taken, he'd assumed his brief return to normality was going fine until his PA had asked if everything was okay with him. That was something he'd never asked him before.

If, as he suspected, Emiliano was monitoring his movements and communications—and someone was because his crack team of experts had found spyware installed in his personal devices—then it was best he play the lovelorn fool. That was the only reason he'd taken to calling Mia daily and sending her messages. That he'd ended their conversations needing to take a cold shower was irrelevant.

That he felt the need for a cold shower now too was also irrelevant. But *Dios*, not only had she greeted him with a smile that made his chest expand to titanic proportions but she smelled fantastic and the summer dress she wore was enough to raise even a celibate's blood pressure. White with tiny red roses patterned over it, it fell to mid-thigh and had buttons running down its length. Flat Roman sandals gave glimpses of her pretty feet and now he kept catching glimpses of smooth golden leg to complement them, which raised his blood pressure that little bit higher.

'How did the audition go?' he asked, determined to ignore the darts running through his skin at the warmth of her hand. Holding Mia's hand like this did not feel like acting.

'Rubbish. I don't think I impressed.'

'Being negative, *mi vida*?'

'Being realistic,' she countered.

They stopped amongst a crowd at a road crossing. Someone jostled into him, pushing him into Mia.

He held his breath until the lights turned green.

Why the hell hadn't he studied the pictures of the four shortlisted actresses more closely and chosen the one who'd jumped out at him the least? He needed to be *focused*, not walking the streets of London fighting the sensation in his loins from turning into anything obvious, a task made harder when the object of his desire's hand was enclosed so tightly in his. Thankfully, they soon arrived at the hotel and he could legitimately drop it.

The hotel's restaurant was busy but Mia wasn't the least surprised that the management were able to fit them in. Damián carried such an air of authority about him that even if he wasn't a gazillionaire she had no doubt they would have been squeezed in regardless.

The bad mood she'd detected developing in Damián during their walk to the hotel continued at the table. Damián studied the menu tight-lipped, not looking at her. It was a complete contradiction to her own mood, which had lightened with every step she'd taken. She decided the glorious weather was the cause of it because who could fail to be cheered with warmth on their skin and bright blue skies above their head? Holding the hand of the sexiest man to walk the earth and who, she'd been discovering, wasn't quite the bastard she'd initially thought had nothing to do with it.

He could easily have kept hold of her criminal record to use as a weapon to ensure she did exactly as she was told. But he hadn't. He'd recognised her distress and given it back to her. For that alone she would give the performance of her life.

'Damián?'

He didn't look up from his menu. 'What?'

'What happened to soft and loving?'

'I'm deciding what to eat.'

She reached for his hand and tried not to be hurt when he flinched at her touch. When all was said and done, Damián was paying her to play a role. So long as she played her part, he could have no complaints if it all went wrong.

'We're supposed to be falling in love, remember?' She could hardly believe she was having to remind him of this. Normally, it was the other way round. She softened her voice and whispered, 'What's wrong?'

'Nothing.' He grimaced, stretched his neck and rolled his shoulders.

'Then wipe the scowl from your face. You're supposed to be wining and dining your new lover, not looking like you're trying to decide who you want to stick your fork into.'

His eyes zipped to hers. To her relief, a smile tugged at his lips.

'That's better,' she said with a grin. Then, because it felt too nice, she moved her hand from his on the pretext of needing a drink of her water.

Once their order had been taken he dived straight into conversation. 'When we have finished eating we will collect your stuff and go straight to my apartment.'

'What do you plan to do with me?'

The gleam that flashed in his eyes at this made her regret her phrasing.

'I meant what plans have you made for us?' she hurried to reiterate, mortified to feel a flush rise up her neck and suffuse her face.

His wide mouth twitched. 'I have a meeting in Frankfurt tomorrow but then my diary is clear. I need to give you the rundown of how the weekend will unfold and plan how you and I are going to handle things. I have the blueprints and virtual tour videos of the villa for you to study. I want you to arrive at the villa knowing exactly what your job is and how I expect things to be played out. I'll have to take you shopping too.'

'What for?'

'Clothes and accessories for you to wear over the weekend—you will need to look the part, *mi vida*.'

'Does that come under expenses?'

'It does.'

She grinned without any effort whatsoever. 'Excellent.'

It was late evening when Damián returned from Frankfurt. After a day spent alone in his apartment studying the blueprints and videos of the villa he'd provided her with, Mia instantly became alert to the front door opening. At the first tread of a footstep her heart exploded and sent the blood whooshing through her veins.

And then he appeared in the living room.

She'd been asleep when he'd left that morning. Only now that he'd returned did she realise she'd been on tenterhooks all day waiting for him.

Frightened at how badly she longed to jump up and throw her arms around him, she hurriedly pretended to tidy some of the papers strewn over the glass dining table where she'd been studying.

'Have you had a good day?' she asked politely as he placed his briefcase on the only available space left on the table.

'I've spent most of it in a board meeting.'

'Exciting!'

Amusement flared in his eyes. 'And you? Have you familiarised yourself with the villa?'

'I think it needs to be renamed as a palace,' she quipped. She had no idea why seeing his amusement made her heart sing but, like with everything else concerning her feelings for Damián, it terrified her. 'Give me a few more days and then you can test me on it.'

His lips twitched. 'I look forward to it. Have you eaten?'

'I've spent the day studying and stuffing my face.' Mia had happily obeyed Damián's edict that she use his concierge service. The only interruption to her studying and constant munching had been a call with her mum where she'd been forced to fend off questions about her new 'relationship'. Her mum's excitement at Mia finally having a man in her life made her feel rotten at her deception. She'd felt compelled to make it clear, while maintaining the upbeat voice she always adopted when speaking to her mum and sister, that it was early days for her and Damián, that they were poles apart socially and financially and that it was very unlikely to work out between them. Even if Damián hadn't been paying her to pretend, it was the truth. It didn't matter what crazy feelings he'd unleashed in her, nothing could ever come of it. Their lives were just too different.

Another gleam of amusement flared. He tugged at his tie to loosen it. The muscles on his biceps bunched. The muscles in her abdomen clenched in appreciation. 'Good. Drink?'

'Yes please.'

'The usual?'

Something warm and fluttery filled her chest at the question and she answered with a nod. *The usual…* Two words without a nip of intimacy in them but with the power to make her feel as if something intimate had passed between them.

Trying to shake off the heady feelings rushing through her, Mia turned her attention back to the papers she'd been studying, but her raging heart had barely found a settled rhythm when Damián reappeared with their drinks and took the seat opposite her, and she found herself trapped in the beauty of his obsidian eyes.

The warm fluttering started all over again, filling her every crevice. She had to fight for breath, fight to open her constricted throat. Fight to stop her fingers, tingling with zings of electricity, from reaching across the table to him.

And in that charged moment while she gazed into his mesmerising stare she had the strongest feeling that he wanted to reach across and touch her too.

She cleared her throat again and broke the lock of their eyes, tugging at her hair and reminding herself in great big capital letters of the reason why she was here with him, and that was to do a job.

'Look, I know you don't want to tell me what the documents contain and I respect that...' After all, he respected her refusal to talk about her drug conviction. 'But I'm wondering how you can be so certain Emiliano's hidden them in the villa.' It was something she'd pondered a lot. Like Damián, Emiliano had homes across the world.

Her question was met with silence.

When she dared look at him again she found his gaze still on her, an unfathomable look in his eyes. He had a long drink of his beer then placed the glass down and bowed his head to knead his skull. 'They were in the villa before my father died.'

'The documents?'

'*Si.*' His fingers moved to rub his temples. 'My father updated his will days before he died. He split his personal wealth between Emiliano and Celeste. His business interests he left to me. The will's gone missing, along with the document he signed transferring control of the entire Delgado Group to me.' He raised his stare to hers. She'd never seen such starkness contained in the dark depths before. 'If those two documents aren't found in the next two weeks the entire business will fall under Emiliano's control.'

Mia's brain pounded as she tried to digest this but nothing computed. 'How can that happen? I didn't think he had any involvement with it.'

According to the internet, Emiliano Delgado preferred horses to finance.

'My father took Monte Cleure citizenship and is bound by its probate laws. By law, six months have to pass there before probate can be granted and the deceased's wishes carried out. If the will isn't found then the laws of intestacy kick in, and in Monte Cleure they are archaic. If there's no legal will then the oldest son inherits everything.'

'And you think Emiliano's hidden the documents to

make this happen? Why would he do that when he has no interest in the business?'

'Revenge,' he answered bleakly. 'Ten years ago, our father put him in charge of a major investment fund. Emiliano screwed up and lost our clients half a billion dollars.'

Realising her mouth had dropped open, Mia quickly closed it. The figures Damián had uttered were almost too mind-boggling to comprehend.

'Emiliano refused to accept responsibility for the losses,' he continued. 'He insisted it was a conspiracy against him.'

'Was it?'

'He had nothing to back his conspiracy claims up. We had no choice but to cut him loose from the business.'

'You sacked him?'

He kneaded his skull vigorously. 'We had to.'

'You were part of the decision?'

'The decision was our father's but I supported it. If his screw-up had got out, the Delgado reputation would have been in tatters. In our business, trust is everything. Emiliano thought we should trust that it wasn't his fault but how could we do that when the facts showed otherwise?'

Hearing the defensiveness in his tone, she said softly, 'You don't have to justify yourself to me.'

'We didn't cut him off without anything. We funded the loss out of our private money and then Father set up a trust fund for him. Emiliano gets ten million dollars a month for life from it but, for all that and for all the success he's made of his life since then, he's never forgiven me or our father for what he sees as us pushing him out of the business.' A pulse throbbed on his temple. 'Nothing would give him greater pleasure than to snatch the Delgado Group from under my nose and publicly sack me. Once he's rid of me, I am certain he will destroy the business. When I said I stand to lose everything, I meant it.'

CHAPTER SEVEN

THINKING HARD, HER heart aching for him, Mia cleared her throat. 'You seem very certain that the documents are still intact. How do you know Emiliano hasn't destroyed them? Have you asked him?'

'Not directly—we haven't spoken since he was fired from the business—but he denied it to Celeste.'

'Hold on—you and Emiliano haven't spoken in *ten years*?'

He shrugged. 'We see each other twice a year but he refuses to even look at me. All communication is done through Celeste.'

She expelled a long breath at this matter-of-fact account of brothers at war. 'So he could have destroyed them?'

'No. Our parents trained us too well for him to do that. They taught us to think like champion chess players: strategically at all times. Anticipate and mitigate any future move your opponent might make. Emiliano would never destroy anything that could prove useful in the future. No, he's hidden them. I know he has.'

'Does Celeste think he's hidden them too?'

'She won't entertain the idea.' Bitterness flashed in the obsidian before he bit out, 'Emiliano is her golden child.'

Although Mia had already gathered the Delgados were a family far removed from the loving family she'd been raised in, to know his own mother had taken his brother's side without a care made her heart wrench for him. No wonder he had such a cold façade.

But that was all it was, she was coming to understand. A façade. Beneath the icy exterior beat a heart capable of great feeling.

Before she could ask anything further about his mother's favouring of his brother, steely black eyes glinted. 'The facts are straightforward. I visited my father at his request three days before he died. He wanted me to read the documents before he had them witnessed. He knew he wouldn't live much longer and wanted me to be prepared. We planned an official announcement about my takeover of the Delgado Group but he didn't live long enough for it to happen.' A sliver of pain cut through the façade. 'Neither of us knew just how short a time he had left.'

She couldn't stop herself from leaning over to cover his hand. She didn't say anything. As she knew all too well, in times like this platitudes were meaningless but human comfort could soothe.

His chest rose sharply as he rolled his neck and moved his hand from hers. Steepling his fingers, he said, 'He told me he was going to keep the documents in his safe. I looked on the day of the funeral and it was empty. At the time, I assumed he'd changed his mind about keeping them there and given them to his lawyer to look after but the family lawyer denies knowing anything about it. I've made contact with every lawyer in Monte Cleure and they deny all knowledge too.'

Rubbing a hand over her face, Mia tried to think. 'Assuming you're right and Emiliano hasn't destroyed them, how do you know they're still in Monte Cleure?'

'He stayed at the villa for a few days after the funeral.' He waited a beat before adding, 'I do have one friend on the inside. He was able to obtain the external surveillance footage of Emiliano from those days but it was too risky for him to get the internal surveillance too. Unless Emiliano got someone to remove the documents for him, they're still there. He didn't leave the estate with anything but his car keys and hasn't been back since. The first thing I'll do when we get there is hack into the villa's security system and try to retrieve the internal footage of the period from my father's death to the weekend following his funeral. The footage, if it can be retrieved, is unlikely to show him hiding them, so I'm going to need to physically search. Which is where I'll need your help. I can't search alone without raising suspicions or risking being caught.'

'Whatever you need me to do, I'll do,' she vowed.

He looked at her for a long, meaningful moment. 'That's what I'm paying you for, *mi vida.*'

'I know.' She swallowed something that felt horribly like disappointment at the cold silkiness of his tone and the pointed reminder of her place in his world. 'I just meant...' Her voice trailed away.

What *had* she meant? That right then she would have sworn to help him even if he wasn't paying her?

'Meant what?' he asked in the same cold, silky voice.

'Nothing.' Her compassion, she realised with a pang as she looked into his expressionless eyes, was not wanted.

Suddenly desperate to be alone, Mia pushed her chair back. 'I hope you don't mind but my brain's fried after all that studying. I need to get some sleep.' And she really needed to get a handle on all these crazy feelings which were growing and mutating by the second but were clearly not reciprocated before she said or did something she'd regret.

The expressionless eyes didn't flicker. *'Buenos noches.'*

She stared at him a moment longer, wondering how he

could confide such secrets one minute then revert to the cold man she'd first met the next.

'Well…goodnight.'

Only when Mia disappeared from sight did Damián relax his jaw, close his eyes and slump forward to cradle his head.

What had possessed him to confide such things? He never spoke about his family on such a familiar level. Whatever went on behind the scenes, a united front was always maintained. Any antipathy was kept within the family. Outsiders might suspect but those suspicions were never confirmed. Discretion was at the heart of all Delgado life, both business and personal.

Admitting vocally for the first time that Celeste had always favoured his brother had been the hardest words he'd ever said…but they'd somehow been the easiest too. He'd stared into Mia's eyes and the words had been sucked from his tongue, just as everything else he'd confided had been.

He downed the rest of his beer and gripped his hair.

What was it with Mia? Was it her proximity while they shared his apartment that was causing him to feel he'd been caught in a spell?

If it was just his apartment she occupied he wouldn't have a problem but she was in his head too when they were apart, constantly shimmering in his vision.

He was paying her to perform a role in a game that would determine his entire future. And even if he wasn't, if they'd met in a more natural way, he still wouldn't want to get involved with her. She was everything he didn't want in a lover. Damián was still holding out hope that one day he would find a lover he could marry, and there was no way he could marry Mia. She was rooted in the UK and he was…

He swore under his breath.

Marriage? Where the hell had that notion come from?

Clenching his fists and jaw and closing his eyes, he

dragged ten large breaths in to expel all the racing thoughts and feelings.

It made no difference.

A large drink. That was what he needed. Something to numb him a little so when he did go to bed he wouldn't lie for hours staring at the ceiling, thinking of the woman occupying the room mere feet from his.

'Where are we starting?' Mia asked brightly when Damián followed her out of the car onto a bustling Bond Street.

'Have you shopped here before?'

'On my wages? You're having a laugh.' When he'd given her the cash to buy herself an outfit for their first date she'd stopped at a boutique that was nowhere near as exclusive as the shops on this street.

'Then take your pick.'

'That's impossible. I want to go in all of them.'

He gave a gruntlike laugh. 'I knew I should have got a personal shopper to select clothes for you and send them to the apartment.'

Keeping the smile on her face and the brightness in her tone, she said, 'Where's the fun in that?'

'You enjoy shopping?'

'Not normally but I've never had an unlimited budget before and I really fancy taking advantage of it. Let's face it, this is an opportunity I'll never have again. Besides,' she added, the darkening of his eyes telling her she'd said the wrong thing, 'you want to be seen with me, remember?'

He gave another grunt in answer and led her to the nearest shop, a designer outlet she'd walked past many times, longing for the day she could afford to do more than ogle the display.

Yearning to see a genuine smile rather than the robotic curving fixture on his face that had hardly met her eyes all morning, she said, 'Do you hate shopping so much that you normally get personal shoppers to buy clothes for your lovers and have them delivered to your home?'

Hand on the shop door, he cast her with a meaningful stare. 'My lovers have their own money.'

The way he said it pulled her up short. 'All of them?'

'All of them. I like my lovers to be financially independent. It means there is no danger of them taking *advantage*—' he stressed the word '—of my bank account, or of me wondering if it's my bank balance they are sharing a bed with.'

Mia had to strain every muscle on her face not to let it crumple. His comment had been too loaded not to have been meant as a warning to her.

'What a horrible, cynical world you live in. No wonder you've had to pay me to be your girlfriend—with that attitude, any rational woman would run a mile from you.'

To her horror, hot tears swelled and stabbed the back of her eyes. The coldness she'd detected in him before she'd gone to bed had carried over to the morning. Although outwardly polite, his tone was clipped, his body language tight, and she had no idea what she'd done to cause it. Not wanting him to see the shimmering tears, she pushed past him and entered the shop. Inside, she took a moment to compose herself, then had to use every acting skill she possessed to turn her face back into the mask of the dewy-eyed, infatuated lover of a billionaire.

A tall, beautiful woman approached them. Naturally, she only had eyes for Damián, who'd silently entered the store a beat after Mia. After establishing she was the manager, the woman whisked Mia off to find the outfits that would transform her from an impoverished actress to a member of the jet-set elite.

The excitement that had bubbled inside her at the thought

of spending hours ogling beautiful clothes and having the once-in-a-lifetime opportunity to try them on and select some for herself had turned to acid.

The clothes that had dazzled her from the outside left her feeling flat and they left the store without her trying anything on. The same thing happened in the next shop. None of the exquisite clothing tempted her. For the first time, she found she couldn't inhabit the role she was playing. All she wanted was to go home.

'What's the matter with you?' Damián asked in an undertone when they left the third shop empty-handed.

'Nothing.' To save herself from further questions, she hurried up the wide steps of a large, world-famous department store. This time, Damián took control of matters.

Approaching a shop assistant, he said, 'My partner would like a selection of outfits.' He explained his requirements and within minutes Mia was being led like a sheep to a changing room so luxurious it wouldn't look out of place in a palace.

She sat on a velvet padded chair to wait for the selections to be brought to her, then jumped back to her feet when the cubicle door opened and Damián appeared.

'Tell me what the matter is,' he demanded through gritted teeth, dark eyes filled with anger.

'*Nothing,*' she spat back in the same low tone he'd adopted.

'Do not lie to me, Mia. It isn't like you to behave like a spoilt brat.'

'No, that's your forte.'

'Do not push me,' he warned.

'Or what?' she hissed. 'You'll dump me?'

His features twisted in anger.

'You hurt me,' she blurted out.

Damián, hating to see the sheen that had appeared in her rapidly blinking eyes, gave an internal curse.

'How?' he asked roughly.

'Don't pretend you don't know. Making out like I'm a gold-digger when you know I only took the job because I thought you were blackmailing me.'

'I did not…' Feeling his temper rise even higher, he cut himself off and dragged his fingers through his hair.

'You *did*. I didn't ask for any of this but I've done everything you've asked of me—I've even lied to my family—and now you're acting as if I'm some greedy cow who needs putting in her place. You might be a noble member of the elite but that does not give you the right to treat me as if I'm less of a person than you.'

He breathed heavily. He didn't know what was causing his chest to constrict so much that getting air into his lungs was an endurance, whether it was her face contorting to stop tears from spilling or the pain lacing her vehemently delivered words.

'I don't think you're less of a person than me,' he eventually bit out.

'You still felt the need to put me in my place though, didn't you? Don't you think your coldness towards me and the fact you flinch every time we touch has spelt out loud and clear that you don't see me as worthy of you? Did you really have to confirm it verbally too?'

'For…' He bit off the curse he wanted to shout and fought to keep his voice to the same venomous whisper they'd conducted the entire conversation in. 'How dare you make me out to be a snob?'

'If the cap fits, wear it. You think you're too good for me. Well, let me tell you something, rich boy. I might be poor but at least I don't judge members of the opposite sex on their net worth before deciding whether they're worth sleeping with, and nor have I ever felt the need to spell out to them why they're unworthy to share my bed.'

This time Damián let the expletives fly free. Damn Mia Caldwell and her beautiful blue eyes and the dignified hurt ringing from them. Damn her for making his tongue reveal things best kept hidden. Damn her for making him feel things he shouldn't.

'I was just being honest,' he said roughly. 'If it came across that I was calling you unworthy then I apologise. That was never my intention...' He swore again and clenched his hands into fists. 'Yes, it damn well was my intention but I wasn't warning you off me—I was warning myself off *you*.'

The damnable beautiful eyes widened.

His body moved before his brain could stop it, taking the one step needed to close the space between them and cup her cheeks in his hands.

'You and I...' Bright colour stained her face. 'Damn it, Mia, every time I touch you or you touch me, my concentration is shot. Don't you see what a dangerous point in my life this is? The Delgado Group has been in my family for three generations and it faces destruction. I stand to lose *everything*. How the hell can I keep my focus when all I can think about is *you*?'

He waited for her to smack his hands away. He waited for her to scream. He waited for her to spit in his face, to do anything that said his touch was unwanted.

But her eyes continued to hold his.

The tips of their noses touched.

'Mia...' Her name fell like a groan from him. 'We are wrong for each other. It could never work. I cannot offer you a future.'

Her lips parted. The tiniest breath escaped from them. It danced over his mouth and slipped into his airwaves.

Back away right now. Let her go. Leave the room.

But he was helpless to heed the warnings in his head. In that moment, all his thoughts and all the heightened feelings rampaging through him were centred round this woman. There was a growing feeling inside him that his entire world could be centred around her…

His mouth dipped to brush against hers. Her eyes closed.

And then the door swung open and they jumped apart to find one of the sales assistants holding a pile of clothing in her arms, a look of utter embarrassment on her face. 'My apologies… I forgot to knock.'

Sucking in a breath at the ache that had formed in his loins, Damián chanced one quick look at Mia. She was holding her cheeks in the exact place he'd just held them. The colour heightening them was the most vivid he'd ever seen.

He took one more deep breath then left the cubicle.

The rest of the day passed in a blur. Mia couldn't remember a single item of clothing she'd chosen. Even the jewellery Damián had bought to complement them was nothing but shadows in her mind.

She had a feeling he'd been in just as big a daze too.

He'd been about to kiss her. And she'd been about to kiss him.

Oh, it was all so confusing. Her feelings were confusing. Making sense of his feelings was confusing. The things he'd said, the way his eyes had turned molten…

The atmosphere in the back of his car on the return journey to his apartment was strained. Heavy traffic meant they were stuck together for almost an hour. Neither of them spoke. Both kept to their own sides, faces turned to the crawling cars outside.

She felt like a tinderbox primed for a match to be struck.

The silence continued in the elevator to the top floor. The chauffeur and concierge came with them, carrying her boxes and bags of purchases: another reminder that Damián was right in saying they were wrong for each other. She'd known it all along but having staff carry her shopping was proof positive that their lives were just too polarised for them to have a future together. Socially, economically and globally, they were on opposite sides of an invisible line. When it came to the most important thing, family, they might as well be of different species.

Why was she even thinking along these lines? She hadn't even considered them having a future until he'd mentioned it.

She didn't want a future with him. Forget all the other reasons why it would never work between them; who wanted a relationship with a man who would always be distrustful of your motivations?

But there was no denying the heated feelings coming close to overwhelming her.

She'd longed for these feelings for so long. James had been her first crush. After him had come Daniel. She hadn't needed to act like a witch to gain Daniel's interest. He'd been her first boyfriend but then her dad had died and their relationship—if you could call holding hands around school and kissing whenever they had a moment of privacy a relationship—had fizzled out. By that point she'd been too caught up in Amy's problems to even think about the opposite sex. By the time she was finally settled in drama school and ready for a relationship she'd become choosy. Dates led to nothing. She'd hated the expectation that a meal together automatically meant ending up in a stranger's bed. What was wrong with waiting to get to know someone first? The longer time had gone and the more disastrous dates she'd endured, the more stubborn she'd become about waiting. What she'd been waiting for she hadn't exactly known but she'd known she was worth more than a quick fling with a stranger.

This feeling of the blood continually whooshing around her body in a torrent and the heavy weight compressing her chest and stomach were what she'd been waiting for, she now realised miserably. A mingling of dread and excitement. A quickening of a pulse. A connection.

To finally have these feelings for the one person in the world she could not have made her want to weep because she *did* want a future. She wanted someone to share her life with.

As Damián had made himself scarce, she sat on her bed and tried to muster the enthusiasm to look through the goodies he'd bought for her. During their shopping trip he'd had some suitcases delivered for her to transport all her new stuff to Monte Cleure in, the cases neatly placed against a wall in her bedroom. She didn't need to examine them to know they were a world-famous designer brand. A fortnight ago she would have squealed with delight to be able to call such fabulous suitcases her own but, as with her new designer wardrobe, she could muster no excitement for them. The horrid feeling of being thought a gold-digger was too raw. The turbulence raging inside her was too strong.

There was a short rap on the semi-open door but she had no time to compose herself before Damián entered the room.

Keeping close to the door, he shoved his hands in his jeans pockets. His chest rose and then fell sharply as his eyes locked onto hers. 'I want to apologise for my behaviour earlier.'

Her heart racing to a canter at the mere sight of him, she swallowed.

'I made a promise not to touch you in private and I broke it. I make no excuses for my deplorable behaviour.'

'A department store's changing room is hardly private,' she muttered, lowering her eyes to the floor so he couldn't see what was in her eyes.

'It will not happen again,' he assured her tautly. 'I give you my word. I apologise too, for implying you are a gold-digger.'

'Good.' She kept her gaze on the floor. 'Because I'm not.'

Damián's throat had closed so tightly it was an effort to say, 'I know.'

And he did know. He'd known even as he'd said it, but he'd wanted to hurt her. To repel her. To reinforce the distance he needed to keep between them.

And then, for those few short minutes in the department store's changing room, he'd lost his head. Never had his control been dismantled like it had been then and he rammed his hands deeper into his pockets to stop them reaching for her again. Would she welcome it? He'd felt the heat radiating off her and seen the look in her eyes...

Dios, his fingers ached to feel her skin beneath them again. His lips tingled to experience the kiss that had never happened.

A lock of her thick blonde hair fell over her bowed face. The urge to sweep it away was almost irresistible.

He breathed in deeply and took a step back. Damián took pride in his word being his bond. To have broken that word once to cradle her face as he'd done had been heinous enough. To break it again would be unforgiveable.

He needed to get out of this room and away from the living temptation that was Mia Caldwell.

He took another step back to the safety of the doorway. She didn't move. The lock of fallen hair still lay over her bowed face. Her dejection tugged at him in a place far different to the place her desirability stirred.

'Mia… I *am* sorry. You were right to say you've done everything I've asked of you. I let my attraction for you get the better of me. I swear I will not let it get the better of me again.'

Her head lifted and her gaze flew to him. What he saw radiating from the bright blue eyes thumped straight through him.

Her voice hardly rose above a whisper. 'What if I want you to let it get the better of you?'

CHAPTER EIGHT

MIA ATE AS much of her Mexican bean stew as she could fit in her tight stomach then pushed her plate to one side. Everything inside her felt tight. Everything except her heart. That was pumping freely, jolting every time she met Damián's stare.

'You don't like it?' he asked in the same conversational tone they'd both adopted since their talk in her bedroom.

'It's lovely. I'm just not very hungry.' Scared he would know why she wasn't hungry, she had a small sip of the Paloma cocktail he'd made for her to complement the food they'd had delivered.

She didn't dare drink too much. Every time she remembered what she'd said in her bedroom she cringed inside. Every time she remembered how he'd stared at her for those long, long moments before turning and walking away, her entire body flushed with humiliation.

She didn't need alcohol to make her tongue run away from her brain. It had proved able to do it all by itself.

Damián had barely touched his drink either.

'Are you going to test me on my villa knowledge tomorrow?' she asked, desperate to fill the developing silence. She couldn't cope with any silence between them. It made her too aware of all the things happening inside her.

'Let's start now. Where is Emiliano's bedroom?'

'East wing. First floor. Last door on the right.'

He bowed his head. 'Very good. What about Celeste's private quarters?'

'Her quarters cover the whole second floor east wing. There's a secret entrance to it through a door in the cellar with stairs that lead up to it.'

'And where's the panic room?'

She had to think hard for this one. 'On the lower ground floor, past the security hub, three doors to the right of the elevator.'

'Two doors to the right,' he corrected, although she detected admiration in his stare. 'I am confident that by tomorrow evening you will be as familiar with the layout as I am. How well prepared do you feel about everything else?'

She shrugged. 'I'm a little nervous about meeting your mum.'

'Celeste is a bitch but hospitality is important to her. She will welcome you.'

She hesitated before saying, 'And Emiliano?'

'His issue is with me, not you. He will treat you with respect.' And if he didn't, Emiliano would answer to him. If *anyone* treated Mia with anything less than respect they would answer to him. If heads needed to be ripped from necks then...

The strength of the sudden protectiveness he felt towards her at these imaginary scenarios shook him. Clenching his hands into fists, he pushed his chair back. He needed distance from her. Rationally, he knew it was the forced intimacy of their situation causing all these heated feelings and wayward thoughts. Being cooped up together with any woman was likely to induce some sense of feeling but when it was a woman as sexy and as beautiful as Mia those feelings would naturally be heightened. It didn't mean anything. It was a pure physical reaction.

But how he wished he could forget her whispered comment. He'd told himself he'd misheard but his ears had not deceived him.

Had her words been an invitation to touch her again? Or had they been hypothetical?

If hypothetical, why say it?

He'd tried hard not to let his gaze focus too much on her that evening but his attention was too tuned in to her that it didn't matter where he rested his eyes. She was always there. He'd gone through his plans again for the weekend, ensuring the tone of his voice was even and professional, but every time she swallowed a bite of her food or a sip of her drink he was aware of it. The awareness was becoming more painful with every passing second.

The times their eyes had locked together…

Those were the moments when the pull between them tugged so hard the truth slapped him hard. All the feelings raging through him were shared. Mia wanted him.

Damn it, he needed to be *focused*. They were going to Monte Cleure in two days. The coming weekend would determine the rest of his life.

But never in his life had he known an ache as powerful as this. His veins burned. His loins burned. His skin felt fevered. His chest kept tightening then blooming wide open in one large pulse.

He got to his feet. 'I've some calls to make and then I'm going to get some sleep.'

She picked her cocktail up but made no attempt to drink it. 'Okay. Well…goodnight.'

'Goodnight, *mi vida*. Sleep well.'

'And you.'

Alone in his office, Damián sat at his desk but, instead of reaching for his phone, he cradled his head. *Dios*, his heart was racing.

A question that had started as a distant whisper had begun repeating itself so loudly he could no longer ignore it.

How the hell was he going to share a bed with Mia for two nights without losing his mind?

Mia had showered. She'd brushed her teeth. She'd brushed her hair. She'd exchanged a dozen messages and played numerous rounds of an online quiz game with her sister. She'd taken three online personality tests since Amy had given up and gone to bed, learned she had the soul of a dolphin, that out of Henry the Eighth's wives she was Catherine of Aragon, and that the best kind of pet for her was a hamster. She'd tried to read her current book but couldn't make it longer than a paragraph before her attention wandered. Intermittently, she'd closed her eyes and tried to sleep but basic tiredness eluded her. She was too wired.

In two nights she would be sharing a bed with Damián.

God help her but the thrumming in her veins at this realisation felt too much like excitement.

Throwing the covers off for the fifth time since going to bed, she decided to get a drink. All this fidgeting and worrying had made her thirsty.

She left her room quietly and, resolutely *not* looking at Damián's bedroom door, tiptoed down the corridor.

In the kitchen she drank some milk and was rinsing the glass out when the strangest sensation ran lightly up her spine.

For the breath of a moment everything inside her stopped functioning.

She placed the clean glass on the drainer and slowly turned.

She stood rooted to the spot, mouth dry, unable to do anything but stare at the magnificence that had appeared like a spectre barely ten feet from her, wearing only a pair of black boxer shorts.

Her insides clenched then melted into molten lava. A sigh escaped her lips.

The clothes she'd always thought enhanced his physique did not do the reality justice. This was a body honed to perfection, hard, muscular and utterly masculine. A light smattering of dark hair covered the navel of his deeply bronzed smooth skin, thickening the lower it went.

Their eyes held. Damián appeared rooted too.

The heat rocketing through her body reached her brain. Her breaths became shallow. A strange weakness had settled in her limbs.

How long they spent like that she could not have said. It could have been seconds. It could have been hours.

She swallowed to clear her constricted throat. 'Sorry... did I wake you?'

He shook his head with the same slowness as when she'd turned to face him.

She swallowed again. 'I should get back to bed.' Did that hoarse voice really belong to her?

He didn't answer. Just continued to stare at her.

Her legs felt so weighted she couldn't have said how she managed to put one foot in front of the other. The closer she got to him the more thunderous was her heart. His eyes did not leave hers.

Four steps from him, he finally blinked and broke the lock ensnaring them. His chest rose. He adjusted his stance so she could pass without their bodies touching.

She took another weighted step. And another. Almost level with him...

A muscular arm suddenly shot out, a large hand pressing against the opposite wall.

Mia stared at the arm blocking her exit, unable to breathe.

MICHELLE SMART   95

She could hear *his* breaths though. Deep. Ragged.

She raised her eyes to his. Saw the deep molten heat swirl. Saw the clenching of his jaw, the flattening of his lips and the flaring of his nostrils. The rise and fall of his chest.

And then the arm lowered. His neck stretched, lips tightened into whiteness, hands fisted into balls. The rise and fall of his chest quickened.

But the lock between them hung suspended.

'Go.'

That one solitary word seemed to be dragged from his throat. His lips barely moved.

Her legs refused to obey. Her eyes refused to break from his.

Damián stood as a statue, not daring to move. The fight against the body that had always served him so well was one he was losing. The vibrations of Mia's skin were like a magnetic charge against his. Her clean scent shrouded him. One wrong move and he risked the danger of them touching.

He should have stayed in his room. He should have stayed in his bed. But he'd heard the gentle movement of her door opening and, like a man possessed, he'd thrown the covers off and followed her.

He wished he could say it had been the short nightshirt she wore that had so captivated him at the kitchen threshold but that would be a lie. He'd have stood rooted if she'd been covered head to toe. It was Mia who captivated him. Everything about her. Her beauty. Her intelligence. Her secrets. He wanted to unwrap it all and open her up to him. He wanted to take possession of her as she had taken possession of him.

Warm fingers tiptoed over his clenched fist, sending a shudder racing through him. His hand loosened under her touch. Tentative fingers laced together.

Her eyes widened. Her throat moved. Their faces drew closer. The vibrations coming from her became a continuous buzz.

The swell of breast brushed against his chest. Had he leaned into her or had she leaned into him…?

Something inside him snapped. With a curse-laden groan he hooked an arm tightly around her slender waist and crushed his mouth to hers. There was a moment of shocked stillness before their closed lips parted like blossoming roses and then he had her pressed against the wall, their mouths fiercely plundering, chest crushed against breast, pelvis against pelvis, all the desire he'd been containing for so long finally unleashed.

Never in Damián's life had he tasted such raw passion as he did in that moment. Mia's arms were wound around his neck, her fingers scraping into his nape and skull, her movements and kisses as urgent as his.

In the dimness of his mind the promise he'd made to her called out. Another broken promise.

He wrenched his mouth from hers and grabbed her wrists from around his neck to press them above her head against the wall. His voice was as ragged as his breaths. 'Mia… *Dios*, I want you. But I gave you my word.'

Her breaths were heavy, her lips plump, eyes dazed. 'I never asked for it,' she croaked before slipping her wrists out of his hold and looping her arms back round his neck to pull him back down for another kiss. The passion and hunger he tasted in it… It was a kiss the like of which he'd never experienced before, more thrillingly electric and sensual than even his deepest fantasies could conjure.

That kiss was the moment he knew he'd lost.

Running a hand roughly down her back, he reached her bottom and dug his fingers into the delectable flesh. *Dios*, but her skin felt like heated satin.

There wasn't a moment of hesitation from her; Mia lifted herself into his arms and wrapped her legs around his waist as effortlessly as if they'd practised the move a thousand times.

Mouths fused together, he carried her to his bedroom, her weight like nothing to him, and half laid, half threw her on the bed. She didn't let go of him, arms and legs tightening as if she were afraid *he* would let go.

Together, they pulled her nightshirt over her head, the cotton fabric discarded, and then their chests were crushed together again, skin against skin. The fever in his flesh deepened.

Never in his life had he wanted to be inside someone as badly as he wanted to be inside Mia, but warring with this was the equally strong need to explore her, to touch and taste every inch and discover all her sensual secrets.

Abandoning her mouth, Damián buried his face in her neck and inhaled the sweet scent of her skin then kissed his way down to her breasts. *Hermosa*, he thought thickly as he covered a puckered pink nipple with his mouth. Beautiful. Perfect.

Mia had fantasised about this many times in unguarded moments but the reality was a thousand times more potent than anything she'd imagined.

Possessively, Damián licked and sucked and bit at her flesh. His hands explored, fingers stroking and kneading. Every movement stoked the inferno inside her.

In her imaginings she'd assumed she'd be inhibited and shy about him seeing her naked but his shameless appreciation and passion overrode her fears. She felt as if she'd been served on a platter for a ravenous Damián to devour and she gloried in it, gloried in the sensations crashing through her, gloried in his unabashed delight in her body and gloried in the urgency of his movements, as if he were afraid she'd be spirited away before he'd tasted every inch of her. The beast beneath the controlled icy façade had been released and it had been unleashed for *her*.

It felt heavenly.

His teeth grazed her hips as they caught hold of her knickers and then he was tugging them down her thighs, exposing the heart of her femininity to him.

Only when he placed his face between her legs and inhaled deeply did she feel a single jolt of uncertainty but his growl of appreciation killed it as quickly as it was born.

She opened herself to him like a budding flower exposed to the brilliant sun and when his tongue found the most potent bud of all she found herself overtaken by the strongest, headiest sensation.

Dear *heaven*.

With a whimper she grabbed hold of the metal bed frame and closed her eyes. Never had she imagined such sensory delights existed. The feelings Damián was evoking were growing in intensity, deeper, stronger, taking her higher and higher until the thrumming pulsations centred in her core erupted and she was flying, soaring and holding onto the brilliant sensations for as long as she could before the inevitable descent back to earth.

Damián was there to catch her.

When she finally opened her eyes, his dark, hooded stare lifted to meet them.

Dazed, she stared back.

Then he gave another growl and gently nipped her belly before licking his way swiftly back up, over her thundering heart and covering her body with his. For the first time she felt the weight of his erection jut against her but there was no time to feel even a frisson of fear because he kissed her so hard and so thoroughly that the tiny part of herself still remaining was lost.

The carnal animal that lived in her had been set free from the imprisonment she hadn't known it was trapped in.

He raised himself onto his elbows and gazed down at her, like a wolf taking one last look at its prey before the proper feast began, and then he kissed her so fiercely all the air was stolen from her before he dragged his mouth over her cheek and whispered something unintelligible in her ear. Only when he reached into his bedside table and produced a small square foil did she realise he'd whispered the word, 'protection'.

Hardly a breath passed her lips between him ripping the foil with his teeth, deftly sheathing himself and then rolling back on her. A large hand slid under her bottom to raise it and then he adjusted himself so his thick, lengthy hardness was right between her legs.

Deep in the recess of her lust-induced daze a voice whispered a warning and she turned her head from the kiss he'd been about to deliver to raggedly whisper into his cheek, 'Be gentle, okay?'

Gentle? Damián had never needed to possess a woman more. This was turning into the most hedonistic experience of his life: not the things they were doing but the feelings consuming him with them.

Never had he wanted to thrust so deeply inside someone. Never had he wanted to crawl into another's skin. Never had his senses been so filled with the essence of another. Mia's taste lay on his tongue, her scent was in every breath he took, her breathy moans echoed in his ears, her fingers burned his skin…

If giving in to his passion for Mia meant he had lost then it was a loss worth taking. How could anything that felt like this be anything but right?

Gripping her hand in his, the fingers of his other hand digging into the flesh of her delicious bottom, he gritted his teeth and carefully inched his way inside her welcoming heat.

And as he groaned with the sheer relief of being so tightly inside her—*Dios*, he'd never known it could be so tight—he heard her suck a sharp breath in.

So deeply under the spell of desire they'd created together was he that it took a beat for his brain to catch up.

A dizzying wave flooded his head, so powerful it took real effort to raise himself onto an elbow so he could look properly at her.

Mia's face was flushed with colour, eyes bright, pupils dilated, lips plump from his kisses. 'Don't stop,' she whispered, her words ragged and breathless, her legs wrapping tightly around his waist as if afraid he would pull out. 'Please. I want this. I want you. Don't stop.'

There was one brief moment when horror at the realisation meant he *would* have pulled out and headed straight into the shower to cool off, but that moment was lost when she cupped the back of his head and pulled him down so her lips could fuse back onto his. The passion and need in that kiss filled him so completely that his greed for her flared instantly back to life.

And he *was* greedy for her, he acknowledged as he clenched his jaw to better control himself. Because as he felt her muscles grip and pull him deeper inside her, and her growing moans of pleasure echoed through him, he could not deny the selfish notion that he was glad no one else had shared this side of her.

Dios. Had anything ever felt so damn *good*?

So *this* was what she'd been put on this earth for, Mia thought dimly as sensation saturated her. One brief moment of distant pain and then *this*. The wonderful things Damián had done to her with his mouth, which she'd thought was the pinnacle of pleasure, had been only the starter. The weight of his body on hers as he drove in and out of her and the feel of his hard thickness inside her had her arching into him, rocking into him, her mouth pressing into his neck, breathing in his scent so the salty muskiness filled her as completely as he did.

She wanted to hold onto this for ever, the sensations *and* the closeness.

Damián's thrusts were becoming more urgent, his groans deeper, and she tightened her hold around him and clung on until the throbbing heat burning so deep inside burst free and she was crying out his name, white-hot, rippling pulsations flooding into every part of her sending her so high that she soared above the stardust. As she floated and stared dazedly down at the stars, her name echoed distantly, a strangled groan from lips buried into her neck and, with great shudders, Damián reached his own climax.

CHAPTER NINE

DAMIÁN LIFTED HIS head to stare into the blue eyes that had captured him before they'd even met. The expression shining from them perfectly matched his own feelings. Drugged. Mia's blonde hair spilled all around her like a silk cloud.

He placed the lightest of kisses to her lips. 'I need to get rid of the condom,' he murmured.

She sighed and dragged her fingers through his hair.

'I'll be right back,' he promised.

For the first time in his life, Damián found his body didn't want to move. Didn't want to break the connection still binding them together.

In the privacy of his bathroom, heart thumping hard, he took a moment to compose himself. He splashed water on his face, patted it dry with a towel and took some deep breaths.

This was for the best, he decided. Making love with Mia. He needed to get these furious feelings for her out of his system before they had to face his family and hunt down the hidden documents.

But when he stepped back into the bedroom and found her sitting upright against the headboard holding the bed-sheets tightly to her chest the thumping in his heart turned to thunder.

Dark colour stained her cheeks. Her voice was husky. 'Do you want me to go to my room?'

He swallowed. 'No.' *Dios*, he needed to touch her again. 'Are you okay?'

She bit her lip. 'I think so.'

'I'm sorry…'

'Don't.' Her hands flew to her burning cheeks. 'Don't apologise. We both wanted it.'

Unbelievably, her words made his blood thicken all over again. 'Why didn't you tell me?'

Her fingers tightened on her cheeks. 'I kind of did.'

He raised a brow, no idea why he found her comment amusing. '"Kind of did"? *Mi vida*, you asked me to be gentle right at the moment. Did you forget to tell me *why* you wanted me to be gentle?'

Now she covered her entire face and groaned. 'I kind of hoped you wouldn't notice.'

'I probably wouldn't have,' he said honestly, climbing onto the bed beside her and pulling her hands off her face to hold them in his. 'I've never bedded a virgin before.'

'Yuck. Bedded? You really do use some strange language.'

'English is not my first language, and you, *mi vida*, are an expert at deflecting.'

'What am I deflecting?'

'Why you didn't tell me you were a virgin.'

'It's not the kind of thing you drop into conversation.'

'True. But that only counts if you're not about to fall into bed with someone.'

'I didn't know I was going to fall into bed with you until it happened.'

That was also true. Neither of them had prepared for it. It had just happened and, for all the self-loathing curdling in his guts at his failure to resist the Mia-shaped temptation, Damián could not bring himself to regret it. 'Are you going to tell me why?'

'I just did...'

'No, *mi vida*, I mean are you going to tell me why you're a twenty-four-year-old virgin? You have to admit, it is a strange thing in the modern world.'

'Don't worry,' she said in a strangely high pitch. 'Just because I've lost my virginity to you does *not* mean I want or expect a ring on my finger.'

'The thought never occurred to me.' At least it hadn't until she said it...

'Good. Because you and I would never work. Not in a million years.'

'And now that we've established that...'

'Re-established it. You're the one who keeps spouting it.'

'Mia...' He sighed. 'Stop being defensive and stop deflecting. I appreciate that you must be feeling...strange... about what we just shared. I am too. I never meant it to happen, you know that, but your virginity changes things. Believe me, I wouldn't care how irresistible you are, I would never have touched you if I knew.'

'Thanks a bunch,' she huffed.

'I do not mean to offend. Waiting as long as you did implies it was something special you were hanging onto.'

'I wasn't hanging onto it,' she clarified quickly. 'I just wasn't prepared to throw it away for some idiot who only wanted a quick fling.'

He put his finger under her chin and forced her to look at him. 'You're beautiful and sexy. Any man would want to bed you, and I'm sure many men have tried, and if you didn't have the history you have, I wouldn't think twice about it.'

Her brow creased. 'What history?'

Now his brow creased, confused at her confusion. 'Your

old drug habit, *mi vida.*' Her eyes widened. The fear he'd detected before shone from them. 'Teenagers who dabble in drugs to the extent that you did usually have lower inhibitions. Sex becomes a commodity...'

'And you know this how?' She twisted her face out of his hold and shuffled back to rest rigidly against the headboard.

'A friend's sister died of a drug overdose when she was a teenager. He set up a charity to help female drug addicts get clean in safe spaces. I've attended many of its fundraisers. So you see, *mi vida,*' he continued, 'I know a lot more about teenage drug abuse and the behaviours attached to it than you might think. I'm not making a judgement call here. I'm just relaying the facts as they have been presented to me.'

Had Amy ever traded sexual favours? This was something that, until that very moment, had never crossed Mia's mind. For many reasons she doubted it, but it was something she would never ask. Seven years on and Amy was happy and content in her life. Why stir the pot by rehashing the past and bringing up all the old pain?

Damián must have seen something of her thoughts on her face for his brows knitted together. 'What are you not telling me?'

She clamped her lips tightly shut.

'You have just shared something incredibly precious with me. Surely you know you can trust me with anything.'

'Do I?' On impulse, she palmed his cheek and stared intently into the obsidian eyes.

In all the time they'd spent together, not once had Damián implied he thought of her as some kind of prostitute. Apart from those early days when their mutual loathing had been like a living entity between them, he'd never made any comment or judgement on her past.

He cupped her face in his hands. 'Talk to me,' he urged, resting his forehead to hers.

How natural it felt to touch like this. And how right.

'I *can't*,' she whispered.

'Why not?'

'It's not my secret to tell.'

He moved his face back a little to gaze more openly at her. A myriad of emotions blazed in the dark depths before he blinked and his features softened. 'It wasn't you, was it?'

Something deep inside her, a tight knot she'd barely been aware of, loosened. She was barely aware of the hot tears filling her eyes either, not until they spilled over and fell onto his hands.

'Your sister?' Damián guessed, and when Mia's whole face crumpled he knew he was right.

Her hands suddenly covered his, her wet eyes stark. 'You can never tell anyone.'

He exhaled a long breath and shook his head, not to deny her but because he understood what it meant to keep things private. Had he not shared things with Mia he'd never dreamed he would share with anyone?

'*Promise* me.'

'I give you my word.'

She closed her eyes and inhaled deeply through her nose. Their hands dropped to rest on her lap, their fingers entwined.

And then she opened her mouth and it all spilled out.

'When Dad died we fell apart. My mum…she suffers with depression, and when Dad died she shut down completely. She was locked away from us. I found solace on the stage. I still don't know how or why that helped but it saved me, but Amy…' She sucked a deep breath in. 'She was only thirteen when he died. We were already worried that she was showing signs of depression like Mum. Dad's death pushed her over the edge and she went completely off the rails.' Her eyes pleaded with him. 'Please, you have to understand—before he died, Amy was the sweetest girl. I'd always been the mouthy one. If you'd put bets on which sister would self-destruct, you would have chosen me.'

Damián gently squeezed her fingers, letting her take a moment to compose herself.

Her throat moved a number of times before she continued. 'She was arrested so many times I lost count. Fighting. Multiple arrests for possession of cannabis. Shoplifting.' She loosened her hand from his and tucked a lock of blonde hair behind her ear. 'About eighteen months after he died, Amy stole a teacher's car and crashed it. No one was hurt but the magistrates at the youth court put an order on her—if Amy was brought before them again for any reason within a year, she would be given a custodial sentence. That was the shock that woke Mum up and it woke Amy up too.'

She tugged her fingers free again to wipe away more tears then looked him in the eye, chin wobbling, biting her lip, swallowing repeatedly. 'She admitted she needed help. She started seeing a grief counsellor and it really *did* help. We started seeing signs of the old Amy. She even dumped her deadbeat boyfriend, which was the best thing she could do because that boy was toxic. Carl was in my year at school and a real nasty piece of work. Anyway, a few months after the magistrates' warning, we walked to school together then split up to go to our classes. I got to the main entrance and I don't know what made me turn around but I did and I saw Amy and Carl standing against a wall having an argument. He had his hand on her arm—it really looked like he was hurting her, so I went straight into Big Sister mode and went charging over but he stormed off before I reached them. Amy wouldn't talk about it and wouldn't let me see her arm. She practically ran away from me.'

For a moment Mia hung her head, lost in a past that still profoundly affected her present.

When she continued, her voice became a whisper. 'We had a school assembly that morning. The head announced that they were going to do a locker search. It was obvious there was something going on. You could feel it.' She swallowed hard. 'I looked at Amy and I saw the panic on her face and I went *cold*. I hadn't paid much attention to it at the time but when she'd run off she was carrying two bags. When we'd left the house she'd only had one. Carl must have given her the other one and I just knew that whatever was in it was bad.'

'You took the bag out of her locker.' He could almost see her doing it.

She nodded. 'I'd stolen her spare locker key when she really started going off the rails so I could check to make sure there was nothing in there that shouldn't be. We were told to line up but I told the softest teacher I knew that I was suffering from women's problems and desperately needed to use the bathroom and she let me go. I was a prefect. She trusted me. I grabbed the bag from Amy's locker but, before I could hide it, the deputy head caught me. There was enough cannabis in that bag to get the whole school high. And scales and deal bags.'

'But surely they must have known it wasn't yours?'

'*Everyone* knew. Even the police knew when they turned up to arrest me. They all knew I was covering for Amy but I stuck to my story and pleaded guilty so there was nothing they could do about it.'

'And your sister let you?' He could hardly compute this monstrous act of selfishness. To allow someone you loved to take the blame and punishment for something you'd done was unforgiveable.

'She wanted to confess but I wouldn't let her. I was just

getting my little sister back and I didn't want to lose her again. She wanted to be fixed. She wanted to make amends and put things right. She was thinking about her future and a career. If I'd let her confess, that would have all been lost. She would have been sent to a young offender institution and her whole life would have been ruined.'

'So she let you ruin yours instead,' he stated flatly.

Her face contorted. '*No.* I insisted. I needed to protect her. I'd learned enough of how the youth courts worked to know I would probably be given a non-custodial sentence and I was right—I was still a minor and had no previous record so I was given a two-year youth rehabilitation order.'

He could hardly believe what she'd just said or the fury that slashed him to hear it. 'You gambled with your freedom on a *probably*?'

'Those drugs were *not* Amy's; they were Carl's. He forced her to take them. The bastard must have heard they were going to do a locker check and tried to frame her, probably because she'd come to her senses and dumped him.'

'All the same, I cannot believe your mother allowed this.'

'You have to understand how ill she'd been. Imagine living in a locked cloud of darkness for eighteen months—that's what it was like for her. She was incredibly fragile. Heaven knows what she would have done if Amy had been sent to prison. I made Mum see that what I was doing was for the best, for everyone.'

'Everyone but you.'

Her features tightened and she shuffled a little further away from him. 'It was the best thing for me too; don't you see that? I'd only just got my mum and sister back and was terrified of losing them again. I knew what I was doing and I would do it again.'

His incredulity almost made his head explode. 'You are not serious.'

'Under the same circumstances, yes, I would.' Her chin jutted, defiance illuminating her beautiful face. 'If Dad hadn't died none of it would have happened. And it's all worked out for the best. Amy qualified as a nurse a few months ago and, with her record, she had to plead her case to be allowed onto the course. If she'd had a custodial sentence it would have been impossible. Her record is something she will have to account for, for the rest of her life.'

'What about your life?' he challenged. 'What about your dream of working on Broadway? You told me yourself that your conviction could prevent you from travelling to America.'

'Amy's mental health is more important than Broadway! And if I did ever make it there I would fall under the spotlight and I can't risk that. We had to move miles away to escape the gossip and pointing fingers, and I don't want to risk people we knew back then being tempted to sell their stories. It doesn't matter whether the press would be allowed to print them or not, social media could see it all being dredged up again. Amy would be dragged into it and then who knows what would happen if her name was splashed everywhere? She's in such a good place now, and Mum is too, and I won't risk their mental health for anything. I *can't.*'

Damián shook his head and tried to control his rapidly rising temper. Or was it despair he was feeling? He didn't know the difference right then, the emotions pushing through him too alien for him to get a handle on. '*Mi vida*, you have the talent and star quality to go as far as your dreams will take you and you're throwing it away.'

'How?' she demanded. 'I have my own home and I'm

making a living doing what I love—how many people can say that?'

'You call that a living? You could be earning a fortune.'

Her defiance blazed as brightly as her fury. 'If being rich means I spend my life cynically doubting the intentions of everyone I meet and being at war with my sibling and having to make an appointment to see my own mother then I'd rather be poor, thank you very much. You can keep your riches and your judgements to yourself.' Jumping off the bed, she picked up her nightshirt and shrugged it over her head.

'What are you doing?'

'Going back to my room.' The blue eyes that had been filled with smouldering desire such a short time ago spat fire at him. 'Goodnight, Mr Delgado. Don't have nightmares.'

She slammed the door shut behind her. A moment later another door slammed.

Mia wrapped herself in the duvet and squeezed her eyes shut, determined not to let any more tears fall.

She'd been an idiot for thinking Damián would understand. The man had been pampered and cosseted his entire life. What would he know about grief? His father had died barely six months ago and, instead of mourning him, he was at war with his brother over who got to run the family business. What would he know about helplessly watching someone you love self-destruct, or the burning need to protect them from themselves? What would he know about depression and the terror evoked by watching someone you love slip further away from you into the darkness?

All Damián knew was how to make money, for himself and the rich people who entrusted their wealth with him. He knew nothing about love and family.

Movement outside her door made her ears prick up and then her door was flung open and Damián's huge looming figure appeared.

'You do not get to run away,' he said harshly.

'Go away.'

'No.'

The bed dipped.

Mia cocooned herself even tighter.

Undeterred, he lay beside her. 'I was not making judgements.'

'Yes, you were.'

For a long time, all she could hear was the heaviness of his breaths and knew he was planning what he was going to say next.

How someone who calculated everything in advance, right down to the words he spoke, could have such passion hidden deep inside him was something she would not have believed if she hadn't experienced it for herself. Just thinking these thoughts was enough for her skin to tingle. She squeezed her thighs tight, trying to fight the quivers now sweeping into her abdomen. How could she still feel such desire for someone so cold?

But he hadn't been cold when they'd been…

And his voice didn't sound cold when he said, 'If I was making judgements it was because I was trying to understand why you did something you knew would affect the rest of your life, and to your detriment.'

'You said I could trust you.'

'I gave my word not to speak about it unless you brought the subject up. I did not give my word to keep my opinions to myself. You would rather I keep silent?'

'It's done. It's in the past. Your opinions don't change anything.'

'That does not stop me from having them. And you have

opinions too. I don't remember going off in a mood when you called my family life a soap opera.'

He had her there. Damn him. And, she had to admit, hearing him be so vocal in his outrage on her behalf had warmed her in a way she couldn't explain.

She couldn't remember the last time anyone had cared about her wellbeing and future, not like that. Her mum and Amy loved her. They cared for her. But they didn't look out for her. With a stab, she realised it was because she never gave them reason to think they needed to. It was her job to look out for them.

Sighing, she loosened the duvet a little to stop herself suffocating. 'I'm sorry for shouting at you. I think... I'm very protective of my family.'

'I've gathered that,' he responded dryly.

She turned her face to his. One look into the obsidian depths and her heart swelled. 'And I'm feeling a little overwhelmed by us...'

'Making love?' he supplied, his eyes crinkling. He tugged at the duvet, loosening it a little more.

Was that what it had been? Making love?

It had felt like making love. It had felt... It had been... wonderful.

'I guess I never expected my first time to be with someone there's not a cat in hell's chance of having a future with,' she said.

He tugged some more at the duvet. 'I thought you had no regrets?'

'I don't.' She turned her face away to stare at the ceiling. 'I guess I never thought I would feel so different.'

'Different how?'

'I don't know. Just different.'

'Good different or bad different?'

'I don't know.' His hand finally burrowed its way beneath the cocooning duvet and rested on her belly. The tingles that had been building up again in her deepened and thickened. She squeezed her eyes shut but that had zero effect on halting the growing sensations.

He brought his mouth to her ear. His voice was caressing, the warmth of his breath swirling deliciously against her sensitised skin. 'If you want me to apologise for not understanding why you willingly admitted to a crime that was not yours then I will apologise.'

'Don't apologise for something you don't mean.'

He kissed the lobe of her ear. 'Not even if it stops you being cross with me?'

'You're just trying to get back in my good books so I don't mess the weekend up.'

For such a large man he was surprisingly agile, rolling on top of her before she had time to hitch a breath. He stared at her with a hungry, wolfish expression. 'No, *mi vida*,' he murmured. 'I'm trying to get back in your good books because I want to kiss your breasts again.'

She tried to glare at him but it was impossible. *He* was impossible.

And then, when he kissed his way down her neck and his mouth found her breasts again, she closed her eyes and sank again into the heady feelings his touch alone evoked in her, as impossible as it should be.

CHAPTER TEN

MONTE CLEURE, THE tiny principality beloved of the rich and famous, was so much more than Mia had imagined. Driving through its pristine streets was a voyage of discovery on how the superrich lived. The shops and cafés and the people bustling through them, all glittering under the weight of gold and diamonds, made Bond Street look downmarket. Even the pocket-sized dogs being walked sparkled in their diamond-encrusted collars. The Mediterranean gleamed under the blazing sun, but not as brightly as the supersized yachts that filled the harbour. For such a small country, everything about it was supersized. Apart from the dogs.

A short drive through verdant countryside and then Damián murmured, 'There it is.'

She squinted. And then her mouth dropped open.

Mostly hidden through the thick trees, her first glimpse of the villa. Having studied it so thoroughly, she'd assumed she knew what to expect. All the pictures and videos in the world could not do it justice. For something that was only thirty-odd years old, it stood like a proud Spanish castle from a bygone age.

Soon the trees thinned and huge iron gates lay before them. And a dozen paparazzo lining the road.

'Turn to me,' Damián murmured, squeezing her hand.

Their hands had been locked the entire journey, from the moment they'd left his apartment.

She did as he said and rested her head on his shoulder, which was no hardship at all. When he wrapped his huge arm around her, she sighed and burrowed her cheek deeper into him, happily breathing in his gorgeous scent.

When he'd thought she would welcome the exposure of being seen on his arm he'd arranged for a car without tinted windows to collect them. He'd since had that replaced with a car with windows that were as dark as they could legally get away with. When the party started tomorrow they wouldn't leave so they could return and make a grand entrance in front of the press. They would stay in the villa. The press were forbidden from passing the iron gates. She would be free from the cameras' lenses.

Gravel crunched beneath the tyres and Mia found her eyes so glued to the villa that the vineyards and olive groves they passed barely registered.

Painted a pale yellow with a terracotta roof, the villa, which had twenty-one luxury suites, was shaped like a squared-off horseshoe with arches and pillars galore. Peeking through the dense perimeter of trees were the terracotta roofs of the adjoining buildings.

As they crawled through landscaped gardens, her heart soared at the abundance of colourful flowers, beautiful fountains and statues all melding together.

The car came to a stop.

'Are you ready for this?' Damián asked.

She met his gaze, swallowed and nodded, but inside she quailed. How was she supposed to pull this off, even if she was wearing an outfit that cost more than her monthly mortgage payment?

Until that moment, Damián's wealth had been too fantastical to be real. The billions he was worth had been mere numbers. Even his apartment, which screamed money, had been just an apartment. This was a whole different ball park that no amount of poring over blueprints and watching videos could have prepared her for. This was the kind of home royalty might live in. There was no doubting that today a prince of the Delgado family had brought a peasant home with him to meet the queen.

Damián saw the fear flit over her face and squeezed her hand again. 'You have nothing to be frightened of, *mi vida*,' he promised softly. 'My family are made of flesh and bone, just as you are.'

Her throat moved before the tightness of her features softened and a smile curved her lips. 'You won't leave me, will you?'

He brought her hand to his lips and grazed a kiss across the knuckles. 'I won't let you out of my sight.'

If Mia's hand hadn't been gripping his so tightly Damián would have believed her nonchalance to be real as they walked up the steps to the villa's main entrance.

Didier, the butler who'd worked for his parents since the villa had been built, greeted them in the reception room. After introductions had been made, he said, 'Your mother is on a call. She will join you for lunch.'

'When will that be?'

Didier looked at his watch. 'In one hour and sixteen minutes. It will be served by the pool.'

'Good. That gives us time to freshen up. Is my brother here yet?'

'He arrived an hour ago. I believe he's in his suite.'

'Have our cases been taken to my suite?'

'Yes, sir. Can I get you any refreshment?'

'A coffee would be great.' He turned to Mia. 'Drink?'

'I'd love a cup of tea, thank you.'

'Have them brought to my suite,' Damián said.

'Very good, sir.'

'Oh, and Didier…?'

'Yes, sir?'

'It's good to see you looking so well.'

For the briefest of moments the elderly butler's austere façade cracked and the widest smile flashed across his face. 'Thank you, sir. Likewise.'

'What was that all about?' Mia whispered as they walked across the reception room.

'What was what about?'

'You and the butler.'

'I don't know what you're talking about.'

She elbowed him in the ribs. 'Yes, you do.'

He grinned. Considering he'd been looking forward to this weekend as much as he'd looked forward to his childhood immunisations, he could hardly believe he was smiling within minutes of his arrival. That was Mia's doing, he recognised. Her natural exuberance and free-spirited air cut through the stiffness of his life. They'd only been lovers a few days but he felt a different man to the one he'd been before he'd met her.

'He's the friend you mentioned, isn't he?'

The friend who'd obtained the external surveillance footage of Emiliano. Not in the least surprised that Mia had put two and two together so quickly, Damián nodded.

'Then why the formality?' she asked.

'Because that is what is expected under this roof…' His words—and smile—came to a sudden halt when they reached the top of the wide, cantilevered stairs and he caught a glimpse of a figure at the end of the east wing corridor.

Across the vast distance, Damián met the baleful stare of the brother he hadn't seen since their father's funeral and with whom he'd not exchanged a word in a decade. Then, like an apparition, Emiliano disappeared into his suite.

'Damián?'

Loosening his clenched jaw, he returned his attention to the woman who was there to help him save his business. And then he found he didn't need to try and loosen his features for her benefit because they loosened for themselves...apart from a certain part of his anatomy which tightened in an adolescent regression.

'Was that Emiliano?' she asked.

'*Si.*'

She smiled. 'That explains why you were trying to break my fingers.'

To his horror, Damián realised he'd squeezed her hand much tighter than was healthy. Hurriedly bringing it to his mouth, he kissed each precious finger. 'I'm sorry, *mi vida.*'

She palmed his cheek and pressed closer him, eyes gleaming with temptation. 'Relax, Señor Delgado,' she murmured. 'We are here for a weekend of fun and frolics, remember?'

'Frolics?' He arched a brow, releasing her hand so he could cup her bottom and pull her closer. 'What are frolics?'

Rising to her toes, she placed her mouth to his ear. 'Take me to your suite and I'll show you.'

Compared to the lovemaking they'd shared over the past two days, this time was short but every bit as passionate and fulfilling. Damián had kicked the door shut behind them and then, before Mia had even had a chance to take stock of his suite, they were tearing each other's clothes off.

Now, catching her breath while she watched her naked lover stride across the beautifully ornate marble floor to the bathroom, Mia blew him a kiss before he disappeared behind the door, then cast her gaze around.

She felt like a princess. The whole villa took her breath away. Damián's room followed the Renaissance theme, blended with modern touches like the rest of the villa. His divan bed, which was the size of Mia's whole bedroom, had a dark brown leather headboard and, a couple of feet from its base, a large leather sofa and a beautiful curved marble-topped table. In the far corner of the room, next to another door, sat a baby grand piano. Heavy drapes covered the three French windows across the left side. The artwork that gracefully adorned the suite was eclectic and totally fitting, the suite as elegant and masculine as the man who inhabited it.

'Do you play the piano?' she asked when a freshly showered Damián returned from the bathroom, disappointingly wearing a towel around his waist.

He pulled a face. 'I had lessons at Celeste's insistence. I think it was her first real lesson in money not being able to buy you everything—in this case, it couldn't buy me a musical ear. I was useless at it.'

'I can't imagine you being useless at anything.'

He winked. 'I assure you, the piano is the only thing I have failed to master.'

She threw a pillow at him. It landed dismally short of its target.

He picked it up and stalked over to the bed. 'I assume you failed to master the art of throwing things?'

'I mastered throwing tantrums, if that counts?'

The grin he flashed could have melted a glacier. Placing the pillow on the bed, he leaned over and hungrily took a nipple in his mouth.

Spent though she'd thought herself to be, his touch sent darts of need spearing through her.

His hand dragged down her belly to her pubis. Gently, he rubbed his thumb over her already swollen bud.

Moaning her pleasure, she groped wildly for his towel and tugged it off. His erection jutted huge and proud before her, but before she could reach out to touch it—he'd shown her during their long bouts of lovemaking just how he liked to be touched—he gave a mock growl and backed away.

Stretching her body as seductively as she could, she waggled a finger at him. 'Don't you want to come back to bed?'

His eyes darkened but his face became stern. 'Move. We are expected for lunch in…' he checked his watch '…twenty-eight minutes. It'll take us ten minutes to get to the pool.'

Pulling a face, Mia got grudgingly off the bed and pretended to strop to the bathroom.

Damián was already dressed, wearing chinos and a grey V-neck T-shirt that covered his muscular frame like a dream when she returned from her shower, and he was waving something that looked like a mobile phone without any buttons around the room.

'What are you doing?' she asked, bemused.

He didn't look at her. 'Searching for bugs.'

'When you say bugs…you don't mean six-legged creatures, do you?'

He shook his head. When he finally looked at her his expression was grim. 'I should have done it as soon as we got here.'

Damián was ready to kick himself. Of all the foolish schoolboy errors he could have made, this was up there with the worst.

But that was exactly why he'd made a schoolboy error—because he'd been thinking like an adolescent and using the brain that wasn't in his head. He hadn't behaved like that even when he'd been an adolescent.

Not only had he failed to check for bugs but he'd forgotten to link his laptop to the villa's security system and now he would have to wait until after lunch to do that because there was no time. Precious hours would be wasted.

The woman who was the cause of his adolescent urges stared at him with wide eyes and tightened the towel she'd wrapped around her. 'Has someone been listening to us?' Horror reflected back at him. 'Or watching us?'

'No. The room's clean. But I should have checked before we christened the bed.'

'Can you trust that thing you're using?'

'Felipe Lorenzi, my security expert, gave it to me. All his equipment is the latest and most sophisticated technology. There is not a bug out there that this cannot detect.'

She blew out a sigh of relief but then doubt clouded her features. 'What if there are bugs when we go searching?'

'I told you before, I have jamming equipment, but I don't expect there to be bugs anywhere in the villa. I know it must look a palace to your eyes but it's a home. Why would Celeste spy on herself?'

'How would I know? She's your mother, not mine.' She tugged at her damp hair. 'I should get dressed. What should I wear?'

'Something casual. Your stuff's been unpacked in the dressing room.'

She went through the door he directed her to, leaving Damián a few minutes alone to compose himself.

So much for making love to Mia getting his crazy hunger for her out of his system.

Damn it, if he hadn't succumbed to her succulent temptation, his focus would have been as clear and crisp as it always was.

At least he wouldn't have to fake his passion for her when they were with his family. They'd been lovers for only two days and already he couldn't keep his hands off her.

Mia held tightly onto Damian's hand as they stepped onto the most pristine, ornate, sprawling terrace she'd ever seen.

A huge rectangular swimming pool beckoned. Laid around it at regular intervals were dozens of sunbeds, each with its own parasol. To the left of the pool and up some wide steps was the outdoor dining area. Six people were sitting around a table. All of them turned their faces as they approached.

An elegant slender woman of indeterminate age with white-blonde hair scraped in a tight bun and whose facially delicate bone structure reminded Mia of a bird, rose to her feet. She was wearing a flowing dark blue sarong dress, her feet bare.

'Mijito,' she purred in greeting. Her face curved into something Mia supposed was meant to be a smile and then she said something in rapid-fire Spanish that she didn't understand but which made Damián's features tighten as he fired something back before pausing, exchanging air-kisses and then taking back hold of Mia's hand and switching to English.

'Celeste, I would like you to meet Mia.'

Obsidian eyes, the only physical resemblance to Celeste's youngest son, fixed on Mia. Something reflecting in them made a shiver run down her spine. It wasn't quite coldness she detected, but a definite coolness. Scrutinising.

Whatever was going on behind the almost beautiful bird-like head, Celeste bestowed her with a smile far friendlier than the one she'd given her son and wafted over to place a kiss on each of Mia's cheeks. Her gracious welcome was only marred by her failure to allow a millimetre of their skin to make contact.

'Delighted to meet you,' she said. Her English was as impeccable as Damián's. 'Let me introduce you to everyone.'

One by one, those seated—Celeste's sister, brother-in-law, two nieces and older son—got to their feet to place dutiful air kisses against Mia's cheeks. The only person whose lips made contact with her skin was Emiliano. As lean and wiry as his brother was broad and muscular, his colouring was a touch lighter, his hair a few shades lighter on the spectrum and his eyes lighter too, although they had Damián's sharp intensity.

'So you're the mystery woman,' he murmured, his voice a lazy drawl. 'Let's hope Damián treats you better than he does the other people he's supposed to love.'

Mia caught Damián's eye. The clenching of his jaw told her his brother's jibe had hit exactly where intended.

'Emiliano, do something about these dogs,' Celeste suddenly snapped.

Until that moment, Mia hadn't noticed the beautiful golden retriever and another smaller dog that looked like it was a variety of breeds. The smaller dog had its teeth in Celeste's sarong and was tugging hard at it, growling.

Emiliano strolled back to his seat, nonchalantly sat back down, winked at Mia, and then finally whistled through his teeth. The dog immediately dropped the sarong and trotted obediently back to its master.

To give Celeste her due, she recovered admirably. She retook her seat and patted the chair beside her, beckoning Mia.

She dropped into it as obediently as the dog had obeyed Emiliano.

Celeste smiled her approval. 'What would you like to drink?'

'Do you have tea?'

A tinkle of laughter. 'Surely a glass of champagne is in order?' She indicated for one of the staff hovering a discreet distance away to open the bottle that was sitting on ice beside her. 'It has been many years since my son has introduced us to one of his lady friends.'

Smiling widely, Mia said, 'Champagne sounds lovely, but I think I'll be better off sticking to soft drinks.'

The clever dark eyes narrowed. 'You're not pregnant, are you?'

'No!' Her denial came out like a bark before she could hold it back and modulate it. For some reason, the beaky lips twitched, which in turn made Mia giggle. 'I'm sorry. No, I'm definitely not pregnant. I just find that drinking alcohol during the day makes me sleepy.'

Celeste waved a dismissive hand. 'So it makes you sleepy? So what? Treat your weekend here as a mini-break. Did Damián tell you I have a spa?'

Mia had studied the villa's blueprints and internal videos so thoroughly she knew exactly where the spa and adjoining beauty rooms were located. 'I think he mentioned it.'

'You *must* use it,' she urged. 'I employ a full-time masseuse. She is the *best*. I have a beautician and hairdresser too, so do make use of them.' Her nose wrinkled, her voice dropping to a conspiratorial level. 'I will tell Gaynor to do something with your hair for tomorrow's party.'

Quite certain she'd been insulted, Mia fought back another giggle. At least Damián had warned her of his mother's bitchy tendencies. 'That sounds wonderful, thank you.'

The champagne opened and poured, Celeste thrust a flute in Mia's hand, cast her eyes around the table for everyone's attention, then raised her own flute. *'Salud!'*

Mutters of *'Salud'* rang out obediently.

Lunch passed at a glacial pace. Fresh fish and salad dishes were served and heartily consumed by the men and picked at by the ladies, apart from Mia who was starving. Celeste held court over the conversation, directing most of it at Mia. 'You *must* tell me, where did you two meet?'

'Damián came to a show I was performing in.'

'Oh, yes, that's right—you're an actress!' Celeste raised her glass to Damián. 'So you've learned there's more to life than numbers and spreadsheets? Congratulations, *mijito*.' She turned back to Mia. 'What show was it?'

'*My Fair Lady.*'

'Did you play Eliza?' At Mia's answering nod, Celeste clutched her chest dramatically. 'No one can better Audrey in that role. I'm sure you were very good too, but Audrey was a goddess. What other roles have you played?'

Stifling another urge to laugh, Mia listed the few professional roles she'd undertaken. Celeste had seen them all, and all the characters had been played by actors who 'illuminated the stage'. Although she was sure Mia was very good too.

The torture seemed to go on for ever, but then, when the last of the dishes had been cleared away, Celeste's phone beeped and she rose to her feet. 'I've booked us a table in the restaurant at the casino for nine o'clock.'

'Which one?' Emiliano asked. They were the first words he'd spoken since their introduction, although a secretive amused smile had played on his lips in the times when he hadn't been sending darts of loathing in his brother's direction.

'The one at the Carlucci. Everyone be ready for eight-thirty. I have appointments so do not disturb me before then.' Then she leaned forward to pinch Mia's cheek. 'You are *adorable*. I will tell Gaynor to expect you in an hour for your first treatment.'

She swished away, leaving a cloud of silence behind her.

Emiliano was the first to break it. 'Well, that was fun,' he commented wryly. Rocking to his feet, he patted his thigh and the dogs burst out from under the table. Saluting at the table in general and throwing another wink at Mia, he strode away, his happy hounds at his side.

to press the keys, her gaze landed on his ring finger. Was that why it appeared pale? Because he'd once worn a wedding band? The thought that Damián had once been married made her heart beat too fast. Had he loved his wife deeply? Where was she now? She wanted to ask so many questions.

But she couldn't. Not without revealing how much she thought about him. And Damián had made it clear that their relationship was merely a charade.

Closing the door behind her, she walked down the hallway. Her heart thumped in her chest as she thought...

CHAPTER ELEVEN

'WHERE, EXACTLY, IS the cubbyhole?' Mia asked when they walked back into Damián's suite. Celeste wasn't to know but her insistence that Mia have spa treatments had been a gift.

According to Damián, there were a dozen secret cubbyholes located throughout the villa. The documents could be in any of them. Or they could be in Emiliano's room. Or... In all honesty, they could be anywhere, which made their task seem daunting, but Damián had shortlisted the most likely places. The spa's cubbyhole was near the top of the shortlist. Emiliano took full advantage of the spa whenever he was at the villa.

'It's behind the towel cupboard on the right side of the door,' Damián said as he unlocked his bureau and removed the black case containing his spyware. He carried it to the marble table, sat on the sofa and put the combination in. 'The cupboard isn't fixed but it's heavy.' He lifted his gaze to her and stared for a moment before pinching the bridge of his nose. 'It might be better for me to look in that one.'

'I'm stronger than I look,' she said lightly. 'Besides, you'll only draw attention to yourself if you book in for a massage.' Damián had never used the spa.

He held her gaze for another moment before nodding and looking back at the laptop. As soon as his fingers began tapping at the keyboard, Mia quietly got on with changing into a bikini in preparation for her task and kept quiet while he worked. This was the moment when they discovered if the instructions he'd been given by his security expert to hack into the villa's security system worked.

She had donned her bikini and monogramed Delgado robe, which had been left in clear wrapping in the bathroom for her, when Damián suddenly punched the air.

'You're in?'

He met her stare and smiled, relief writ large on his face.

She sat beside him and found herself staring at a split screen, one side showing the corridors of the spa area, the other the corridors outside their own suite. She hardly had time to blink before Damián showed her the images from the other cameras placed throughout the villa. The only people to be seen were staff.

'You're sure there aren't any cameras or bugs in the rooms themselves?' she asked.

'I'm positive. Celeste has never liked them being in the corridors but accepts it as a necessary evil.' Damián caught the way Mia was chewing her bottom lip and recognised her anxiety.

'I have a spare detector.' He reached into the case and removed it for her. Now that they were here and their task had become real, he would not take any chances. Not with Mia. There was no danger for either of them if they were caught. The worst that would happen would be Celeste banishing them. And yet…

The thought of Mia being cornered made his guts cramp.

'Take it with you,' he ordered. 'When you're alone, cover the surfaces with it like you saw me doing earlier. If there's anything there, it will flash.' He plucked out the diamond stud earrings from the case and handed them to her. When she'd put them on and he'd put the microphone cufflinks on, he sent her to the bathroom. 'Close the door behind you,' he instructed.

When the door was closed, he whispered, 'Can you hear me?'

The door burst back open and, a beaming smile on her face, Mia came charging back out. 'Yes!'

The hunt for the missing documents got off to a dismal start. Mia's beauty treatments had been great but she'd been unable to relax properly, waiting for the call Damián had promised would come, which would see the beautician excuse herself long enough for Mia to search the hidden cubbyhole. When the call had come, a huge burst of adrenaline had shot through her and she'd sprung into action. Damián had watched the surveillance cameras outside the rooms on his laptop, his voice constantly in her ear. But the cubbyhole had been empty.

Never mind, she thought with a sigh as she paced the suite while waiting for him to finish shaving; tomorrow the villa would be packed with hundreds of staff setting up for the party and they would be able to search properly, hidden in plain sight.

It would be the last full day they spent together but it would be spent surrounded by people, with little time to be alone. As lovers, this was their last real day together.

Needing a distraction from the surge of fierce panic this thought induced, she shakily picked up a framed photo on the piano that had caught her eye earlier. It was a picture of Damián and his father.

Eduardo Delgado looked exactly as she imagined Damián would in forty years: a handsome silver fox, a man who would always command attention.

The bathroom door opened and Damián stepped out, neck and jaw shaved, goatee trimmed, and as sexy as she'd ever seen him. 'Shouldn't you be getting dressed…? What are you looking at?'

Knowing there was no time to make love before they left for the evening, Mia contented herself with leaning into him and filling her lungs with his scent before handing him the photo.

He smiled sadly and rubbed his thumb over his father's face. 'This is my favourite picture of us.'

'You look so much like him.' She looked again at it. 'It's strange but I can't see anything of Emiliano in him.'

His brows drew together in obvious surprise. 'Emiliano wasn't his biological child.'

That took her aback. 'Seriously?'

'Didn't it come up in any of your searches?'

'I only searched your name.' And she'd been too greedy to learn everything about Damián to do more than give a cursory glance at any information not directly concerning him.

'My father adopted him when he married Celeste. His father was an Argentinian polo player called Alessandro. Celeste married him when she was twenty but he died in a freak horse accident when Emiliano was a few months old. Celeste married my father a year after that.'

'How come you've never mentioned it? You always refer to him as your brother, never your half-brother.'

'Because I never think about it like that. To me, he is my brother.' His tone became grim. 'He thinks differently though. He's always hated me.'

'Always?'

He gave a tight nod.

'But why?'

'I think Emiliano resented me for being Father's biological child, which is ludicrous because when we were growing up he was as distant and remote with me as he was with Emiliano. It's just the way Father was. If anyone should be resentful it's me—Celeste never denied loving Emiliano more than me.'

Mia blanched. 'Please tell me you're joking.'

His head shook slowly. Grimly. 'Celeste is never anything less than honest. Brutally so. Alessandro was the love of her life. When he died she poured that love into Emiliano. He's the reason she married my father.'

'Your father knew that?'

'Neither of my parents married for love. My father was a bachelor until he was forty-five because he was wary of gold-diggers. Trust me, there are many of them around. Celeste comes from an old, noble Spanish family with great wealth. Her upbringing was very strict and controlled. When Alessandro died, her parents wanted her back under their roof but she'd had a taste of freedom and refused. As I'm sure you've seen for yourself, Celeste is not a passive woman and despises being pigeonholed by her sex. She knew she would never love another man but she wanted a father for Emiliano and a husband who would give her freedom and treat her as his equal, and that's what my father offered her. She never hid her reasons for marrying him, just as Father never hid his reasons for marrying her—he wanted someone with breeding, independent wealth and proven fertility. My father took great care in his selection of a wife and Celeste took great care in her selection of husband number two. Their marriage worked. They were a formidable team.'

'Is that what you want in a wife?' she asked softly.

He shrugged. 'I don't care about breeding. That's an outdated notion. But I do want a wife with independent wealth and intelligence.'

To cover the heavy weight in her heart his honesty provoked, Mia adopted an airy tone. 'I suppose someone wealthy but dim would bore you.'

His eyes actually crinkled with amusement. 'God forbid I marry someone who bores me.'

What did she expect? she thought as she gazed into his eyes and tried not to let her sudden despondency show. A marriage built on love and passion was not for a man with Damián Delgado's upbringing.

Frightened of the wrenching in her heart at the knowledge that the most a woman like her could hope for from a man like him was something akin to mistress status, she found herself needing to fill the growing silence.

'Have you ever spoken to Emiliano about his issues with you?'

'It's not easy to speak to someone who looks at you as if you're something they've trodden on.'

'I know that feeling. That's how Amy used to look at me when she was going through her destructive phase.'

'That's how he's looked at me since I was old enough to form memories.'

'It's never too late,' she said softly. 'Maybe you should think about forcing him to talk and open up about why he hates you. It's too simplistic to blame it on biology. Talking with him might pave the way to you two making an agreement about the business, especially if we don't find the documents.'

'We will find them.'

'Even so…'

His stare became shrewd. '*If* I were to talk to him, would you be prepared to sit down with your mother and sister and talk to them?'

'What for?' she asked, thrown by the question.

'About the fact that you're still paying the price for the sacrifice you made all those years ago.'

She tried not to bristle. 'I'm not.'

'Yes, you are. The world could be yours if you allowed yourself to reach for it. From what you tell me, your sister and your mother have both found happiness. Would they not want that for you too?'

Happiness? That was something Mia hadn't felt in a long time. Not true happiness of the kind when you woke in the morning and sunshine blazed in your heart regardless of the weather outside. The kind of happiness she'd found these past days with Damián...

'They already think I'm happy,' she whispered while her heart made another huge wrench.

'Are you?'

I'm happy with you. Happier than I have ever been.

She closed her eyes to stop his astute gaze from reading them. 'It's always there in the back of my mind, what we went through. When I see them, when I speak to them... it always feels like I'm performing, keeping up the happy face.'

She never had to perform for Damián, she realised. With him, she was never anything but entirely herself. Until she'd been pulled into his world, she hadn't known how much she wanted someone to see *her* and not the roles she played or the happy face she displayed to her family.

'You are scared it will upset them to see you as vulnerable?'

Damián had seen her vulnerable. He'd seen her angry. He'd seen her scared. In the short time they'd been together, he'd seen all the components that made her Mia, the good and the bad.

'Something like that.' She met his stare. 'When Mum saw the damp on my walls I was so worried that she'd start worrying that I made a big joke about buying a hazmat. I could never tell her about the times I was terrified I wouldn't meet my mortgage payments. I never tell them anything that could make them worry.'

And yet she could tell this stuff to Damián. She could tell him anything.

He gently smoothed a stray strand of her hair off her forehead. 'If you're always looking after them and protecting them, who's out there looking after you?'

She wished his question didn't make her want to cry. 'I'm a big girl. I look after myself.'

'You should talk to them, *mi vida*. If they love you as much as you love them, they will want to support you as you have supported them.'

She rested a hand against his freshly smooth cheek. 'I'll talk to them if you'll talk to Emiliano.'

'Let's see how tomorrow unfolds.' He looked at his watch. 'You should get dressed. We leave for dinner in fifteen minutes.'

'I'll be ready in five,' she promised.

Mia thought she'd never felt as glamorous as she did in her glorious red dress which swept over one shoulder and ruched beneath the other, cinching at the waist and falling gracefully to mid-calf. She'd definitely never been anywhere as glamorous as the Carlucci. And never in her entire life had she dreamed she would watch people gamble thousands of euros on the spin of a ball or the turn of a card, give a nonchalant shrug when they lost and then gamble thousands more on the next game.

The evening had started off awkwardly, with Celeste insisting everyone travel to the hotel casino in her stretch limo. Making Damián and Emiliano share a confined space was, in Mia's opinion, asking for trouble. However, Celeste ignored the frostiness in her own inimitable way, enthusing over Mia's much improved appearance at the hands of her beautician and admiring her dress, which was, 'Just like one I had when the boys were small. You do carry if off well, even though your waist is thicker than mine was back then.'

How small had Celeste's waist been? The size of a baby courgette?

A critical eye had then passed over Mia's obviously too-thick waist before Celeste had encouragingly said, 'I will put you in touch with my personal trainer. Two hours of yoga a day will soon knock that puppy fat off you.'

Damián had immediately come to her defence. 'Mia is perfect as she is,' he'd said in a voice that made even Mia quail.

Celeste had laughed. 'No one is perfect, *mijito*. Not without work.'

Damián had replied to this in their native language. Whatever he'd said to his mother did the trick for she'd kept her mouth shut for the rest of the journey, with the expression of someone sucking a particularly sour lemon.

By the time they'd taken their seats for dinner, Celeste had forgotten to be cross with Damián and held court in the same manner she had over lunch. Mercifully, Mia was seated between Damián and one of his cousins so was saved from Celeste's attention. Less mercifully, she sat opposite Emiliano, so spent much of the meal trying not to flinch at the appraising glances he kept throwing at her and the daggers he kept throwing his brother.

Where Damián reminded her of a panther, Emiliano brought to mind a cheetah: sitting there, saying nothing, simply biding his time until he pounced. She didn't need to know the brothers' history to guess it would be Damián's jugular he'd aim for.

If Damián was bothered by his brother's coldness, he didn't show it. But then, after a lifetime, he would be used to it.

Mia shivered. She would die if Amy ever showed such coldness to her again. And she would die if her mum were to say, however nonchalantly, that she loved Amy more than her.

The one thing she was looking forward to after this weekend was never having to see or speak to Celeste again. She just could not comprehend the casual cruelty of telling your own child you loved their sibling more. It made her want to weep for Damián and the small boy he'd once been. No wonder he was so cynical.

Money really did not buy happiness.

And then the meal had finished and everyone split up to see who could blow the most of their fortune in one night. Damián placed a hand in the small of her back and gave her a tour of the casino and a brief rundown on how each game was played.

After ordering drinks for them both from a passing waiter, he said, 'I'm going to play poker. Do you want to join in?'

'I'm happy to watch.'

He dug his wallet out of his back pocket and pulled out a wad of fifty-euro notes. 'In case you change your mind. Let me know if you run out.'

Despite the amiable words, Mia detected a frostiness in his voice. There was the tell-tale tightness of his jaw. Damián was angry about something. She'd felt it since their meal had finished. 'Are you okay?'

'Yes.' He tried to press the cash into her hand.

'I don't want it.' She didn't need money. She didn't want to gamble and drinks in the casino were free.

He shrugged and put the notes back in his wallet. 'Suit yourself. I will be at one of the poker tables if you need me.' And then, first pressing a hard, possessive kiss to her lips, he strode away, snatching his glass of Scotch from the returning waiter as he went.

Mia watched him melt into the crowd, wondering what the heck she was supposed to have done to anger him. Or was she imagining it?

Yes, she decided, she was imagining it. Damián was bound to be tense. A night out with his brother giving him the evil eye could not be pleasant.

Rum and Coke in hand, Mia wandered back to the roulette table. Damián's aunt was playing, a huge pile of black chips stacked in front of her. Also playing were people she'd never met in her life but who she recognised. Famous faces.

'You don't fancy a flutter yourself?' a drawling voice asked.

Emiliano had come to stand with her.

She had a large sip of her drink and shook her head. 'I'm having fun watching everyone else play.'

He produced a handful of black chips. 'Red or black?'

Figuring there must be ten thousand euros in his hand, she laughed at the absurdity of her deciding the colour that would determine whether that money remained his. 'No way. Choose for yourself.'

'In that case I choose red. To match your dress.'

'Don't blame me if it lands on black.'

She held her breath as the ball spun. After bouncing a number of times on the wheel, it eventually landed on black.

Emiliano gave a rueful shake of his head and quirked an eyebrow. 'Black to match Celeste's heart.'

Not willing to fall into a trap by responding to that, she finished her drink.

'Another?' he asked as he placed another pile of chips on red.

'Sure.'

He lost again.

Their fresh drinks arrived as he tried his luck on red for a third time. This time he won.

Emiliano raised his glass to her. 'You must be my lucky charm. *Salud.*'

She smothered a laugh. 'Hardly. You've already lost more than you've just won.'

He grinned. 'Pick a number.'

'You're doing a great job of blowing your money without my help.'

His grin widened. 'I see why my brother is so smitten with you.'

At the mention of Damián she darted a glance at his table. As if he felt her gaze on him, he raised his stare to her, then, without acknowledging her, dropped his attention back to the cards in his hand.

Mia made a valiant attempt not to let her hurt show on her face and quickly changed the subject. 'Who's looking after your dogs tonight?'

'I employ a full-time dog-sitter. Where the boys go, she goes.' He placed a pile of chips on red thirty-eight.

'They're gorgeous. You've trained them so well.'

'You like dogs?'

'I love them. We had them when I was growing up.'

'You should get one.'

'I live in a little flat without a garden. It wouldn't be fair.'

He drained his drink. 'Get Damián to buy you a house with a garden. Then you can get yourself a dog or two and when you come to your senses and dump him you'll have the most loyal and loving creatures to help you pick up the pieces.'

'You're very cynical, aren't you?'

He laughed. 'It's a family trait.'

'So I've noticed.'

'Red thirty-eight,' the croupier called.

Emiliano's eyes gleamed and then, before she knew what he was doing, he placed a smacker of a kiss to her cheek. 'See? I said you were my lucky charm. I've just won ninety thousand euros.'

Her laughter at this died when Damián suddenly appeared at her side. Ignoring his brother, he took Mia's hand. 'My driver's on his way.'

'We're going?' she asked, surprised both at the suddenness of his decision and the coldness in his voice.

'I've had my fill of gambling for one night.'

CHAPTER TWELVE

'Are you going to tell me what's wrong?' Mia asked as soon as they were back in Damián's suite.

The drive back had been tense, like it had been between them before they'd become lovers. Every time she'd tried to strike up conversation he'd either answered in monosyllables or ignored her.

'There is nothing wrong,' he answered tersely.

She stalked towards him and placed a hand on his chest. He brushed it away with a scowl.

'See! I *knew* it. You're angry with me about something. You hardly looked at me all evening…'

'I'm surprised you noticed,' he snapped, 'considering how cosy you were with my brother.'

The moment the words left his mouth, Damián regretted them.

Damn it, but he could not believe the rancid feelings that had played in his guts throughout the evening. It had been bad enough seeing Mia's gaze darting towards his brother during the meal, but to then see her laughing and enjoying his company had made the bile rise up his throat. It still lingered on his taste-buds. It was like nothing he'd ever felt or tasted before.

Mia's eyes widened, her mouth opening and closing before she shook her head and folded her arms across her breasts. 'What are you accusing me of here?'

'I'm not accusing you of anything. I'm merely observing that Emiliano seems very taken with you,' he said sardonically.

'That's not the vibe I got.'

'Really? And what *vibe* did you get from him?'

'Curiosity. He was sizing me up, like everyone else has been.'

'Knowing my brother, he was sizing you up to see which of his beds he wanted to take you in.' And Mia was exactly Emiliano's type, he thought grimly. Physically, at least. The only thing to differentiate her from his usual women was her intelligence. Brain cells lacking or not, his brother never had a shortage of women throwing themselves at him. While Damián was choosy about the women he bedded, he doubted his brother had spent more than a handful of nights alone since he'd turned eighteen.

'Like I said, that is not the vibe I was getting from him.' From the tone of her voice she was fast losing patience. 'And, even if it was, why get angry with me about something your brother was doing?'

'Because I am paying you to act as *my* lover for the weekend, not flirt with the man who's doing his damnedest to steal my future.'

Her jaw dropped. 'I was *not* flirting!'

'He kissed you.'

'Yes!' Outrage vibrated from her pores. '*He* kissed *me*. He kissed my cheek, and only because he'd just won a shedload of money.'

He gave her the stare he usually reserved for staff he suspected of covering their tracks when they'd made an accounting error. 'You couldn't keep your eyes off him during the meal.'

She put her hands on her hips and glared at him. 'He sat opposite me! If I was supposed to sit like a good little Victorian maid and keep my head bowed then you should have told me that before we left.'

'I saw you staring at him during lunch too.'

'You really do want to police where I look!' Now she threw her hands in the air. 'I tell you why I kept looking at him—it was like watching a horror movie, that's why. The whole situation. Everyone sat around pretending to have a jolly old time and, in the midst of it all, the lone wolf secretly plotting the demise of one of the other characters. If I kept looking at Emiliano it's because I was trying to figure out if he really is the lone wolf.'

'We both know the lone wolf you describe is my brother and that it's my demise he's plotting.'

'I assumed that too but the more I look and talk to him, the less convinced I am. I wouldn't be at all surprised if the lone wolf was your mother.'

'Celeste?'

'The way Emiliano looks at you reminds me of the way Amy looked at our mum when she was going through her self-destruct phase. She hated everyone but she had special hatred for Mum.'

'Then that completely negates your argument,' he said coldly. 'If Celeste was behind it, she would be open about it. She would tell me to my face. To her, it would be a challenge, an invitation for me to try to best her.'

'I don't pretend to understand the sick dynamics of your family,' she said as she tugged her hair free of the chignon and mussed it with her fingers. 'But when I see how Emiliano looks at you I see Amy, and I see the hurt and pain she carried. Amy's pain was made worse by Mum locking herself away from us. She needed her but she couldn't reach her. From what I've seen of you two, you ignore him as much as he ignores you. How do you know he hasn't spent the past ten years waiting for you to reach out to him?'

A throbbing pulse pounded in his head at this observation.

'All communication between you and Emiliano in the past decade has been through Celeste. How do you know she hasn't been stoking the feud?'

Rage filtered through him. 'Why are you taking his side?'

'I'm not.' She muttered something that sounded remarkably like a curse and stormed to the bathroom. 'You might be acting like a jealous idiot but I will always be on your side and always have your back, but if you're so confident you're right, talk to him. Even if you're not, be the bigger man and talk to him anyway because this stupid feud has gone on for long enough.'

Head held high, she stepped into the bathroom and slammed the door behind her, leaving Damián alone with his anger. He didn't know what infuriated him the most, Mia's insinuations about his mother or her laughable words about him being jealous.

He'd never felt an ounce of jealousy in his life, had always been contemptuous of those who tried to control the people they claimed to love while lacking control over their own emotions.

Ripping his clothes off, he paced the suite, fighting the urge to kick the bathroom door down and carry Mia out over his shoulder and stare into her eyes for so long that he imprinted his image in her so she could never again look at another man without seeing him...

He came to an abrupt halt.

What in hell was he thinking?

Were these not the thoughts of someone irrational and possessive? Someone jealous?

He slumped onto the edge of the bed and hung his head, kneading his temples vigorously.

And as he sat there his fury slowly ebbed away and reason came back to him. It was a reasoning that only made him feel sick to the pit of his stomach.

Mia hadn't done anything wrong. This was all on him. Again.

What was it with her? How could one woman evoke so many wild emotions in a man who'd turned self-control into an art form?

After a scalding-hot shower that failed to rinse away the anger, Mia brushed her teeth vigorously and wished she had a punch bag to hand.

Damián's behaviour had shocked her. The man who was always in full control of every situation had behaved like a jealous teen...

She paused brushing.

Had he been jealous?

The angry beats of her heart became skittish. The vibrations from them danced into her stomach and pushed against her lungs.

She was still standing with the toothbrush static in her mouth when he knocked on the door.

'Mia?' She heard him sigh. 'I'm sorry.'

Unexpected hot tears filled her eyes.

'I had no right to accuse you of flirting with him. I...' Another sigh. 'Emiliano brings out the worst in me. I think we bring out the worst in each other.'

Desperately blinking the tears away, hands suddenly trembling, she rinsed the toothpaste out and patted her mouth dry, all the while trying hard to breathe through a body contracting in on itself.

'I've behaved abominably. I am under immense pressure and I took it out on you.'

She opened the door.

Damián stood at the threshold, shirt and socks removed, trousers unbuttoned, hair mussed. One look at his face showed her the sincerity of his apology.

She tried to smile but the muscles of her face wouldn't work, not when they were too busy trying to hold the tears at bay.

Why did she want to cry?

He burrowed a hand into her hair. 'Forgive me?'

She swallowed hard. 'I am not your enemy,' she whispered.

'I know you're not, *mi vida*.' He brought his forehead to rest against hers. 'You said things I did not want to hear… but I think I needed to hear them.' He pressed his lips to hers and held them there, eyes closed, breathing her in.

Tentatively, Mia looped an arm around his neck and returned the pressure of the kiss. When his lips parted, hers moved with them, her tongue sliding into his mouth as his slid into hers, her arms tightening around him as his tightened around her.

But there was no comfort to be found in his touch, only a rising desperation and a growing ache that she couldn't take comfort because their time together was coming to an end.

The desperation in her bones was matched by the desperation she found in Damián's touch and the rawness of his kisses. Her towel fell to the floor and she pressed herself even closer so her breasts flattened against his hard chest.

She didn't want this to be over. She didn't want to leave this villa in less than two days and never see him again.

His hands roamed her body, fingers biting as they

clenched her buttocks then scraped up her back as if trying to penetrate her skin. And she found herself doing the same, a fraught urgency in her fingers to touch every part of him they could reach, a need to imprint every inch of him onto her memories as something to cherish for the rest of her life because in her heart Mia knew it would be impossible to recreate what they shared with anyone else.

They fell onto the bed in a tangle of limbs and entwined tongues, their kisses broken when he wrenched his mouth from hers to bury his face in her neck, sending darts of tingling pleasure over her sensitised skin. When he cupped a breast and centred an erect nipple against the palm of his hand before kneading it, she gasped, her gasps soon turning into moans when he made his way down to her abdomen and then lower still, bringing her quickly to a peak with nothing more than his tongue.

And then it was her turn to take him in her hand and cover him with her mouth and revel in his appreciative moans, her other hand skimming over his thighs and stomach, the need to touch and remember every part of him burning deeper and deeper in her.

Her name fell from his lips like a groan and speared right through her. How she loved to hear him say her name and the richness in his voice as it rolled off his tongue.

He moaned her name again when, sheathed and rockhard, he thrust inside her and filled her with that most wonderful fulfilling sensation that was like nothing else on this earth.

Please don't let this be over, she silently begged through their fevered kisses. *I don't think I can bear to say goodbye. Not yet. I'm not ready.*

But, just as with all the best things in life, she knew they must end, just as their lovemaking had to end, the swell of her orgasm too strong to deny, her body too needy and responsive to Damián's touch to do anything but what it was designed for, and, as hard as she tried to make her climax last for ever, as hard as she clung to him, as tightly as she wrapped her limbs around him, her body was soon spent and she was left sated yet bereft.

In the aftermath, as Damián lay on her and inside her, the mocking words she'd said to him what felt a lifetime ago echoed in her ears.

Our love will burn like a flame and then it will, sadly, extinguish itself.

Oh, the cruelty of words said in jest. Her flame for Damián blazed brighter by the day. The danger of it turning into an inferno was something she'd become powerless to stop and, unless there was a miracle, she saw no way of extinguishing it before they said goodbye.

Damián adjusted his black bow tie and tried to relax his features out of the glower tightening his face.

The day had proven unbelievably frustrating. His plan to search the villa's secret hiding places for the documents had gone better than he could have hoped but had ultimately proved fruitless, one dead end after another. The few hidden suitcases he'd found had contained millions in cash but no documents.

He was frustrated with himself too, for wasting that time making love to Mia when they'd first arrived at the villa rather than hacking straight into the security system. Felipe Lorenzi's team were at the top of their game but they couldn't perform miracles, and he'd been four hours late getting into the system and linking them to it. He debated calling Felipe for an update but then figured it would be a waste of time. If they'd retrieved the interior villa footage for the period around his father's death they would have notified him immediately.

He thought hard about where else Emiliano would be likely to hide the documents. He didn't want to search his suite but was coming to see he had no other option.

He didn't have to wait much longer for Mia to return, wearing her robe and with a strange towel-like thing wrapped around her head. Under his mother's instructions, Gaynor and the other beauticians had been working on her for the last two hours.

'Don't look at me,' she said by way of greeting, hand covering her face as she zipped straight past him to the dressing room.

Just her presence was enough to lighten his mood. 'Why not?'

'Because you need the full effect for when I put the dress on.' She shut the door behind her.

He opened it a touch so he could speak through the gap. 'What's that thing around your head?'

'I told you not to look.'

'But I like looking at you.'

'Good. Because I like looking at you. Now go away.' She shut the door again.

He opened it again. 'I won't look until you're ready.'

'You'd better not. Anyway, I have gossip.'

'Oh?'

'Yep. Celeste sent your cousins for beauty treatments too. The younger one…what's her name?'

'Cordelia.'

'That's the one. She was telling me that she saw Emiliano a month ago in England for some polo competition he was in. They went out for dinner and he basically spent the meal banging on about his horses. Apparently, he's fallen out with one of his players and is going to find someone new to replace him for the American season.'

She skimmed past the small gap in the door. He only

caught a brief glimpse but it was enough to distract him from what she was saying, mainly because she had only a pair of lacy black knickers on.

He adjusted his position so his back was to the wall by the door and tried not to imagine peeling those knickers off with his teeth.

Oblivious to the effect she was having on him, she continued. 'Cordelia also mentioned the Delgado Group and how she's going to ask you for a job. So that makes me wonder—why is she going to ask *you* for a job if Emiliano is poised to take over? And if Emiliano *is* planning to take over the Delgado Group, why is he going full-throttle for preparations for the next polo season when the current season isn't finished yet and the takeover should be taking all his attention?'

Those were excellent questions, he conceded grimly, resting his head against the wall and expelling a long breath.

For the first time, Damián considered the validity of Mia's suggestion that Celeste could be behind it all. It was a consideration that made his guts tighten unbearably.

Celeste couldn't be behind it. That she had always loved Emiliano more than him was merely a statement of fact, but that didn't mean she would actively conspire against him... Did it?

'Are you okay?' Mia called from behind the door. He heard the concern in her voice and closed his eyes as a wave of nausea swept through him.

He had to force his vocal cords to work. '*Si*. All good. Just impatient to see your beautiful face.'

'Almost done.'

Less than a minute later, the door opened. If he hadn't jumped out of the way it would have slammed into him.

Mia stood before him and spread her arms out. 'Well? What do you think of the newly improved Mia Caldwell?'

What did he think?

For long moments he couldn't breathe, let alone think. For those long moments the agony of imagining his mother's betrayal was cast aside as his greedy eyes soaked in every inch of the sparkling beauty before him.

Her rose-pink dress, covered in silver and crystal jewels, was strapless and skimmed her cleavage to caress her beautiful body and fell to mid-thigh, displaying her gorgeous legs, which were a couple of shades darker than they'd been when he'd kissed her goodbye before her beauty treatments. Covering the dress was a sheer silk toga-style piece, which skimmed her shoulders and fastened at the waist with a diamond-encrusted button, then split to fall at her pretty feet. With sultry make-up, hair loose and tumbling in waves, the end result was something that managed to be both elegant and fun, which, to Damián's mind, summed Mia up perfectly.

The glow in her eyes slowly dimmed. 'Are you sure you're okay?'

He swallowed and nodded. 'You look…beautiful. Perfect.'

He looked beautiful too, Mia thought, her heart exploding as she drank in his raw masculinity. In his black velvet tuxedo, he looked so handsome it should be illegal.

But, the longer she stared into Damián's dark eyes and saw the torture reflecting back at her, the heavier the weight in her chest grew until the torture became her own.

A swell of tears burned the back of her eyes and, using the pretext of squirting some perfume on, she hurried back into the dressing room so she could blink them away without destroying her make-up.

All day she'd kept a happy front. She'd turned the search for the missing documents into a thrilling adventure, imagining herself in some kind of spy movie. It had been easier to do that than confront the deep ache rooted in her chest, a pain so familiar she could hardly bear to acknowledge it.

It was the pain she used to carry when she feared she would lose Amy and when she'd been fearful *for* Amy.

She wasn't afraid of losing Damián. Losing him was a given, written in black and white the fateful day she'd been summoned to him. She'd never imagined then that she would spend the eve of their parting desperately throwing herself into her task, terrified to give herself any time to think because the pain of what was to come for her was already too big to cope with.

But she was afraid for Damián too. Afraid he would never find those documents. Afraid he *would* find them. Afraid of his security expert finally retrieving the footage of the time of his father's death and what that footage would reveal. Afraid of her hunch that his mother was behind it all. Of all the things she feared, that was at the forefront. Celeste might defy all the laws of nature when it came to mothering but surely there were limits? She prayed there were limits.

Something told her that by the end of the night there would be no more secrets.

CHAPTER THIRTEEN

DAMIÁN HAD TO give Celeste her due—she knew how to throw a party. There was a reason why invitations to her annual summer party were considered gold dust. Each year outdid the year before.

Tonight, hundreds of guests spilled out of the villa's vast rooms, hundreds more basking in the evening warmth in its vast gardens. The guests, all so beautifully dressed now, would leave hours later much the worse for wear and stagger to their waiting cars or helicopters—the grounds had two helipads—clutching their goody bags. This year's goody bags contained, amongst other delights, diamond-encrusted bracelets for the ladies and diamond-encrusted cufflinks with matching tiepins for the gentlemen. Anyone found selling or trading their gifts would be banned from attending again, a fate that had befallen a Hollywood superstar who'd made the mistake of listing the motorcycle he'd been given on an auction site. That had been the year each guest had been given a set of vehicle keys.

For two hours Damián and Mia mingled, slowly sipping their champagne while everyone else guzzled theirs, making small talk, avoiding the biggest bores where possible and generally looking as if they were having a marvellous time. Because that was expected. Everyone had to have a marvellous time.

Mia, as he'd known she would, threw herself into it. Having her by his side made the whole thing easier to endure and kept the demons inside his head at bay. If he wasn't on such tenterhooks he would be enjoying himself. Who could fail to enjoy Mia's company? She was vivacious and funny and in her element when under the spotlight, which, as the first woman he'd brought to one of his mother's parties, she was. Everyone wanted to meet her. Everyone was curious about her.

Damian had introduced only one of his lovers to his family, his first serious lover many years ago, long before his relationship with Emiliano had detonated. He'd ended that relationship weeks later and decided not to introduce anyone else to his family until he found the perfect woman to settle down with. He hadn't imagined then that well over a decade later he would still be looking for her. Choosy in forming relationships, he'd been even choosier at keeping them. One lover had ended the relationship because of his refusal to bring her to Celeste's summer party. With hindsight, he could see he'd hurt her feelings. At the time, he'd assumed she was only with him for what she could get and so he hadn't considered that she might have had any real feelings for him.

Perfect on paper though his lovers had been, that perfection had soon bored him. Until Mia had come into his life, he hadn't understood the boredom for what it was, had just sensed when things weren't working and ended the relationship.

Everything with Mia felt different. Better.

And then he remembered, with something akin to shock, that the only reason Mia was here was because he was paying her. That she'd become his lover was an accident.

Ice crept up his spine as he remembered that she wasn't with him for *him* any more than his previous lovers had been. She desired him, that was not in dispute, but were his power and wealth her aphrodisiacs? Would she have looked twice at him if he were an ordinary man? Would her ready affection be more muted if she wasn't surrounded by the trappings of his success?

She was an actress. A damn good one. Something he should not have forgotten.

The group they were talking with burst into laughter. Mia tugged at his hand, bringing him back to the here and now, and he joined in, not having a clue what he was supposed to be laughing at.

He looked into her smiling face, which couldn't mask the concern in her eyes.

Was that concern real?

She said something that had them all barking out more laughter, and then she hooked an arm around Damián's neck and kissed his cheek, a display of affection that punched through his chest and filled it with something that made him feel drunk.

'Excuse me a moment,' she said cheerfully to the group, 'but I need to powder my nose.'

Her fingers lingered on his before she disappeared into the increasingly raucous throng.

The moment she left his sight, his chest tightened and he had to concentrate harder than ever to keep up with the conversation.

She returned within minutes but they were the longest minutes he'd endured in a very long time.

She smiled at everyone as she took his hand. 'Apologies, but I need to steal Damián from you. He's promised me a tour of the bell tower.'

The way she said it left no one in any doubt that she was dragging him away for less cultural purposes, and their knowing laughter echoed behind them as they walked away.

'What's wrong?' he asked in an undertone.

She looked over her shoulder then put a hand to his shoulder so she could whisper into his ear. 'Your brother's in the swimming pool with a load of women.'

He gazed into the bright blue eyes, saw the trepidation in them and exhaled slowly. Then he swallowed and nodded. 'Let's do it.'

Her mouth curved in understanding before she pressed a sweet, gentle kiss to his mouth. Even with his cynicism breathing freely, her kiss loosened the angst knotting in him.

For the next hour he needed to keep his growing cynicism on lockdown. He still needed Mia's help for what came next.

Hands clasped together, they sidestepped dancing couples and waiting staff balancing trays of champagne and canapés, Damián making the 'one minute' sign to anyone who tried to catch his attention. Celeste, he knew, would be holding court as she always did in her special Art Room, where she displayed the best of her extensive collection, the pieces refreshed every year so no guest ever saw the same artworks displayed twice. He remembered her overseeing the packing of a Titian to replace it with the work of a graffiti artist. As far as he knew, the Titian was still stored in a vault in Switzerland. She thought it didn't 'fit' in any of the other rooms.

With his brother and mother both busy, now was the perfect time to strike. They wouldn't miss their presence.

Damián climbed the stairs two at a time, Mia hurrying alongside him. No one watching would have any doubt where they were going and what they intended to do when they got there.

Except when they got to the top of the stairs they turned left instead of right.

A chaise longue was one of the elegant pieces lining this particular corridor and they sat on it for a moment while Damián checked his phone, which he'd linked to the security system. As the screen was much smaller than the laptop, it was pointless aiming to split screen, but he set it for the camera in the foyer at the bottom of the stairs and gave it to Mia.

'Stay here and keep watch.' He didn't have to tell her what to keep watch for.

'Sure you don't want me to search with you?'

His throat going dry, he shook his head. 'It's bad enough that I'm invading his privacy in this way without dragging you into it. Just keep watch for me. I won't be long.' Then he swallowed and met her apprehensive stare. 'If I don't find anything, I will search Celeste's quarters.'

She closed her eyes and nodded her understanding but he could see from the frown etching her face that she felt as bad about what he was about to do as he did. And that she understood why he had to do it.

Or was that merely what she wanted him to think? That she was pushing aside her scruples—the very scruples he'd selected her for in the first place, thinking they were non-existent—for him?

He dug his fingers hard into the nape of his neck and ground his teeth together. Why was he doubting her, and why now, when it was imperative he keep his mind clear?

It was this place, he thought. The villa. And being with his family. It messed with his head.

'Have you got the bug checker?' she asked.

He patted his jacket pocket. He also had a kit to unlock doors if Emiliano had locked his. He hoped he'd paid good enough attention to Felipe's instructions on how to use it.

Her shoulders rose. He could see the length of the breath that she took.

He put his hand on the door but found he couldn't turn it. It wasn't that the handle was stuck; it was that his hand didn't want to co-operate.

'Great time to develop a conscience,' he muttered to the offending hand.

Nausea roiled again in his stomach. He forced his hand to work and turn the damned handle.

And that was when Mia suddenly shouted, 'I think Felipe's retrieved the footage! He's sent you a video.'

Mia could hardly breathe. She couldn't hear Damián breathing either.

He had the phone in his hand. The accompanying message was in Spanish. Whatever he read in that message made his hand shake. His thigh, pressed tightly to hers, juddered. She put a hand on it and gently squeezed.

He pressed play.

The footage started with Celeste carrying a glass of something that looked like Scotch out of her quarters. Rapid shots with time stamps in the bottom right hand corner showed her progress and then entry into the sun room, which she left less than a minute later, empty-handed. The next shot, time stamped thirty-one minutes later, showed her returning to the sun room. Four minutes after that the corridor suddenly filled with staff. Noise rang out of the phone in Damián's hand, making her jump. Shouts. Calls for help.

Coldness crept through her bones as the realisation she was watching the afternoon of Eduardo Delgado's death suddenly dawned on her.

The screen blurred before her eyes but she forced them back into focus to see the body, mercifully wrapped in a black body bag, being respectfully carried out of the villa.

And then the next shot came. Four hours later. The villa

was dark. Eduardo's private quarters. Celeste appeared. Unlocked the door. This time the footage stayed still, the timestamp ticking rapidly in the bottom right corner.

Mia pressed herself closer to Damián and covered her mouth, dreading what she feared would be shown next.

She couldn't help the moan of despair that ripped out of her throat when the heavy door opened again and Celeste stepped out. Under her arm, a pile of papers.

Whoever had retrieved the footage had zoomed in. Although the documents were written in Spanish, Damián's sharp intake of breath told her they were looking at his father's will.

And then the final cruelty. Celeste entering the drawing room with the documents and leaving two minutes later without them.

They had searched the drawing room that morning. It was the most sparsely furnished room in the whole villa. But it had a huge open fire. Eduardo had died in winter.

Damián could not breathe. The corridor was spinning around him, faster and faster, nausea rising from deep inside and lining his throat.

Blinking hard for focus, he rewound the video and forced himself to watch the damning footage again. Beside him, he felt Mia shaking.

The nausea abated. In its place was a lead weight, pushing down, numbing him.

'What's going on?'

Raising his head from the screen in his hand, Damián found his brother, his hair and tuxedo soaking wet, standing a foot away, looking him in the eye for the first time in a decade.

Wordlessly, he held the phone out to him.

Emiliano's right brow rose in question but he took it from him.

'You might want to sit down,' Damián muttered.

Emiliano pressed his back against the wall and slithered down until he reached the floor. He pressed play.

The only sounds in the corridor were the heaviness of the Delgado brothers' breathing and Mia's quiet sobs.

What was she crying for? This was nothing to do with her. She was only here because he'd paid her.

When the shouts for help rang out of the phone, Emiliano flinched. A minute later, he put the phone on the floor and buried his face in his hands.

'Answer me one thing,' Damián said in their native tongue. 'Were you in on it?'

His brother's haunted face looked at him. 'You have to ask?'

'Yes.'

Something ugly contorted the handsome features. 'This was all *her*. It has always been her. Everything. Don't you see that?'

'She did it for you.'

In a flurry of venomous curses, Emiliano jumped to his feet and slammed his fist into the wall. 'Don't put this on me. If she did it for anyone, she did it for herself.'

'She always loved you more than me—'

'You call that love? I call it manipulation.'

'What the hell does that mean?'

'That her love is for her ego, so she can pretend she is a good mother when the truth is she's a narcissistic bitch. I let her manipulate me because I *had* to—I got nothing in the way of love or respect from your father.'

'That's crap. He took you in as his own. He gave you his name—'

'He did that for *her*. Not for me. Everything I did was a disappointment to him. I couldn't even tie my shoelaces right in his eyes! I bent myself to Celeste's will for years but only because I knew what the alternative would be, and I was right—the first chance the pair of you got, you threw me out of the company. You appointed yourselves judge, jury and executioner without even listening to my side of things, but if you think for a damned minute that that means I was in on *this*...' Rage blazed across his face as he stood eyeball to eyeball with his brother. 'Never. I hated him. I hated you. But this? No way. I've made a good life for myself. I don't need your damned money or your damned business and I don't need her manipulating me any more—I haven't in over a decade.'

Damián's hands clenched into fists. 'Without my damned money you wouldn't have this good life!'

'Stop it!'

Mia's plea brought them both up short.

Shooting his brother one last venomous look, Damián slowly turned to her.

On her feet, white-faced and red-eyed and rubbing her arms, she said in a quieter voice, 'Please. Both of you. Just stop. This isn't helping.'

Mia hadn't understood a word of what they'd said but she'd known from the tone of their voices and their body language that the venom being exchanged was close to spilling over into something physical.

Her heart broke for them both but it bled for Damián. Everything inside her bled for him and she wished with all her broken heart that she could whisper some magic words and make his pain disappear.

This was the ultimate treachery. His own mother. The woman who'd carried him in her womb and given birth to him had set out to destroy him. She hardly dared think about the implications of Celeste taking that drink to Eduardo.

The brothers faced each other again. The rage that had

blazed so brightly dulled to a simmer before Damián's great shoulders rose and he looked at Mia again.

The coldness in her bones turned to ice when she saw the expression in his eyes. 'Go to our suite and wait for me.'

'What are you going to do?' she whispered.

But she knew what he was going to do.

Together, the Delgado brothers marched downstairs and her heart broke all over again to see them united for the first time in such horrific circumstances.

Damián switched the main lights on as he strode into the Art Room at the same moment Emiliano clapped his hands. 'Everybody out!'

Celeste sat in a Queen Anne armchair amongst a gaggle of sycophants blinking at the sudden strong light in their eyes around her. She jumped to her feet. 'What's happened?'

Damián folded his arms across his chest. 'Get rid of them. Now. Or I kick everyone out.'

The room quickly cleared. He didn't care that those expelled would already be spreading the news that a confrontation was taking place. Let them talk. He no longer cared.

At that moment, he cared for nothing but the truth.

He thrust his phone at her. 'Watch this.'

'Mijito...'

'I said *watch*!'

Her poise intact, she sat back down and made a big song and dance of pressing play.

He watched her closely.

Not a flicker of emotion passed over her face.

'Just tell me why,' he said flatly when the video finished.

Her black eyes met his. They were filled with contempt. 'I don't answer to you.'

'Answer me or answer to the police.'

She had the temerity to laugh. 'The police? On what charge?'

It was Emiliano who said, 'You killed our father.'

The laughter died. 'Have you both taken leave of your senses? That is the most ridiculous thing I've ever heard. Your father was an old man!'

'The evidence is there. You made a drink for him in your quarters and carried it through the villa to give to him. Considering you've never lowered yourself to pour yourself a glass of water before, that alone would be suspicious, but that he was dead thirty minutes later is damning.'

Eyes glittering, she folded her arms and crossed her legs. 'Prove it.'

'You destroyed the will and the documents giving me control of the Delgado Group,' said Damián.

'I repeat. Prove it.'

'It's on the footage.'

'No, darling, all that's on the footage is me taking the documents out of your father's office.'

'You deny destroying them?'

'Of course.'

'Then where are they? If you haven't destroyed them they must be around somewhere.'

Her lips formed a tight line.

'You burned them, didn't you?'

The lips became white.

'We know why you did it.' God alone knew how Damián managed to keep control of his voice. 'Father allowed you great influence in the running of the business but he never gave you the power you craved. You knew any influence you had would be lost when I took over and so engineered things for Emiliano to have it, knowing damn well he didn't want it, knowing he hated me so much he'd rather see me on the street than let me stay on the board and would hand over the running of it to you.'

Her face taut, she got back to her feet. 'I think we've had enough games for one evening. Please excuse me, but this is a party. I suggest you both have a strong drink and put this nonsense out of your minds. You're letting your grief get the better of…'

'You're a *monster*!' The roar came from Emiliano. 'You know what you did and we know what you did. You're a monster, do you hear me? A monster! You pitted brother against brother from the moment we could speak and all so you could control us. That ends *now*. You'd better not have destroyed those documents because if they're not found and I'm declared heir, I will cut you off. You won't even have the half share of father's personal wealth that he left you because it won't exist. You will have nothing.'

Her face twitched. *'Mijito…'*

But he was already at the door. He flung it open. 'I hope you rot in hell.'

Her composure unravelling before his eyes, Celeste looked to her youngest son.

Before she could open her mouth, Damián cut her off. 'Save your breath. I don't want to hear it. From this moment on, you're dead to me.'

CHAPTER FOURTEEN

MIA PACED THE suite frantically, alternating from looking out of the windows into the grounds to walking the corridor, trying to hear above the noise in her own head.

What was happening down there? She prayed it had all been a big misunderstanding and that Celeste had a valid explanation for everything. That the drink she'd given her husband half an hour before his death was a provable coincidence. That she'd been suffering amnesia and could magically produce the documents. Anything—*anything*—that would spare Damián the pain of knowing his mother was a monster.

She stepped onto the balcony again in time to see a helicopter fly overhead. The pretty garden lights that had illuminated the grounds so beautifully had been turned off. Were the guests leaving?

She paced again until heavy footsteps approached on the corridor.

She swung the door open before Damián reached it and flung her arms around him. 'I've been so worried. Are you okay?' An inane question, she knew, but one she couldn't help but ask.

He stood rigid. She felt the strength of his heartbeat, ragged against her ear. He'd lost his tuxedo jacket and bow tie since he'd gone to confront his mother.

Unwrapping her arms from his waist, she gazed up at him. His gaze was focused over her head, jaw rigid.

'What's happened?' she whispered, resting her hands on his shoulders, silently pleading with him to look at her.

Slowly, his giant hands covered hers. They lingered for a moment before he pushed her hands off and stepped past her into the suite.

'Damián?'

'You need to leave.'

Certain she'd misheard or misunderstood, she stared at him. His eyes stayed fixed above her.

'Tell me. Please?' she begged. 'What's happened?'

As rigid as a statue, he said tonelessly, 'The Richmonds are waiting for you. Get your passport. They're flying back to London and will give you a lift home. I'll have the staff pack the rest of your stuff together and get it couriered to you.'

She swallowed, uncertain how to respond. 'Okay... But you'll call me?'

His gaze suddenly found hers. The coldness in it made her quail. 'What for?'

'Because I'll worry about you.' She was already worried about him. Desperately worried.

'I'm not paying you to worry about me. I am paying you to do a job. That job has been fulfilled and now it is time for you to leave.'

'You know you mean more to me than a job,' she whispered.

Obsidian eyes flashed. 'Do I? If you are after a bonus payment for the extra services you provided then name your price and I will pay it with the remainder of what I owe you.'

She flinched, his words landing like a physical blow. 'You don't mean that.'

'Don't I? Do not think sharing my bed means you know me or that I owe you anything other than money.'

'Don't do this,' she pleaded. 'Please. Don't. I know you're hurting. Let me help you. I want to help you…'

In the numb void that was Damián's head, Mia's words penetrated with the effect of nails being scraped down a chalkboard. His body suddenly springing to life, he clutched her biceps. 'Which part of *leave* don't you understand?' he snarled into her face. 'I don't want your help. I want nothing more from you. You are nothing to me.'

'Well, you're something to *me*.'

He dropped his hands from her arms as if they'd been scalded. *He* felt scalded, as if his body were being licked by the flames of his mother's monstrous betrayal, and here was Mia, gazing at him as if he meant something to her when her every action was a lie he'd paid for. None of her affection and empathy had been genuine, and he'd been a fool if he'd ever thought it was.

'I know exactly what I am to you,' he said scathingly. 'A cash cow. The fulfiller of designer clothes and luxury travel. You think because I have been brought low that you can take advantage of it. You think you can be my shoulder to cry on? *Si?*'

Her eyes filled with tears at his harsh words but he didn't care. Mia was an actress, just like his mother. At least Celeste had never pretended to care for him. He'd given her credit for being honest but her honesty had been an act like everything else, given only when it suited her. She'd manipulated all of them and he, a man who prided himself on his cynicism and nose for lies, had fallen for it.

Never again.

Mia had given him her virginity. She'd confided her secrets to him. She'd made him feel that he was the only man in the world for her without having to say a word. *That* was how good an actress she was.

And he'd been close—so damn close—to falling for it. To falling for her.

What could she possibly want from him, other than the gifts his bank account could lavish on her?

Crushing the emotions smothering him, he controlled his voice to an icy clip. 'I will give you the briefest of details to satisfy your curiosity. Celeste killed my father. She poisoned him before my takeover of the business could be announced and the papers making it official lodged because she wanted it for herself. She wanted Emiliano to inherit it, knowing damn well he would pass it onto her to run on his behalf. Celeste hacked my communications and did all the other things I blamed my brother for. I can prove none of this. My father was cremated. His death was attributed to natural causes. I will have to spend the rest of my life knowing what she's done and knowing there is not a damned thing I can do to bring justice for my father.'

He took a deep breath, his features twisting. 'So there you have it. All the sordid details, and now is your moment to show your compassion for the man whose mother never loved him.' He leaned into her, staring her right in the eye. 'That is what you want from all this, is it not? For me to be so grateful to you for your understanding and compassion that I never want to let you go? For me to be so desperate for love and affection that I grab hold of what a two-bit actress can give me?' His laughter was short. 'Do you think I forget you are an actress? I never forget, *mi vida*. I never forget what you are. Now, I thank you for the excellent job you have done for me and for all the extra services you provided, but it is time for you to leave.'

Mia clutched her flaming cheeks, too horror-struck to care that hot tears were streaming down her face.

This was not the Damián she knew. This was not the man she'd fallen in love with. This was a stranger: a monster who'd taken possession of him. But oh, dear God, his words and the venom behind them hurt, ripping through her shattered heart like a hot blade.

'I'm sorry she hurt you,' she said through the tears. 'I'm sorry for everything she's done to you and your family, and the cynical bastard she's forged you into, but that doesn't give you the right to turn it around and inflict your pain on *me*. I wanted to help you through this, not for what I could get from you—if you haven't learned by now that money means nothing to me then you haven't learned a thing—but because I can't bear to see someone I love in so much pain and not try to help.'

The mouth that had kissed her with such passion curved cruelly. 'Yes, you're a regular saint, aren't you? Always sacrificing yourself. Give yourself a criminal record to save your sister and now what? Cosy up to me and be my pet and keep the perks of being my lover going a bit longer?'

'That's not fair and it's not true,' she said, distraught he could say such things. 'I never asked to be brought into this, remember? I was prepared to hate you and thought faking love for you would be my greatest achievement, but I never had to act for you. Right from the start, I was nothing but myself with you—I couldn't be anything else.'

'How would I know that? You're a great actress. The best. Almost as good as Celeste.'

His words landed like a slap. 'You're comparing me to *her*? My God...'

Fearing she could be sick, she stepped to the bureau and opened the drawer. She removed her passport with a shaking hand, blinking rapidly, trying desperately to stop the tears falling.

'I never expected forever from you,' she choked, gripping the bureau to stop her legs giving way beneath her. 'I knew that couldn't happen. Our lives are just too polarised, but I thought you respected me. I thought we had something special. You made me feel things I've never felt in my *life* and I thought you felt the bond as deeply as I did. I thought we would part on good terms and that you were someone I would always be able to call a friend.'

'Then you're as big a fool as I am.'

Swallowing back the nausea rising up her throat, Mia wiped away the last of her tears, shoved the drawer shut and spun back around to look at Damián one last time.

How she wanted to hate him for his cruel words. How she wished she didn't still want to put her hands to his face and stroke the desolation etched beneath the coldness away.

'I thought beneath your cold exterior lay a warm heart but that was just wishful thinking, wasn't it? You don't think you're worthy of love. I get it. I really do. You push people away before they can get too close and hurt you, like your mother hurt you every day of your life, but Damián, keep doing what you're doing and soon you'll find your heart's so cold that no one will be able to touch it, even if you want them to.'

Trying her hardest to stop her legs from collapsing and trying her hardest not to look at him, Mia walked out of the door and out of his life.

Damián got unsteadily to his feet and almost tripped over one of his brother's dogs, who was snoozing by the sofa. Unsurprising, since he'd shared nearly a bottle and a half of Scotch with Emiliano since eleven that morning and it was now only five in the afternoon. They'd holed themselves up in their father's study and drank to his memory.

Celeste had gone. She'd joined the exodus of guests and slipped away three days ago. They'd both laughed bitterly at the irony of this. The Monte Cleure villa was the only property in her sole name. All the other assets had been in their father's name: the Swiss lodge, the penthouse apartment in Manhattan, the villa in St Barts, all the magnificent townhouses dotted in the world's leading capitals. Celeste had abandoned her only home. When she returned, which she would have to, she would find there was an arrest warrant for her. Neither of them expected her to be charged. The evidence was all circumstantial. But let her have the indignity of being arrested.

'We need food,' Damián said, then laughed to hear the slur in his voice.

Emiliano hiccupped. 'Eating's cheating.'

'What?'

'That's what the Brits say.'

'Oh.' He sat back down, took another swig out of the bottle then passed it over.

Emiliano's head suddenly lifted. 'Where's your Brit gone?' His eyes peered around the room, as if Mia might have spent the past three days hiding in there.

'Gone.'

'Gone where?'

'Home.'

'Which home?'

'Give me the bottle.'

'Not until you tell me which home. One of yours or hers?'

'Hers. Now, give me the bottle.'

Emiliano passed it to him. 'Why her home?'

'She doesn't live with me.'

'How long have you two been together?'

'We're not together.'

'You looked like you were together.'

'I paid her.'

'What?' Emiliano, who'd snatched the bottle back and put it to his lips, now missed his mouth and spilled the amber liquid over his chin. 'I thought she was an actress?'

'She is an actress.' A superb one. Wasting her talent in provincial theatres for fear of what fame could do to her family. 'I paid her to pretend to be in love with me.'

'Why?'

'I needed help finding Father's will. I thought you'd hidden it somewhere.'

Emiliano's face puckered. 'I guessed Celeste had taken it.'

'Did you?'

'You were hardly likely to have hidden it, were you?'

Damián shrugged. 'I can't believe she burned it.'

'I can.' Now Emiliano shrugged. 'You're single-minded when you want something. She knew you'd find it if she didn't destroy it.'

'Do you know what else I can't believe?'

'What?'

'That I'm sitting here and getting drunk with my brother.'

'Strange, huh?' Emiliano passed the bottle back. 'We should do this more often.'

Damián raised the bottle in agreement and took another swig.

'So when are you going to see her again?'

'Who?'

'Your actress.'

'I'm not.'

'Why not?'

'The job's done.'

'And?'

'And what?'

'You're nuts.'

'What?'

'I've spent my life studying you and I have *never* seen you look at anyone the way you look at her.'

'I was acting too.'

'Whatever, Pinocchio. I know what I saw between you two and that was not fake…'

Emiliano's voice drifted out of focus as a memory of calling Mia Pinocchio sprang back to him. Why had he called her that? His addled brain couldn't remember. Didn't want to remember. *He* didn't want to remember. No. Must. Keep. Her. Out.

'Earth to Damián.' Emiliano leaned over and clicked his fingers in front of Damián's face.

He blinked.

'Where did you go?'

'Mia.' Her name slipped off his tongue. 'I sent her away.'

'Call her back. She's fun.'

'No.' He clamped his lips together to stop his tongue spilling anything else.

It wasn't that he didn't want his brother to hear it. More that he didn't want to hear it himself. He wanted to lock her away in a compartment in his brain and never let her out again.

If he allowed himself to remember the harsh words of their parting he was afraid…

He didn't know what he was afraid of. Only knew that he had to keep her locked away far from the memories in his brain and never let her out.

'Fancy joining us for some lunch?'

Mia blinked and focused on Tanya, standing before her. 'I'm not hungry,' she said, conjuring a tired smile.

'Sure?'

'Sure.'

'Okay… Well, see you at the next one.'

The next audition. For another provincial theatre. In her hand sat a theatre magazine that had listings for open auditions. A young company that was making a real name for itself was hosting auditions for actors for a production of the musical *Annie*. Mia quite fancied trying out for the role of Miss Hannigan. She was fed up of only trying for 'nice' characters. It used every acting skill she possessed to be happy and cheery, left her exhausted and more miserable than ever. But the show would be in the West End. The company had a buzz about it. It would be guaranteed to get press attention.

She rested her head back against the wall and closed her eyes.

Maybe Damián was right. Maybe it was time to talk to her mum and sister. She needed to give them more credit for the progress they'd made with their lives instead of living in fear of the dark days. Amy was a goodhearted woman now, not a grieving self-destructive teenager. Her mum had regular therapy. They both loved her. She needed to let *them* decide how equipped they felt to cope if the spotlight ever did fall on Mia, and the potential repercussions that might come with it. It was a conversation they needed to have.

Whatever the outcome of the conversation, Mia's family came first every time. The Delgados were the antithesis of what a family should be, each concerned with only their own selfish desires.

She just wished she'd seen that about Damián before giving him her…

She whipped her head forwards and clutched at her hair. Why was she still giving that man room in her head? The way things were going, she was going to have to start charging him rent.

She hadn't seen or heard from him in nine days. She

hadn't expected to. But she'd found her fingers hovering over her phone numerous times, ready to call him and offer her support since all the stories had surfaced. The spectacular fallout between the uber glamorous and fabulously rich Celeste Delgado and her two gorgeous billionaire sons at her high society party had been gossip fodder for three days. Speculation was rife as to the cause of it. Rumours were flying around about doubts over the death of Eduardo Delgado. Maybe, the gossips all said, his death wasn't as natural as had been presumed.

For a man as private as Damián, this intrusion must be horrific and, though she knew in her heart that it was folly, she longed to reach out and tell him she would always be on his side and always be there for him, that she knew his cruel words to her had come from a place of deep, deep pain.

But he didn't want her. He didn't want anyone.

And she didn't know what to do with herself. She went through the motions of living but inside she felt dead. She'd gone out last night with a group of friends. She'd drunk some shots and thrown herself with abandon onto the dance floor but she might as well have been a humanoid for all the emotion she'd felt. She'd acted the whole night away, smiling and happy on the outside, dead and cold inside. She needed to find a way through this. She needed to move on. Her head accepted that she and Damián were over—her head had accepted it before they'd even started—but her heart…

Oh, her heart ached for him. It ached for the pain he was going through and it ached at his rejection. She'd given it to him, her whole heart, not even realising she'd gift-wrapped it for him until it was too late to take it back.

She wished she could hate him. Maybe this pain would be easier to endure then.

So lost in her thoughts was she that it wasn't until the

casting director stopped to ask if she was okay did she realise the auditions were over and they were closing up.

She nodded, too tired now to even fake a smile.

Slipping her bag over her shoulder, she trudged to the exit. When she stepped outside it was to a hail of camera lenses flashing in her face.

It was good to be home. It felt like a lifetime had passed since he'd last been in Buenos Aires rather than a mere fortnight.

Damián headed straight to his bar and poured himself a Scotch, the first alcoholic drink he'd had since he'd got so drunk with his brother that the pair of them had fallen asleep on the sofa and he'd woken to find Emiliano's feet in his face. What a mess they'd got into. Both of them. But it had been necessary. A lifetime of antipathy, ten years of which had been spent as real enemies, could not be breached overnight. Words for men as proud as the Delgado brothers did not come easily. Sometimes alcohol helped to loosen lips.

He switched his phone on, checked his emails, replied to the few that mattered then opened his news app, filtered so only business news was fed into it. He had no wish to read the spurious speculation about his family currently entertaining the world.

He read a report on one of his clients, a shipping magnate, and his plans for five new cargo ships. It was a huge relief to know he could still call him a client. The six months from his father's death had passed and Emiliano had inherited everything. That same day, Emiliano had signed the Delgado Group and all its holdings over to Damián. Agreement between the brothers had come easily—Emiliano would keep their father's personal assets, Damián the businesses.

That was the only good thing in this whole mess, he

thought. He finally had the makings of a proper relationship with his brother and, for the first time, he understood where Mia's deep need to protect her sister came from and why she would make the same sacrifice. Now, if he was given the choice of the business or his brother, he would choose his brother. Every time. He should have chosen his brother ten years ago and fought his corner with their father. That he hadn't, and that he'd allowed their estrangement go so far, was something he would regret for the rest of his life.

If Mia had been in his life back then, she would never have allowed it to go so far. She would have talked sense into him, made him talk to his brother, forced him to listen rather than condemning him straight away.

He sucked in a sharp breath. He would not think of Mia. They had known from the start they had no future together. How could they?

But *Dios*, the pain in his heart whenever her face floated before him. The pain was becoming constant. The more he tried to lock her away, the stronger her image grew and the stronger the pain in his chest. And it was always the image of her beautiful face crumpling at the cruel words he'd thrown at her.

Why had he been so cruel? And to her? The one person in the whole world who'd truly been on his side.

He would never forgive himself for the way he'd ended things between them.

He could only hope that one day soon the throbbing in his heart would lessen and he would find a way to stop thinking about her. And stop missing her so much.

CHAPTER FIFTEEN

MIA PRESSED HER fingers to her ears to drown out the hammering on her door. Whoever it was should have taken the hint when she'd ignored the first quieter knock. She'd thought these people, with the assistance of an official harassment complaint, had finally got the message that she wouldn't speak to them.

The hammering got louder. She switched her television on and turned the volume up.

Her phone buzzed. With a sigh, she picked it up. It wouldn't be her mum or Amy. Her mum had gone away for the weekend with friends and Amy was working.

And then she saw the name on the screen and her heart almost punched out of her ribcage.

Her hand shook as she swiped to read the message.

I know you are home. Please let me in. I will only take a few minutes of your time. D

It seemed to take forever for the spinning in her head to slow enough for her to get to her feet. Feeling as if she'd been drugged, she walked to her front door and put her eye to the spyhole.

She rested her forehead to the door, clutched her chest and breathed deeply.

She wasn't prepared for this.

And then Damián's deep voice vibrated through the door, penetrating straight into her. 'Please, Mia. I need to talk to you. I swear I won't stay long, but please just let me say what I need to say to you.'

She took one more huge breath for luck and opened the door.

It felt as if a truck had been slammed into her. There was the face she'd dreamed about every night since their parting. The face she thought about every minute of the waking day. As darkly handsome as she remembered. But more gaunt. The toll of everything he'd been through these past few weeks was etched right there.

For the longest time they just stared at each other.

Eventually she dragged one syllable out. 'Hi.'

His throat moved. 'Hi.'

Wrapping her oversized fluffy wrap tightly around her so he couldn't see the black vest she wore beneath it, which she hadn't changed out of for two days, she stepped aside to admit him into her home. His exotic scent filled her senses with such acute familiarity that she pressed herself against the wall and ground her toes into the floor.

She thought back to the first time she'd let him into her home. She'd wanted to throw the roses he'd brought her in his face, terrified even then of the feelings he evoked in her.

She should have paid better attention to those feelings. Protected herself better. Sealed her heart up.

He led the way to her living room. 'May I sit?'

She nodded and carefully curled herself into the armchair, letting him have the sofa. Too late, she realised she had the newspaper cuttings all over the coffee table.

He followed her gaze and his brow creased. 'What is this?'

'Our affair.'

Shocked eyes met hers. 'The press know?'

'They've known for four days. One of your guests tipped them off. They had a photo of us together.'

He muttered a curse. Such a familiar sound. It had always made her laugh, the way he cursed, as if he couldn't quite bring himself to say it out loud. As with the familiarity of his scent, hearing it felt like a knife in her heart.

'I'm sorry. I didn't know.' He raised his shoulder and looked her in the eye. 'I've been avoiding everything but business news. My staff had instructions not to talk of the gossip about my family with me.'

'Don't worry about it. They've gone now.'

'The press have been here?'

'It doesn't matter.' She managed something she hoped looked like a smile. 'I've been offered TV work off the back of it. The Damián Delgado effect worked as you said it would.'

He kneaded his temples. 'I'm sorry. I know it isn't what you want. Have there been repercussions?'

'Not yet.' Her next smile came a little easier. 'I think they've got the message that I won't speak to them. And I had a heart-to-heart with Mum and Amy the other day. They want me to push forward with my career and stop holding myself back for their sake. If anything from the past gets dredged up, we'll deal with it then.'

'That's good to hear. You're too talented not to reach for the stars.'

She couldn't hold the smile up any longer. 'Why are you here?'

Damián put more pressure on his temples. Being here with Mia was even harder than he'd thought it would be. So many powerful feelings ran through him, all threatening to overwhelm him. Underlying it all was a sense of devastating loss at what could have been.

'I am here to apologise.'

She closed her eyes. 'You don't have to apologise.'

'I do.' He sucked a breath in to gather his thoughts. If he didn't say what needed to be said he feared he would never sleep again. The guilt and despair had grown too big. 'What I said to you… Mia, it was unforgiveable.'

Her eyes opened. To see them glisten with unshed tears only cut the gaping wound in his heart deeper.

'Whenever I think back to that night, I want to grab hold of myself and stop the words from forming. I was out of my mind. I didn't want to believe my own mother could do something so evil. I knew she didn't love me as she loved Emiliano but…she couldn't have loved me at all. The woman who gave me life feels nothing for me. I don't see how she can feel anything for anyone, even Emiliano.'

The wound in his heart slashed wider to see Mia's chin wobble and her chest heave. Even after all the cruel things he'd said to her, her compassion blazed from her eyes as strongly as ever.

Why had he been such a fool to think any of it had been fake?

'We will never be able to prove it, but she killed our father. How can someone do that? To live with someone for thirty-seven years and bear his child and build a life together and then take that life without a cent of remorse.'

Needing another moment to compose himself, he covered his face. When he looked back at her, Mia had huddled tighter into herself, her cheeks now damp with tears.

'And then I think of their marriage. How separate they were. They married each other for power and money. Love and feelings had nothing to do with it. I always thought it worked well but I didn't understand how badly I misjudged it because I had never experienced love for myself. If I were married to you I would want to be with you always.

I would do whatever it took to be with you. If that meant giving up the business and living in London permanently, then I would do it because I love you and when you love someone you do whatever it takes to make them happy and protect them. You taught me that.' He swallowed. 'I'm sorry I haven't been here to protect you from the press. If I had known, I swear to you I would have been. For you, I would do anything.'

Something hot burned the back of his eyes. He pinched the bridge of his nose and inhaled deeply, trying to hold it back. 'I need you to know that I will always be in your debt. What you have given to me is immeasurable. Until I met you, I always thought success was valued in monetary terms. In assets. Now I see it comes from cherishing the ones you love and taking pride in watching them thrive. In protecting them. I should have protected you that night, as I should have been here to protect you from the press. Instead, I lashed out, and I lashed out at the one person who, more than anyone in the world, did not deserve it. I took my pain and my grief and I threw it at you. At the time, all I could think was what were you doing there? How could you try to comfort me? *Why* would you try and comfort a man whose own mother didn't love him?'

Something hot and wet rolled down his cheek. He closed his eyes and tried to suck it back. '*Mi vida*, what you said about me pushing people away is true. I push them away before they can hurt me. But you were wrong about my heart being too cold for anyone to touch it. *You* touched it. You touched it and you brought it to life. I think you brought me to life too, and I thank you. I thank you for teaching me how to love. I thank you for bringing my brother back to me. And I thank you for doing all this and not even knowing you were doing it. I am a better man for knowing you.'

Throughout this outpouring of his feelings, Mia simply

stared at him, eyes wide, her fingers grasping tightly at the wrap huddled around her, the only movement the tears falling soundlessly down her face.

Drying his eyes with the palms of his hands, Damián got to his feet. 'Thank you for giving me your time and listening. All I have left to say is this—please, *mi vida*, reach for the stars. If Broadway ever calls, let me know. I have friends who will help you with the visa. If ever you or your family need help with *anything*, you call me. Okay? The debt I owe you will take ten lifetimes to repay.'

Her wrap fell off a shoulder as she released her grip on it and straightened. 'You're leaving?'

'I have said what I came to say, and I promised not to take too much of your time.' Terrified of the desperate need to touch her, to take her face in his hands and touch the skin he'd missed so much and breathe the scent that had imprinted in his memories, he forced his legs to move. He'd purged his conscience and now it was time to leave and find some privacy to release the agony in his heart.

'Don't go. Please.'

His back to her, he took a shuddering breath. 'I have to.'

'When you said that you love me... Did you mean it?' Her voice dropped to a stifled whisper. 'Or were you talking hypothetically?'

'I meant it. I love you. I will always love you.'

A hand touched his shoulder.

A huge shudder racked him. 'Please, *mi vida*, let me leave. Don't make this any harder for me, I beg you.'

'Please, look at me.'

His throat closing tightly, he choked, 'I can't.'

Her hand brushed over his neck as she moved to stand in front of him.

He closed his eyes tightly. 'Don't do this.'

Cold hands slowly cupped his face. A slender body pressed against his.

'Please, Damián, *look* at me.'

He opened his eyes.

Her face was inches from his. She tightened her hold on his face and brought hers even closer, so the tips of their noses touched. 'I love you too,' she whispered. 'Haven't you realised that?'

His heart thumped loudly, both at her words and the tenderness reflecting from her eyes.

She gave a pained smile. 'I haven't been warm since we parted. I…' She swallowed. 'Those press cuttings on my table… I keep them because they're all I have of you. I torture myself staring at them. I stare at your face even when I know I shouldn't, when I know that I'm making things worse for myself.'

Her warm breath danced over his mouth before she placed the lightest of pressure to it. A tear that could have come from either of them fell over their lightly locked mouths.

'That night… I knew you were lashing out at me. I knew you didn't mean half of what you said. I've seen grief and pain that strong before, with Amy. And, just like with Amy, all I wanted was to take that pain from you and protect you and smother you with so much love that you never felt unloved or unwanted again. Because *I* love you. *I* want you. I want to be with you. I want to wake up with you every day for the rest of my life. I want to be there for you, in good times and bad.'

Damián continued to stare into the tear-filled eyes, still hardly able to breathe, hardly daring to believe. 'You love me?' he whispered hoarsely. 'How?'

'You have to ask?' She sighed then gave a smile of such brilliance that it dived straight into his battered heart. She pressed a lingering kiss to his mouth before giving another sigh. 'I love you because you are everything to me. You make me feel like I can take on the world and win, but if I stumble on the way you'll be there to catch me. I love you because with you I can be *me*. Just me. You make my heart sing and when I'm with you, when I'm not with you, all I want is to rip your clothes off and feel your heart beating against mine. You make me feel so many things I never knew I could feel, and I don't want to go through the rest of my life never feeling like this again. So please, if you feel you still must go…take me with you.'

A crack rent through his chest and then, in a rush that knocked out what little air he had left in his lungs, a tsunami of joy filled the crevice, flooding into all the parts of him he'd thought would never feel again. 'You love me?'

'I love you. So much it hurts to breathe.'

'Mi vida…' Crushing his mouth to hers, he wrapped his arms tightly around her and when her arms wrapped tightly around him and he felt all her feelings for him in the heat of her kisses he became suffused with the sweetest feeling imaginable: the love of the woman he would worship for the rest of his life.

EPILOGUE

MIA HOOKED A leg out of the bathroom door. 'Ready, Señor Delgado?'

'*Si*, Señora Delgado.' The excitement in Damián's rich voice was palpable.

She poked her head around the door. 'Are you sure?'

He pulled the bedsheets back and slapped his hand on the mattress. 'Stop teasing me.'

She pouted. 'I like teasing you.'

'And I like you naked in my arms, so come here.'

She shimmied to him, as unashamedly naked as he, revelling in the hooded expression in his eyes and the erection that had sprung to attention. After three years of marriage, the potent effect they had on each other remained undiminished.

As soon as she reached the bed he pounced. Seconds later, she was flat on her back, covered by his gorgeous body. 'Tell me,' he murmured, nibbling her neck in the way that never failed to turn her on.

For the past year of their marriage they'd been trying for a baby. Mia had tried out for the role of Miss Hannigan and, to her surprise, got the part. Whether that had been down to her talent or her famous husband—back then her famous lover—hadn't mattered in the end. She'd been determined to prove herself worthy of the role and she had. She'd also discovered, while spending all that time with the kids in the show, that she really wanted children. They'd decided to wait for a while and enjoy their marriage.

Damián had restructured his business, which now had its headquarters in London. They'd had a glorious time exploring the world together. They'd travelled and made love under so many different skies that she'd lost count. They'd partied. They'd spent time with their families. Celeste was rarely mentioned between them but they saw a lot of his brother. Damián had bought Mia's mum and sister a new house each. Naturally, they adored him. The exposure Mia had feared for her family had never materialised and she no longer worried about it. Her sister had fallen in love too and would be marrying that summer.

He nipped her neck then raised himself up and pinned her arms above her head. With his sternest expression in place, he said, '*Tell* me.'

But the gleam in his eyes told her he already knew the answer.

He knew her well enough to know she wouldn't dramatize a negative result, not when they'd been through four false hopes.

The magnitude of what she was carrying inside her suddenly hit her and, without any warning whatsoever, tears filled her eyes. Sniffing them back, she loosened one of her hands from his hold and palmed his cheek. 'We're going to be parents.'

Even though he'd already guessed, hearing it from her left him momentarily stunned. 'For real?'

She nodded and pulled his head down to kiss him. And then she wrapped her legs around him and burst into laughter. 'We're going to be parents!'

He kissed her and laughed into her mouth before springing down to kiss her naked belly. 'I'm going to be a father.'

Chin resting lightly on her abdomen, he grinned so wide and with such force she was certain their tiny little nutmeg must be able to feel it. 'I love you, Señora Delgado.'

She stroked the top of his hair tenderly. 'Not as much as I love you.'

'I love you more.'

'No, I love you more.'

'No, I love *you* more.'

'No, *I* love *you* more.'

Some time later, having tried to prove who loved each other the most the best way they knew, they conceded that they loved each other equally.

* * * * *

MILLS & BOON

Coming next month

CLAIMING HIS BOLLYWOOD CINDERELLA
Tara Pammi

The scent of her hit him first. A subtle blend of jasmine and her that he'd remember for the rest of his life. And equate with honesty and irreverence and passion and laughter. There was a joy about this woman, despite her insecurities and vulnerabilities, that he found almost magical.

The mask she wore was black satin with elaborate gold threading at the edges and was woven tightly into her hair, leaving just enough of her beautiful dark brown eyes visible. The bridge of her small nose was revealed as was the slice of her cheekbones. For a few seconds, Vikram had the overwhelming urge to tear it off. He wanted to see her face. Not because he wanted to find out her identity.

He wanted to see her face because he wanted to know this woman. He wanted to know everything about her. He wanted... With a rueful shake of his head, he pushed away the urge. It was more than clear that men had only ever disappointed her. He was damned if he was going to be counted as one of them. He wanted to be different in her memory.

When she remembered him after tonight, he wanted her to smile. He wanted her to crave more of him. Just as he would crave more of her. He knew this before their lips even touched. And he would find a way to discover her identity. He was just as sure of that too.

Her mouth was completely uncovered. Her lipstick was

mostly gone leaving a faint pink smudge that he wanted to lick away with his tongue.

She held the edge of her silk dress with one hand and as she'd lifted it to move, he got a flash of a thigh. Soft and smooth and silky. It was like receiving a jolt of electricity, with every inch he discovered of this woman. The dress swooped low in the front, baring the upper curves of her breasts in a tantalizing display.

And then there she was, within touching distance. Sitting with her legs folded beneath her, looking straight into his eyes. One arm held the sofa while the other smoothed repeatedly over the slight curve of her belly. She was nervous and he found it both endearing and incredibly arousing. She wanted to please herself. And him. And he'd never wanted more for a woman to discover pleasure with him.

Her warm breath hit him somewhere between his mouth and jaw in silky strokes that resonated with his heartbeat. This close, he could see the tiny scar on the other corner of her mouth.

"Are you going to do anything?" she asked after a couple of seconds, sounding completely put out.

He wanted to laugh and tug that pouty lower lip with his teeth. Instead he forced himself to take a breath. He was never going to smell jasmine and not think of her ever again. "It's your kiss, darling. You take it."

Continue reading
CLAIMING HIS BOLLYWOOD CINDERELLA
Tara Pammi

Available next month
www.millsandboon.co.uk

COMING SOON!

We really hope you enjoyed reading this book. If you're looking for more romance, be sure to head to the shops when new books are available on

Thursday 15th October

LET'S TALK
Romance

For exclusive extracts, competitions and special offers, find us online:

 facebook.com/millsandboon

🐦 @MillsandBoon

📷 @MillsandBoonUK

Get in touch on 01413 063232

For all the latest titles coming soon, visit
millsandboon.co.uk/nextmonth

JOIN US ON SOCIAL MEDIA!

Stay up to date with our latest releases, author
news and gossip, special offers and discounts, and
all the behind-the-scenes action
from Mills & Boon...

 millsandboon

 millsandboonuk

 millsandboon

It might just be true love...